A
DAUGHTER'S
DEVOTION

A DAUGHTER'S DEVOTION

George MacDonald

Michael R. Phillips, Editor

BETHANY HOUSE PUBLISHERS

MINNEAPOLIS, MINNESOTA 55438

A Division of Bethany Fellowship, Inc.

Cover illustration by Dan Thornberg,
Bethany House Publishers staff artist.

Originally published in 1881 as MARY MARSTON
by Sampson Low Publishers, London.

Published by Bethany House Publishers
A Division of Bethany Fellowship, Inc.
6820 Auto Club Road, Minneapolis, Minnesota 55438

Printed in the United States of America

Library of Congress Cataloging-in-Publication Data

MacDonald, George, 1824–1905.
  A daughter's devotion.

  Rev. ed. of: Mary Marston. 1881.
  I. Phillips, Michael R., 1946–   .
II. MacDonald, George, 1824–1905. Mary Marston. III. Title.
PR4967.M37 1988   823'.8   88–19256
ISBN 0-87123-906-X   CIP

Scottish Romances by George MacDonald retold for today's reader by Michael Phillips

The two-volume story of Malcolm:
The Fisherman's Lady
The Marquis' Secret

Companion stories of Gibbie and his friend Donal:
The Baronet's Song
The Shepherd's Castle

Companion stories of Hugh Sutherland and Robert Falconer:
The Tutor's First Love
The Musician's Quest

Companion stories of Thomas Wingfold:
The Curate's Awakening
The Lady's Confession
The Baron's Apprenticeship

Stories that stand alone:
The Gentlewoman's Choice
The Highlander's Last Song
The Laird's Inheritance
The Maiden's Bequest
The Minister's Restoration
A Daughter's Devotion

The George MacDonald Collector's Library—
beautifully bound hard-cover editions:
The Fisherman's Lady
The Marquis' Secret

A New Biography of George MacDonald by Michael Phillips

George MacDonald: Scotland's Beloved Storyteller

Contents

8

Introduction

If any single label can be applied to George MacDonald's novels as a whole, it might well be the term "character studies." It is MacDonald's probing, insightful glimpses into human nature, and the responses of men and women as spiritual forces operate upon them that so distinguish MacDonald's fiction.

Though MacDonald's genius as a storyteller originates from his ability to skillfully weave character interaction and growth through a complex and sometimes mysterious plot, it is usually the characters themselves who linger longest in the memory after the events of the story have faded. Indeed, a lack of plot altogether hardly seems to diminish the impact a George MacDonald novel can have: the characters are equally real, their growth just as fascinating, and their responses to God just as imperative— even if nothing "exciting" happens to them.

In 1881, at the very height of his literary career, George MacDonald published a novel centered about the life of a simple shopkeeper's daughter, whose name, and the book's title, was *Mary Marston*, here reissued in the Bethany House series as *A Daughter's Devotion*. The book followed the publication of *Paul Faber Surgeon* (renamed *The Lady's Confession*), and one wonders if something of the same writing "mood" carried over from the one to the other, for they are very similar in certain ways. Both can be seen as "extended sower parables," in which the broad range of human responses to the gospel is seen in the various individuals of the story— from those in whom the seed strikes no root, to those in whom it is choked out by worldly cares, to those whom Satan has in his grasp, to those others whose soil is rich and in whom God's priorities flourish.

In *Mary Marston*, MacDonald sets up an intriguing array of diverse characters, gives us something of their background and their present situations, and then proceeds to let them live their lives in interaction with one another. The threads between them are occasionally loose; some of the main twelve to fifteen persons never cross paths with certain of the others. There is not a tightly woven plot that interconnects them all. Yet taken together, what follows makes fascinating reading. The individuals are so diverse, sometimes so petty and foolish, their intertwining relationships so humorous at times. And as we watch Mary, Tom, Hesper, Letty, Sepia, Joseph, Mr. Turnbull, Mr. Redmain, Godfrey, Mrs. Perkin, Mewks, and the others, we are able to observe the growth process at work—sometimes forward, sometimes backward, but there is always progression. As I read this book again recently, I found myself enjoying it not primarily for the story, but rather because of my engrossment with each of the many individuals. At the end I did not want to stop; I wanted to keep reading about them all. I didn't care about their activities; I just wanted to know how they were doing—inside.

I found myself identifying with all the characters at different times. As I sat back and observed and analyzed, I could see pettiness within myself, false priorities, motives of self. What lessons I discovered here for my own life! We all get so unknowingly wrapped up in such small things (rings and dresses and how we look and what people think of us and the status of our bank accounts) that we lose sight of the priorities of the kingdom, which are eternal. I found myself hungry anew to rid myself of such trivial concerns, so that God's life within me might live more fully.

A number of other factors struck my attention as I was working on *A Daughter's Devotion*. Perhaps foremost, I noticed again how far in advance of his era MacDonald was. Over a hundred years ago he was writing about women in a manner most contemporary to the 1980s. MacDonald always gave women their full and respectful due. Like Jesus, he understood the role of women (and men and children and animals and nature) as God created them to function in the world, without the modern, perverted exultation of self-rights so rampant, not merely within the women's movement but throughout all of society today. But in addition to respect, which MacDonald always gave women, he subtly makes a host of women's issues primary ingredients in *A Daughter's Devotion*: women in the workplace, the role of love and submission to an ungodly husband, a marriage where husband and wife both work, women as spiritual leaders over men, a marriage where the woman takes the lead in certain aspects of the relationship. No Victorian chauvinist was MacDonald! His lead character here is a woman who teaches and counsels the men of the story in very humble fashion. Indeed, it is Mary who is the "priest" (Christ's representative) in one of the most powerful deathbed scenes since *The Fisherman's Lady*. The development of these women's themes, as we watch Mary mature and come into independence, are particularly interesting when we reflect on how many years ago this book was written.

Humble and obedient servanthood is again emphasized—as it is in all of MacDonald's books—as the one true path to godliness, to relationship, to growth, and to true status and significance. Capturing perhaps the essence of her character, if not the book's fundamental theme, when Mary suffers from typical Victorian snobbery at the hands of those above her on the social scale and those of her peers who do not understand the spiritual perspectives behind her decisions and attitudes, her view is: "What can it matter to me . . . whether they call me a lady or not, as long as Jesus says *daughter* to me?"

And there is an imaginative interpretation of the composition and meaning and meaning and spiritual power of music that is positively unlike anything I have ever heard before. To have written what he did, George MacDonald truly had to "feel" the emotion of music moving him deep in his soul. One doesn't dream up something like that; it proceeds only from the heart!

In this age of succinct recipes for growth and compact formulas to supposedly unlock spiritual birth—in neither of which MacDonald placed much trust—the concept of "goodness" has come to connote almost the exact opposite in certain Christian circles. To listen to some zealous evangelizers talk, one would think that goodness has itself become a spiritual evil. Quoting "there is none righteous, no not one," and "we are all sinners"—true, of course—we are told in no uncertain terms that "being a good person is not good enough." Goodness, in fact, will lead us astray if we are not careful and blind us from a "saving faith." Well, certainly it is not "enough"; fulfillment as a spiritual being is a multi-faceted process of deepening growth. Man must be properly related to God by living in His grace and obeying His commands, and this does truly involve more than being good and kind.

But goodness *is* a good thing. Over and over Jesus extolled the "good" man—saying not a word about his spiritual state in many cases. For Jesus, if a man was good, that was a *good* thing. Because where does goodness come from in the first place? Goodness cannot originate anywhere but in the goodness of God. That's why goodness is one of the fruits of the Spirit, and why, in the New Testament, we are commanded to "be good" some thirty times, whereas we are commanded to "trust God," "follow Jesus," and "be righteous" less than half that many. According to the New Testament, only the commands, "love," "pray," and "be watchful" are more frequently stressed than "be good!"

In short, *goodness* is scripturally a good thing—a very good thing. Far from being a spiritual vice that will blind us from God's truth and keep us from heaven (which some amateur fundamentalist theologians would have it), goodness is something Jesus commands of us as one of the supreme messages of His life. It is good to be a good person!

George MacDonald understood this truth clearly. He brought into his books none of the spiritualized baloney and pious fog of his day that still lingers in our own. He understood the Bible, and he understood God's priorities. Whereas goodness in and of itself is not an end-all, he understood that it is an essential starting point toward Christlikeness.

Therefore, the notion that some of his characters are "too good" for believable fiction is at root a meaningless statement to make. It is precisely because MacDonald's characters run the gamut from good to bad that they can serve meaningfully as models as we ourselves attempt to conform our lives to that supremely good Man who was and is the central figure in the most dramatic and exciting story ever told.

All this is by way of saying that in *A Daughter's Devotion* we encounter a "good" lead character. Mary is a good young lady. Too good? Not for me. Why do we love Jesus? Because He possessed a tragic fatal flaw and was therefore a great Shakespearean hero? No. It is because He was the perfectly good man sent from God—God's Son.

I like good heroes. How else can I learn to submit more and more of my daily life to the lordship of Christ than by surrounding myself with friends and acquaintances who help that process along, who show me how to yield in many diverse circumstances? Mary Marston, like so many of her colleagues in MacDonald lore, is my friend, and thus helps me toward that end.

Not every one of the people you will meet herein, however, views life from quite this perspective. MacDonald offered no syrupy fiction where all the characters in the end reform their ways, repent, and join the straight and narrow path. There is a realism here. These men and women are true to life. Not everyone repents. Not everyone responds equally to the seeds of gospel truth that are sown.

Hearkening back to *The Lady's Confession*, Faber, though he is the lead character, by the end of the book has only come to the point where he is listening, thinking, and growing more open to truth. This is the most appropriate ending MacDonald could have given to such a parable on sin and man's need for God. For in the end it always boils down to a choice. Each man and woman stands before God in the silence and emptiness of their own heart and must choose whether they will say yes or no to Him. With such endings, MacDonald emphasized that very point. In the same way that each reader must decide for himself what he think's Faber's choice will be, MacDonald is revealing the fact that each must make that choice for himself. Even MacDonald, as Faber's creator, cannot make that determination for the doctor. The choice remains Faber's alone.

Similarly, in this parable of seed sown, of different human soil, of responses to God, and of elevation or denial of self, all the individuals we get to know so well—Hesper, Tom, Letty, the Turnbulls, Mr. Redmain— must make choices that will determine in which direction their growth will progress. The variety of their responses—to Mary, to their fellow creatures, to husbands and wives, and to the still small voice of God in their hearts— illustrate once again that timeless truth of "the secret of the kingdom of God" which Jesus clarified in Mark 4:13–20: different people respond in different ways. And MacDonald will not take away from the impact of that truth by doctoring the responses of his people. As much as Mary longs to see a breaking of self in Mr. and Mrs. Redmain, she knows that in the end, each must decide for himself. Will we live our lives conscious of the invisible kingdom of God that surrounds and fills the world, or will we waste away these few precious earthly years consumed with how we look, what others think of us, with wealth and gain and importance and status? Will we live for others or for ourselves?

As interest in George MacDonald has grown in recent years, a variety of editions of his work have been released in many formats. Those of us who love MacDonald welcome this diversity, rejoicing to see MacDonald's novels, fairy tales, and sermons penetrating into markets and lives where they previously had not been available. This Bethany series alone has found its way onto every continent in the world and has been translated into four languages other than English, including Chinese. MacDonald's work was all published in the nineteenth century, making it public domain. And it is this that makes possible the truly worldwide impact of his message. Undoubtedly this republishing of MacDonald's work will continue, and, as was the case in his own day, no doubt many distinctive editions, often of the same book, will continue to be released.

Since the very beginning of this project more than thirteen years ago, it has been my personal dream to see a uniform set of MacDonald's novels available. This has been the commitment of Bethany House since 1981 when they gave that dream reality. Since that time, we have worked jointly to bring the novels out one at a time, hoping ultimately to see the entire set completed. However, as the Bethany series has expanded and as MacDonald's popularity has increased, it has become inevitable that overlap between various publishers would occur, given that there are at present no less than fifteen publishers in the U.S. currently publishing George MacDonald titles.

Yet every publisher, every editor, every illustrator will bring his or her distinct interpretations to MacDonald's work; occasional redundancy is but the inevitable outcome of each series' uniqueness. In the case of *The Princess and the Goblin* and *At the Back of the North Wind*, both titles have been published by upwards of two or three dozen publishers over the years, and at this moment are available from at least six apiece. In the case of edited works (there are to my knowledge some seven or eight individuals who are editing MacDonald's work for contemporary readers), every editor will view differently his task of being faithful to MacDonald's original priorities. There is room for such diversity because the reading public responds differently to distinctive editions of any great author.

I view all this as an exciting outgrowth of MacDonald's new burst of popularity as new generations of readers discover Scotland's beloved nineteenth-century storyteller for themselves. Therefore, in whatever formats and editions you are enjoying the works of George MacDonald, all of us involved in making them available to you rejoice in the experience with you. MacDonald has spoken to each one of us; that is why we are burdened to share his work. I'm certain I speak for all editors and publishers of MacDonald when I say that we are with you in your adventure. We pray it is a fulfilling and fruitful one, and we all welcome your responses and thoughts.

May God bless you as you read . . . grow . . . learn . . . and enjoy!

Michael Phillips
℅ One Way Book Shop
1707 E Street
Eureka, California 95501

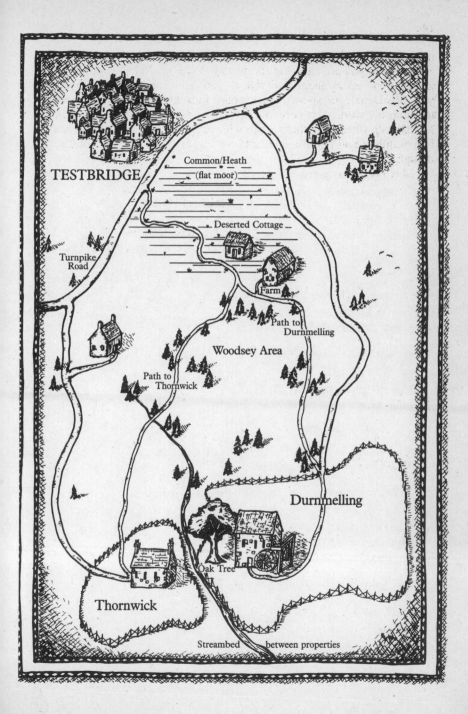

The Cast of Characters_____

At the Shop in Testbridge

Mary Marston
William Marston
George Turnbull
John Turnbull
Mrs. Turnbull
Beenie—William and Mary's housekeeper

At the Mortimer Estate of Durnmelling

Mr. Mortimer
Lady Margaret Alice Mortimer
Hesper Mortimer
Sepia Yolland—Hesper's cousin

At the Wardour Estate of Thornwick

Godfrey Wardour
Mrs. Wardour—Godfrey's mother
Letty Lovel—Mrs. Wardour's cousin

Also in Testbridge

Tom Helmer
Mrs. Helmer—Tom's mother

At the Redmain House on Glammis Street in London

Mr. Redmain
Mrs. Redmain
Mrs. Perkin—chief housekeeper
Jemima—lady's maid
Mrs. Folter—Mrs. Redmain's maid
Mr. Mewks—Mr. Redmain's man-servant

Also in London

Ann Byrom
Joseph Jasper—Ann's half-brother
Count Galofta

1 / The Shop

It was an evening early in May. The sun was low, and the street was blotched with the shadows of its cobblestones—worn smooth enough, but far from evenly set into the ground. The sky was clear, except for a few clouds in the west, hardly visible in the dazzling of the huge setting light. The sun lay among the clouds, just above the horizon, like a radiant liquid that had broken its vessel and was pouring over the fragments. The street was almost empty, and the air was chilly. The spring was busy, and the summer was at hand; but the wind was blowing from the north.

The street was neither commonplace nor uninteresting. There were features of interest in the shadowy fronts of almost each of its picturesque old houses. Indeed, many of them wore something like human expression, the look of having both known and suffered. From many a porch and many a latticed oriel window, a long shadow stretched eastward, like a death-flag streaming in a wind the body could not feel—or a fluttering leaf, ready to drop and flit away after the vanishing light, and add one more drop to the mound of blackness gathering on the horizon's edge. It was the main street of an old country town, dwindled by the rise of larger and more prosperous places, but holding and exercising a charm none of them would ever gain.

Some of the oldest of its houses, most of them with more than one projecting story, stood about the middle of the street. The central and oldest of these was a draper's shop.

The floor of the shop was lower than the street, and thus the windows of the ground floor descended very close to the pavement, encroaching a little on it. But though they had glass on three oriel sides, they were not much used for displaying what was to be found inside. A few ribbons and gay handkerchiefs, mostly of cotton, for the eyes of the country people on market days, formed the chief part of their humble show. The door was wide and very low, the upper half of it glass—old, and bottle-colored, and its threshold was a deep step down into the shop.

As a place for purchases it might not look promising to some eyes, but both the ladies and the housekeepers of Testbridge knew that rarely could they do better in London itself than at the shop of Turnbull and Marston, whether in variety, quality, or price. And whatever the first impression, the moment the eyes of a stranger began to grow accustomed to its gloom, the size and abundance of the shop looked hopeful indeed. It was low, and the walls could therefore accommodate few shelves. But the ceiling was therefore low enough as to be itself available for stowage by means of well-contrived slides and shelves attached to the great beams crossing it in several directions.

The shop had a particularly high reputation for all kinds of linen goods, from cambric handkerchiefs to towels, and from table-napkins to sheets. But almost anything else in the way of draperies was to be found in it, from Manchester moleskins for trousers, to Genoa velvet for a dowager's gown, and from Horrocks's prints to Lyons silks. It had been enlarged at the back, and that part was a little higher and a little better lighted than the front; but the whole place was still dark enough to have awaked the envy of any swindling London shopkeeper. Its owners, however, had so long enjoyed the confidence of the town and its neighborhood, that faith readily took the place of sight with their customers. Seldom, except in a question of color or shade, was an article carried to the door to be confronted with the day so that its quality could be verified. It had been just such a shop, untouched of even legendary change, as far back as the memory of the sexton reached. And he, because of his age and his occupation, was the chief authority in the local history of the place.

On this evening, as there were few people in the street, so there were few in the shop, and preparations were underway for its closing: they were not particular there to a good many minutes either way. Behind the counter to the left stood a youth of about twenty, young George Turnbull, the son of the principal partner, leisurely occupied in folding and putting away a number of things he had been showing to a farmer's wife who had just left. He was an ordinary looking lad, with little more than business in his high forehead, fresh-colored, good-humored, and self-satisfied cheeks. His keen hazel eyes kept wandering from his not very pressing occupation to the other side of the shop, where a young woman stood behind the opposite counter, attending to a well-dressed youth who had just chosen a pair of driving gloves. His air and carriage were conventionally those of a gentleman—a gentleman, however, more than ordinarily anxious to please a young woman behind a counter. She answered him with politeness, and even friendliness, and seemed unaware of anything unusual in his attentions.

"They're splendid gloves," he said, making small talk, "but don't you think the price is rather high for a pair of gloves, Miss Marston?"

"It *is* a good deal of money," she answered in a sweet, quiet voice. The tone suggested simplicity and straightforwardness. "But they will last you a long time. Just look at how well-made they are, Mr. Helmer. It is much more difficult to stitch them like these are, one edge over the other, than to sew the two edges together, as they do with ladies' gloves. But I'll go and ask my father whether he marked them himself."

"He did mark those, I know," said young Turnbull, who had been listening to all that went on, "for I heard my father say they ought to be sixpence more."

"Ah then!" she returned with an assenting tone, and laid the gloves on the box before her, the question settled.

Helmer took them and began to put them on.

"They certainly are the best quality gloves where there is much handling of reins," he said.

"That is what Mr. Wardour says of them," rejoined Miss Marston. "He has used this very brand for years."

"By the way," said Helmer, lowering his voice, "when did you last see anybody from Thornwick?"

"Their old man was in town yesterday with the dogcart."

"Nobody with him?"

"Miss Letty. She came in for just two minutes or so."

"How was she looking?"

"Very well," answered Miss Marston, with what to Helmer seemed indifference.

"Ah," he said with a look of knowingness, "you girls don't see each other with the same eyes as we. I grant Letty is not very tall, and possibly not as beautiful as some, but where did you ever see such eyes?"

"You must excuse me, Mr. Helmer," returned Mary with a smile, "if I don't choose to discuss Letty's merits with you. After all, she is my friend."

"What would be the harm?" rejoined Helmer. "I would not say anything against her. You know perfectly well I admire her beyond any woman in the world. I don't care who knows it."

"Even your mother?" suggested Mary.

"Come now, Miss Marston! Don't you turn my mother loose on me. I shall be of age in a few months, and then my mother may think as she pleases. I know, of course, with her notions, she would never consent to my courting Letty—"

"I should think not!" exclaimed Mary. "Who ever thought of such a thing for one in your position? What would your mother say to hear you?"

"Let mothers mind their own business!" retorted the youth angrily. "I shall mind mine. My mother ought to know that by this time."

Mary said no more. She knew Mrs. Helmer was not a mother to deserve her boy's confidence, any more than to gain it. She treated him as if she had made him, and was not satisfied with her work.

"When are you going to see Letty again, Miss Marston?" resumed Helmer, after a brief pause to let his anger subside.

"Next Sunday evening probably. I usually walk out to Thornwick then."

"Take me with you."

"Take you with me! Are you serious, Mr. Helmer?"

"I would give my bay mare for a good talk with Letty Lovel," he returned.

Mary made no reply.

"So you won't take me with you?"

"No," she answered quietly, but with sober decision.

"What would be the harm?" pleaded the youth, in a tone of mingled argument, begging, and humiliation.

"One is not bound to do everything there would be no harm in doing," answered Mary. "Besides, Mr. Helmer, I don't choose to go out walking with you on a Sunday evening."

"Why not?"

"For one thing, your mother would not like it. You know she would not."

"Never mind my mother. She can't bite—ask the dentist. Come, come, that's all nonsense. I shall be at the stile over the fence beyond the turnpike-gate all afternoon—waiting till you come."

"The moment I see you—anywhere on the road—I shall turn back. Do you think I would endure having all the gossips of Testbridge talk of my going out on a Sunday evening with a boy like you?"

Tom Helmer's face flushed a bright red. He grabbed the gloves, threw the price of them on the counter, and walked angrily from the shop without another word.

"What's this!" cried George Turnbull from the other counter. "What did you say to the fellow to send him off like that? If you don't like the business, Mary, you don't need to scare the customers away besides."

"You know I like the business well enough, George. And if I did scare a customer," she added laughing, as she dropped the money in the till, "it was not until after he was done buying."

"That may be. But we must look to the future as well as today. When is Mr. Helmer likely to come near us again after whatever you must have said to make him rush off like that?"

"Tomorrow, I imagine, George," answered Mary. "He won't be able to bear the thought of having left a bad impression on me. There's something about him I can't help liking. Though I said nothing that ought to have upset him so. I only called him a boy."

"Let me tell you, Mary, you could not have called him a worse name."

"Why, what else is he?"

"A more offensive word a man could not hear from the lips of a woman," replied George loftily.

"A man, I dare say. But Mr. Helmer can't yet be nineteen."

"How can you say that? He told you himself he would be of age in a few months. The fellow is older than I am. You'll be calling me a boy next."

"What else are you? You at least are not twenty-one."

"And how old are you?"

"Twenty-three."

"A mighty difference indeed!"

"Not so much—only all the difference, it seems to be, between sense and absurdity, George."

"That may be all very true of a fine gentleman, like Helmer, who does nothing from morning to night but try to get loose from his mother's apron strings. But you don't think it applies to me, Mary, I hope!"

"That's as you behave yourself, George. If you don't make it apply, it won't apply of itself. But if young women had not more sense than most of the young men I see in the shop—on both sides of the counter, George— things would soon be in a fine pass. Nothing better in your head than in a peacock's!—only that a peacock *has* the fine feathers he's so proud of."

"If it were Mr. Wardour now, Mary, who was spreading his tail for you to see, you would not complain."

A vivid rose blossomed instantly in Mary's cheeks. Mr. Wardour was hardly even an acquaintance of hers. Though he was Letty Lovel's cousin, she had never spoken to him except in the shop. "It would not hurt you, George, to learn a little respect for your superiors," she returned. "Mr. Wardour is hardly to be compared with the kind of young men we were talking about. Mr. Wardour is not a young man, and he *is* a gentleman."

She took the glove box and turned around to place it on a shelf behind her.

"Just so!" remarked George a little bitterly. "Any man you don't choose to count a gentleman, you look down upon. What have you got to do with gentlemen I should like to know?"

"To admire one when I see him," answered Mary.

"And I suppose you call *yourself* a lady," rejoined George contemptuously.

"I do nothing of the kind," returned Mary sharply. "I would *like* to be a lady. And inside of me, if it pleases God, I *will* be a lady. But I will leave it to other people to call me this or that. It matters little what anyone happens to be *called*."

"All right, all right," returned George, a little cowed. "Only just tell me why a well-to-do tradesman like myself shouldn't be a gentleman as well as a small yeoman like Wardour."

"Why don't you say—as well as a squire, or an earl, or a duke?" replied Mary.

"There you are deriding me again! It's hard enough to have every fool of a lawyer's clerk or a doctor's boy looking down on me, and calling me but a counter-hand. But it's even worse when a girl in the same shop hasn't a civil word for a fellow, just because he isn't what she counts a gentleman! Isn't my father a gentleman? Answer me that, Mary."

It was one of George's few good points that he had a great opinion of his father, though the grounds of it were hardly such as to enable Mary to answer his appeal in a way he would have counted satisfactory. She thought of her own father, and was silent.

"Everything depends on what a man is within himself, George," she answered at length. "Mr. Wardour would be a gentleman all the same if he were a shopkeeper or a blacksmith. I do not count Mr. Wardour intrinsically of more worth than Mr. Jasper down the street, though his hands may not be so black."

"So then why shouldn't I be as good a gentleman as Mr. Wardour, if I had been born with an old tumbledown house on my back, and a few acres of land I could do with as I liked? Or *more* a gentleman than your blacksmith Joseph Jasper! Come, answer me that."

"If it be the house and the land that made the difference between gentlemen and others, then you would, of course, be one in such a case," answered Mary.

Her tone implied, even to George's rough perceptions, that there was a good deal more of a difference between them than lay therein. But common people, whether lords or shopkeepers, are slow to understand that possession—whether in the shape of birth, or lands, or money, or intellect—is a small thing when it comes to the difference between men.

"I know you don't think me fit to hold a candle to him," he said. "But I happen to know, for all he rides such a good horse, he's not above doing the work of a laborer, for he polishes his own stirrup-irons. I've even seen him in the blacksmith's shop helping the big rough fellow shoe one of his horse's hoofs."

"I'm very glad to hear it," rejoined Mary. "Both he and Mr. Jasper must be more of gentlemen yet than I thought them."

"Then why should you count Wardour a better gentleman than me?"

"I'm afraid, for one thing, that you would go with your stirrup-irons rusty, rather than clean them yourself, George. But I will tell you one thing Mr. Wardour would not do if he were a shopkeeper: he would not, like you, talk one way to the rich and another way to the poor—all submission and politeness to the one, and familiarity and rudeness with the other. If you go on like that, you'll never come within sight of being a gentleman, George—not if you live to the age of Methuselah.''

"Thank you, Miss Mary! It's a fine thing to have a lady in the shop! Shouldn't I be just like my father to hear you! I don't know how a fellow is to get on with you! If we're not friends, it is certainly not *my* fault.''

Mary made no reply. She knew what George meant, and she flushed with honest anger from brow to chin. But while her dark-blue eyes flamed with indignation, her anger was not such as to render her face less pleasant to look upon. There are as many kinds of anger as there are of the sunsets with which they ought to end: Mary's anger had no hate in it.

As plainly as I see her in my mind's eye, it is impossible to give a portrait of Mary with words; I can but cast her shadow on the page. She was a dainty, medium-height young woman, neither tall nor short, dressed in a plain, well-fitting dress of black silk, with linen collar and cuffs, who rose behind the counter, standing, in spite of displeasure, calm and motionless. Her hair was dark, and fixed in the simplest manner, without even a reminder of the hideous occipital structure then in style—especially with shopwomen, who in general choose for imitation and exorbitant development whatever is ugliest and least ladylike in the fashion of the day. Mary's hair had a natural wave in it, which broke the too straight lines it would otherwise have made across a forehead of sweet and composing proportions. Her features were regular—her nose straight—perhaps a little thin; the curve of her upper lip carefully drawn, as if with design to express a certain firmness of modesty; and her chin well shaped, perhaps a little too sharply defined for her years, and rather large.

Everything about her suggested the repose of order satisfied, of unconstrained obedience to the laws of harmonious relation. The only fault honest criticism could have suggested, merely suggested, was the presence of just a possible *nuance* of primness. Her boots, at this moment unseen by any eye, fitted her feet as her feet fit her body. Her hands were especially good. There are not many ladies interested in their own graces, who would not have envied her seals to her natural patent of ladyhood. Her speech and manner corresponded with her person and dress; they were direct and simple, in tone and inflection, those of one at peace with herself. Neatness was more notable in her than grace, but grace was not absent. Good breeding was more evident than delicacy, yet delicacy was there. And unity was plain throughout.

George put the cover on the box he had left open with a bang, and shoved it into its place as if it had been the backboard of a cart, shouting as he did so to a boy in another room to make haste and put up the shutters. Mary left the shop by a door on the inside of the counter, for she and her father lived in the house. As soon as the shop was closed, George went home to the villa his father had built in the suburbs.

2 / A Business Saturday

The next day was Saturday, a busy one at the store. From the neighboring villages and farms many people came to Testbridge to shop. Early in the day ladies from the countryseats around began to arrive at Turnbull and Marston. The whole strength of the establishment was called out to help wait on them.

Busiest in serving was the senior partner, Mr. Turnbull. He was a stout, florid man, with a bald crown, a heavy watchchain of the best gold festooned across the wide space between waistcoat-button hole and pocket, and a large hemispheroidal carbuncle on a huge fat finger, which yet was his little one. He was close-shaved and double-chinned, and had cultivated an ordinary smile to such an extraordinary degree that, to use the common exaggeration, it reached from ear to ear. He was good-tempered by nature and genial. But having devoted all his mental as well as physical energies to the making of money, what few drops of spiritual water were in him had to go with the rest to the turning of the mill-wheel that ground the universe into coin. In his own eyes he was a strong churchman, but the only sign of it visible to others was the strength of his contempt for dissenters.* Except for his partner and Mary, however, he spoke this contempt to no one but fellow Church of Englanders, for he would do nothing to drive their business away. As he often remarked, once it was in his till, a dissenter's money was as good as the best churchman's.

To the receptive eye, he was a sight not soon to be forgotten as he bent over a piece of goods outspread before a customer, one hand resting on the stuff, the other on the yard-measure, his chest as nearly touching the counter as the protesting adjacent parts would permit, his broad smooth face turned up at right angles, and his mouth, eloquent even to solemnity on the merits of the article, now hiding, now disclosing a gulf of white teeth. No sooner was anything brought into stock, than he bent his soul to the selling of it, doing everything that could be done, saying everything he could think of saying, short of plain lying about its quality: that he would not do. To buy well was a care to him, to sell well was a greater. But to make money, and as speedily as possible, was his greatest care, and his whole ambition.

In his gig, as he drove along the road to the town, and then through the street approaching his shop, John Turnbull would have shown himself to a

---

*Members of various non-Church of England churches.

chance observer as a man who knew himself of importance, a man who might have a soul somewhere inside that broad waistcoat. As he drew up, threw the reins to his stableboy, descended upon the pavement, and then stepped down into the shop, he looked like a being in whom a son or daughter might feel some honest pride. But the moment he was behind the counter and in front of a customer and in a position to exact a profit from the transaction, he changed to a creature whose appearance and carriage were painfully contemptible to any lover of mankind. Immediately he would lose the upright bearing of a man, and cringed like an ape. But I fear it was in so doing that he gained a portion at least of his favor with the countryfolk, many of whom much preferred his ministrations to those of his partner. A glance, indeed, from the one to the other, was enough to reveal which must be the better salesman—and to some particularly discerning eyes the better man as well.

In the narrow walk of his commerce—behind the counter, I mean—Mr. Marston stood up tall and straight, lank and lean, seldom bending toward the counter, but doing everything necessary upon it notwithstanding, from the unusual length of his arms and bony hands. His forehead was high and narrow, his face pale and thin, his hair long and thin, his nose curved like an eagle's, his eyes large, his mouth and chin small. He seldom spoke a syllable more than was needful, but his words breathed calm respect to every customer. His conversation was usually all but over as he laid something for approval or rejection on the counter: he had already taken every pain to learn just what the man or woman wanted, and what he then offered he submitted without comment. If the thing was not judged satisfactory, he removed it and brought another.

Many did not like this mode of service. They would rather be helped to buy. Unequal to the task of making up their minds, they welcomed any aid toward it; and therefore preferred Mr. Turnbull, who gave them every imaginable and unimaginable assistance, groveling before them like a man whose many gods came to him one after the other to be worshiped. Mr. Marston, on the other hand, shot up straight as a poplar in a sudden calm the moment he had presented something on the counter, his visage bearing witness that his thoughts were already far away—in heavenly places with his wife, or hovering like a perplexed bee over some difficult passage in the New Testament. Mary could have told which, for she knew the meaning of every shadow that passed or lingered on his countenance.

His partner and like-minded son despised him. His unbusiness-like habits, as they counted them, were the constantly recurring theme of their scorn. But Mary saw nothing in them that did not raise her father in her eyes above all other men she knew.

To mention one thing, which may serve as typical of the man, he frequently sold things under the price marked by his partner. Against this breach of fealty to the firm, Turnbull never ceased to level his biggest guns of indignation and remonstrance, though always without effect. He even lowered himself in his own eyes so far as to quote Scripture like a canting dissenter, and remind his partner of what came to a house divided against itself. He did not see that the best thing for some houses must be to come to pieces.

"But, Mr. Turnbull, I thought it was marked too high," was the other's invariable reply.

"William, you are a fool," his partner would rejoin for the hundredth time. "Will you never understand that if we get a little more than the customary profit upon one thing, we get less upon another? You must make the thing even, or come to the workhouse."

To this, for the hundredth time also, William Marston would reply: "That might hold, I daresay—but I am not sure—if every customer always bought an article of each of the two sorts together. But I can't make it straight with my conscience that one customer should pay too much because I let another pay too little. Besides, I am not at all sure that the general scale of profit is not set too high. I fear you and I will have to part, John."

But nothing was further from Turnbull's desire than that he and Marston should part ways. He could not keep the company going without his money, not to mention he never doubted that Marston would immediately go out and open another shop. And even if he did not undersell him, he would certainly take from him all their dissenting customers; for the junior partner was deacon in a small Baptist church in the town—a fact which, although like vinegar to the teeth and smoke to the eyes of John Turnbull in his villa, was invaluable in the eyes of John Turnbull behind his counter of business.

Whether William Marston was right or wrong in his ideas about the rite of baptism—probably he was both—he was certainly right in his relation to that which alone makes it of any value—that, namely, which it signifies. Buried with his Master, he had died to selfishness, greed, and trust in the secondary; died to evil, and risen to good—a new creature. He was just as much a Christian in his shop as in the chapel, in his bedroom as at a prayer meeting.

But the world was not now much temptation to him, and, to tell the truth, he was getting a good deal tired of the shop. Oftener and oftener he had to remind himself that in the meantime it was the work given him to do. And more frequently he had to take the strengthening cordial of a glance across the shop at his daughter. Such a glance passed through the dusky place like summer lightning through a heavy atmosphere, and came to Mary like a glad prophecy; for it told of a world within and beyond the world, a region of love and faith, where struggled no antagonistic desires, no counteracting aims, but unity was the visible garment of truth.

The question may well be asked—How could such a man be so unequally yoked with such another as Turnbull? To this it may be replied that Marston's inner spiritual strength exercised a certain silent power upon his partner, so that Turnbull was never at his worst in his presence. Marston never thought of his former friend as he truly was, never saw the degeneration that had occurred in his selfish soul over the years—indeed he flattered himself that poor John was gradually improving, and coming to see things more and more as he would have him look on them. But this false hope was just one more evidence of Marston's character: he always looked for the best in every man, even though in this present case, that best was largely an illusion. Add to all this the fact that they had been childhood friends, and had been in the business together almost from boyhood, and much will be explained. As their characters had diverged through the years since then, the immediate temporal needs of the shop had yet bound them together. And thus together they still found themselves.

An open carriage, with a pair of showy but ill-matched horses, looking unfit for country work on the one hand, as for Hyde Park on the other, drew up at the door. A visible wave of interest ran from one end of the shop to the other, for the carriage was well known in Testbridge. It was that of Lady Margaret Mortimer. She did not herself like the *Margaret*, and signed only her second name *Alice* at full length, whence her so-called friends generally called her Lady Malice to each other. She did not leave the carriage, but continued to recline motionless in it, at an angle of forty-five degrees, wrapped in furs, for the day was cloudy and cold. Her pale, handsome face looked inexpressibly as indifferent in its regard of earth and sky and the goings of men, as that of a corpse whose gaze is only on the inside of a coffin-lid. But the two ladies who were with her got down. One of them was her daughter, Hesper by name, who, from the dull, cloudy atmosphere that filled the doorway, entered the shop like a gleam of sunshine, dusky-golden, followed by a glowing shadow, in the person of her cousin, Miss Yolland.

Turnbull hurried to meet them, bowing profoundly. They turned aside to where Mary stood, and in a few minutes the counter was covered with various fabrics for some of the smaller articles of ladies' attire.

The customers were hard to please, for they wanted the best things at the price of inferior ones, and Mary noted that the desires of the cousin were farther reaching and more expensive than those of Miss Mortimer. But, though in this way hard to please, they were not therefore unpleasant to deal with. And from the moment she looked Hesper in the face, whom she had known as a girl but had not seen for a long time, Mary could hardly take her eyes off her. All at once it struck her how well the unusual name her mother had given her suited her, and as she gazed, the feeling grew.

Large and grandly made, Hesper stood straight and tall, with the carriage of a young matron. Her brown hair was abundant on her head. Her eyes were large and hazel; her nose cast gently upward, answering the carriage of her head; her mouth decidedly large, but so exquisite that the loss of a centimeter of its length would to a lover have been as the loss of a kingdom; her chin a trifle large, and grandly lined; for a woman's, her throat was massive, and her arms and hands were powerful. She was large in both size and *presence*. Her expression was frank, almost brave, her eyes looking full at the person she addressed. As she gazed, a kind of love she had never felt before kept swelling in Mary's heart.

Her companion impressed her very differently.

Some men, and most women, counted Miss Yolland strangely ugly. But there were also men who exceedingly admired her. Not especially slight for her stature, and above average height, she still looked small beside Hesper. Her skin was very dark, with a considerable touch of sallowness. Her eyes, which were large and beautifully shaped, were as black as eyes could be, with light in the midst of their blackness, and more than a touch of hardness in the midst of their liquidity. Her eyelashes were singularly long and black, and she seemed conscious of them every time they rose. She did not use her eyes habitually, but when she did the thrust was sudden and straight. Like Hesper's, her mouth was large and good, with fine teeth. Her chin projected a little too much; her hands were finer than Hesper's, but bony.

Her name was Septimia. Lady Margaret called her Sepia, and the contraction seemed suitable to so many that it had been generally adopted. She appeared to be in mourning, with a little crape. At first glance she seemed as unlike Hesper as she could be. But as she stood gently regarding the two, Mary gradually became aware of a singular likeness between them. Sepia was a few years older and in less flourishing condition, and her features were therefore sharper and finer, and by nature her complexion was darker; but if one was the evening, the other was the night. Their manner, too, was similar, but Sepia's was the haughtier, and she had an occasional look of defiance, of which there appeared nothing in Hesper. When she first came to Durnmelling, Lady Malice had once alluded to the dependence of her position—but only once: there came such a flash into rather than out of Sepia's eyes that made any repetition of the insult impossible, and Lady Malice wished that she had left her distant niece a wanderer on the face of Europe.

Sepia was the daughter of a clergyman, an uncle of Lady Malice, whose sons had all gone to the bad, and whose daughters had all vanished from society. Shortly before this time, however, one of the latter, namely Sepia, the youngest, had reappeared, a fragment of the family wreck, floating over the gulf of its destruction. Nobody knew with any certainty where she had been in the interim: nobody at Durnmelling knew anything but what she chose to tell, and that was not much. She said she had been a governess in Austrian Poland and Russia. Lady Margaret had become reconciled to her presence, and Hesper attached to her.

Of the men who, as I have said, admired her, some felt a peculiar enchantment in what they called her ugliness; others declared her devilishly handsome; and some shrank from her as if with an undefined dread of perilous entanglement, if she should but catch them looking her in the face. Among some of them she was known as Lucifer, in antithesis to Hesper.

The ladies, on their part, especially Hesper, were very pleased with Mary by the simplicity of her speech and manner, by the pains she took to find the exact thing they wanted, and by the modest decision with which she answered every question. When their purchases were ended, Hesper took her leave with a kind smile, which went on glowing in Mary's heart long after she had vanished.

"Home, John," said Lady Margaret the moment the two younger ladies were seated. "I hope you have gotten all you wanted. I fear we shall be late for luncheon. I would not for worlds keep Mr. Redmain waiting—a little faster, John, please."

Hesper's eyes darkened at the mention of the name. Sepia eyed her from under the mingling of ascended lashes and descended brows. The coachman pretended to obey, but the horses knew very well when he did and when he did not mean them to, and took not a step faster than before. John had a special regard for the splendid-looking black horse on the near side which was weak in the wind, and cared little for the anxiety of his mistress. To him, horses were the final peak of creation—or if not the horses, the coachmen, whose they are; masters and mistresses were the merest parasitical adjuncts. He got them home in good time for luncheon, notwithstanding—more to Lady Margaret's than Hesper's satisfaction.

Mr. Redmain was a bachelor of fifty, to whom Lady Margaret was endeavoring to make the family agreeable, in the hope he might take Hesper off their hands. I need not say he was rich. He was a common man with good cold manners, which he offered you like a handle. He was selfish, capable of picking up a lady's handkerchief, but hardly a wife's. He was attentive to Hesper; but she scarcely concealed such a repugnance to him as some feel at sight of strange fishes—being at the same time afraid of him, which was not surprising, as she could hardly fail to perceive the fate intended for her.

"Isn't Miss Mortimer a stunner?" said George Turnbull to Mary, when the tide of customers had finally ebbed from the shop.

"I don't exactly know what you mean, George," answered Mary.

"Oh, of course, I know it isn't fair to ask any girl to admire another," said George. "But I mean no offense to you. Miss Mortimer hasn't got your waist, nor your hands, nor your hair, though you don't have her size."

He looked up from the piece of fabric he was smoothing out, and saw he was alone in the shop.

3 / Sunday at Thornwick

The next day was Sunday at last, a day dear to all who do anything like their duty during the week, whether they go to church or not. It was Mary's custom to go to the Baptist chapel, a practice made holy by the companionship of her father. On this particular day she stood, knelt, and sat through the routine of observance with more than ordinary restlessness and lack of interest, for old Mr. Duppa was certainly duller than usual. How could he be anything but dull when he had been preparing to spend a mortal hour in descanting on the reasons which necessitated the separation of all true Baptists from all brother-believers?

The narrow, high-souled little man—for a soul as well as a forehead can be both high and narrow—was dull that morning because he spoke out of his narrowness, and not out of his height. Mary was better justified in feeling bored than even when George Turnbull plagued her with his attentions. When at last they were out, she could hardly help skipping along the street by her father's side. How much better than chapel would be their nice little cold dinner together, in their only sitting-room, smelling so pleasantly of the multifarious goods piled around it on all the rest of the floor. Greater yet was the following pleasure—of making her father lie down on the sofa, and reading him to sleep, after which she would doze a little herself, and dream a little, in the great chair that had been her grandmother's. Upon awakening they had their tea, and then her father always went to see the minister before chapel in the evening.

When he was gone, Mary would put on her pretty straw bonnet and set out to visit Letty Lovel at Thornwick. Some of the church-members thought this habit of taking a walk instead of going again to the chapel for the evening service very worldly, and did not scruple to let her know their opinion. But so long as her father was satisfied with her, Mary did not care a straw for the world's thoughts. She was too much occupied with obedience to trouble her head about opinion, either her own or other people's. Not until a question comes puzzling and troubling us so as to paralyze the energy of our obedience is there any necessity for its solution, or any probability of finding a real one. A thousand foolish doctrines may lie unquestioned in the mind, and never interfere with the growth or bliss of him who lives in active subordination of his life to the law of life: obedience will in time exorcise them, like many another worse devil.

It had drizzled all the morning from the clouds as well as from the pulpit, but just as Mary stepped out of the kitchen-door, the sun stepped out of the last rain-cloud. She walked quickly from the town, eager for the fields and the trees, but in some dread of finding Tom Helmer at the stile, where she must climb over the fence. He was such a fool, she said to herself, that there was no knowing what he might do, for all she had said. But he had thought better of it, did not come out to meet her, and she was soon crossing meadows and cornfields in peace, by a path which, with many a winding and many an up and down, was the nearest way to Thornwick.

The saints of old did well to pray God to lift on them the light of his countenance: has the Christian of the new time learned of his Master that the clouds and the sunshine come and go of themselves? If the sunshine fills the hearts of old men and babes and birds with gladness and praise, and God never meant it, then they are all idolaters, and have but a careless Father.

Sweet earthly odors rose about Mary from the wet ground; the rain-drops glittered on the grass and the corn-blades and hedgerows. A soft, damp wind breathed rather than blew about the gaps and gates. With an upward springing, like that of a fountain momentarily gathering strength, the larks kept shooting aloft, like music-rockets, to explode in showers of glowing and sparkling song; while all the time and over all, the sun as he went down kept shining in the might of his peace. And the heart of Mary praised her Father in heaven.

Where the narrow path ran westward for a little way, so that she could see nothing for the sun in her eyes, in the middle of a plowed field she would have run right into a gentleman had he been as blind as she. But since his back was to the sun, he saw her coming perfectly, and stepped out of her way into the midst of a patch of stiff soil, where the rain was still standing between the furrows. She saw him then, and as he lifted his hat and stepped aside, she recognized Mr. Wardour.

"Oh, your nice boots!" she cried, in the childlike distress of a simple soul discovering itself the cause of catastrophe, for his boots were smeared all over with yellow clay.

"It only serves me right," he returned with an amused laugh. "I shouldn't have put on such thin ones at the first of summer when the ground is still so wet."

Again he lifted his hat and walked on.

Mary also continued on her way along the path, regretting that someone should have had to step up to the ankles in mud on her account. As I have said, she had never before spoken to Mr. Wardour except in the shop a time or two, and he did not even recognize at first who she was.

The friendship that now drew Mary to Thornwick, Godfrey Wardour's place, was a fairly recent one. Though she and Letty Lovel had known each other for some time, it was only very recently that their acquaintance had ripened into something better. Godfrey's mother, Mrs. Wardour, the aging matriarch of the estate, did not particularly like Mary and steadfastly protested the growth of the intimacy she perceived between the two young women. She often let the remark fall that the society of a shopwoman was far from suitable for one like Letty, who, as the daughter of a professional man, might lay claim to the position of a gentlewoman. The difference in class between her and Mary, according to the prejudices of Mrs. Wardour, was like night and day. For Letty was the orphan daughter of a country surgeon, Mrs. Wardour's cousin, and she had come to stay at Thornwick upon her father's death. At the same time, however much Mrs. Wardour would have considered her the superior of Mary Marston, she by no means treated Letty as her own equal, and Letty could not help being afraid of her aunt, as she called her.

The well-meaning woman was in fact possessed by two devils—the one the stiff-necked devil of pride, the other the condescending devil of benevolence. She was kind, but she must have credit for it. And Letty, though the child of a beloved cousin she had known since childhood, must not presume upon that, or forget that the wife and mother of long-descended proprietors of certain acres of land was greatly the superior of any man who lived by the exercise of the best-educated and most helpful profession. She counted herself a devout Christian, but her ideas of rank at least—and not a few other ideas as well—were absolutely opposed to the Master's teaching: they who did least for others were greatest in her eyes of what constituted the aristocracy.

Letty was a simple, true-hearted girl, a little slow it is true, who honestly tried to understand her aunt's position with regard to her friend. "Shopgirls," her aunt had said, "are not fitting company for you, Letty."

"I do not know any other shop-girls than Mary, Aunt," Letty replied. "But she at least is downright good; indeed she is."

"That may well be," answered Mrs. Wardour, "but it does not make a lady of her."

"I am sure," returned Letty, feeling a little bewildered, "on Sundays you could not tell the difference between her and any other young lady."

"Any other well-dressed young woman, my dear, you should say. Just because shop-girls call their companions young ladies does not justify the use of the word. If the word 'lady' should sink to common use, we must find some other word to express what *used* to be meant by it."

"Is Mrs. Cropper a lady, Aunt?" asked Letty, after a pause, in which her brains were not half so muddled concerning the morass of social distinction as she thought them.

"She is received as such," replied Mrs. Wardour, but with doubled stiffness, through which ran a tone of injury.

"Would you receive her, Aunt, if she called upon you?"

"She has horses and servants, and everything a woman of the world can desire. But I should feel I was bowing my knee to mammon were I to ask her to my house. Yet such is the respect paid to money in these degenerate days that many will court the society of a person like that, who would think me or your cousin Godfrey unworthy of notice because we no longer have a tenth of the property the family once possessed."

The lady forgot that there are many kinds of mammon worship, both among those who have money, and those who would like to have more.

"God knows," she went on, "how that woman's husband made his money! But that is a small matter nowadays, except to old-fashioned people like myself. Not *how* but *how much* is all the question now," she concluded, flattering herself she had made a good point.

"I am really trying to understand Aunt—but if Mrs. Cropper is not a lady, how can Mary Marston not be one? She is as different from Mrs. Cropper as one woman can be from another."

"Because she does not have the position in society," replied Mrs. Wardour, enveloping her empty arguments in flimsy reiteration and self-contradiction.

"And Mrs. Cropper has the position?" ventured Letty.

"Apparently so," answered Mrs. Wardour. But Letty did not feel much enlightened.

Letty did not have the logic necessary to think the thing out completely, or to discover that, like most social difficulties, hers was merely one of the upper strata of a question whose foundation lies far too deep for what is called Society, and sadly in many cases the Church as well, to perceive its very existence.

But although such were her reasonings, Mrs. Wardour's heart had so far overcome her prejudices after Mary's first few visits—for she could not help but perceive her high tone and good influence—that she allowed herself to see her as often as she came. She always played the grand lady on these occasions, with a stateliness that seemed to say, "Because of your individual worth, I condescend and make an exception, but you must not imagine that I would automatically receive your class at Thornwick." Yet she did cease almost entirely to make any further remarks of class distinction to Letty.

On her part, Letty had opened the question to Mary a number of times, and this same Sunday afternoon, as they sat in the arbor at the end of the long yew hedge in the old garden, it had come up again between them.

"I cannot trouble my mind about it as you do, Letty," Mary said.

"Society is neither my master nor my servant, and so long as she does not bar my way to the kingdom of heaven, which is the only society worth getting into, I feel no right to complain of how she treats me. I do not acknowledge her laws—hardly her existence, and she has no authority over me. What can it matter to me, Letty, whether they call me a lady or not, so long as Jesus says *daughter* to me? It reminds me of what I heard my father say once to Mr. Turnbull, when he had been protesting that none but church members ought to be buried in the churchyards.

" 'I don't care a straw about it, Mr. Turnbull,' my father said. 'The Master was buried in a garden.'

" 'Ah, but don't you see, things are different now,' said Mr. Turnbull.

" 'I don't go by things, but by my Master,' said my father. 'Besides, you must not think it of any real consequence yourself, or you would never want to keep your brothers and sisters out of such nice quiet places!'

"Mr. Turnbull then gave his kind of grunt, and said no more."

After passing Mary, Mr. Wardour did not go very far before he began to slacken his pace. A moment or two more and he suddenly wheeled round and began to walk back toward Thornwick. Two things had combined to produce this change of purpose—the first, the state of his boots, which, now beginning to dry in the sun and wind as he walked, grew more and more hideous at the end of his new gray trousers; the other, the occurring suspicion that the girl must be Letty's new shopkeeping friend, Miss Marston, on her way to visit her. *What a sweet, simple young woman she was*, he thought. Immediately he began to say to himself that it would be more pleasant to spend the evening with Letty and her friend than at his own friend's, smoking and lounging about the stable.

Mary had, of course, upon her arrival, told of her small adventure, and the conversation had again turned upon Godfrey just as he was nearing the house.

"How handsome your cousin is," said Mary, with the simplicity natural to her.

"Do you think so?" returned Letty.

"Don't *you* think so?" rejoined Mary.

"I have never thought about it," answered Letty.

"He looks so manly and has such a straightforward way with him," said Mary.

"There is something about him that used to make me afraid of him," said Letty.

"Does he talk to you?"

"Oh, yes—now. It was a long time before he began to though. He is always giving me books to read and then questioning me to see if I have understood what I read."

Here she gave a little cry. For through the narrow gap in the yew hedge, near to the arbor, Godfrey had entered the walk and was coming toward them.

He was a well-made man, thirty years of age, rather tall, sun-tanned, and bearded, with wavy brown hair and gentle approach. His features were not regular, but that is of little consequence where there is unity. His face indicated intelligence and feeling, and there was much good nature, shadowed with memory of suffering, in the eyes which shone so blue out of the brown.

Mary rose respectfully as he drew near.

"What treason were you talking, Letty, that you were so startled at the sight of me?" he said with a smile. "You were not complaining of me as a hard master were you?"

"No indeed, cousin Godfrey," answered Letty, not without a little shaking in her voice and coloring in her face as she spoke. "I was only saying I could not help being frightened when you ask me questions about what I had been reading. I am so stupid, you know."

"Pardon me, Letty," returned her cousin. "I know nothing of the sort. You are very far from stupid. Nobody can understand everything at first sight, and you understand more than your share. But you have not introduced me to your friend."

Letty bashfully murmured the names of the two.

"I guessed as much," said Wardour. "Please, sit down, Miss Marston. For the sake of your dresses, I will go and change my boots. May I come and join you afterward?"

"Please do, cousin Godfrey. And bring something to read to us," said Letty. "It's Sunday, you know."

"Why you should be afraid of him, I can't imagine," remarked Mary, when his retreating steps had ceased to sound on the gravel. "He is delightful!"

"I don't like to look stupid," said Letty.

"I shouldn't mind how stupid I looked so long as I was learning," returned Mary. "I wonder you never told me about him."

"I couldn't talk about cousin Godfrey," said Letty, and a pause followed.

Letty was a rather small and freckled girl, with the daintiest of rounded figures, a good forehead, and fine clear brown eyes. Her mouth was not pretty, except when she smiled—and she did not smile often. When she did, it was not infrequently with tears in her eyes, and then she looked lovely. In her manner there was an indescribable charm, of which it is not easy to give an impression. I think it sprang from a constitutional humility, partly ruined into a painful and haunting sense of inferiority, for which she imagined herself to blame. Hence there dwelt in her eyes an appeal that few hearts could resist. When they met another's, they seemed to say: "I am nobody, but I am not pretending to be anybody. I will try to do what you want, but I am not clever. Only be gentle with me." To Godfrey, at least, her eyes spoke thus.

In ten minutes or so he reappeared, far at the other end of the yew-walk, approaching slowly, with a book in his hand, in which he seemed thoughtfully searching through the pages as he came. When they saw him the girls instinctively moved farther from each other, making large room for him between them, and when he came up he silently took the place thus silently assigned him.

"I am going to try your brains now, Letty," he said, and tapped the book with a finger.

"Oh, please don't!" pleaded Letty, as if he had been threatening her with a small amputation of a finger, or the loss of a front tooth.

"Yes," he persisted, "and not your brains only, but your heart and all that is in you."

Even Mary could not help feeling a little intimidated at such a beginning.

With a few words of introduction, Godfrey read Carlyle's translation of one of the finest of Jean Paul's dreams. Slowly, with due inflection and emphasis, he read to the end, stopped, and lifted his eyes.

"There, Letty," he said, "what do you think of that?"

Letty was looking altogether perplexed, and not a little frightened.

"I don't understand a word of it," she answered, gulping back her tears.

He glanced at Mary, but she said nothing.

Godfrey picked up the book and read the passage again. The second reading affected Mary more than the first—because, of course, she took in more. And this time a glimmer of meaning broke on the slower mind of Letty.

"I can't be completely stupid after all, cousin Godfrey," admitted Letty when he had finished, "for something kept going through and through me. But I cannot yet say I understand it.—If you will lend me the book," she continued, "I will read it over again before I go to bed."

He shut the volume, handed it to her, and began to talk about something else.

Mary rose to go.

"You will take tea with us, I hope, Miss Marston," said Godfrey.

But Mary said she would not. What she had heard was working in her mind with a powerful fermentation, and she longed to be alone. In the fields, as she walked, she would come to an understanding with herself.

She knew almost nothing of the higher literature, and felt like a dreamer, who, in the midst of a well-known and ordinary landscape, comes without warning upon the mighty cone of a mountain, or the breaking waters of a boundless ocean.

"If one could but get hold of such things, what a glorious life it would be!" she thought. The reading had given her a glimpse of a world beyond the present, and already as a result all things were new. The sun set as she had never seen him set before. The wind visited her cheek like a living thing, and loved her. The skylarks had more than reason in their jubilation. For the first time she heard the full chord of intellectual and emotional delight.

What a place her room would be if she had such things to read! Might Mr. Wardour lend her the book? Had he other books as good? Were there many books to make one's heart go as that one did?

Under the enchantment of her first true literary joy, she walked home like one intoxicated—a being possessed for the time with the awful imagination of a grander soul, and reveling in the presence of her loftier human kin.

4 / Godfrey Wardour

The property of which Thornwick once formed a part was at that time large and important. But it had by degrees, generation following generation of unthrift, dwindled and shrunk and shriveled, until at last it threatened to disappear from the family altogether. Then came one into possession who had some element of salvation in him. Godfrey's father not only held the poor remnant together, but, unable to add to it, improved it so greatly that at length, in the midst of the large properties around, it resembled the diamond that lies in the center of inferior stones. Had he been able to use his wife's money, he would have spent it on land. But it was under trustees for her and her children, and indeed would not have gone far in the purchase of English soil.

Considerably advanced in years before he thought of marrying, he died while Godfrey, whom he intended bringing up to a profession, was yet a child. His widow, carrying out his intention, had educated the boy with a view to the law. Godfrey, however, had positively refused to embark on studies toward a career he detested. And as time went on it was not especially difficult for him to reconcile his mother to the idea of a change in plans, when she found that his sole desire was to settle down with her, and manage the two hundred acres his father had left him.

Therefore Godfrey took his place in the county as a yeoman farmer—nonetheless a gentleman by descent, character, and education. But while in genuine culture and refinement he was the superior of all the land proprietors in the neighborhood, he was also the superior of most of them in this also, that he counted it no diminishing of his dignity to put his hand to any piece of work required about the place.

His nature was too large, however, and its needs therefore too many, to allow his spending all his energies on the property. And he did not brood over anxieties. How much time is wasted in what people *call* thought, but is merely care—an anxious idling over the fancied probabilities of result. Of this fault, I say, Godfrey was not guilty—more, however, from healthy leanings in other directions, than from any inbred wisdom he possessed. This other bent was namely this: he was a *reader*. In his reading Godfrey nourished certain of the higher tendencies of his nature, but did not read with the highest aim of all—the enlargement of reverence, obedience, and faith in God. He had never yet turned his face full in the direction of infinite growth—the primal end of a man's being is that he may return to the Father,

39

gathering truth as he goes. Yet by the simple instincts of a soul undebased by self-indulgence or low pursuits, he was drawn ever toward things lofty and good. And life went calmly on, bearing Godfrey Wardour toward middle age, unruffled neither by anxiety nor ambition.

To the forecasting affection of a mother, the hour when she would have to yield the first place both of her son's attention and in-house affairs must often have presented itself in dread to Mrs. Wardour. But as year after year passed and Godfrey revealed no tendency toward marriage, her anxiety changed sides, and she began to fear lest with Godfrey the ancient family should come to an end. And yet, however, she had not ventured to speak openly to him on the subject. All the time she had never thought of Letty as either thwarting or furthering her desires. She looked upon her as some-one Godfrey could never condescend to be familiar with, except with the sort of kindness one shows to those immeasurably below him. She had neither curiosity nor care about what might pass in Letty's mind. If she had thought about it, she might have been more careful about speaking of Godfrey with such words of motherly pride. But as it was, Letty could hardly escape coming to regard her cousin as one of the very best of men.

It added force to the veneration of both mother and cousin that there was about Godfrey an air of the inexplicable, or at least the unknown, and therefore mysterious. The elder woman, not without a pang at knowing herself excluded from his confidence, correctly attributed this to some passage in his life at the university. To the younger it merely appeared as greatness itself, in intellect, in courage, and in being above the ordinary world.

The passage in Godfrey's life to which I have referred, I need not present in more than merest outline: it belongs to my history only as a component part of the soil whence it springs, and as in some measure necessary to the understanding of Godfrey's character. In the last year of his college life he had formed an attachment, the precise nature of which I do not know. What I do know is that the bonds of this love were rudely and suddenly broken, and what remained was disappointment and pain, doubt and distrust.

It would have been well for him if he had been left with only a wounded heart, but in that heart lay wounded pride as well. He hid it carefully, and no stranger could have suspected what lay in Godfrey's heart beneath the calm manner he wore. Under that bronzed countenance, with its firm-set mouth and powerful jaw—below that clear blue eye, and that upright easy carriage—lay a faithful heart haunted by a sense of having been wronged. He who is not perfect in forgiveness must be haunted thus. Forgiveness is the only cure of wrong. And hand in hand with Sense-of-injury walks ever the weak sister—demon Self-pity, so dear, so sweet to many—both of them the children of Love-of-Self, not of Agape.

But there was no hate, no revenge, in Godfrey, and his weakness he kept concealed. For the rest, his was a strong poetic nature—a nature that half unconsciously always turned toward the best, and away from the low and worldly. Yet there was in him a profound need of redemption into the love of the truth for the truth's sake. He had the fault of thinking too well of himself—which who has not who thinks of himself at all? At the age of thirty, Godfrey Wardour had not yet become so displeased with himself as to turn self-roused energy upon betterment. And until then all growth must be of doubtful result. The point on which the swift-revolving top of his thinking and feeling turned was still his present conscious self, as a thing that *was* and *would be*, not as a thing that had to *become*. Naturally the pivot had worn a socket, and such a socket is sure to be sore. His friends, notwithstanding, gave him credit for a great easy-going nature. But in such willfully unemotional men the evil burrows the more insidiously that it is masked by a constrained exterior.

5 / Godfrey and Letty

Being an Englishman with land of his own, Godfrey could not fail to be fond of horses. For his own use he kept two, but had no groom. Therefore, now and then, strap and steel, as well as hide and hoof, would get partially neglected. His habits in the use of his horses were fitful, and sometimes it would even be midnight when he rode from his home, seeking the comfort of desert as well as solitary places. But since he had no one to help him, it was not surprising if at times, going to the stable to saddle one, he should find its gear in something less than spick-and-span condition.

One night, meaning to start for a long ride early in the morning, he had gone to the stable to see how things were; and, soon after, it happened that Letty, attending to some duty before going to bed, caught sight of him cleaning his stirrups. From that moment she took upon herself the silent and unsuspected supervision of the harness-room. When she found any part of the riding equipment neglected, she would draw a pair of housemaid's gloves on her pretty hands and polish away like a stable-boy.

Godfrey had begun to notice how long it had been since he had found anything dirty or rusted or unfit, and to wonder what might have caused the change. One morning, some months before this present time, he walked hastily into the harness-room to get a saddle, and came upon Letty who had imagined him out in the fields with the men. She was energetic upon a stirrup with a chain-polisher. He started back in amazement, but she only looked up and smiled.

"I will be done in a moment, cousin Godfrey," she said, polishing away harder than before.

"But, Letty, I can't allow you to do things like that. What on earth put it into your head? Why shouldn't I clean my own harness if I like?"

"Oh surely, if you like," she answered. "But do you like to?"

"Better than to see you doing it."

"But not better than I like to do it, that I am sure of. Hands like yours that write poetry are not fit for work like this."

"How do you know I write poetry?" asked Godfrey displeased, for she touched a sensitive spot.

"Please don't be angry with me," she replied. "I couldn't help seeing it when I went to do your room."

"Do my room! Does my mother—?"

"She doesn't want to make a lady of me, and I shouldn't like it if she

42

did. I have no head, but I can work with my hands. But I didn't read a word of it. I wouldn't have dared do that, however much I might have wished to."

A childlike simplicity looked out of the clear eyes, and Godfrey's heart could not but be touched by her devotion. At the same time he was not a little puzzled how to carry himself; what would be a proper way of thanking her and showing how highly he esteemed this act of her ladyhood? For, although Letty did make beds and chose to clean harnesses, Godfrey was enough of a gentleman not to think her less of a lady because of such things. I will not say he had gotten so far on in the great doctrine concerning the washing of hands as to be able to think her *more* of a lady for thus cleaning his stirrups. He laid his hand on her head and said: "I ought to be a knight of the old times, Letty, to have a lady serve me so."

"You're just as good, cousin Godfrey," she rejoined, polishing away.

He turned from her and left her at her work.

He had taken no real notice of the girl before—had felt little interest in her. Neither did he feel much now, except as owing her something and wishing there might be something he could do for her. She was a fresh, bright girl—that he seemed to have just discovered.

"There must be *something* in the girl," he said to himself. Then suddenly he reflected that he had never seen a book in her hand, except her prayer book. If only he might get her to read, and be interested in books! Perhaps, if he could make her drink once, she would drink again. To do so he must first find out what sort of spiritual and literary drink would be most to her taste, and would entice her to want to read on her own. There must be some seeds lying cold and hard in her uncultured garden; what water would soonest make them grow? Not all the waters of Damascus will turn mere sand sifted of eternal winds into fruitful soil. But Letty's soil could not be such. And then literature has seed to sow as well as water for the seed sown. She had shown a shadow of respect for poetry—perhaps that might be the place to start.

Thus pondering, he forgot all about his ride, and went up to the study he had contrived for himself in the rambling roof of the ancient house, and began looking along the backs of his books, in search of some suggestion of how to approach Letty. He found a volume of verse—a selection of English lyrics—and took it back to the saddle room at once.

Letty was not there. He went in search of her, thinking she might be in the dairy.

That was the very picture of an old-fashioned English dairy—green-shadowy, dark, dank, and cool—floored with great irregular slabs, mostly of green marble, polished into smooth hollows by the feet of generations of mistresses and dairymaids. Its only light came through a small window shaded with shrubs and ivy, which stood open, and let in the scents of bud and blossom, weaving a net of sweetness in the gloom, through which, like a silver thread, shot the twittering song of a bird, which had inherited the gathered carelessness and bliss of a long ancestry in God's aviary.

Godfrey came softly to the door, which he found standing ajar, and peeped in. There stood Letty, warm and bright in the middle of the dusky coolness, skimming the cream in a great red-brown earthen pan. He pushed the door a little, and at its screech along the uneven floor, Letty's head turned quickly and she saw Godfrey.

"Letty," he said, "I have just come upon this book in my library: would you like to have it?"

"You don't mean to keep for my own?" exclaimed Letty, hastily wiping her hands in her apron. Her face flushed rosy with pleasure, and she hesitantly took the rich morocco-bound book from Godfrey's outstretched hand. Daintily she opened it and peeped inside.

"Poetry!" she cried in a tone of delight. "Is it really for me, cousin Godfrey? Do you think I shall be able to understand it?"

"You can soon settle that question for yourself," answered Godfrey with a pleased smile, as he turned to leave the dairy.

Letty stood motionless, the book in her hand. Slowly she flipped through the pages, reading snatches from poem after poem. She read more that very night in her bed, and before many days had taken a fresh start in intellectual and spiritual growth.

Whenever possible after that evening, Godfrey took the opportunity of asking her about what she was reading. He set himself in earnest to the task of developing her intellectual life, and almost daily grew more interested in the endeavor. His main object was to make her think; and for that high purpose, chiefly but not exclusively, he employed verse.

The main obstacle to success he soon discovered to be Letty's great distrust of herself. I do not mean she had too little confidence in herself; of that no one can have too little. Some will answer that you must have either self-distrust or self-confidence. "You must have neither," I reply. You must follow the truth, and in that pursuit, the less one thinks about himself, the pursuer, the better. Let him so hunger and thirst after the truth that the dim vision of it occupies all his being, and leaves no time to think of his hunger and thirst. Self-forgetfulness is the healthiest of mental conditions. One has to look to his way, to his deeds, to his conduct—not to himself. In such losing of the false, or the merely reflected, we find the true self. There is no harm in being stupid, so long as a man does not think himself clever; no good in being clever, if a man thinks himself so, for that is a short way to the worst stupidity. If you think yourself clever, set yourself to do something, and you will have a chance of humiliation.

With good faculties and fine instincts, Letty got on fairly well in spite of always thinking she must be wrong about something. And as she did, her devotion to Godfrey grew as well. By that, I do not mean what in novels is commonly called love. Godfrey Wardour was at least ten years older than Letty, and she had no other male relative in the world besides him—neither had she mother or sister on whom to let out her heart. And she was a little afraid of Mrs. Wardour, who was more severe on her than on anyone else. Thus, though it might not be love in the fictional sense, it came that cousin Godfrey grew and grew in her imagination, until he represented to her everything great and good—the idea of him naturally growing as she herself grew under his influences. To her he was the heart of wisdom, the head of knowledge, the arm of strength.

Godfrey began to be more and more interested in her, especially after he had made the discovery that the moment she laid hold of a truth—the moment, that is, when it was no longer another's idea only but her own perception as well—it began to sprout in her in all directions of practice. By nature she was not intellectually quick. But because such was her character, the ratio of her progress was of necessity an increasing one.

Godfrey saw in his new relation to Letty no possibility of falling in love and reviving those feelings he had supposed forever extinguished. He behaved to her with almost a tutorial distance, insisting on a precision in all she did that might with some natures have roused defeat and resentment in the mind of a less childlike learner. But just as surely, however, did the sweet girl make a nest for herself in his soul—what kind of a nest for a long time he did not know, and for long did not think to inquire. He was more than satisfied to occupy the relationship with her of an elder brother to a younger sister. But how far any man and woman may have been made capable of loving without falling in love can be answered only after question has yielded to history. In the meantime, Mrs. Wardour, who would have been indignant at the very notion of any equal bond between her idolized son and her patronized cousin, neither saw nor heard nor suspected anything to rouse uneasiness.

Such was the state of things when the growing friendship of Letty and Mary Marston led Letty to ask Mary one day if she would come visit her at Thornwick on Sunday. The moment she had said the words, she thought with dread of her aunt, and almost regretted having made the invitation. She did not withdraw it, however. Mary came, the difficulty with her aunt was gotten over, and the visit became weekly. The friendship of Godfrey also had not run into that of the girls, and Mary's visits were continued, with pleasure to all. Her Sunday visit became to Mary the one foraging expedition of the week—that which going to church ought to be, and so seldom can be.

The mainstay of Mary's spiritual life was her father. From books and sermons she had gotten little good, for in neither had the best come near her. She did very nearly her best to obey, but she was yet, in relation to the gospel, much as the Jews were in relation to their law. They had not yet learned the gospel of their law, and she was yet only serving the law of the gospel. But she was making progress, in simple and pure virtue of her obedience. Show me the person ready to step from any, let it be the narrowest sect of Christian Pharisees into a freer and holier air, and I shall look to find in that person one who, in the midst of the darkness and selfish worldliness—mistaken for holiness—around them, has long been living a life more obedient than the rest.

And now Godfrey was sent to Mary's aid, a teacher actually far behind his pupil, inasmuch as he was more occupied with what he was than what he had to become. The weakest may be sent to give the strongest help, and Godfrey presented Mary to men greater than himself, whom in a short time she would understand even better than he. Book after book he lent her, introducing her without even realizing it to much spirituality that was good in the way of literature as well. Only where he delighted mainly in the literature, she delighted more in the spirituality.

But Godfrey, as he led the talk on the Sunday afternoons, was by no means confined either to religious or to English literature. His seclusion from what is called the world had brought him into larger and closer contact with what is really the world. The breakers upon reef and shore may be the ocean to some, but he who would know the ocean indeed must leave them afar, sinking into silence, and sail into wider and lonelier spaces. Through Godfrey, Mary came to know of a land never promised, yet open— a land of the spirit, a land of which the fashionable world knows little. As thankful as she was, however, Mary did not trouble herself much to show Godfrey her gratitude. We may spoil gratitude as we offer it, by insisting on its recognition. To receive honestly is the best thanks for a good thing.

Mary did receive honestly, and Godfrey was not without payment for what he did: the revival of ancient benefits, a new springtime of old flowers, and the fresh quickening of one's own soul are the spiritual wages of every spiritual service. In giving, a man receives more than he gives, and the *more* is in proportion to the worth of the things given.

Mary did not encourage Letty to call at the shop. She knew the rudeness of the Turnbulls was certain to break out on her once she left, as it did one day upon Godfrey. When he entered the shop in quest of something for his mother, he naturally shook hands with Mary over the counter. No remark was made so long as her father was in the shop, for, with all their professed contempt of him and his ways, the Turnbulls stood curiously in awe of him: no one could tell what he might do, and there were reasons for avoiding offense. But the moment he retired, which he usually did earlier than the rest, their words soon caused Mary a burning cheek and indignant heart. Yet despite their uncivil tongues, the great desire of Mr. Turnbull was a match between George and Mary, for that would, whatever might happen, secure the Marston money to the business.

But their low natures could not long keep down the wellspring of her own peace, which, deeper than anger could reach, soon began to rise again in her spirit, fed from that water of life which underlies all care. In a few moments it had cooled her cheek, stilled her heart, and washed the wounds of offense.

6 / Tom Helmer

When Tom Helmer's father died, his mother, who had never been able to manage him, sent him to school to be rid of him. She lamented his absence till he returned, then writhed and fretted under his presence until he went again. Never thereafter did mother and son meet, whether from a separation of months or of hours, without at once falling into obstinate argument. When the youth was at home, their sparring, to call it by a mild name, went on from morning to night, and sometimes almost from night to morning.

Primarily, of course, the fault lay with the mother; and things would have gone far worse, had not the youth, along with the self-will of his mother, inherited the good nature of his father. At school he was a great favorite, and mostly had his own way, both with boys and teachers. For although he was a fool, he was a pleasant fool, clever, fond of popularity, and compliant with everybody—except always his mother, the merest word from whom would at once rouse all the rebel in his blood.

In appearance he was tall and loosely knit, with large joints and extremities. His face was handsome and vivacious, expressing far more than was in him to express, and giving ground for expecting more out of him than he had ever met. He was by no means an ill-intentioned fellow, preferred doing well and acting fairly, and neither at school nor at college had gotten into any serious scrape. But he had never found it imperative to reach out after his own ideal of duty or obedience. He had never been worthy of the name of student, or cared much for anything beyond the amusements the universities provide so liberally, except dabbling in literature. Perhaps his only vice was self-satisfaction, which few will admit to be a vice. Self-evaluation or disapproval never reached him. To himself he was always in the right, judging himself only by his feelings and vague intents, never by his actions; that these had little correspondence never struck him. It had never even struck him that they ought to correspond, and that actions might somehow be the truest measure of a man. In his own eyes he did well enough, and a good deal better. Gifted not only with fluency of speech, that crowning glory and ruin of a fool, but with plausibility of tone and demeanor, a confidence that imposed both on himself and on others, and a certain superficial impressionableness that made him seem and believe himself sympathetic, nobody could well help liking him.

He was now in his twenty-first year, at home, pretending that nothing should make him go back to Oxford, and enjoying more than ever the sport of plaguing his mother. A soul-doctor might have prescribed for him a course of smallpox, to be followed by intermittent fever, with nobody to wait upon him but Mrs. Gamp. After that, his mother might have had a possible chance with him, and he with his mother. But, unhappily, he had the best of health—supreme blessing in the eyes of the fool whom it enables to be a worse fool still; and was altogether the true son of his mother, who consoled herself for the absolute failure in his moral education with the reflection that she had reared him sound in wind and limb. It will be clear that a good deal of his foolishness he inherited from her, for it is only the foolish parent who thinks it his or her sole duty to offer a home and food for a growing child, as if that were all he needed to truly become the adult God intended, paying little attention to the silent and steady growth of character through the years. Mrs. Helmer had paid little attention to it, and was now reaping the reward of seeing in her grown son a reflection of her own shortsightedness.

Plaguing his mother, amusing himself as best he could, riding about the country on a good mare, of which he was proud, he was living in utter idleness, affording occasion for much wondering that he had never yet disgraced himself, and one whom Solomon might well have observed before writing the Proverbs. He talked with everybody who would talk to him, and made friends with anybody on the spur of the moment's whim. He would sit on a log with a gypsy, and bamboozle him with lies made for the purpose, then thrash him for not believing them. He called here and called there, made himself especially agreeable everywhere, went to every ball and evening party to which he could get admittance, and flirted with any girl who would let him.

He meant no harm, neither had done much, and was imagined most incapable of doing any. The strange thing to some was that he stayed on in the country, and did not go to London and run up bills for his mother to pay. But the mare accounted for a good deal, and the fact that almost immediately on his recent return he had seen Letty and fallen in love with her at first sight accounted for a good deal more. Not since then, however, had he yet been able to meet her alone; for Thornwick was one of the few houses of the middle class in the neighborhood where he was not encouraged to show himself. Therefore, he was constantly on the watch for a chance of seeing her, and every Sunday went to church for that reason and no other.

Letty knew nothing of all this. For although Tom, as we have heard, confessed to her friend Mary Marston his admiration of her, Mary had far too much good sense to make herself his ally in the matter.

7 / Celebration at Durnmelling ─────────────

In the autumn, Lady Margaret's husband, Mr. Mortimer of Durnmelling, decided to give a feast for his tenants to celebrate the successful completion of the harvest. Under the covering of the occasion, he resolved also to invite a good many of his neighbors and some of the townsfolk of Testbridge, whom he could not well ask to dinner under other circumstances: it happened to be politically expedient for him to do so with respect to certain ambitions he cherished. Many whom Lady Margaret had never called on or in any way ever acknowledged were invited, but the knowledge of what it meant did not cause most of them to decline the questionable honor. Mrs. Wardour accepted for herself and Letty; but in their case Lady Margaret did call, and in person gave them the invitation. Godfrey positively refused to accompany them. He would not be patronized; he said; "—and by an inferior," he added to himself.

Mr. Mortimer was the illiterate son of a literary father who had reaped both money and fame. The son spent the former, and on the strength of the latter married an earl's daughter, and thereupon began to embody in his own behavior his ideas of how a nobleman ought to carry himself. From being only small, therefore, he soon became an objectionable man as well. He had never demonstrated the least approach to neighborliness with Godfrey, although their houses were almost within a stone's throw of each other. Had Wardour been an ordinary farmer, and therefore low enough never to think to presume upon the friendship of one so much higher, Mortimer would doubtless have behaved differently. But as Wardour had some pretense toward being a gentleman in his own right—namely, old family, a small, though indeed *very* small, property of his own, a university education, good horses, and the habits and manners of a gentleman—the men scarcely even saluted when they met. The Mortimer ladies, indeed, had more than once remarked—but it was in solemn silence, each to herself only—how well their neighbor sat on his horse. But not once until now had so much as a greeting passed between them and Mrs. Wardour.

It was therefore not so surprising for Godfrey to choose not to accept their invitation. But his mother was distressed at having to go to the gathering without him, and agitated in mind about what would be thought of his absence and what would be the most appropriate excuse to make for him. Therefore, Godfrey resolved to go to London a day or two before the event and make a long-promised visit to a clerical friend.

The relative positioning of the stone-and-lime houses of Durnmelling and Thornwick was curious. That they had at one time formed part of the same property might have suggested itself to any beholder. Durnmelling was built by an ancestor of Godfrey's who forsook the old nest for the new, and had allowed Thornwick to sink into a mere farmhouse, in which condition it had afterward become the sole shelter of the withered fortunes of the Wardours. In the hands of Godfrey's father, it had been restored to something like its original modest dignity.

Durnmelling, too, had in part sunk into ruin, and had been but partially recovered from it; still it swelled important beside its antecedent Thornwick. Nothing more than a deep stream-bed separated the two houses, of which the older and smaller occupied the higher ground. Between it and the stream was nothing but grass—in front of the house enough and well enough kept to be called lawn. On the lower, the Durnmelling side of the fence, were trees, shrubbery, and some out-buildings; the chimney of one of them, the laundry, gave great offense to Mrs. Wardour, when, as she said, wind and wash came together. But although they stood so near, there was no easy means of getting between the houses except the road; and the mile that it took was seldom indeed passed by any of the unneighborly neighbors.

The father of Lady Margaret would at one time have purchased Thornwick at twice its value; but the present owner could not have bought it at half its worth. He had lately been losing money heavily—whence, in part, arose Lady Margaret's anxiety not to keep Mr. Redmain fretting for his lunch.

The house of Durnmelling, new compared with that of Thornwick, was yet, as I have indicated, old enough to have passed also through many changes, and a large portion of the original structure had for many years been nothing better than a ruin. Only a portion of one side of its huge square was occupied by the family, and the rest of that side was not habitable. Lady Margaret, of an ancient stock, had gathered from it only pride, not reverence. Therefore, while she valued the old, she neglected it, and what money she and her husband at one time spent upon the house was devoted to addition and ornamentation, not to preservation or restoration. They had enlarged both dining room and drawing rooms to twice their former size, when half the expense, with a few trees from a certain outlying oak plantation of their own, would have given them a room fit for a regal assembly. For a portion of the same section of the house in which they lived was roofless, laying open to every wind and snow that blew. In this area was an ancient hall that connected the habitable portion of the house with another part, less ruinous than itself, but containing only a few rooms in occasional use for household purposes. It was a glorious ruin, of nearly a hundred feet in length, and about half that in width, the walls complete despite the fallen roof, and thick enough to walk around in safety. Their top was accessible from a tower, which formed part of the less ruinous portion, and contained the stair and some small rooms.

Once the hall had contained portraits and armor and arms, with fire and lights, and state and merriment. Now, however, the sculptured chimney lay open to the weather, and the sweeping winds had made its smooth hearthstone clean as if fire had never been there. Its floor was covered with large flagstone, a little broken.

It was Miss Yolland's idea to use the great roofless hall for the festivities, and to her was committed the responsibility of its preparation and decoration for the occasion, in which Hesper gave her assistance. A few workmen were leveling, patching, and replacing stones in the floor. The tables would be set here, and there was to be dancing after the meal. With colored blankets, carpets, and a few pieces of old tapestry, they managed to clothe the walls to the height of six or eight feet, and thus gave the weather-beaten skeleton an air of hospitable preparation and respectful reception.

The day came and the hour arrived. It was a hot autumn afternoon. In all sorts of horse-drawn vehicles they came. As they arrived they mostly scattered about the place. Some loitered on the lawn, some visited the stables or the farm, with its barns and dairy, some went to the neglected greenhouses, and some walked along the equally neglected paths of the grounds, with their clipped yew trees and their moss-grown statues. No one belonging to the house was anywhere to receive them until the great bell at length summoned them to the plentiful meal spread in the ruined hall. "The hospitality of some people has no roof to it," Godfrey said when he heard of the preparations. "Ten people will give you a dinner, for one who will offer you a bed and a breakfast."

At last their host made his appearance, and sat down at the head of the table. The ladies, he said, were to have the honor of joining the company afterward. They were at the time—but he did not tell his guests this—giving another stratum of society a less ponderous, but yet tolerably substantial, refreshment in the dining room.

By the time the eating and drinking were nearly over, the shades of evening had gathered. But even then some few of the farmers, capable of little besides drinking, grumbled at having their potations interrupted for the dancers. They were presently joined by the company from the house, and the great hall was quite crowded.

Much to her chagrin, Mrs. Wardour had a severe headache from having worked half the night on her dress, and was forced to remain at home. But she allowed Letty to go without her, which she would never have done had she not been so anxious to have news of what she could not lift her head to see. She sent her with an old servant—herself one of the invited guests—to gather and report. They did not go to the dinner, and the dancing had begun before they reached the hall.

Tom Helmer had arrived among the first, and had joined the tenants in their feast, faring well and making friends, such as he knew how to make with everybody in his vicinity. When the tables were removed and the rest of the company began to come in, he went about searching anxiously for Letty's sweet face, but it did not appear. And when she did arrive, she stole in without his seeing her and stood mingled with the crowd about the door.

It was a pleasant sight that met her eyes. The wide space was gaily illuminated with colored lamps. Overhead the night sky was spangled with clear pulsing stars, afloat in a limpid blue. Outside it was dark. The moon was not yet up; she would rise in good time to see the scattering guests to their homes.

Tom's heart had been sinking, for he could see Letty nowhere. Now at last, he had been saying to himself all day, had come his chance. It is true that he knew nothing of her nature; but what was that to one who knew nothing, and never troubled himself to know anything, of his own?

All at once he saw her! Yes it was she—lost in a humble group near the door! His heart gave a great bound. She was dressed in white muslin, from which her white throat rose warm and soft. Her head was bent forward, and a gentle dissolved smile was over all her face, as with loveliest eyes she watched eagerly the motions of the dance, and her ears drank in the music of the band. He seized the first opportunity of getting nearer to her. He had scarcely spoken to her before, but that did not trouble Tom. He had plenty of confidence in his carriage and manner, and knew how to act the part of a gentleman.

Mr. Mortimer had opened the dancing by leading out the wife of his principal tenant, a handsome matron, whose behavior and expression were such as to give a safe, homelike feeling to the shy and doubtful of the company. But Tom knew better than to injure his chance by being too eager: he would wait until the dancing was more general and the impulse to movement stronger, and then offer himself. Therefore, he stood near Letty for some time, talking to everybody, and making himself agreeable all around. Then at last, as if he had just caught sight of her, he walked up to where she stood flushed and eager, and asked her to favor him with her hand in the next dance.

By this time Letty had become familiar with his presence, had recalled her former meeting with him, had heard his name spoken by not a few who evidently liked him, and was quite pleased when he asked her to dance with him.

In the dance, nothing but commonplaces passed between them. But Tom had a certain pleasant way of his own in saying the commonest, emptiest things—an off-hand, glancing, skimming way of brushing and leaving a thing, which made it seem for the moment as if he had said something. Even if his companion was capable of discovering the illusion, there was no time; Tom was instantly away, carrying him or her with him to something else. There was a certain bit of the poetic element in Tom. In the presence of a girl that pleased him, there would rise in him a poetic atmosphere, full of a rainbow kind of glamour, which passed out from him and called up a similar atmosphere about many of the girls he talked to. This he could no more help than the grass can help smelling sweet after the rain.

Tom was a finely projected, well-built, unfinished, barely furnished house, with its great central room empty, where yet the devil, coming and going at his pleasure, had not yet begun to make any great racket. There might be endless embryonic evil in him, but Letty was aware of no repellent atmosphere about him, and did not shrink from his advances. He pleased her, and why should she not be pleased with him? Was it a fault to be easily pleased? The truer and sweeter any human self, the readier it is to be pleased with another self—except, indeed, something in it grates on the moral sense. To Tom, therefore, Letty responded with smiles and pleasant words, even grateful to such a fine youth for taking notice of her small self.

The sun had set in a bank of cloud, which, as if he had been a lump of leaven to it, immediately began to swell and rise, and now hung dark and thick over the still, warm night. Even the farmers were unobservant of the change: their crops were all in, they had eaten and drunk heartily, and were merry, looking on or sharing in the multiform movement, their eyes filled with light and color.

Suddenly the wind rose, and within but moments a deluge of rain, mingled with large, half-melted hailstones rushed straight into the hall upon the gay company. In an instant or two scarcely a light was left burning. The merrymakers scattered like flies—into the house, into the tower, into the sheds and stables in the court behind, under the trees in front—anywhere out of the hall, where there was no shelter at all.

At that moment Letty was dancing with Tom, and her hand happened to be in his. He clasped it tight, and as quickly as the crowd and the confusion of the shelter-seeking would permit, led her to the door of the tower. But many had run in the same direction, and already its lower story and stair were crowded with refugees—the elder bemoaning the sudden change, and folding tight around them what poor wraps they were fortunate enough still to have with them; the younger merrier than ever, notwith-standing the cold gusts that now poked their spirit-arms hither and thither through the openings of the half-ruined building. To them even the destruction of their finery was but added cause of laughter. But a few minutes before, its freshness had been a keen pleasure to them, brightening their consciousness with a rare feeling of perfection. Now crushed and rumpled, soiled and wet and torn, it was still fuel to the fire of gaiety. But Tom did not stay among them. He knew the place well. On through the crowd he led Letty up the stair to the first floor. Even here were a few couples talking and laughing in the dark. With a warning, by no means unnecessary, to watch where they stepped, for the floors were bad, he passed on to the next stair.

"Let us stop here, Mr. Helmer," said Letty. "There is plenty of room here."

"I want to show you something," answered Tom. "You need not be frightened. I know every nook and cranny of the place."

"I am not frightened," said Letty, and made no further objection.

At the top of that stair they entered a straight passage, in the middle of which was a faint glimmer of light from an oval aperture in the side of it. To this Tom led Letty, and told her to look through it.

Beneath them lay the great gulf, wide and deep, of the hall they had just left. This was the little window, high in its gable, through which, in distant times past, the lord or lady of the mansion could oversee at will whatever went on below.

The rain had ceased as suddenly as it came on, and already lights were moving about in the darkness of the abyss.

"Are you cold?" asked Tom. "Of course you must be, with nothing but that thin muslin! Shall I run down and get you a shawl?"

"Oh, no. Don't leave me, please. It's not that," answered Letty. "I don't mind a bit of wind. It's rather pleasant. It's only that the look of the place makes me miserable. It looks as if no one had danced there for a hundred years."

"I suppose no one has until tonight," said Tom. "What a fine place it would be if only it had a roof to it! I can't imagine how anyone could live beside it and leave it in such condition."

But Tom lived a good deal closer to a worse ruin, and never spent a thought on it.

Letty shivered again.

"I'm quite ashamed of myself," she said, trying to speak cheerfully. "I can't think why I should feel like this—just as if something dreadful were watching me. I'll go home, Mr. Helmer."

"I fear you have caught cold," replied Tom, rejoiced at the chance of accompanying her. "I shall be delighted to see you safely there."

"There is no occasion for you to trouble yourself, thank you," answered

Letty. "I have an old servant of my aunt's with me—somewhere about the place. The storm is quite over now: I will go and find her."

Tom made no objection, but helped her down the dark stair, hoping, however, that the servant might not be found.

As they went, Letty seemed to herself to be walking in some old dream of change and desertion. The tower was empty as a monument. Not a trace of the crowd was left, which a few minutes before had filled it. The wind had risen in earnest now, and was rushing about, like a cold wild ghost, through every cranny of the desolate place. Had Letty, when she reached the bottom of the stairs, found herself on the rocks of the seashore, with the waves dashing up against them she would only have said to herself, "I knew it was a dream!"

The wind had blown away the hail-cloud and the stars were again shining down into the hall. One or two forlorn-looking searchers were still there; the rest had scattered like gnats. A few were already home; some were harnessing their horses to go, not even waiting for the man in the moon to light his lantern; some were already trudging on foot through the dark. Hesper and Miss Yolland were talking to two or three friends in the drawing room; Lady Margaret was in her boudoir, and Mr. Mortimer smoking a cigar in his study.

Letty could find Susan nowhere. She was in the farmer's kitchen behind. Tom suspected as much, but did not hint at the possibility. Letty found her cloak, which she had left in the hall, soaked with rain, and thought it best to search for Susan no further but go home at once. Therefore she accepted Tom's renewed offer of his company.

They were just leaving the hall, when a thought came to Letty.

"Oh," she said, "I know a shorter way home." Without waiting for any response from Tom, she turned and led him in the opposite direction from the road, by the back of the court, and into a field. There she made for a huge oak, which gloomed in the light of the now-rising moon by the sunk fence parting the grounds. By the slow strength of its growth, and the spreading of its roots, it had gradually broken and crumbled the stone wall so as to make a little way through it, leading to the top of the other side of the stream-bed. Letty scampered through the wall and up the bank. She turned to bid Tom good night, but there he was, following close behind her, insisting on seeing her safe to the house.

"Is this the way you always come?" asked Tom.

"I have never been on Durnmelling land before," answered Letty.

"How did you know about the short-cut, then?" he asked. "It certainly doesn't look as if it is used much."

"Of course not," replied Letty. "No one walks between Durnmelling and Thornwick now. It was all ours once, though, cousin Godfrey says.

Did you notice how the great oak sends its biggest arm over our field?"

"Yes."

"Well, I often sit under it when I'm thinking over my lessons, and can't rest in the house. That's how I know about the crack in the stone-dike."

She said it innocently, but Tom perked up his ears.

"Are you still taking lessons?" he asked. "Do you have a governess?"

"No," she answered in a tone of amusement. "But cousin Godfrey teaches me many things."

Tom was thoughtful. Little more was said, and when they reached the gate of the yard behind the house, she would not let him go any farther.

8 / Under the Oak _____

In the morning, as Letty narrated the events of the evening, she told her aunt about her acquaintance with Tom, and that he had seen her home. This information did not please the old lady, as, indeed, without knowing any reason, Letty had expected. Mrs. Wardour knew all about Tom's mother, or thought she did, and knew little good. She knew also that, although Tom was a general favorite about the neighborhood, her own son had a very poor opinion of him. Therefore, she sharply rebuked the poor girl for having anything to do with such a fellow, and said that if she ever permitted him so much as to speak to her again, she would do something which she left in a cloud of vaguest suggestion.

Letty made no reply. The chastisement hurt her. Not that she was so attached to Tom; it hardly mattered to her whether she saw him again, but how could her aunt have the right to compel her to behave rudely? All day she felt weary, and after the merrymaking of the night before, the household work was irksome. But she would soon have gotten over both weariness and tedium had her aunt been kind. But all day she kept driving Letty from one thing to another, and not once showed the least satisfaction with anything she did, calling her an ungrateful girl, and by the evening had rendered her more tired and dispirited than she had ever been in her life.

But Mrs. Wardour was only doing what all of us have done, and ought to be heartily ashamed of. Oppressed by her headache, and annoyed that she had spent time and money in preparation for nothing, she had allowed the cistern of her bitterness to fill to overflowing and then spill out upon Letty. Like some of the rest of us, she never stopped to think how her evil mood might affect others, never stopped to consider that all things work for good in the end. Another night's rest, it is true, sent the evil mood to sleep again for a time, but did not exorcise it permanently; for there are demons that will not go out without prayer, and a bad temper is one of them—a demon as contemptible, mean-spirited, and unjust as any in the peerage of hell—much indulged, nevertheless, and excused, by us poor lunatics who are possessed by him. Mrs. Wardour was a lady, as are so-called by those of this world, but a poor lady for the kingdom of heaven: I should wonder much if she ranked as more than a very common woman there.

The next day all was quiet, and a visit by Mrs. Wardour's sister set Letty at such liberty that she had all afternoon to read in the book Godfrey had given her, in which he had set her one of Milton's smaller poems to study. She went out with the book, and again sought the shadow of the Durnmelling oak.

It was a lovely autumn day, the sun glorious as ever in the memory of Abraham, or the author of Job. But there was a keenness in the air as well, which made Letty feel a little sad without knowing why. She sat down and tried to fix her attention on her task, but not altogether successfully, when a yellow leaf dropped on the very line she was poring over. She brushed it away and began to read again, when a second leaf fell. Again she threw it off the book. But not another half-minute had passed when down on the same spot fell a third leaf.

Letty looked up. There was a man in the tree over her head. She jumped to her feet. At the same moment he dropped on the ground beside her, lifting his hat as coolly as if he had met her on the road. She stood silent, her face white with fear from the shock of seeing him so suddenly.

"I hope I haven't frightened you," said Tom. "Do forgive me. You were so kind to me the other night, I could not help wanting to see you again."

"You gave me such a start!" gasped Letty, with her hand pressed on her heart.

"I didn't know what to do but hide in the tree," answered Tom. "I was certain if you saw me coming you would run away."

"Why would you think that?" asked Letty, the color gradually coming back to her face.

"Because I was sure they would be telling you all manner of things against me. But there is no harm in me—really, Miss Lovel—nothing, that is, worth mentioning."

"I am sure there isn't," said Letty, and then there was a pause.

"What book are you reading, may I ask?" said Tom.

Letty had by now remembered her aunt's injunctions against Tom. But partly from a kind of paralysis caused by his coolness, and from mere lack of presence of mind, not knowing what to do, yet feeling she ought to run back to the house, instead she sat down again on the grass. Instantly Tom threw himself at her feet, and lay there looking up at her with eyes of humble admiration.

Confused and troubled, she began to turn over the pages of her book, asking something about why he stared at her so.

"I can't help it. You are so lovely."

"Please don't talk such nonsense to me," she rejoined. "I am not lovely and I know it."

She spoke a little angrily now.

"I speak the truth," said Tom, quietly and earnestly. "Why should you think I do not?"

"Because nobody ever said so before."

"Then it is quite time somebody should," returned Tom.

"I wish you wouldn't talk to me about myself!" said Letty, feeling confused and improper, but not altogether displeased. "I don't want to hear about myself. It makes me so uncomfortable!"

Despite her uneasiness at the position in which she found herself, and the discomfort of conscious disobedience of her aunt's threats, still she did not move.

"I am very sorry to have upset you," said Tom, seeing her evident trouble. "I didn't mean to do so, and I promise not to say a word of that kind again—if I can help it. But tell me, Letty," he went on again, changing his tone and look and manner with such simplicity that she never even noticed his calling her by name, "do tell me what you are reading."

"There!" said Letty, almost crossly, handing him her book and pointing to the sonnet, as she rose to go.

Tom took the book and sprang to his feet. He had never read a word of Milton in his life, but he stood as if devouring it. He was doing his best to understand what he read quickly, for there Letty stood, with her hand held out to take the book again, ready to leave for home.

Silent and motionless he read and reread. Letty was restless and growing impatient, but still Tom read, gradually making a kind of superficial sense out of some of the words and phrases, but by no means taking possession of the poem. Not until we downright love a thing can we truly know or understand it, or call it our own.

"It is a beautiful poem," he said at last.

"I am sure it must be," said Letty, "but I have hardly gotten hold of it yet." Again she stretched out her hand a little farther, as if to proceed with its appropriation and her leave-taking.

But Tom was not yet prepared to part with the book. He knew as soon as it was gone, so was the girl. Thus he proceeded instead, in fluent speech and not inappropriate language, to set forth not the power of the poem, but the beauty of those phrases and turns of expression that particularly pleased him, giving the illusion that he grasped far more than he actually did about its deeper meaning. He also commented on rhyming, which was not altogether perfect according to his expert knowledge gained from an early habit of scribbling in ladies' albums.

About these surface affairs, Godfrey—understanding them better and valuing them, in their proper place, even more than Tom—had yet taught Letty nothing, judging it premature to teach polishing before carving. Hence this little display of knowledge on the part of Tom impressed Letty to a greater degree than was appropriate—so much so, in fact, that she began to regard him as on a level with her cousin Godfrey.

Question followed question, and answer followed answer, Letty feeling all the time that she *must* go, yet standing like one in a dream who cannot break the spell—for in the act only is the ability and the deed born. Repeatedly she stretched out her hand to take back the book. But although he saw the motion, he held on to the book as to his best anchor, hurriedly turning its leaves and searching for something more to his mind than anything of Milton's. Suddenly his face brightened.

"Ah!" he said—and remained silent a moment, reading. "I don't wonder," he resumed, "at your admiration of Milton. He's very grand, of course, and very musical too. But one can't always be listening to an organ. Not that I prefer merry music always, for the tone of all the beauty in the world is sad." Much Tom Helmer knew of beauty or sadness either! But ignorance is no reason with a fool for holding his tongue. "But there is the violin! Listen to this. This is the violin after the organ—played as only a master can."

With this brief introduction, he read a song of Shelley's, and read it well, for he had a good ear for rhythm and cadence, and prided himself on his reading of poetry.

Now the path to Letty's heart through her intellect was neither open nor well trodden. But there was something in the tone of the poem that suited the pitch of her spirit-chamber. And, if Letty's heart was not easily found, it was the readier to confess itself when found. Her eyes filled with tears. "He must be a poet himself to read poetry like that!" she said to herself, and felt at once sure that her aunt had wronged him greatly by her judgment against him.

As thus her thoughts went on interweaving themselves with the music, all at once the song came to an end. Tom closed the book, handed it to her, said, "Good morning, Miss Lovel," and ran down the break in the dike and through the stream-bed. By the time Letty came to herself again, she heard the soft thunder of hoofs on the grass. She ran to the edge, looked over, and saw Tom on his bay mare in full gallop across the field on the other side. She watched him as he neared the hedge and ditch that bounded it, saw him go flying over, and lost sight of him behind a thicket of small hazel trees. Slowly she turned and went back to the house, vaguely aware that a wind had begun to flow in her atmosphere, although only the faint sound of it had yet reached her.

9 / Letty's Confusion _____

From that moment Letty's troubles began.

For the first time she began to feel like a target for many arrows sent against her. At first sight—and if we do not look a long way ahead of what people stupidly regard as the end when it is only a horizon—it seems hard that so much we call evil, and so much that *is* evil, should result from that unavoidable, blameless, foreordained, and essential attraction which is the law of nature, that is the will of God, between man and woman.

Even if Letty had fallen in love with Tom at first sight, who dares blame her? And who will dare say that Tom should be judged for seeking the society and friendship, even the love, of a young woman whom in all sincerity he admired, or for using his wits to get into her presence? There are reasons infinitely deeper than any philosopher has yet fathomed, or is likely to fathom, why a youth such as he, and a sweet and blameless girl such as Letty, should exchange regards of admiration and wonder. That which moves them, and goes on to draw them closer and closer, comes with them from the very source of their being, rooted in all the gentle potencies and sweet glories of creation, and not unworthily watered with all the tears of agony and ecstasy shed by lovers since the creation of the world. What it is, I cannot tell; I only know it is not that which the young fool calls it, still less that which the old sinner thinks it.

As to Letty's disobedience of her aunt's extravagant orders concerning Tom, I must leave that to the judgment of the just, reminding them that she was taken by surprise. But Letty now found herself very uncomfortable, because she knew her aunt would be very displeased if she found out what had passed that afternoon. Yet when she recalled how unkindly, how unjustly Mrs. Wardour had spoken against Tom, she began to wonder whether she truly was under obligation to tell her everything that had happened.

Supposing it remained Letty's duty to acquaint her aunt with what had taken place, I must still assert that the old people, who make it hard for the young people to do right, may be twice as much to blame as those youths they arraign for a concealment whose very heart is the dread of their known selfishness, fierceness, and injustice. If children have to obey their parents or guardians, those parents and guardians are over them in the name of God, and they must look to it. If in the name of God they act instead in the place of the devil, that will not prove a light thing for them to answer to. The causing of the little ones to offend hangs a fearful woe about the neck of the causer. Seeing there is One who judges fairly in all things, it is a hard as well as a needless task for a parent to set forth how far the child is to blame, when the parent is first of all utterly wrong, yea out of true relation, toward the child.

Not, therefore, is the child free. Obligation remains—modified, it may be, but how difficult, alas, to fulfill! And whether Letty and such as act like her are excusable or not in keeping attentions paid them a secret, this sorrow for them remains: that next to a crime, a secret is the heaviest as well as the most awkward of burdens to carry. It has to be carried always, and all about. From morning to night it hurts in tenderest parts, and from night to morning hurts everywhere.

At any expense, let there be openness. Take courage, my child, and speak out. Dare to speak, I say, and that will give you strength to resist, should disobedience become a duty.

Letty's first false step was here: she said to herself *I cannot*, and did not. She lacked courage—not to be wondered at in her case, but a lack just as serious notwithstanding; for courage of the true sort is just as badly needed to the character of a woman as a man. Had she spoken, she might have heard true things of Tom, sufficient to alter her opinion of him at this early stage of their relationship, and to alter the set of her feelings, which were now pointed straight for him. It may be that the exercise of such courage as it would have taken to tell her aunt might have rendered the troubles that were now to follow unnecessary to her development. But shrinking from her duty, and from the growth to her character doing that duty would have induced, Letty had now to be taken on another path toward that character—a longer route, it is true, and more painful, but one just as sure to bring about the required growth in the end.

From that time on she went about with the haunting consciousness that she was one who might be found out, that she was guilty of what would justify the hard words she had so resented. Already the secret had begun to work conscious destruction in her heart. She managed to quiet herself with the idea, rather than the resolve, that as soon as Godfrey came home, she would tell him everything, even confessing that she did not have the courage to tell his mother. She was sure he would forgive her and would set her at peace with herself.

In the meantime, she would take care not to go where she might meet Tom again. And the resolve was no less genuine that with the very making of it rose the memory of that delightful hour more enticing than ever. How beautifully and with what feeling he read the lovely song!

Nevertheless, she kept to her resolve. And although Tom left his horse now here now there, to avoid attracting attention, and almost every day visited the oak, he looked in vain for her approach. Disappointment increased his longing: what would he not have given to see once more one of those exquisite smiles break out in its perfect blossom! He kept going and going—haunting the oak, but without success. It was the first time in his life he had followed one idea for a whole two weeks.

At length Godfrey returned from his visit to London. But although all the time he was away Letty had thought about the idea of making her confession to him, the moment she saw him she felt such confession to be impossible. It was a sad discovery to her. Up till then Godfrey had been the chief source of the peace and interest in her life, at least that portion of her life to which all the rest of it looked as the sky—and now she felt like a culprit. She had done something he would undoubtedly be displeased with. And if only that was all! For in addition she felt like a hypocrite: she had done something she could not confess.

Again and again in Godfrey's absence she had tried to convince herself that the help Tom had given her with her task with Milton would at once make Godfrey feel favorable toward him. But now that she looked in Godfrey's face, she was aware—she did not know why, but she was aware it would not be so.

The moment Godfrey saw her, he knew something was the matter. But there had been that going on in him which put him on a false track for the explanation. Scarcely had he turned his back on Thornwick for London before he found his thoughts full of the one he was leaving behind. Every hour of his absence he found his heart obsessed with the sweet face and ministering hands of his humble pupil. Yet he still was unaware that he was in love with her. He thought of her only as his younger sister, loving, clinging, obedient. So dear was she to him, he thought, that he would rejoice if he could make her happy at any cost to himself—even the cost of giving her to a better man. But such a crisis was far away, and there was no *certainty* of such a need, only the possibility.

He must be careful, he said to himself, how he carried himself, so as not to lead her into error. He was not afraid she might fall in love with him; he was not so full of himself as that. But he recoiled from the idea that she might imagine him in love with her. It was not merely that he had loved once and had determined never to love again. But it was not for him, a man of thirty years, to fall in love with a girl of eighteen—a child in everything except outward growth. Not for a moment would he be imagined by her a courtier for her favor.

Thus, even in the heart of one so far above ordinary men as Godfrey, and with respect to the sweetest of child-maidens, pride had its evil place. And no good ever comes of pride, for it is the meanest of mean things, and no one but he who is full of it thinks it grand. Therefore, this wise man was firmly resolved on caution. And so when at last they met, it was not with the former abandon of simple pleasure as before, but with a visible restraint that was enough to make Letty, whose heart was now beating in a very thicket of nerves, at once feel it impossible to carry out her intent—impossible to confess to him any more than to his mother. Godfrey perceived her uncomfortable shyness and embarrassment, attributed them to his own wisely guarded behavior, and continued his caution. Thus the pride, which is of man, mingled with the love, which is of God, and polluted it. Because of the change they saw less of each other than before, yet for the next month, inconsistent as it may seem, Godfrey spent every leisure moment in working on the copying out of a present for her.

Their awkward meeting called into operation another disintegrating force: the moment Letty knew she could not tell Godfrey, and was aware that a wall had arisen between him and her, that moment woke in her the desire as she had never felt it before, to see Tom Helmer. She could no longer bear to be shut up in herself; she must see somebody, get near to somebody, talk to somebody. Otherwise her secret would choke her. And who was there to think of but Tom—and Mary Marston?

She had never once gone to the oak again. But she had not altogether avoided a certain little cobwebbed gable-window in the garret, from which it was visible. Neither had she withheld her hands from cleaning a pane in that window, that through it she might see the oak. And there, more than once or twice, she had seen someone who could be nobody other than Tom on the watch for her. He must surely be her friend, she reasoned, or else why would he care to make such an attempt to visit her—she who was such a nobody in all other eyes but his? It was so good of Tom! She would call him Tom; everybody else called him Tom, and why shouldn't she—to herself, when nobody was near?

As for Mary Marston, she treated her like a child! When she told her that she had met Tom at Durnmelling, and how kind he had been, she looked as grave as if it had been wicked to be nice to him. Then Mary had told her in return how he and his mother were always quarreling: that must be his mother's fault, she was sure—it could not be Tom's; anyone might see that at a glance! His mother must be something like her aunt!

After that, how could she see Mary any more? It would not be fair to Tom. If only they had all been more kind to her, she would have told them everything—Mary, Godfrey, her aunt. But they all frightened her so, she could not speak. It was not her fault if Tom was the only friend she had! She would ask his advice; he was sure to advise her to do the right thing. He had read that sonnet about the wise maiden with such feeling and such force, he must know what a girl ought to do, and how she ought to behave to those who were unkind and would not trust her.

Poor Letty! She had no root in herself yet. Certainly no human being ought, even if it was possible, to be enough for himself; each of us needs God and every human relationship he has given us. But we each ought to be able to endure for a time, even though we don't have enough. Letty was not to blame that she desired the comfort of humanity around her soul; but I am not sure that she was not to blame in not being fit to walk a few steps alone, or even to sit still and listen expectantly. With all his learning, Godfrey had not taught her what William Marston had taught Mary. And now her heart was like a child left alone in a great room.

But the moment Letty's heart had thus cried out against Mary, something else cried out against her own false judgment, telling her that she was not being fair to her friend, and that Mary and no other was the proper person to advise her. She had no right to turn from her because she was a little afraid of her. Perhaps Letty was on the point of discovering that to be unable to bear disapproval was an unworthy weakness. Praise was to her a precious thing, but disapproval a misery, because it made her feel as if she never could do anything right. She had not yet learned that the right is the right, come of praise or blame or whatever. The right will produce more right and be its own reward—in the end a reward altogether infinite, for God will meet it with what is deeper than all right, namely, perfect love.

The more Letty thought, the more she was sure she must tell Mary. And disapprove as she might, Mary was still down-to-earth, still her friend, and a very different object of alarm than either her aunt or her cousin Godfrey.

Therefore, the first afternoon on which she thought her aunt could spare her, she asked to be allowed to go and see Mary. Mrs. Wardour yielded, but not very graciously. She could admit that Mary was not like other shopkeepers, but that did not make her favor the deepening of the friendship.

10 / The Hut in the Field

When Letty entered the shop Mary immediately saw trouble in her eyes, and without a moment's hesitation drew her inside the counter, and into the house. She led the way to her own room, up stairs and through passages which were indeed lanes through masses of merchandise, like those cut through deep-drifted snow. Everywhere all over the house it was a store, till they came to the door of Mary's room, which, opening from such surroundings, had upon Letty much the effect of a chapel—and rightly, for it was a room not unused to having its door shut. It was small and plainly but daintily furnished, with no foolish excess of the small refinements on which girls so often set value.

"Sit down, Letty dear, and tell me what is the matter," said Mary, placing her friend in a straw chair, and seating herself beside her.

Letty burst into tears and sat sobbing.

"Come, dear, tell me all about it," insisted Mary. "They'll be calling me soon."

Letty could not speak.

"Then I'll tell you what," said Mary. "You must stay with me tonight, that we may have time to talk it over. You stay here and amuse yourself as best you can till the shop is shut, and then we will have a good talk. I will send your tea up here."

"Oh, but I can't!" cried Letty. "My aunt would never forgive me."

"I didn't mean to keep you without sending word to your aunt to let her know."

"She wouldn't let me stay," persisted Letty.

"We will try her," said Mary confidently, and without more ado, left Letty, went to her desk, and wrote a note to Mrs. Wardour. This she gave to Beenie to have sent by messenger to Thornwick; after which she told her to take a nice tea up to Miss Lovel in her bedroom. Mary then resumed her place in the shop, under the frowns and side-glances of Turnbull, and the smile of her father.

In an hour or so, the boy-messenger, whom Beenie had taken care not to pay beforehand, destroyed the hope of a pleasant evening, for he brought a note from Mrs. Wardour absolutely refusing to allow Letty to spend the night away from home: she must return immediately, so as to get in before dark.

The rare anger flushed Letty's cheek and flashed from her eyes as she read. For in addition to the prime annoyance, her aunt's note was addressed to her and not to Mary, whom it did not even mention. Letty felt deeply hurt, and her displeasure with her aunt added yet a shade to the dimness of her judgment. She rose at once.

"Will you not tell me first what is troubling you, Letty?" said Mary.

"Not right now," replied Letty, caring a good deal less about the right ordering of her way than when she entered the house. Why should she care, she said to herself—but it was the anger within her speaking now—how she behaved, when she was treated so abominably?

"Then I will come and see you on Sunday," replied Mary. "And then we shall manage to have our talk."

They embraced and parted—Letty unaware that she had given her friend a less warm hug than usual. There can hardly be a plainer proof of the lowness of our nature, until we have laid hold of the higher nature that belongs to us by birthright, than this, that even a just anger tends to make us unjust and unkind. Letty was angry with every person and thing at Thornwick, and unkind to her best friend, for whose sake in part she was angry. And though the anger toward Mrs. Wardour may have in part been justifiable in human terms, the root of Letty's trouble lay as much in her own poor choices as anywhere. But she did not look inside herself, for anger always seeks others to blame and blinds us from our own responsibility. Thus, with glowing cheeks, tear-filled eyes, and indignant heart, Letty set out on her walk home, in more hospitable condition than when she came for the welcoming of demons, which sought her undoing in worse ways than the anger that stood holding the door open for them.

It was a still evening, with a great cloud rising in the southwest; from which, as the sun drew near the horizon, a thin veil stretched over the sky between, and a few scattered drops of rain came now and then. All was in complete harmony with Letty's mood. Her soul was clouded, and her heaven was only a place for the rain to fall from. Annoyance, doubt, her new sense of constraint, and a wide-reaching, undefined feeling of homelessness, all combined together to make her mind a chaos out of which misshapen things might rise, instead of an ordered world in which gracious and reasonable shapes appear. For as the state of our mind and emotions is, such will be the thoughts that spring from within us. Not until all is divine peace in our souls shall we think with absolute reasonableness.

About halfway to Thornwick, the path crossed a little heathy field. Just as Letty left the hedge-guarded field-side, the wind came with a burst and brought the rain in earnest. It was not yet very heavy, but heavy enough, with the wind at its back, to wet her thoroughly before she could reach any shelter. But in truth, she had no desire for shelter, and bent her head to the blast and walked on. She would like to get wet to the skin, take a violent cold, go into consumption, and die in a fortnight. The wind whistled about her bonnet, the rain drops dashed all about her, and made her skirts cling to her like chains. She could hardly keep going, when suddenly in the middle of the field there came a lull. For from behind her and over her head had come an umbrella, and now came a voice and an audible sigh of pleasure.

"I little thought when I left home this afternoon," said the voice, "that I should have such a happiness before night!"

At the sound of the voice Letty gave a cry, which ran through all the shapes of alarm, surprise, and delight; and it was not much of a cry either.

"Oh, Tom!" she said, and clasped the arm that held the umbrella. How her foolish heart bounded! Here was help come to her. Her aunt would no doubt expect her to run from under the umbrella and away from him, but she would do as she pleased this time. Here was Tom getting all wet for her sake, and counting it a happiness! Oh, to have a friend like that—all to herself! She would not reject a friend like that for all the aunts in creation. Besides, it was her aunt's own fault; if she had let her stay with Mary, she would not have met Tom. It was not her doing; she would take what was sent her, and enjoy it!

"What a night for you to be out in," said Tom. "How lucky it was I chose the right place to watch in at last. I was sure if only I persevered long enough I should be rewarded."

"Have you been waiting for me long?" asked Letty, with foolish acceptance.

"Two weeks and a day," answered Tom with a laugh. "But I would wait a long year for such another chance as this." He pressed to his side the hand upon his arm. "Fate is indeed kind to me tonight."

"Hardly in the weather," said Letty.

"What?" said Tom, with seeming pretense of indignation. "Let anyone but you dare to say a word against the weather of this night and he will have me to reckon with. It is the sweetest weather I ever walked in. I will write a glorious song in praise of showery gusts and bare fields."

"Do," said Letty, careful not to say Tom this time, but unwilling to revert to Mr. Helmer, "and be sure you bring the umbrella into it."

"That I will! See if I don't!" answered Tom.

"And make it real poetry, too?" asked Letty, looking round the stick of the umbrella.

"Thou shalt thyself be the lovely critic, fair maiden!" answered Tom.

And thus they were already on the footing of somewhere about a two years acquaintance—thanks to the pain of ill-usage in Letty's heart, the gaiety in Tom's, the sudden wild weather, the quiet heath, the gathering shades, and the umbrella. The wind blew cold, the air was dank and chill, the west was a low gleam of wet yellow, and the rain shot stinging in their faces. But Letty cared as little for it all as Tom did, for her heart, growing warm with the comfort of the friendly presence, felt like a banished soul that has found a world, and a joy as of endless deliverance pervaded her being. Within that umbrella, hovered and glided with them an atmosphere of bliss and peace. In the midst of storm and coming darkness, it closed warm and genial around the pair. Tom meditated no guile, and Letty had no deceit in her. Yet Tom was no true man, or sweet Letty much of a woman. Neither of them was yet *of the truth.*

At the other side of the field, almost upon the path, stood a deserted hut. Door and window were gone, but the roof remained. Just as they neared it, the wind fell, and the rain began to pour down.

"Let us go in here for a moment," said Tom, "and catch our breath for a new fight."

Tom felt Letty's reluctance, but she said nothing. She fancied that refusal would be more unmaidenly than consent, and allowed Tom to lead her in. And there, within those old and crumbling walls, with the twilight sinking into a cheerless night of rain, encouraged by the very dreariness and obscurity of the place, she told Tom the trouble of mind their meeting at the oak was causing her, saying that now it would be worse than ever, for it would be altogether impossible to confess that she had met him yet again that evening.

So now indeed Letty's foot was in the snare: she had a secret with Tom. Every time she saw him, liberty had withdrawn a pace. There was no room for confession now. If a secret held is a burden, a secret shared is a chain. But Tom's heart rejoiced within him.

"Let me see . . .—How old are you, Letty?" he asked gaily.

"Just past eighteen," she answered.

"Then you are fit to judge for yourself. You're not a child, and they are not your mother and father. What right have they to know everything you do? I wouldn't let any such nonsense trouble me."

"But they give me everything, you know—food, and clothes, and all."

"Ah, and what do you do for them?"

"Nothing."

"Why, what are you about all day?"

Letty gave a brief sketch of her day.

"And you call that nothing!" exclaimed Tom. "Isn't that enough to pay for your food and your clothes? Do your private affairs have to make up the difference? What pocket money do they give you?"

"Pocket money?" returned Letty, as if she did not quite know what he meant.

"Money to do with what you like," explained Tom.

Letty thought for a moment.

"Cousin Godfrey gave me a sovereign last Christmas," she answered. "I have still got ten shillings of it left."

Tom burst into a merry laugh.

"You dear creature!" he cried. "What a sweet slave you make. Even the lowest servant on the farm gets wages, and you get none: yet you think yourself bound to tell them everything, because they give you food and clothes, and a sovereign last Christmas!"

Here a gentle displeasure arose in the heart of the girl, up to then so contented and grateful. She did not care about money, but she resented the claim her conscience made for them upon her confidence. She did not reflect that such claim had never been made by them, nor that the fact that she felt the claim proved that she had been treated, in some measure at least, like a daughter of the house.

"Why," continued Tom, "it is nothing but downright slavery! Of course, you are not to do anything wrong, but you are not bound not to do anything they may happen not to like."

Thus he went on, believing he spoke the truth. His heart was exultant in the thought that he now possessed this lovely creature to direct and guide. Through her sweet confidence he would set her free from the unjust oppression that was taking advantage of her simplicity. But in very truth he was giving her just the instruction that goes to make a slave—a slave in heart, who serves without devotion, and serves unworthily. Yet as Tom went on with his poverty-stricken, swine-husk arguments, Letty seemed to hear a gospel of liberty. She hardly needed the following injunctions from Tom to firmly resolve not to utter a word concerning him. To do so would be treacherous to him, and would be to give up the liberty he had taught her. Thus, from the neglect of a real duty, she became the slave of a false one.

"If you say anything," said Tom, "I will never see you again: they will set everyone about the place to watch you, like so many cats after one poor little white mouse, and on the least suspicion you will be gobbled up before you can get to me to take care of you."

Letty looked up at him gratefully.

"But what could you do for me if I did?" she asked. "If my aunt were to turn me out of the house, your mother would not take me in!"

Already Letty was not herself now; she was herself and Tom—by no means a healthy combination.

"My mother won't be mistress long," answered Tom. "When I am twenty-one she will have to do as I tell her, and that will be in a few months." Tom did not know the terms of his father's will. "In the meantime, we must keep quiet, you know. I don't want a row—I have plenty of that with her as it is. You may be sure I shall tell no one how I spent the happiest hour of my life. How little circumstance has to do with bliss!" he added with a philosophical sigh. "Here we are in a wretched hut, roared and rained upon by an equinoctial tempest, and I am in paradise!"

"I must go home," said Letty, recalled to a sense of her situation. Yet still she sat, trembling with pleasure at his words. "See, it is getting quite dark."

"Don't be afraid, my white bird," said Tom. "I will see you home. But surely you are as well here as there anyhow! Who knows when we shall meet again?"

Scarcely were the words past his lips when a tall shadow—no shadow either, but the very person of Godfrey Wardour—passed the opening in the wall of the hut where there had once been a window, and the gloom it cast into the dusk within was awful and ominous. The moment he saw it, Tom threw himself flat on the clay floor of the hut as if to hide in case Godfrey looked in, hoping he had not heard his last speech.

Godfrey stopped at the doorless entrance, stood on the threshold, and bent his head to clear the lintel as he looked in. Letty's heart seemed to vanish from her body. A strange feeling shook her. The question Tom had so recently asked with triumph, where was the harm, seemed to have no heart in it now. For a moment that had to Letty the feel of a year, Godfrey stood peering into the inner darkness.

Not a little to his displeasure, he had heard from his mother of her refusal to grant Letty's request, and had set out in the hope of meeting her and helping her home, for by that time it had begun to rain and looked stormy.

He had indeed heard nothing, but in the darkness he saw something white, and as he gazed, it grew to become Letty's face. The strange, scared, ghastly expression of it bewildered him.

Letty became aware that Godfrey could not see clearly into the darkness of the hut, and hope sprung up in her that he might not see Tom at all. But she could not utter a word, and stood returning Godfrey's gaze like one fascinated with terror.

At length came Godfrey's voice into the gloom. "Is it really you, my child?" he said in an uncertain voice—for, if it was indeed she, why did she not speak, and why did she look so scared at the sight of him?

"Oh, cousin Godfrey!" gasped Letty, finding a little of her voice, "you gave me such a start!"

"Why should you be so startled at seeing me, Letty?" he returned.

"You came all at once," replied Letty, "blocking up the door with your shoulders so that no ray of light fell on your face, and how was I to know it was you, cousin Godfrey?"

From a paleness grayer than death, her face had now grown red as fire;

it was the burning of the lie inside her. She felt all a lie now: that was the good that Tom had brought her! But the gloom was friendly. With a resolution new to her usually reticent character, she went up to Godfrey and said: "If you are going to the town, let me walk with you, cousin Godfrey. It is getting so dark."

She felt as if an evil necessity were driving her. But the poor child was not half so deceitful inside as the words seemed to her issuing from her lips. It was such a relief to be assured Godfrey had not seen Tom that she felt she could almost forego the sight of Tom ever again. Her better feelings rushed back, her old confidence and reverence, and in the altogether nebula-chaotic condition of her mind, she felt as if, in his turn, Godfrey had just appeared for her deliverance.

"I am not going into town, Letty," he answered. "I came to meet you, and we will go home together. It is no use waiting for the rain to stop. I have brought your rain-jacket, and we must just take the weather as it comes."

The wind was up again, and the next moment Letty, on Godfrey's arm this time, was struggling with the same storm she had so lately encountered leaning on Tom's, while Tom was only too glad to be left alone on the floor of the dismal hut, from which he did not venture to rise for some time, lest some improbable thing should happen to bring Mr. Wardour back. He was as mortally afraid of being discovered as any young thief in a farmer's orchard.

He had a dreary walk back to the public house where he had stabled his horse. But he trudged it cheerfully, brooding with delight on Letty's beauty, and her lovely confidence in Tom Helmer—a personage whom he had begun to feel nobody trusted as he deserved.

"Poor child!" he said to himself—for he as well as Godfrey patronized her—"what a doleful walk home she will have with that stuck-up old bachelor fellow!"

And indeed it was not a particularly comfortable walk home she had, although Godfrey broke the force of the wind in front of her as best he could. A few weeks ago she would have thought the walk and the talk and everything delightful. But after Tom's airy converse on the same level with herself, Godfrey's sounded indeed wise—very wise—but dull, so dull! It is true the suspicion, hardly awake enough to be troublesome, lay somewhere in her that in Godfrey's talk there was a value of which in Tom's there was nothing. But then it was not wisdom Letty was in want of, she thought, but somebody, though she did not say this even to herself, to be kind to her and pamper her a little, to humor her and not require too much of her. Physically Letty was not in the least lazy, but she did not enjoy being forced to think much. She could think, and occasionally to good purpose. But as yet she had no hunger for the possible results of thought, and how then could she care to think?

Seated on the edge of her bed, weary and wet, she recalled, and pondered, and as much as she was capable of, compared the two scarce comparable men, until the voice of her aunt, calling her to make haste and come to tea, made her start up from her reverie, and quickly removed her drenched clothes. The old lady imagined from her delay that Letty was upset because she had made her come home. But when she appeared, she was so ready, so attentive, and so quick to help, that, a little repentant, she said to herself, "Really the girl is very good natured!" as if then for the first time she had discovered the fact. But Thornwick could never again to Letty feel like a home. Not at peace with herself, she could not be in rhythmic relation with her surroundings.

The next day the old manner of life began again. But it was only the old manner, not the old life. That was gone forever, like an old sunset, or an old song, and it could not be recalled from the dead. We may have better, but we can not have the same. Time and growth and relationships march ever forward. God only can have the same. God grant that our new may enwrap our old!

Letty labored more than ever to lay hold of the lessons Godfrey set before her, but success seemed further from her than ever. She was all the time aware of a weight, an oppression, which seemed to belong to the task, but was in reality her self-dissatisfaction. She was like a poor Hebrew set to make brick without straw, but the Egyptian that had brought her into bondage was the feebleness of her own will. Now and then would come a break—a glow of beauty, a gleam of truth. For a moment she would forget herself; for a moment a shining pool would flash on the clouded sea of her life. But then almost immediately her heart would send up a fresh mist, the light would fade and vanish, and the sea lie dusky and sad. She tried diligently to serve both her aunt and Godfrey. But even this conscience of service did not make her happy. Duty itself could not, where faith was wanting, where the heart was not at one with those to whom the hands were servants. She would cry herself to sleep, and rise early to be sad. At last she resolved, and seemed to gain strength and some peace from the resolve, to do all in her power to avoid Tom.

Thus it went on. Her aunt saw that something was amiss. She began to watch her even more closely, and this added still further to Letty's discomfort. But the only thing Mrs. Wardour was able to discover was that the girl was eager to please Godfrey, and the conviction began to grow within her that she was indulging in the impudent presumption of being in love with her peerless cousin. Then maternal indignation misled her into the folly of dropping hints that should put Godfrey on his guard: men were so easily taken in by designing girls! She did not say much; but she said a good deal too much for her own ends, when she caused her fancy to present itself to the mind of Godfrey.

He had not failed to observe the dejection that had come upon her and now ruled every feature of her countenance. Again and again he asked himself whether she might be thinking him displeased with her. But watching her now with the misleading light of his mother's lantern, and not quite unwilling to accept the truth of the thing she implied, he became by degrees convinced that she was right in her assessment of Letty's behavior.

Up to this point perhaps, the man was pardonable in that his mother had caused him to err. But for what followed he could not be excused. He had a true and strong affection for the girl, but it was an affection as from conscious high to low, an affection not unmixed with patronage, even condescension—a bad thing, far worse in fact than it can possibly seem to the heart that indulges it. Good fellow as Godfrey was, he thought much too much of himself; and, unconsciously comparing it with Letty's, altogether overvalued his worth. Noble as in many ways Wardour was, and kind as he thought he was to Letty, he was not yet generous to her; he was no Prince Arthur, no unselfish Knight. Had he now brought himself as severely to task as he ought, he would have discovered that he was making no objection to the little girl's loving him; but he would not love her in the same way in return; and where was the honor in that?

But though his actions were perhaps not as kind as they should have been on one level, on another he continued to do what he could for her betterment. When in London he had ransacked the bookstores for dainty editions of many of his favorite authors in order to make a nice little library for Letty. And on his return he had set a cabinetmaker in Testbridge to work making a small set of bookshelves for them. When they were ready, one afternoon when she was out he took them to her room, fastened them to the wall, and filled them with the books. He never doubted that she would rush to find him the moment she saw them. Therefore, when he was done he retreated to his study, there to sit in readiness to receive her and her gratitude with gentle kindness. But there he sat expectantly in vain. When they met at tea, in the presence of his mother, with embarrassment and broken sentences, she tried to thank him.

"Oh, cousin Godfrey!" she said, ". . . it is so much more than I deserve, I dare hardly thank you." She paused, shook her pretty head, then went on as best she could. "I don't know—I seem to have no right to thank you; I ought not to have such a splendid present. Indeed, I don't deserve. You would not have given it to me if you knew how naughty I am."

These broken sentences were altogether misinterpreted by both mother and son. Hearing about Godfrey's present now for the first time, the mother was filled with jealousy, and began to revolve thoughts of dire disquietude: was the hussy actually beginning to gain upon his affections and steal from her the heart of her son? Who was *she*, Mrs. Wardour said to herself with growing evil pride, to wriggle herself into an old family and property? Had *she* been born to such things? Well, she would teach her who she was! When dependents began to presume upon their betters, it was time they had a lesson.

Letty could hardly bear the sight of the books and their shelves. The very beauty of the bindings was a reproach to her. From the misery of this freak burden, this new stirring of her sense of hypocrisy, she began to wish herself anywhere out of the house, and away from Thornwick. It was torture to her to think how she had deceived cousin Godfrey at the hut, and now the books sat on the beautiful shelves he had made for her like an embodied conscience, gazing out at her from the wall of her chamber.

The next day was Sunday, and they all went to church. Letty felt that Tom was there too, but she never raised her eyes to glance at him.

He had been looking out in vain for a sight of her all this time—now from the oak tree, now from his bay mare's back, as he haunted the roads about Thornwick, now from the window of the little public-house where the path across the fields joined the main road to Testbridge. But not once had he caught a glimpse of her.

When Sunday came he had seated himself where he could not fail to see her if she was there. How ill she looked, he thought when at last she came into view. His heart swelled with indignation.

"They are being cruel to her!" he said to himself. "I *must* see her somehow."

If Letty had but had a real friend to strengthen and advise her, much suffering might have been spared her, for she was a teachable girl. She was, indeed, only too ready to be advised, too ready to accept for true whatever friendship offered itself. But none but the friend who will strengthen us to stand is worthy of the name. Such a friend Mary would have been, but Letty did not yet know what she needed. The unrest of her conscience made her shrink from one who was sure to side with that conscience, and help it to trouble her. It was sympathy Letty longed for instead, not strength, and therefore she was afraid of Mary.

She came to see her, as she had promised, the Sunday after that disastrous visit; but the weather was still uncertain and gusty, and she found both Letty and Godfrey in the parlor; and Letty did not give her a chance of speaking to her alone. The poor girl had now far more on her mind that needed help than when she went to Mary's house in search of it, but she would seek it no more from her. For the more she thought about it, the surer she felt that Mary would insist on her making a disclosure of the whole foolish business to Mrs. Wardour, and would admit neither her own fear nor her aunt's harshness as a sufficient reason for continuing to keep quiet. *More than that,* thought Letty, *I can't be sure that she wouldn't go and tell her all about it herself! And then what would become of me? I would be a hundred times worse off than if I had told her myself.*

11 / William Marston

The clouds were gathering over Mary too—deep and dark, but of altogether another kind from those that enveloped Letty. No troubles are for one moment to be compared with those that come of the wrongness, even if it be not wickedness, that is our own. Some clouds rise from stagnant bogs and pools; others from the wide, clean, large ocean. But either kind, thank God, will serve the angels to come down by. In the old stories of celestial visitants the clouds do much; and it is oftenest of all that down the misty slope of griefs and pains and fears, the most powerful joy slides into the hearts of men and women and children. Beautiful are the feet of the men of science on the dust-heaps of the world, but the patient heart will yield a myriad times greater thanks for the clouds that give foothold to the shining angels.

Few people were interested in William Marston. Of those who saw him in the shop, most turned from him to his jolly partner. But there were a few who, some by instinct, some by experience, did seek him out when they came in. Yet strange as it may seem, Marston was the one whom the worldly-wise of Testbridge called the holier-than-thou hypocrite, and Turnbull the plain-spoken, agreeable, honest man of the world, pretending to be no better either than himself or other people. The few friends that Marston had, however, loved him as not many are loved: they knew him, not as he seemed to the casual eye, but as he was. Never did man do less to conceal or to manifest himself. He was all taken up with what he loved, and that was neither himself nor his business. These friends knew that when the faraway look was upon him he was not indifferent to his presence or heedless of their existence; it was only that his thoughts were out, like heavenly bees, foraging. A word spoken directly to him brought him back in a moment, and his soul would return to them with a smile. He stood as one on the keystone of a bridge, and held communion now with these: on this side of the river and on that, both companies were his own.

He was not a man of great education, in the common use of the word. But he was a good way on in that education, for the sake of which, and for no other, we are here in this world—the education which, once begun, will sooner or slower lead knowledge captive, and teaches nothing that has to be unlearned again, because every flower of it scatters the seed of one better than itself. The main secret of his progress, the secret of all wisdom, was, that with him action was the beginning and end of thought. He was not one of that cloud of false witnesses, who, calling themselves Christians, take no trouble for the end for which Christ was born, namely, their salvation from unrighteousness. Such a class of so-called believers may be divided into the insipid and the offensive, both regardless of obedience.

It may well seem strange that such a man should have gone into business with one such as John Turnbull; but the latter had been for many years growing more and more self-centered, while Marston had been growing more and more refined, by which I mean out of himself. Still from the first, it was an unequal yoking of believer with unbeliever. And it had been a great trial: punishment had not been spared—with best results in patience and purification; for so are our false steps turned back to good by the evil to which they lead us.

Turnbull was ready to take every advantage he thought he could risk safely to gain for himself from his partner's comparative carelessness about money. He drew a larger proportion of the profits than belonged to his share in the capital, justifying himself on the ground that he had a much larger family, did more of the business, and had to keep up the standing of the firm. He made Marston pay more than what was reasonable for the small part of the house he and his daughter lived in. Far worse than this, he had for some time been risking the whole affair by private speculations.

It is true that alone Marston would hardly have made much money. But he would have gotten through this life, and would have left his daughter the means of getting through also; for he would have left her in possession of her own peace and the confidence of her friends, which will always prove enough for those who confess themselves to be strangers and pilgrims on the earth—those who regard it as a grand staircase they have to climb, not a plain on which to build their houses and plant their vineyards.

As to the peculiar doctrines of the church to which he had joined himself, right or wrong in themselves, Marston, after having complied with what seemed to him the letter of the law concerning baptism, gave himself no further trouble. He had for a long time known—for, by the power of the life in him, he had gathered from the Scriptures the finest of the wheat, where so many of every sect, great churches and small ones, gather only the husks and chaff—that the only baptism of any avail is the washing of the fresh birth, and the making new by that breath of God, which, breathed into man's nostrils, first made of him a living soul. When a man *knows* this, potentially he knows all things.

One evening George had gone home early because of a party at *the villa*, as the Turnbulls always called their house. The boy who worked in the shop had also for some cause gotten permission to leave early, and thus Mr. Marston was left to shut the shop himself. Mary, who was in some respects the stronger of the two, was assisting him. When he had shut the last shutter, he dropped his arms with a weary sigh. Mary, who had been fastening the bolts inside, met him in the doorway.

"You look worn out, Father," she said. "Come and lie down, and I will read to you."

"I will, my dear," he answered. "I don't feel quite like myself tonight. The seasons are telling upon me now. I suppose the stuff of my tabernacle is wearing thin."

Mary looked anxiously at him, for, though never a strong man, he seldom complained. But she said nothing, and led him through the dark shop to the door into the house, hoping to herself that a good cup of tea would restore him. When they arrived at their little sitting room at the top of the stairs, she quickly made the sofa comfortable for him. He lay down, and she covered him with a blanket, then ran to her room for a book, and read to him while Beenie was getting the tea.

The tea was brought and he drank a cup of it, but could not eat. And as he could not, neither could Mary.

"I want a long sleep," he said, and the words went to his child's heart— she dared not question herself why. When the tea-things were removed, he called her.

"Mary," he said, "come here. I want to speak to you."

She knelt down beside him.

"Mary," he said again, taking her hand in his two long, bony ones, "I love you, my child, more than I know how to say. And I want you to be a Christian."

"So do I, Father dear," answered Mary simply, the tears rushing into her eyes. "I want to be a Christian too."

"Yes, my love," he went on. "It is not that I do not think you a Christian. I do think you one. It is that I want you to be a downright real Christian, not one that is only trying to feel as a Christian ought to feel. I have lost so much precious time in that way!"

"Tell me," said Mary, clapping her other hand over his. "What would you have me do?"

"I will tell you," he replied. "At least I will try. A Christian is one that does what the Lord Jesus tells him. Neither more nor less than that makes a Christian. It is not even understanding the Lord Jesus that makes one a Christian. It is doing what he tells us that makes us Christians, and that is the only way to understand him. Peter says that the Holy Spirit is given to them that obey him: what else can that be but just actually, really doing what he says—just as if I were to tell you to go and fetch me my Bible, and you would get up and go. Did you ever do anything, my child, just because Jesus told you to do it?"

Mary did not answer immediately. She thought for a moment, then spoke.

"Yes, Father," she said, "I think so. Two nights ago, George was very rude to me—I don't mean anything bad, but you know he can be very rough."

"I know it, my child. And you must not think I don't care because I think it better not to interfere. I am with you all the time."

"Thank you, Father. I know it. Well, when I was going to bed, I was still angry with him, so it was no wonder I found that I could not pray. Then I remembered how Jesus said we must forgive or we should not be forgiven. So I forgave George in my heart, and then I found I could pray."

The father stretched out his arms and drew her to him, murmuring, "My child! My Christ's child!" After a little pause, he began to speak again.

"It is a sad thing to hear those who desire to believe themselves Christians, talking and talking about this question and that, the discussion of which makes only for strife and not for unity—not a thought among them of the one command of Christ to love one another. I fear some are hardly content with not hating those who differ from them."

"I try, Father—and I think I do love everybody who loves him."

"Well, that is much—though it is not enough, my child. We must be like Jesus, and you know that it was while we were yet sinners that Christ died for us. Therefore, we must love all men, whether they are Christians or not."

"Tell me, then, what you want me to do, Father dear. I will do whatever you tell me."

"I want you to be just like the Lord Jesus, Mary. I want you to look out for his will, and find it, and do it. I want you not only to do it, though that is the main thing, when you think of it, but to look for it, to actively seek it that you may do it. This is not a thing to be talked about much. You may think me very silent; but I do not always talk even when I am inclined to, for the fear that I might let my feelings out through talk, instead of doing something he wants of me with it. And how repulsive are those generally who talk the most. Our strength ought to go into conduct, not into talk—least of all into talk about what they call the doctrines of the gospel. The man who does what God tells him, sits at his Father's feet, and looks up in his Father's face. Such a man is a true Christian. And men had better be careful in how they criticize such a one, for he cannot greatly mistake his Father, and certainly will not displease him, when he is thus walking in obedience. Look for the lovely will of God, my child, that you may be its servant, its priest, its sister, its queen, its slave—as Paul calls himself. How that man did glory in his Master!"

"I will try, Father," returned Mary, tears spreading down her cheeks. "I do want to be one of his slaves."

"You are bound to be. You have no choice but to choose it. It is what we are made for—freedom, the divine nature, God's life, a grand, pure, open-eyed existence! It is what Christ died for. You must hardly talk about *wanting* to; it is all *must*."

Mary had never heard her father talk like this, and notwithstanding the endless interest of his words, it frightened her. An instinctive uneasiness crept up and laid hold of her. The unsealing hand of Death was opening the mouth of a dumb prophet.

A pause followed, and he spoke again.

"I will tell you one thing now that Jesus says. He is unchangeable; what he says once he says always. I mention it now because it may not be long before you are especially called upon to remember it. It is this: *'Let not your heart be troubled.'* "

"But did he not say that to his disciples only for one particular occasion?" said Mary, willing, in her dread, to give the conversation a turn.

"Ah, Mary," said her father with a smile, "will you let the questioning spirit deafen you to the teaching one? Ask yourself, the first time you are alone, what the disciples were troubled about, and why they were not to be troubled about it.—I am tired, and should like to go to bed."

He rose, stood for a moment in front of the fire, winding his old doublecased silver watch. Mary took from her side the little gold one he had given her, and, as was her custom, handed it to him to wind for her. The next moment he had dropped it on the floor.

"Ah, my child!" he cried. He stooped over, gathered up the dying thing, whose watchfulness was all over. The glass was broken, the case was open; it lay in his hand a mangled creature. Mary heard the rush of its departing life, as the wheels went whirring, and the hands circled rapidly.

They stood motionless. She looked up in her father's face with a smile. He was looking concerned.

"I am very sorry, Mary," he said. "But if it is past repair, I will get you another—you don't seem too upset!" he added, and smiled himself.

"Why should I be, Father dear?" she replied. "When one's father breaks one's watch, what is there to say but 'I am very glad it was you that did it'? I shall like the little thing the better for it."

He kissed her on the forehead.

"My child, say that to your Father in heaven, when he breaks something for you. He will do it from love, not from blundering. I don't often preach to you, my child—do I? but somehow it comes to me tonight."

"I will remember, Father," said Mary. And she did remember.

She went with him to his bedroom, and saw that everything was right for him. When she went again, before going to her own, he felt more comfortable, he said, and expected to have a good night. She left him relieved. But her heart continued to be heavy. A shapeless sadness seemed pressing it down; it was being gotten ready for what it had to bear.

When she went to his room in the middle of the night, she found him slumbering peacefully. She went back to her own and slept better. When she went again in the morning, he lay white, motionless, and without a breath.

It was not in Mary's nature to give sudden vent to her feelings. For a time she was stunned. The sorrow was too huge for entrance. The thing could not be! Not until she stooped and kissed the pale face did the stone in her bosom break, and yield a torrent of grief.

But already she knew that it was not he that lay where she had left him the night before. He was gone, and she was alone. She tried to pray, but her heart seemed to lie dead in her chest, and no prayer would rise from it. It was the time of all times when, if ever, prayer must be the one reasonable thing—and yet pray she could not.

In her dull stupor she did not hear Beenie's knock. The old woman entered, and found her on her knees, with her forehead on one of the dead hands, while the white face of her master lay looking up to heaven, as if praying for the living not yet privileged to die. Then first was the peace of death broken. Beenie gave a loud cry, and turned and ran, as if to warn the neighbors that Death was loose in the town. Thereupon the sanctuary of the dead was invaded by unhallowed presence, and the poor girl, hearing voices she did not love coming up the stairs, raised herself from her knees and crept from the room and away to her own.

"Follow her, George," said his father, in a loud, eager whisper. "You've got to comfort her now. That's your business. Now's your chance!"

The last words he called from the landing of the stair, as George sped up after her.

"Mary! Mary, dear," he called as he ran.

But Mary had the instinct to quicken her pace, and lock the door of her room the moment she entered. As she turned from it, her eye fell upon her watch—where it lay silent and disfigured, on her dressing table. With the sight, the last words of her father came back to her. She fell again on her knees with a fresh burst of weeping, and, while the foolish youth was knocking unheard at her door, cried, with a strange mixture of agony and comfort, "Oh, my Father in heaven, give me back William Marston!" Never in her life had she thought of her father by his name. But death, while it made him dearer than ever, set him away from her so that she began to see him in his larger individuality, as a man before the God of men, a son before the Father of many sons: Death turns a man's sons and daughters into his brothers and sisters. And while she kneeled, and, with exhausted heart, let her brain go on working of itself, as it seemed, there came a dreamy vision of the Savior with his disciples about him, reasoning with them that they should not give way to grief. "Let not your heart be troubled," he seemed to be saying, "although I die, and go out of your sight. It is all well. Take my word for it."

She rose, wiped her eyes, looked up, and said, "I will try." She left the room, called Beenie, and sent her to ask Mr. Turnbull to come up and speak with her.

She knew her father's ideas, and that he would want to have the funeral as simple as possible. It was a relief to have something, anything, to do in his name.

Mr. Turnbull came, and the man was kind. Though it went considerably against the grain with him to help plan what he called a pauper's funeral for the junior partner in the firm. But he was more desirous than ever to conciliate Mary, and therefore promised all that she wished.

"Marston was a poor-spirited fellow," he said to his wife when he told her; "the thing is a disgrace to the shop, but it's fit enough for him—and it will save money," he added, while his wife turned up her nose, as she always did at any mention of the shop.

Mary returned to her father's room, now silent again with the air of that which is not. She took from the table the old silver watch. It went on measuring the time by a scale now useless to its owner. She sat down by the bedside. Already, through love, sorrow, and obedience, she began to find herself drawing nearer to him than she had ever been; already she was able to recall his last words, and strengthen her resolve to keep them. And, sitting thus, holding vague companionship with the merely mortal, the presence of that which was not her father, which was like him only to remind her that it was not he, and which must so soon cease to resemble him, there sprang, as in the very footprint of Death, yet another flower of rarest comfort—a strong feeling, namely, of the briefness of time, and the certainty of the messenger's return to fetch herself.

Her soul did not sink into peace, but a strange peace awoke in her spirit. She heard the spring of the great clock that measures the years rushing rapidly down with a feverous whir, and saw the hands that measured the weeks and months careering around its face; while Death, like one of the white-robed angels in the tomb of the Lord, sat watching, with patient smile, for the hour when he should be bid to go for her.

I will not linger much over the crumbling time. It is good for those who are in it, especially good for those who come out of it chastened and resolved. But I doubt if any prolonged contemplation of death is desirable for those whose business it now is to live, and whose fate it is before long to die. It is a closing of God's hand upon us to squeeze some of the bad blood out of us, and, when it relaxes, we must live the more diligently— not to get ready for death, but to get more alive. I will relate only one thing yet which belonged to this twilight time.

12 / Mary's Dream

That night, and every night until the dust was laid to the dust, Mary slept well, and through the days she had great composure. But when the funeral was over there came a collapse and a change. The moment it became necessary to resume her former relations with the world as if nothing had changed, a fuller sense of her lonely desolation manifested itself. When she said good night to Beenie, and went to her room, she felt as if she went walking along to her tomb.

That night was the first herald of the coming winter, and blew a cold blast from his horn. All day the wind had been out. Wildly it had pulled at the long grass in the churchyard, as if it would tear it from its roots in the graves. It had struck vague sounds, as from a hollow world, out of the great bell overhead in the huge tower. And it had beat loud and fierce against the corner-buttresses that went stretching up out of the earth, like arms to hold steady and fast the lighthouse of the dead above the sea, which held them drowned below. Despairingly had the gray clouds drifted over the sky. And like white clouds fastened below, and shadows that could not escape, the robe of the ministering priest and the garments of the mourners had flapped and fluttered as if in captive terror. The only things remaining still were the coffin and the church—and the soul that had risen above the region of storms in the might of him who abolished death.

At the time Mary had noted none of these things. But now, as she slowly went up the stair and heard the same wind, she recalled them all in minute detail. The smell of the linen about her, and of the blue cloth and brown paper—things no longer to be handled by those tender, faithful hands—was dismal and strange. It seemed as if everything had gone dead, as if it had exhaled the soul of it, and retained but the odor of its mortality. The passages through the merchandise, left only wide enough for one, seemed like those she had read of in Egyptian tombs and pyramids.

When she opened the door of her room, the bright fire, which Beenie had made for her, startled her: the room looked unnatural, uncanny, because it was cheerful. She stood for a moment on the hearth, and in a sad, dreamy mood listened to the howling swoops of the wind, making the house quiver and shake. Now and then would come a greater gust, and rattle the window as if in fierce anger at its exclusion, then go shrieking and wailing through the dark heaven. Mechanically she took her New Testament, seated herself in a low chair by the fire, and tried to read it. But she could not fix her thoughts, or get the meaning of a single sentence. When she had read it, there it lay, looking at her just the same, like an unanswered riddle.

The region of the senses is the unbelieving part of the human soul; and out of that now began to rise fumes of doubt and question into Mary's heart and brain. Death was a fact. The loss, the ceasing were incontrovertible. She was sure of them: could she be sure of anything else? How could she? She had not seen Christ rise; she had never looked upon one of the dead; never heard a voice from the other bank across the river.

These were not her thoughts; she was too weary to think. They were but the thoughts that steamed up in her, and went floating about before her. She looked on them calmly, coldly, as they came and passed, or remained—saw them with indifference—there they were, and she could not help it. At last she fell asleep, and in a moment was dreaming diligently. This was her dream, as nearly as she could recall it, when she came to herself after waking from it with a cry.

She was one of a large company at a house where she had never been before—a beautiful house with a large garden behind. It was a summer night and the guests were wandering in and out at will, and through house and garden, amid lovely things of all colors and odors. Every now and then she came on a little group, or met a party of the guests, as she walked, but none spoke to her, or seemed to see her, and she spoke to no one.

She found herself at length in a long avenue of dark trees. She went walking along it, meeting no one, crossing strange shadows from the moon. At the end of the walk she found herself in a place of tombs. Indescribable terror and dismay seized her. She turned and fled back to the company of humankind at the house. But for a long time she sought it in vain; she could not reach it. The avenue seemed interminably long. At last she was again on the lawn, but no man nor woman was there, and in the house only a light here and there was burning. Every guest was gone. She entered. The servants, soft-footed and silent, were busy carrying away the vessels of hospitality and restoring order, as if already they were preparing for another company on the morrow. No one heeded her. She was out of place and obviously unwelcome. She hastened to the great door. She reached the hall. A strange, shadowy porter opened it to her, and she stepped out into a wide street.

That, too, was silent. No carriage rolled along, no one walked along either side. Not a single light shone from window or door, except what they gave back of the yellow light of the moon. She was lost—lost utterly, with an eternal loss. She knew nothing of the place, had nowhere to go, nowhere she wanted to go. She had no home, no direction, no desire; she knew of nothing she had lost, nor of anything she wished to gain. She had nothing left but the sense that she was empty, that she needed some goal, and had none. She sat down upon a stone between the wide street and the wide pavement, and saw the moon shining gray upon the stone houses. It was all deadness.

Presently from somewhere in the moonlight appeared the only brother she had ever had, walking up to her where she sat in eternal listlessness. She had lost him years and years before, and now she saw him. He was there and she knew him, but not a throb went through her heart. He came to her side, and she gave him no greeting. "Why should I heed him?" she said to herself. "He is dead. I am only in a dream. Everything is an empty dream of loss. I know it and there is no waking."

Then came the form of her mother, and bent over that of her brother. "Another ghost of a ghost!" she said to herself. "She is nothing. If I speak to her, she is not there."

With that came her father and stood beside the others, gazing upon her with still, cold eyes, expressing only a pale quiet. She bowed her face on her hands and would not look at him. Even if he were alive, her heart was past being moved. It was all settled into stone. The universe was sunk in one of the dreams that haunt the sleep of death. And if these were all ghosts, they were ghosts walking in their sleep.

But one of the dead seized one of her hands, and another the other. They raised her to her feet and led her along, and her brother walked before her. Thus was she borne away captive of her dead, neither willing nor unwilling, equally careless of life and death. Through the moonlight they led her from the city, and over fields, and through valleys, and across rivers and seas—a long journey. She did not grow weary, for there was not life in her to be made weary. The dead never spoke to her, and she never spoke to them. Sometimes it seemed as if they spoke to each other, but if it was actually so, it concerned some shadowy matter, no more to her than the talk of grasshoppers in the field, or of beetles that weave their much-involved dances on the face of the pool. Their voices were even too thin and remote to rouse her to listen.

At length they came to a great mountain, and, as they were going up the mountain, light began to grow, as if the sun were beginning to rise. But she cared as little for the sun that was to light the day as for the moon that had lighted the night, and closed her eyes, that she might cover her soul with her eyelids.

All of a sudden a great splendor burst upon her, and through her eyelids she was struck blind—blind with light rather than darkness, for all was radiance about her. She was like a fish in a sea of light. But she neither loved the light nor mourned the shadow.

Then were her ears invaded with a confused murmur, as of the mingling of all sweet sounds of the earth—of wind and water, of bird and voice, of string and metal—all afar and indistinct. Next arose about her a whispering, as of winged insects, talking with human voices. But she listened to nothing, and heard nothing of what was said: it was all a tiresome dream, out of which it hardly mattered whether she woke or died.

Suddenly she was taken between two hands, and lifted, and seated upon knees like a child, and she felt that someone was looking at her. Then came a voice, one that she never heard before, yet with which she was as familiar as with the sound of the blowing wind. And the voice said, "Poor child! Something has closed the valve between her heart and mine." With that came a pang of intense pain. But it was her own cry of speechless delight that woke her from her dream.

13 / Hesper's Fate

The same wind that rushed about the funeral of William Marston in the old churchyard of Testbridge also howled in the roofless hall and ruined tower of Durnmelling, and dashed against the plate-glass windows of the dining room, where the three ladies sat at lunch. But something very different was on the mind of the elder of them than the thoughts that had been occupying Mary of late. The moment the wind ceased, Lady Malice rose, saying: "Hesper, I want a word with you. Come to my room."

Hesper obeyed, with calmness, but without a doubt that evil awaited her there. To that room she had never been summoned for anything she could call good. And indeed she had a premonition of what evil it was she was sure to face. When they reached the boudoir, rightly so called, for it was more in use for sulking than for anything else, Lady Margaret, with back as straight as the door she had just closed, led the way to the fire, seated herself, and motioned Hesper to a chair. Hesper again obeyed, looking as unconcerned as if she cared for nothing in this world or any other. If only we were all as strong to suppress hate and fear and anxiety as some ladies are to suppress all show of them!

"Well, Hesper," said her mother, "Mr. Redmain has at last come to the point, my dear child."

"What point, Mama?"

"He had a private interview with your father this morning."

"Indeed."

"Foolish girl. Do you think to tease me by pretending indifference?"

"How can a fact be pretending, Mama? Why should I care what passes in the study? I was never welcome there. But I will pretend. What important matter was settled in the study this morning?"

"Hesper, you provoke me with your affectation!"

Hesper's eyes began to flash. Otherwise she was still and silent—not a feature moved. The eyes are more untamable than the tongue. When the wild beast cannot get out at the door, nothing can keep him from the windows. But Hesper continued silent, and indeed looked so utterly void of interest that her mother quailed before the evil spirit she had herself sent on to the generations to come, and finally yielded and spoke out.

"Mr. Redmain has proposed for your hand, Hesper," she said, in a tone as indifferent in her turn as if she were mentioning the appointment of a new clergyman to the family living.

For one moment, and one only, the repose of Hesper's faultless upper lip gave way—to return presently to a grander bend than before. In a tone that emulated, and more than equaled, the indifference of her mother's, she answered: "And Papa?"

"He has referred him to you, of course," replied Lady Margaret.

"Why?"

"I do not understand you," answered the mother.

"If Mr. Redmain is such a good match in Papa's eyes, then why does he refer him to me?"

"That you may accept him, of course."

"How much has the man promised to pay for me?"

"Hesper!"

"I beg your pardon, Mama. I thought you approved of calling things by their right names."

"No girl can do better than follow her mother's example," said Lady Margaret, with vague sequence. "If *you* do, Hesper, you will accept Mr. Redmain."

Hesper fixed her eyes on her mother and let them flash and burn as they pleased.

"As you did Papa?" said Hesper.

"As I did Mr. Mortimer."

"That explains a good deal, Mama. Tell me, would *you* marry Mr. Redmain?"

"That is a foolish question. As a married woman, I could not even consider it without impropriety. Knowing the duty of a daughter, I did not put the question to you. You are yourself the offspring of duty."

"If you were in my place, then, Mama," reattempted Hesper.

"In any place, in every place, I should do my duty," her mother replied.

It was not only born in Lady Malice's blood, but from earliest years it had been impressed on her brain that her first duty was to her family, and mainly consisted in getting well out of its way—in going peaceably through the fire to Moloch, that the rest might have good places in the Temple of Mammon. In her turn, she had trained her children to the bewildering conviction that it was duty to do a certain wrong, if it should be required. That wrong thing was now required of Hesper—a thing she scorned, hated, shuddered at.

"*Duty*, Mama!" she cried, her eyes flaming. "Can it be that women were born for such things? How *could* I, how could any woman with an atom of self-respect, consent to occupy the same *room* with Mr. Redmain?"

"Hesper! I am shocked. Where did you learn to speak, not to say *think*, of such things? Have I watched my child like a very angel, as anxious to keep her mind pure as her body fair, and is *this* the result?"

Upon what Lady Margaret founded her claim to a result more satisfactory to her maternal designs, it would be difficult to say. She had known nothing about the development of her daughter since the nursery, and nothing of the real character of the governesses and schoolmistresses she gave charge of Hesper's upbringing.

"Was it your object, then, to keep me innocent so that I might have the necessary lessons in wickedness first from my husband?" said Hesper rudely.

"Hesper, you are vulgar!" exclaimed Lady Margaret. She was, indeed, genuinely shocked. That a young lady of Hesper's birth and position should talk like this was a thing unheard of in her world. What innocent girl could dare allude to such matters?

"You are a married woman, Mama," returned Hesper in a tone inconsistently calm, "and therefore must know a great many things I neither know nor wish to know. For anything I know, you may be a better woman than I for having learned not to mind things that are a horror to me. But I appeal to you as a woman: for God's sake, save me from marrying that beast!"

"Girl! Is it possible you dare to call the man whom your father and I have chosen for your husband a beast?"

"Is he not a beast, Mama?"

"If he were, how should I know it? What has any lady to do with a man's secrets?"

"Even if he wants to marry her daughter?"

"That makes little difference. If he should not be altogether what he ought to be—and which of us is?—then you will have the honor of reclaiming him to the side of virtue. But men settle down when they marry."

"And what comes of their wives? Oh, Mother! How dare a man like that even desire in his heart to touch an innocent girl?"

"Because he is tired of the other sort," said Lady Malice, half unconsciously to herself. What she said to her daughter was ten times worse: the one was merely a fact concerning Redmain; the other revealed a horrible truth concerning herself. "He will give you three thousand pounds a year, Hesper," she said with a sigh, "and you will find yourself mistress."

"I don't doubt it," answered Hesper, in bitter scorn. "Such a man is incapable of making any woman a wife."

But all her mother could think, misinterpreting her daughter's innocence from her own familiarity with evil, was: what right had a girl to think at all for herself in such matters?

Thank God, the day will come—it may be thousands of years away—when there shall be no such things for a man to think of, any more than for a girl to shudder at! There is a purification in progress, and the kingdom of heaven will come, thanks to the Man who was holy, harmless, undefiled, and separate from sinners. You have heard a little, probably only a little, about him at church sometimes. But when that day comes, what part will you have had in causing evil to cease from the earth? The only way to increase in righteousness is to stay away from evil, not to become familiar with it, thinking—as so many delude themselves—that by first-hand knowledge will they the better avoid sin.

There had been a time in the mother's life when she herself regarded her approaching marriage, with a man she did not love, as a horror to which her natural maidenliness had to be compelled and subjected. She eventually got used to the horror, however, and thereby lost much of what purity she had once had. One thing only she knew now—and that was that her husband's affairs were so involved as to threaten absolute poverty. And what woman of the world would not count damnation better than that? And Mr. Redmain was rolling in money. Whatever there might have been to know about his bad character, this one fact would have covered all.

In Hesper's useless outburst, the mother did not fail to recognize Sepia's influence, without whom, she believed, Hesper could not have been nearly so awake to the bad side of the world. She was afraid of Sepia, but she did not think she would work to thwart the marriage. On that point she would speak to her.

"I will leave your father to deal with you, Hesper," said her mother, and rose.

"Give me a few hours first, Mama," begged Hesper. "Don't let him come to me just yet. For all your hardness, you feel for me a little—don't you?"

"Duty is always hard, my child," said Lady Margaret. She entirely believed it, and looked on herself as a martyr, a pattern of self-devotion and womanly virtue. But never once in her life had she done or abstained from doing a thing *because* the thing was right or was wrong. Such a person, be she as old and has hard as the hills, is mere putty in the fingers of Beelzebub.

Hesper rose and went to her own room. There she sat—for a long hour. Sat without moving, almost without thinking. She neither stormed nor wept; her life went smoldering on.

I fancy Hesper would have been a little shocked if one had called her an atheist. She went to church most Sundays. But if anyone had suggested to her a certain old-fashioned use of her chamber door, she would have inwardly laughed at the absurdity. But then, you see, her chamber was no closet, but a large and stately room. And besides, how, alas! *could* the child of Roger and Lady M. Alice Mortimer know that in the silence was hearing—that in the vacancy was a power waiting to be sought? Hesper was not much alone, and here was a chance it was a pity she should lose. But when she came to herself with a sigh, it was not to pray; and when she rose, it was to ring the bell and send for Miss Yolland.

14 / Ungenerous Benevolence_____

In the meantime, across the field, Letty saw nothing more of Tom, and began to feel that the danger was past. She would never again place herself in circumstances where she had to conceal the truth. She began, much too soon, to feel as if she were newborn; but nothing worthy of being called a new birth can take place anywhere but in the will, and poor Letty's will was not yet old enough to give birth to anything; indeed, it scarcely existed. The past was rapidly receding, that was all. But her existence continued uninteresting, and therefore who could blame her if the idea of Tom's friendship was still pleasant in her memory. A kiss from Mrs. Wardour or a little teasing from cousin Godfrey would have done far more than intellectual labor upon her to lift her feet above such snares as she was now walking in. She needed some play—a thing far more important to life than a great deal of business. Many a matter, over which grown people look important, long-faced, and serious, is folly compared with the merest child's frolic, in relation to the true affairs of existence.

All during this time Letty had not in the least neglected her house-duties. And again her readings with Godfrey had begun to revive in interest. He grew kinder and kinder to her, and more fatherly.

But the mother had lost no time in taking measures for his protection. In every direction, she secretly was inquiring through friends for some situation for Letty: she owed it to herself, she said, to find the right thing for the girl. In the true spirit of benevolent tyranny, she said not a word to Letty of her design. She had the chronic distemper of concealment, where Letty had but a feverish attack. In the meantime, she kept her lynx-eye upon the young people.

Having caught a certain expression in the said eye, Godfrey vowed more than ever to watch what he was about and keep himself thoroughly in hand. And yet he was so much drawn to the girl, that he gave her the manuscript of his own verses—a volume exquisitely written and bound expressly for her own eyes.

At length, news of something that seemed likely to suit her ideas for Letty came to Mrs. Wardour's ears, whereupon she thought it time to prepare the girl for the impending change. Therefore, as one day she sat knitting, she opened the matter.

"I am getting old, Letty," she began, "and you can't stay here forever.

You are a thoughtless creature, but I suppose you have the sense to see that.''

"Yes, indeed, aunt," answered Letty.

"It is high time you should be thinking how you are to earn your bread," Mrs. Wardour went on. "If you waited until I was gone, you would find it very awkward, for you would have to leave Thornwick at once, and I don't know who would take you while you were looking for something. I must see you comfortably settled into a position before I go."

"Yes, aunt."

"There are not many things you could do."

"No, aunt; very few. But I should make a better housemaid than most. I do believe that."

"I am glad to find you willing to work. But I trust we shall be able to do a little better for you than that. A situation as housemaid would reflect little credit on my plans for you—it would hardly be in keeping with the education you have had."

Mrs. Wardour referred to the fact that Letty was for about a year a day-boarder at a ladies' school in Testbridge, where no immortal soul could have taken the least interest in the chaff and chopped straw that composed the provender there offered.

"It is true," her aunt went on, "that you might have made a good deal more of it, if you had cared to do your best. But such as you are, I trust we shall find you a very tolerable situation as governess."

At the word, Letty's heart ran halfway up her throat. She could not have imagined a more dreadful proposal. She knew she was utterly incapable of such an office: how could she teach anything?

"You don't seem to relish the proposal, Letty," said Mrs. Wardour. "I hope you had not taken it into your head that I meant to leave you independent. What I have done for you, I have done purely for your father's sake. I was under no obligation to take the least trouble about you. But I have more regard to your welfare than I fear you give me credit for."

"Oh, Aunt! it's only that I'm not fit to be a governess. I wouldn't mind a bit being a dairymaid or housemaid. I would go to such a place tomorrow if you liked."

"Letty, your tastes may be vulgar, but you owe it to your family to at least look like a lady."

"But I am not scholar enough to be a governess."

"That is not my fault. I sent you to a good school. Now, I will find you a good situation, and you must find a way to keep it."

"Oh Aunt! let me stay here—just as I am. Call me your dairymaid or your housemaid. It is all one—I do the work now."

"Do you mean to reflect on me that I have required menial offices of you? I have been to you like a mother. It is for me, not for you, to make the choice of your path in life."

"Do you want me to go at once?" asked Letty, her heart sinking again.

"As soon as I have secured for you a desirable situation—not before," answered Mrs. Wardour, in a tone generously protective.

Her affection for the girl had never been deep, and the moment she fancied a danger between her and her son, she considered her duty to Letty well discharged. There are those who never learn to see anything except in its relating to themselves. And, this being a withering habit of mind, they keep growing drier and older and smaller and deader the longer they live—thinking less of other people and more of themselves and their past experience, all the time as they go on withering.

But Mrs. Wardour was in some dread of what her son would say when he came to know what she had been doing; for when we are not at ease with ourselves, when conscience keeps moving as if about to speak, then we dread the disapproval of others. Therefore, she kept silent toward him about her plans. If she had spoken, things might have gone very differently. It might have roused him to speak on Letty's behalf, or even his own.

For her part, Letty believed her cousin Godfrey regarded her with pity and showed her kindness from a generous sense of duty; she was a poor, dull creature for whom her cousin must do what he could. One word of genuine love from him would have caused her nature to shoot heavenward and spread out earthward so rapidly it would have astonished him.

But now she felt crushed. The idea of undertaking something for which she knew herself so ill-prepared was not merely distasteful but frightful to her. She was ready enough to work, but it must be real, not sham work. She must talk to Mary! This was quite another matter from Tom. She would have to find the first opportunity to see her.

15 / A Meeting in the Moonlight

When Letty went to her room that night, she walked mechanically to the window, and with the candle in her hand stood looking out. It was a still, frosty night, with a full moon. The window looked on an open, grassy yard, where there were a few large ricks of wheat, shining yellow in the cold, far-off glow of the sun's reflection. Between the moon and the earth hung a faint mist, which the thin clouds of her breath seemed to mingle with. There lay her life—out of doors—dank and dull; all the summer faded from it—all the atmosphere a growing fog. It was six weeks since she had seen Tom. He had probably stopped thinking of her altogether by this time.

Suddenly something struck the window with a slight, sharp clang. It was winter, and there were no moths or other insects flying about. What could it be? She put her face close to the pane and looked out.

There was a man in the shadow of one of the ricks! He had his hat off and was beckoning to her. Who could it be but Tom?

The thought sent a pang of mingled pleasure and pain to her heart. He must want to speak to her. How gladly she would, but then would come again all the troubles of conscious deceit: how was she to bear that all over again! Still, if she was to be turned out of the house so soon, what would it matter? If her aunt was going to compel her to be her own mistress, what was the harm if she began it a few days sooner? What did it matter anyhow what she did? But she dared not speak to him; Mrs. Wardour's ears were as sharp as her eyes.

She opened the lattice softly, gently shook her head, and began to close it again, when the man stepped into the moonlight making frantic signs with his hands. It was plainly Tom.

This was too dreadful! He might be seen at any moment! She shook her head again, but, without making a sound, he continued to entreat her. With sudden resolve, she nodded and then left the window.

Her room was in a little wing, projecting from the back of the house, over the kitchen. The servants' rooms were in another part, but Letty forgot a tiny window in one of them, which also looked out upon the ricks. There was a back stair to the kitchen, and in the kitchen a door to the farmyard. She stole down the stair and opened the door with absolute noiselessness. In a moment more she had stolen on tiptoe around the corner and was creeping like a ghost among the ricks. Not even a rustle betrayed her as she came up to Tom from behind. He still stood where she had left him, looking up to her window, which gleamed like a dead eye in the moonlight. She stood for a moment, afraid to move, lest she should startle him and he should cry out, for the slightest noise about the place would bring Godfrey down. The next moment, however, Tom became aware of her presence, and turned around and sprang to her and took her in his arms. Still possessed by the one terror of making a noise, she did not object even by a contrary motion, and when he took her hand to lead her away and out of sight of the house, she yielded at once.

When they were safe in the field behind the hedge, she finally spoke.

"Why did you make me come down, Tom?" she whispered, half choked with fear, looking up in his face, which was radiant in the moonshine.

"Because I could not bear it one day longer without seeing you," he answered. "All this time I have been trying to get a word with you, and yet even at church you would never even look at me. It is cruel of you."

"Do speak a little lower, Tom; sound goes so far at night! I didn't know you would want to see me," she answered, looking up in his face with a pleased smile.

"Didn't know!" repeated Tom. "I want nothing else, think of nothing else, dream of nothing else, you darling Letty!"

"But I must go back, Tom. I have no business to be out of the house at this time of the night. If you hadn't made me think you were in some kind of trouble, I wouldn't have dared come."

"And aren't I in trouble enough—trouble that nothing but seeing you and talking to you could get me out of? To love your very shadow, and not be able to get so much as a peep even of that—isn't that trouble enough?"

Letty's heart leaped up. So he loved her! She would be afraid of nothing any more! They might say or do what they pleased—she did not care, if he loved her—really loved her! And he did!

"I didn't know you loved me, Tom!" she said, simply, and with a little gasp.

"And I don't know yet whether you love me," returned Tom.

"Of course, if you love *me*," answered Letty, as if everybody must give back love for love.

Tom took her again in his arms, and Letty was in greater bliss than she had ever dreamed possible. From being a nobody in the world, she now felt like a queen. From being utterly friendless, she had the heart of Tom Helmer for her own.

Yet in the midst of her thoughts, as she eluded the barriers of Tom's arms, shot to her heart, sharp as an arrow, the thought that she was forsaking cousin Godfrey. She did not attempt to explain it to herself; she was in too great confusion, even if she had been capable of the necessary analysis. It came, probably, of what her aunt had often told her concerning her cousin's opinion of Tom. She had often told herself that, of course, cousin Godfrey must be quite mistaken in not liking Tom; she was sure he would feel differently if he knew him as she did. Yet to act against his opinion cost her this sharp pang, and not a few that followed. To soften it for the moment, however, came the vaguely reproachful feeling that, seeing they were about to send her out into the world, they had no more right to make demands on her loyalty.

"Now, Tom, you have seen me and spoken to me, and I must go," said Letty.

"Oh, Letty!" cried Tom, "now when we at last understand each other, will you leave me in the very moment of my supremest bliss? I was never so happy in all my life, and now you want to leave me all alone in the middle of the night, with only the moon to comfort me? Do as you like, Letty!—but I won't leave this blessed spot till the morning. I will lie in sight of your window all night."

The idea of Tom out on the cold ground, while she was warm in bed, was too much for Letty's childish heart. Had she known Tom better, she would not have worried about him. She would have known that he would indeed do as he had said, and lie down under her window, and there remain, even to the very moment when he began to feel miserable, and a moment longer, but not more than two. Then he would get up, and with a last look start home for bed.

"I will stay a little while, Tom," she consented at last, "if you will promise to go home as soon as I leave you."

Tom promised.

They went wandering along the farm lanes, and Tom spoke words of love to her. I do not wish to be understood that he did not love her—with such love as lay in the immediate power of his development. But it was not love in any true sense. Being a sort of poet, such as a man may be who loves the form of beauty but not the indwelling power of it, that is, the truth, he *fashioned* forms of love, and offered them to her. And she accepted them, and found the words of them very dear and very lovely. For she had not gotten far enough, with all Godfrey's endeavors toward her development, to love rightly the ring of the true gold, and therefore was not able to distinguish the dull sound of the gilt brass Tom offered her. Poor fellow! it was all he had. But compassion itself can hardly urge that as a reason for accepting it as genuine. What rubbish most girls will take for poetry, what polish they will take for refinement, what mere gallantry for love!

In justice to Tom, he was no intentional deceiver; he was so thoroughly self-deceived that, being himself a deception, he could be nothing but a deceiver—at once the most pardonable, and perhaps the most dangerous of deceivers.

With all his fine talk of love, to which he now gave full flow, it was characteristic of him that, although he saw Letty without hat or cloak, just because he was himself warmly clad, it never dawned on him that she might be cold, until the arm he had thrown round her waist felt her shiver. At that point he was kind, and insisted that she should go in and get a shawl. But when she positively refused to go in and come out again, he offered her his coat. His action sprung from no conscious sense of putting her needs above his own, but only so that she might be able to stay out a little longer. But she prevailed upon him to let her go. He therefore brought her to the nearest point not within sight of any of the windows, there left her, and set out at a rapid pace for the inn where he had put up his mare.

When Tom was gone, and the bare night like a diffused conscience all about her, with a strange fear at her heart, though she had done nothing wrong in its mere self, Letty stole back to the door of the kitchen.

She had left the door an inch ajar so that there might be less risk of making a noise in reopening it. But as she approached it, she saw plainly that it was closed, and her heart turned sick. Between cold and terror she shuddered from head to foot, and stood staring at it.

After a moment or two she recovered a little, and said to herself that some draft must have blown it shut. If so, there was danger that the noise had been heard; but in any case, there was not a moment to lose. She went to the door and lifted the latch slowly. But horror of horrors! in vain. The door was locked. She was shut out. She must lie or confess! The least perilous thing to do would now have been to let the simple truth appear; Letty ought immediately to have knocked at the door. But that was just the kind of action of which, truthful as was her nature, poor Letty was incapable. She dared not encounter the anger and condemnation of her aunt. She sank, more than half fainting, upon the doorstep.

The moment she came to herself, her apprehension changed into active dread, and then into uncontrollable terror. She sprang to her feet, and, the worst thing she could possibly do, fled like the wind after Tom—now, indeed, she imagined, her only refuge! She knew where he had put up his horse, and knew he could hardly take any other way than the footpath to Testbridge. He could not be but a little ways ahead of her, she thought.

Presently she heard him whistling, she was sure, as he walked leisurely along, but she could not see him. The way was mostly between hedges until it reached the common: there she was sure to catch sight of him. On she went as fast as she could, still fancying at intervals that she heard his whistle in front of her and even his step on the hard frozen path. It was bitingly cold, but, in her eager anxiety to overtake him, she felt neither the chilling air nor the fear of the night and the loneliness. Dismay was behind her and hope before her.

On and on she ran. But when, now with failing breath, she reached the common, and saw it lie so bare and wide in the moonlight, with the little hut standing on its edge, like a ghastly lodge to nowhere, the horror of her deserted condition and the terrors of the night began to crush their way into her soul. What might not be lurking in that ruin, ready to wake at the lightest rustle, and, catching sight of the fleeing girl, start out in pursuit and catch her by the hair that now streamed behind her! And there was the hawthorn tree, so old and grotesquely contorted, reminding her of an old miser, decrepit with age, pursued and unable to run! Miserable as was her real condition, it was made all the more awful by these terrors of the imagination. The distant howl of a dog which the moon would not let sleep, the muffled low of a cow, and a certain strange sound coming again and again, which she could not account for, all turned things unnatural and therefore frightful. But more frightful than all possible dangers was the old house she had left, standing silent in the mist, holding her room inside it empty, the candle burning away in the face of the moon! She could do nothing but continue on! Therefore, across the common she glided like a swift wraith.

If Tom had come this way, Letty thought she would have overtaken him by now! But perhaps she had lain longer than she realized at the kitchen door. Who could tell but that Tom was already at home! Alas! she was lost utterly!

The footpath came to an end, and she found herself on the main road. There was the inn where Tom generally put up! It was silent as the grave. The clang of a horseshoe striking a stone came through the frosty air from far along the road. Her heart sank into the depths of the infinite sea that encircles the soul, and Death passing by gave her an alms of comfort, and she fell down insensible on the edge of the same road along which Tom, on his bay mare, went singing his way home.

16 / Godfrey's Search

At Thornwick Tom had been seen in the yard by one of the servants—a woman not very young, and not altogether innocent of nightly interviews. Through the small window of her closet she had seen, and having seen she watched—not without hope she might be herself the object of the male presence, which she recognized as that of Tom Helmer, whom almost everybody knew. In a few minutes, however, Letty appeared, and with the sight a throb of evil joy shot through her bosom. What a chance! to find Miss Letty out in her naughty secret! to have her in her power!

She had not a thought of betraying her: there would be no fun in that. She would, of course, tell Letty everything—and then what privileges would be hers, and what larks they two would have together!

To make sure of Letty and her secret, partly also in pure delight of mischief, she stole down the stairs and locked the kitchen door—the bolt of which, for reasons of her own, she kept well oiled. Then she sat down in an old rocking chair, and waited—I cannot say watched, for she fell fast asleep. Letty lifted the latch almost too softly for her to have heard even had she been awake. But on the doorstep, had she been capable of listening, Letty might have heard her snoring. When the young woman awoke in the cold gray of the morning and came to herself, her conscience seized her. She opened the door softly, went out and searched everywhere, and, discovering no trace of Letty, left the door unlocked and went to bed, hoping she might yet find her way into the house before Mrs. Wardour was down.

When that lady awoke at the usual hour and heard no sounds of stirring, she put on her dressing-gown, and went angrily to Letty's room. There, to her amazement and horror, she saw that the bed had not been lain in all night. She hurried to the room occupied by the girl who was the cause of the mischief. Roused suddenly by the voice of her mistress, she got up half awake and sleepy-headed. Assailed by a torrent of questions, in her confusion, before she was well awake, she had told all she had seen from the window, but nothing of what she had done herself.

Mrs. Wardour hurried to the kitchen, found the door on the latch, believed everything she had heard and much more, went straight to her son's room, and in a calm rage, woke him up, and poured into his unwilling ears a torrent of mingled fact and fiction, wherein floated side by side with Letty's name every bad adjective she could bring the lips of propriety to utter. Before he quite came to himself, the news had practically driven him mad. There stood his mother, dashing her cold hailstorm of contemptuous wrath on the girl he loved. He had been dreaming of her with the utmost tenderness, when his mother woke him with the news that she had gone in the night with Tom Helmer, the poorest creature in the neighborhood.

"For God's sake, Mother," he cried, "go away, and let me get up!"

"What can you do, Godfrey? What is there to be done? Let the jade go to her ruin!" cried Mrs. Wardour. "You can do nothing now. She has made her bed, and now she must lie in it."

Her words were torture to him. He sprang from his bed and proceeded to pull on his clothes. His mother fled from the room.

Godfrey could hardly dress himself from the agitation. Anger fought with unbelief in his mind. It was all incredible and shameful, yet not the less miserable. He had been silently worshiping an angel with wings not yet matured to the spreading of themselves to the winds of truth. Those wings were a little maimed, and he had been tending them with precious balms and ointments. Now all at once she had turned into a bat, a skin-winged creature that flies by night, and had disappeared into the darkness! Of all possible mockeries, for her to steal out at night into the embraces of a fool—a weak-headed idle fellow who did nothing but ride the country on a horse too good for him, and quarrel with his mother from Sunday to Saturday! For such a man she had left Godfrey Wardour—a man who would have lifted her to the height of her nature—whereas the fool Helmer would sink her to the depth of his own merest nothingness! The thing was inconceivable!

He knew *now* that he loved the girl. In a rage, he grabbed his hunting whip from the wall and rushed out of the house.

Like many in the neighborhood, he thought worse of Tom Helmer than he yet deserved. He had no character, it is true, and was a fool, a good-for-nothing sort of fellow. But that was the worst that as yet was true of him. And better things might with equal truth have been said of him, had there been anyone that loved him enough to know them.

Godfrey ran to the stable, threw the saddle over the back of his fastest horse, but in the midst of his passion his hands trembled so that he failed repeatedly in passing the straps through the buckles of the girths. But the moment he felt the horse under him, he was stronger, and set his head straight for the village of Warrender, where Tom's mother lived. His flight led him across the field at the back of the house of Durnmelling. Hesper, who had not slept well, saw him from her window. She called Sepia, who for a few nights had slept in her room, to the window.

"There now!" she said, "there is a man who looks like a man. Good heavens! how recklessly he rides! I don't believe Mr. Redmain could keep on a horse's back if he tried."

"Something is wrong with the proud yeoman!" Sepia returned. "We shall no doubt hear more of this morning's ride! That's a man I should like to know," she added carelessly. "There is some go in him. I have a weakness for the kind of man that could shake the life out of me if I offended him."

"Are you so anxious to be a good, submissive wife?" said Hesper.

"Heavens no! I would take the first opportunity of offending him. It would be worth one's while with a man like that."

"Why? What would be the good of that?"

"Just to see him fly into a passion. To know that you have the man's heartstrings stretched on your violin, and that with one dash of your bow you can make him shriek—there is nothing on earth so scrumptious."

"Sepia!" said Hesper, "I think Darwin must be right, and some of us at least *are* come from—"

"Tiger cats?" suggested Sepia, with one of her scornful half-laughs.

But the same instant she turned white as death and sat down softly on the nearest chair.

"Good heavens, Sepia! what is the matter? I did not mean it," said Hesper, thinking she had wounded her.

"It's not that, Hesper, dear. You could say nothing that would hurt me," replied Sepia, drawing in a sharp breath. "It's a pain that comes sometimes—a sort of picture drawn in pains—something I saw once."

"What was it?"

"Oh nothing. It's gone now. Someday, when you are married and a little more used to men and their ways, I will tell you. My little cousin is much too innocent now."

"But you have not been married, Sepia. What could you know about disgraceful things?"

"I will tell you when you are married, and not until then, Hesper. That's a bribe to you to do as you must—that is, as your father and mother and Mr. Redmain would have you!"

While they talked, Godfrey had quickly become a speck in the distance and now vanished from their sight.

By this time he had collected his thoughts a little. But instead of reproaching himself that he had not drawn the poor girl's heart to his own, he tried to congratulate himself on the pride and self-important delay that had preserved him from yielding his love to one who counted herself of so little value.

Arriving at the house—a well-appointed cottage, with out-buildings larger than itself—he dismounted, went through the gate, and rang the bell in a porch covered with ivy. The old woman who opened the door said Master Tom was not up yet, but she would take his message. Returning presently, she asked him to walk in. He declined the hospitality, and remained in front of the house.

Tom was no coward, in the ordinary sense of the word; but he did confess to not feeling "particularly well" when he heard who was below: there was but one thing it could mean, he thought—that Letty had been found out, and here was her cousin come to make a row. But what did it matter, so long as Letty was true to him? As soon as he was of age, he would marry her and spite them all!

While Godfrey waited, it was all he could do to keep his contempt within the bounds of reason. He kept walking up and down the little lawn, making a futile attempt to look unconcerned, and the next moment striking fierce, objectless blows with his whip. Catching sight of him from a window on the stair, Tom was so little reassured by his demeanor that he took from the stand in the hall a thick oak walking stick—poor odds against a hunting whip in the hands of one like Godfrey.

Tom's long legs came doubling carelessly down the steps, and swinging his cudgel as if he were just going out for a stroll, he coolly greeted his visitor. But the other, instead of returning the salutation, stepped quickly up to him.

"Mr. Helmer, where is Miss Lovel?" he said, in a low voice.

Tom turned pale, and his voice betrayed genuine anxiety as he answered: "I do not know. What has happened?"

Wardour's fingers gripped convulsively his whip-handle, and the word *liar* had almost escaped his lips. But through the darkness of the tempest raging in him, he yet read truth in Tom's scared face and trembling words.

"You were with her last night," he said fiercely.

"I was," answered Tom, looking more scared still.

"Where is she now?" demanded Godfrey again.

"I hope to God you know," answered Tom, "for I don't."

"Where did you leave her?" asked Wardour, in the tone of an avenger rather than a judge.

Without a moment's hesitation, Tom described the place exactly—a spot not more than a hundred yards from the house.

"What right had you to come sneaking about the place?" hissed Godfrey, a vain attempt to master an involuntary movement of the muscles of his face, at once clinching and showing his teeth. At the same moment he raised his whip unconsciously.

Tom instinctively stepped back and raised his stick in an attitude of defense. Godfrey burst into a scornful laugh.

"You fool!" he said. "You need not be afraid. I can see you are speaking the truth. You dare not tell me a lie."

"It is enough," returned Tom with dignity, "that I do not tell lies. I am not afraid of you, Mr. Wardour. What I dare or dare not is neither for you nor me to say. You are the older and stronger and every way better man, but that gives you no right to bully me."

This answer brought Godfrey to a better sense of what became himself. He spoke the next in a tone calm even to iciness.

"Mr. Helmer," he said, "I will gladly address you as a gentleman if you will show me how it can be the part of a gentleman to go prowling about his neighbor's property after nightfall."

"Love acknowledges no law but itself, Mr. Wardour," answered Tom, inspired by the dignity of his honest affection for Letty. "Miss Lovel is not your property. I love her, and she loves me. I would do my best to see her, if Thornwick were the castle of Giant Blunderbore."

"Why not walk up to the house, like a man, in the daylight, and say you wanted to see her?"

"Should I have been welcome, Mr. Wardour?" said Tom, significantly. "You know very well what my reception would have been; and I know better than to throw difficulties in my own path."

"Well, we must find her now anyhow. And then you must marry her."

"*Must!*" echoed Tom, his eyes flashing. "Must?" he repeated, "when there is nothing in the world I desire more? How do you dare tell me what I *must* do, even if I care for nothing but to marry her? But tell me what it all means, Mr. Wardour; I tell you, I am utterly in the dark."

"It means just this—that the girl was seen in your company late last night, and has neither been seen nor heard of since."

"My God!" cried Tom, now first laying hold of the fact; and with the word he turned and started for the stable. But halfway there, he turned back.

"Mr. Wardour," he said, "what should we do? If we raise a cry, it will set people saying all manner of things, pleasant neither for you nor for us."

"That is your business, Mr. Helmer," answered Godfrey bitterly. "It is you who have brought this shame on her."

"You are a cold-hearted man," said Tom. "But there is no shame in the matter. I will soon make that clear—if only I knew where to go after her. The thing is utterly mysterious to me. What *can* have happened to her?"

He turned his back on Godfrey for a moment, then, suddenly wheeling around, broke out: "I will tell you what happened! I see it all now. She realized that she had been seen and was too terrified to go back into the house again!—Mr. Wardour," he continued, with a new look in his eyes, "I have more reason to be suspicious of you and your mother than you have to suspect me. Your treatment of Letty has not been of the kindest."

So Letty had been accusing him of unkindness! It was a fresh stab to

Godfrey's heart. Was this the girl for whom, in all honesty and affection, he had sought to do so much? How could she say he was unkind to her?— and say it to a fellow like this? It was humiliating indeed!

But he would not defend himself. He would carry himself with pride. Though she had plunged his heart into a pitcher of gall, he would do everything he could for her sake. And then he would have done with her and all women forever, except his mother!

He looked at Tom full in the eyes, and made no answer.

"If I don't find Letty this very morning," said Tom, "I shall apply for a warrant to search your house: my uncle Rendall will give me one."

Godfrey smiled a smile of scorn, turned from him as a wise man turns from a fool, and went out of the gate.

He had just retrieved his horse when he saw a young woman coming hurriedly across the road, from the direction of Testbridge. Plainly she was on urgent business. She came nearer, and he saw it was Mary Marston. The moment she recognized Godfrey she began to run to him. But when she came near enough to take notice of the look on his face, as he stood with his foot in the stirrup, with no word of greeting or look of reception, her haste suddenly dropped. Her flushed face turned pale, and she stood still, panting. Not a word could she utter, and was but just able to force a faint smile, with intent to reassure him.

17 / The Next Morning

Letty would perhaps never have come to herself in the cold of this world had it not been for an outcast mongrel dog, which came wandering masterless and hungry along the road. He came upon her where she lay seemingly lifeless, and, recognizing with pity his neighbor in misfortune, he began at once to give her what help and healing might lie in a warm, honest tongue. Diligently he set himself to lick her face and hands.

By slow degrees her misery returned, and she sat up. Rejoiced at his success, the dog kept dodging about her, catching a lick here and a lick there, wherever he saw a spot of bare within his reach. By slow degrees, next, the knowledge of herself joined on to the knowledge of her misery, and she knew who it was that was miserable. She threw her arms round the dog, laid her head on his, and wept. This relieved her a little, for weeping is good. But she was cold to the very marrow, almost too cold to feel it, and when she rose, she could scarcely put one foot in front of the other.

Not once, for all her misery, did she imagine a return to Thornwick. Without a thought of where she was going, she moved on, unaware that she was even moving in the direction of the town. The dog, delighted to believe that he had raised up to himself a mistress, followed humbly at her heel. But always when she stopped, as she did every few paces, ran round in front of her, and looked up in her face, as if to say, "Here I am, mistress! Shall I lick again?"

Slowly the two went on, with hardly enough motion to keep the blood moving in their veins. Had she not been in fine health and strength, despite all her recent depression, Letty could hardly have escaped death from the cold of that night. But although she never forgot this part of the terrible night, her memory could not join it to the next part, for again she lost consciousness, and could recall nothing between feeling the dog once more licking her face and finding herself in bed.

When Beenie opened her kitchen door in the morning to let in the fresh air, she found seated on the step, and leaning against the wall, what she took first for a young woman asleep, and then for the body of one dead: for when she gave her a little shake, she fell sideways off the door-step. Beenie's heart smote her, for during the last hours of her morning's sleep she had been disturbed by the howling of a dog, apparently in their own yard, but she had paid no attention to it other than that of repeated mental objurgation. And now there stood the offender, looking up at her pitifully. When the girl fell down, he darted at her, licked her cold face for a moment, then stretching out a long, gaunt neck, uttered from the depth of his skinny frame the most melancholy appeal imaginable.

When Beenie stooped, and peered more closely into the face of the girl, she recognized, though faintly, a known face. She too uttered a kind of howl, and straightway raised Letty's head and did what she could to draw her into the house. It is the mark of an imperfect humanity that personal knowledge should be necessary to spur hospitality: what difference does our knowing or not knowing make to the fact of human need? The good Samaritan would never have been mentioned by the mouth of the True, had he been even an old acquaintance of the "certain man." But it is thus we learn; and, from loving this one and that, we come to love all at last, and then is our humanity complete.

Letty could hardly move one frozen muscle. Beenie grew terrified and flew up the stairs to her mistress. Mary sprang from her bed and hurried down. There, on the kitchen floor, lay the body of Letty Lovel. A hideous dog was sitting on his haunches at her head. The moment she entered, again the animal stretched out a long, bony neck, and sent forth a howl that rang penetrative through the house. They raised Letty and carried her to Mary's room. There they laid her in the still-warm bed, and did everything they could to restore heat to her and renew her circulation.

When Beenie returned to the kitchen to get hot water, she found the dog still sitting there motionless with his face turned toward the door by which they had carried Letty out. Not realizing that he had already done more to save Letty's life than they yet had, she drove him from the kitchen and out into the street. God rest all such of His creation!

It took some time, but eventually Letty began to revive again. It was resolved between the two nurses that, for the present, they would say nothing of what happened until they learned more, and would keep the affair to themselves, a conclusion affording much satisfaction to Beenie, in the realization that therein she would have the better of the Turnbulls, against whom she cherished an ever-renewed indignation.

But when Mary set herself to find out from Letty what had happened, she found her mind so far gone that she could understand nothing she said to her. She kept murmuring almost inarticulately, but, to Mary's uneasiness, every now and then plainly uttered the name *Tom*. What was she to make of it? A single false step might do no end of mischief! She must see Tom Helmer: without betraying Letty, she might get from him some enlightenment. She had a better opinion of him than many had, and was a little nearer the right of him. The doctor should be called, but if possible she would see Tom first.

It was not more than a half hour's walk to Warrender, and she set out quickly. She must get back before George Turnbull came to open the shop.

When she got near enough to see Mr. Wardour's face, she read in it at once that he was there from the same cause she was, though neither of them appeared to know the complete story. But there was no good news to be drawn from his expression: she read there not only anxiety, but also suppressed anger, and possibly a distrust directed at her as well. The sole acknowledgment he made of her approach was to withdraw his foot from the stirrup and stand waiting.

"You know something," he said, looking cold and hard in her face.

"About what?" returned Mary, recovering herself. For Letty's sake, she was careful to feel her way.

"I hope to goodness," returned Godfrey, almost fiercely, yet with a dash of rude indifference, "that *you* are not concerned in this—business!"—he was about to use a bad adjective, but suppressed it.

"I *am* concerned in it," said Mary, with perfect quietness.

"You knew what was going on?" cried Wardour. "You knew that fellow there came prowling about Thornwick like a fox about a hen-roost? By Heaven! if I had but suspected it—"

"No, Mr. Wardour," interrupted Mary, already catching a glimpse of light, "I knew nothing of that."

"Then what do you mean by saying you are concerned in the matter?"

Mary thought that he was behaving so unlike himself that a shock might be of service.

"Only this," she answered, "—that Letty is now lying in my room, whether dead or alive I am in doubt. She must have spent the night in the open air—and without a cloak or hat."

"Good God!" cried Godfrey. "And you left her?"

"She is attended to," replied Mary. "There are worse evils to be warded off than death, otherwise I should not be here; there are hard judgments and evil tongues. Will you come and see her, Mr. Wardour?"

"No," answered Godfrey gruffly.

"Shall I send a note to Mrs. Wardour, then?"

"I will tell her myself."

"What would you have me do about Letty?"

"I have no concern in the matter, but I suppose you had better send for a doctor. Talk to that fellow there," he added, pointing with his whip toward the cottage, and again putting his foot in the stirrup. "Tell him he has brought her to disgrace—"

"I don't believe it," interrupted Mary again. But Godfrey went on without heeding her.

"And tell him to marry her—for, by God! he *shall* marry her, or I will kill him."

He spoke looking round at her over his shoulder, a scowl on his face, and his foot in the stirrup. Mary stood white but calm, and made no answer. He swung himself into the saddle, and rode away. She turned to the gate.

From behind the shrubbery, Tom had heard all that passed between them. Meeting her as she entered, he led the way to a sidewalk, then said: "Oh, Miss Marston! what is to be done? This is a terrible business! I am so glad you have gotten her, poor girl. I heard all you said to that brute, Wardour. Thank you! Let me tell you all I know."

He had not much to tell, however, beyond what Mary knew already.

"She keeps calling out for you, Mr. Helmer," she said when he had finished.

"I will go with you. Come," he answered.

"You will leave a message for your mother?"

"Never mind my mother. She's good at finding out for herself."

"She ought to be told," said Mary. "But I can't take time to argue it with you. Certainly your first duty is to Letty now. Oh, if only people wouldn't hide things!"

"Come along," cried Tom, hurrying ahead of her. "I will soon set everything right."

"How shall we manage with the doctor?" said Mary, as they went. "We cannot do without him, for I am sure she is still in some danger."

"She will be all right when she sees me," said Tom. "But we will go by the doctor's on our way, and prepare him."

When they came to the doctor's house, Mary walked on, and Tom told the doctor he had met Miss Marston on her way to him, and had come instead that Mary might hurry back to her patient. She wanted to let him know that Miss Lovel had come to her quite unexpected that morning, that she was delirious, and had apparently wandered away from home in the middle of the night.

18 / The End Result

Everything went very tolerably, so far as concerned the world of talk, in the matter of Letty's misfortunes. It is true that rumors—and more than one of them strange enough—did go gloating about the country. But none of them came to the ears of Tom or Mary, and Letty was safe from hearing anything. Thus the engagement between her and Tom soon became generally known.

Mrs. Helmer was very angry, and did all she could to make Tom break it off—it was so much below him! But in nothing could the folly of the woman have been more apparent than in her fancying, with the experience of her life to assist her judgment, that any opposition of hers could be effectual in anything but to the confirmation of her son's will. She was so short-sighted as to originate most of the reports that showed Letty in a poor light.

Mrs. Wardour took care to say nothing unkind of Letty. She was of her own family, and besides, not only was Tom a better match than she could have expected, but she was more than satisfied to have Godfrey's dangerous toy thus drawn away beyond his reach. As soon as the doctor gave his permission, she went to see her. And although she did not utter one unkind word, her visit was so plainly disturbing in its effect on Letty, that it was long before Mary would consent to a repetition of it.

Letty's recovery was very slow. The spring was close at hand before the bloom began to reappear in her cheek. But neither her gaiety nor her usual timidity returned. A certain sad seriousness had taken the place of both, and she seemed to look out from deeper eyes. I cannot think that Letty had begun to perceive that there actually is a Nature shaping us to its own ends, but I think she had begun to feel that Mary lived in the conscious presence of such a power. To Tom she behaved very sweetly, but more like a tender sister than a lover, and Mary began to doubt whether her heart was altogether Tom's. She turned from all talk of approaching marriage with a nervous, uneasy haste.

Mary could not help wondering if the enforced calmness of suffering had opened Letty's eyes to anything in Tom. The doubt filled her with anxiety. At length, after much thought, she resolved to speak to Godfrey Wardour on the subject, even though it was a delicate matter to meddle with, and despite the lack of sympathy he had demonstrated.

Therefore, one Sunday evening she went to Thornwick, and requested to see him.

It was plainly an unwilling interview he granted her, but she was not deterred from opening her mind to him.

"I fear, Mr. Wardour," she began, "—I know I come altogether without authority—but I fear Letty has been rather hurried in her engagement with Mr. Helmer. I think she dreads being married—at least so soon."

"You would have her break it off then?" said Godfrey, with cold restraint.

"No," replied Mary, "that would be unjust to Mr. Helmer. But the thing was so hastened, indeed, hurried by that unhappy incident, that she scarcely had time to know her own mind in the matter."

"It is entirely her own fault, Miss Marston—all and entirely her own fault."

"But surely," said Mary, "it will not do for us to insist on it because she deserves it. That is not how we are treated ourselves."

"Is it not?" returned Godfrey angrily. "My experience is different. I am sure my faults have come back upon me pretty sharply. She *must* marry the fellow or her character is gone."

"I cannot agree with that, Mr. Wardour. It was wrong in her to have anything to say to Mr. Helmer without your knowledge, and a foolish thing to meet him as she did. But Letty is a good girl, and you know country ways are old-fashioned, and in itself there is nothing wicked in having a talk with a young man after dark."

"You speak, I dare say, as such things are regarded in—certain strata of society," returned Godfrey coldly. "But such views do not hold in that to which either of them belong."

"It seems to me a pity they should not then," said Mary. "I know nothing of such matters, but, surely, young people should have opportunities to talk and understand each other. Anyhow, marriage is a heavy penalty to pay for such an indiscretion. A girl might like a young man well enough to enjoy a talk with him now and then, and yet find it hard to marry him."

"Did you come here to dispute social customs with me, Miss Marston?" said Godfrey. "I am not prepared, nor sufficiently interested to discuss them with you."

"I will come to the point at once," answered Mary, who was frightened at her own boldness, even though she gave the appearance of speaking so collectedly. "Would it not be possible for Letty to return here? Then the thing might take its natural course, and Tom and she know each other better before they went so far as to marry. They are little better than children now."

"The thing is absolutely impossible," said Godfrey, and haughtily rose from his chair like one in authority ending an interview. "But," he added, "you have been put to great expense for the foolish girl, and when she leaves you, I desire that you will let me know her bill, that I——"

"Thank you, Mr. Wardour!" said Mary, who had risen also. "As you have now given a turn to the conversation which is not in the least interesting nor complimentary to me, I wish you a good evening."

With the words she left the room. He had finally made her angry. She trembled so much that the moment she was out of sight of the house, she had to sit down and catch her breath.

Godfrey remained in the room where she left him, full of indignation. Ever since that frightful waking, he had brooded over the injury—the insult, he counted it—that Letty had heaped upon him. A great tenderness toward her, unknown to his conscious mind, remained in his spirit. When he passed the door of her room, returning from that terrible ride, he locked it and put the key in his pocket, and from that day no one entered the chamber. But had he loved Letty as purely as he had loved her selfishly, he would have listened to Mary pleading in her behalf, and would have thought first about her well-being, not about her character—and his standing—in the eyes of the world. But in Godfrey Wardour love and pride went hand in hand. Not for a moment could he any more love a girl capable of being interested in Tom Helmer. In addition, it would have been torture to him to see Letty about the place, to pass her on the stair, to come upon her in the garden. Even were she to give up Tom, she could never be anything more to him. She had behaved too deceitfully, too heartlessly, too ungratefully for him ever to think of her in the previous way again. Yet was his heart torn every time the vision of the gentle girl rose before his inward eye, when he saw those hazel depths looking half sorrowful in his face, as with a sadly comic sense of her own stupidity she listened while he explained or read something he loved. But no—nothing else would do than for him to act the part of the mere honest guardian.

Mary returned with a sense of utter failure.

Now and then Mary tried to turn Tom's attention a little toward the duty of his spiritual self in relation to God and his son Jesus Christ. Tom received the attempt with gentle amusement and merry jests. It was all very well for girls! Like most men, he was so well satisfied with himself that he saw no occasion to take trouble to be anything better than he was. Never suspecting what a noble creature he was meant to be, he never saw what a poor creature he was. In his own eyes he was a man any girl might be proud to marry. He had not yet, however, sunk to the altogether lower depth of those who have caught a glimpse of what they can and should become, perhaps even admit the obligation upon them to become more than they are, but move no inch to fulfill it. It seems to me that such must one day make acquaintance with *essential* misery—a thing of which they have no conception.

Day after day Tom passed through Turnbull and Marston's shop to see Letty, and in the same little sitting room where for so many years Mary had listened to the slow, tender wisdom of her father, the clever young man continued to speak of love to the simple and ignorant recovering young girl, whom he did not half understand or half appreciate, all the time feeling himself the greater and wiser of the two.

The whole Turnbull family, self-constituted judges of the two Marston's from the beginnings of things, were not the less critical of the daughter now that the father had been taken from her. There was grumbling in the shop every time she ran up to see Letty, every one regarding her and speaking of her as a servant neglecting her duty. Yet all knew well enough that she was co-proprietor of the business and the stock. And the elder Turnbull knew besides that, if the lawyer to whose care William Marston had committed his daughter were at that moment to probe into the affairs of the partnership, he would find that Mary had a much larger amount of money actually in the business than he.

Mary was ignorant, however, of all matters connected with the business except her own department. Her father had never neglected his duty, but he had so far neglected what the world calls a man's interests as to leave his affairs much too exclusively in the hands of his partner. He had been too much interested in life itself to look too sharply after anything less than life. He acknowledged no worldly interests at all: either God cared for his interests or he himself did not. Whether he might not have been more attentive to the state of his affairs without danger of deeper loss, I do not care to examine; the result of his life in the world was a grand success on the only plane that matters.

Now since Mary's feeling and judgment with regard to *things* was identical with her father's, Turnbull, instructed by his natural and acquired greed, argued thus—unconsciously almost, but not the less argued—that what Mary valued so little, and he valued so much, must, by necessary deduction, be more his than hers—and *logically* ought to be *legally*. So gradually he began to steal, arguing that such and such things are only lying about, and nobody cares for them anyway.

But even though Turnbull perceived that reason was on his side, he knew that it was not safe to act on such a conclusion, and thus for some time he had been anxious to secure himself safe from investigation and possible disaster by the marriage of Mary to his son George.

For the first time, Tom Helmer now learned that his father's will, no doubt made under the influence of his mother, provided for him to have but a very small annuity so long as she lived. He determined to marry in spite of this, confident in his literary faculty, which, he never doubted, would soon raise it to a very sufficient income. Nor did Mary attempt to dissuade him; for what could be better for a disposition like his than to be forced to care for the needs of others dependent on him. Besides, there seemed to be nothing else now possible for Letty.

So in the early summer they were married. Mrs. Wardour was the only relative present. Mrs. Helmer and Godfrey both declined their invitations. Mary was Letty's bridesmaid. Mr. Pycroft, a school and college friend of Tom's who was now making a bohemian livelihood in London by writing for the weekly press, was the groom's man.

After the ceremony, and a breakfast provided by Mary, the young couple took the train for London.

19 / Mary in the Shop_____

The fullness of summer had again come to Testbridge. To the careless eye, things were unchanged, though in fact nothing was the same, and nothing would be the same again. For were not the earth and the sun a little colder? Had not the moon crumbled a little? Had not the eternal warmth, unperceived but by a few, drawn a little nearer—the clock that measures the eternal day ticked one tick more to the hour when the Son of Man will come? But the greed and the groveling did go on unchanged in the shop of Turnbull and Marston, seasoned only with the heavenly salt of Mary's good ministration.

But Mary could not help being very lonely. Her father was gone, and now Letty was gone. And the link between her and Mr. Wardour was not only broken, but a gulf of separation was in its place. Not the less remained the good he had given her. No good is ever lost. The heavenly porter was departed, but had left the door wide. She had seen him but once since Letty's marriage, but his salutation was cold; for in his sore heart he still imagined her the confidant of Letty's deception.

Yet the shadow of her father's absence swallowed all the other shadows. The air of warmth and peace and conscious safety that had till now surrounded her was gone. The moment her father departed, malign influences concentrated themselves upon her: it was the design of John Turnbull that she should not be comfortable so long as she did not irrevocably cast in her lot with his family. And the rest of those in the shop being mostly creatures of his choice, by a sort of implicit understanding proceeded to make her uncomfortable as well. So long as they confined themselves to silence, neglect, and general exclusion, Mary little heeded their behavior. But when they advanced to positive rudeness, it became hard to endure. At first they began to find fault with what she had done or said the moment a customer was gone. But when it led in the end to the insolence of doing the same in the presence of the customer, she found it more than she could bear. For Mary was naturally quick-tempered, and the chief trouble they caused her was the potential loss of her self-control in this area. Not every one who can serve unboundedly can endure patiently, and the more gentle some natures, the more they resent the rudeness that springs from an opposite nature. Absolutely courteous themselves, they flame at discourtesy, and thus lack of the perfection to which patience would and must raise them. When Turnbull, in the narrow space behind the counter, would push his way past her without other pretense of apology than something like a sneer, she did often feel for a moment as if evil were about to have the victory over her. And when Mrs. Turnbull came in, which happily was but seldom, she felt as if from some black hole in her mind a very demon of anger sprang to meet her. For that lady behaved to her worst of all with her airs and vulgar looks.

From the height of her small consciousness, Mrs. Turnbull looked down on the shop as a small country store. She never bought a dress at the shop, but took pains to let her precious public know that she went to London to make her purchases. If she did not mention also that she made them at the same warehouses where her husband was a customer, procuring them at the same price he would have paid, it was because she saw no occasion.

One day a short time before her marriage, delayed by the illness of Mr. Redmain, Miss Mortimer happened to be in the shop and was being served by Mary, when Mrs. Turnbull entered. Paying no attention to the customer, she walked straight up to her, and in a haughty tone asked Mary to bring her a reel of marking-cotton. Now it had been a principle with Mary's father, which she had thoroughly learned, that whatever would be counted a rudeness by *any* customer, must be shown to *none*. "If all are equal in the sight of God," he would say, "how dare I leave an unlovely person to serve a lovely, how dare I leave the poor to serve the rich? My business is to sell in the name of Christ."

"Excuse me, ma'am," said Mary, therefore, "I am waiting on Miss Mortimer. I will get your reel presently."

Mrs. Turnbull flounced away, a little abashed, not by Mary, but by finding who the customer was, and carried her commands across the shop. After a moment or two, however, imagining, in the blindness of her surging anger, that Miss Mortimer was gone, whereas she had only moved a little farther on to look at something, she walked up to Mary in a fury.

"Miss Marston," she said, her voice half choked with rage, "I am at a loss to understand what you mean by your impertinence."

"I am sorry you should think me such," answered Mary. "You saw yourself that I was engaged with a customer."

"Your tone was inexcusable!" What more she might have said I can not tell, for just then Miss Mortimer resumed her place in front of Mary. She had no idea who Mrs. Turnbull was, but hearing the interchange felt compelled to interfere.

"Miss Marston," she said, "if you should be called to account by your employer, will you please refer him to me? You were perfectly civil both to me and to this—" she hesitated a perceptible moment, but ended with the word, "*lady*," but not without a peculiar intonation.

"Thank you, ma'am," said Mary with a smile, "but it is of no consequence.'' This answer would have almost driven the woman out of her reason—already, between annoyance with herself and anger with Mary, her hue was purple: something she called her constitution required a nightly glass of brandy and water—but she was so dumbfounded by Miss Mortimer's defense of Mary, which she looked upon as an assault on herself, and so painfully aware that all eyes in the shop were now fixed on her, and mortified with the conviction that her husband was enjoying her discomfort, that, with what haughtiness she could summon, she made a sudden spin about, and walked from the vile place.

Now George never lost a chance of recommending himself to Mary by siding with her—but only after the battle. He came up to her now with an unpleasant look, intended to represent sympathy, and, approaching close, said confidentially: ''What made my mother speak to you like that, Mary?''

''You must ask her yourself,'' she answered.

''There you are, as usual,'' he protested. ''You will never let a fellow take your part.''

''If you wanted to take my part, you should have done so when there would have been some good in it.''

''How could I, in front of Miss Mortimer, you know?''

''Then why do it now?''

''Because I don't want to see you ill-used. What did you say to Miss Mortimer that angered my mother?''

His father heard him, and, taking the cue, called out rudely: ''If you think, Mary, you're going to take liberties with customers because you've got no one over you, the sooner you find you're mistaken the better.''

Mary made him no answer.

On her way home, spurred by spite, Mrs. Turnbull had gotten hold of the same idea as George, only that she invented where he had but imagined it, and when her husband came home in the evening she fell out upon him for allowing Mary to be impertinent to his customers.

''There she was talking away to that Miss Mortimer as if she were Beenie in the kitchen! She'll be the ruin of the business, with her fine-lady-airs! Who's *she*, I should like to know?''

''I shall speak to her,'' said her husband. ''But,'' he went on, ''I fear you will no longer approve of marrying her to George if you think she's an injury to the business.''

''You know as well as I do that is the readiest way to get her out of it. Make her marry George, and she will fall into my hands. If I'm not able to make her repent of her impudence then, you may call me the fool you think me.''

Mary knew well enough what they wanted of her. But of the real financial cause at the root of their desire she had no suspicion. Recoiling altogether from Mr. Turnbull's theories of business, which were in flat contradiction to the laws of Him who alone understands either man or his business, she yet had not a doubt of his honesty as the trades and professions count honesty. Her father had left the money affairs of the firm to Mr. Turnbull, and she did the same. It was for no other reason than that her position had become almost intolerable, that she now began to wonder if she was bound to this mode of life, and whether it might not be possible to forsake it in favor of something more pleasant.

Greed is the soul's thieving. Where there is greed, there cannot be honesty. John Turnbull, it is true, was not only proud of his reputation for honesty, but prided himself on being an honest man. Yet not the less was he dishonest.

Like most of his kind, he had been neither so vulgar nor so dishonest from the first. In the prime of youth he had had what the people about him called high notions. But it was not their mockery of his tall talk that turned him away from his original goals. It was simply that he had never set his face in the right direction. The seducing influence lay in himself. It was not the truth he had loved but rather the external show of fine sentiment. He had never set himself to be better, and the whole mountain-chain, therefore, of his notions sank and sank, until at length their loftiest peak was nothing more than the maxim, *Honesty is the best policy*—a maxim which, true enough in fact, will no more make a man honest than the saying, *The supply equals the demand* will teach him the niceties of social duty. Whoever makes policy the ground of his honesty will discover more and more exceptions to the rule. Therefore, the career of Turnbull of the high notions had been a gradual descent to the level of his present dishonesty.

Things went a little more quietly in the shop after this for a while: Turnbull was probably afraid of precipitating matters and driving Mary to seek counsel—from which much injury might arise to his condition and prospects. As if to make amends for past rudeness, he even took some pains to be polite, putting on something of the manners with which he favored his best customers. This of course rendered him all the more odious in Mary's eyes, and ripened her desire to free herself from the circumstances to which she found herself tied by the past. She was, however, too much her father's daughter to do anything in haste.

She might have been more content with her lot had she had any close friends like-minded with herself. But she had always been rather a private person, and so was little known even among the religious associates of her father. There are few of the so-called religious who seem able to trust either God or their neighbor in matters that concern these two and no other. Nor had she had opportunity of making acquaintance with any who believed and lived like her father in any of the other churches of the town. But she had her Bible, and when that troubled her, as it did sometimes, she had God himself to cry to for such wisdom as she could receive. And one of the things she learned was that nowhere in the Bible was she called on to believe in the Bible, but in the living God in whom is no darkness, and who alone can give light to understand his own intent. All her troubles she carried to him.

It was not always the solitude of her room that Mary sought to get out of the wind of the world. Her love of nature had been growing stronger after her father's death. If the world is God's, every true man and woman ought to feel at home in it. Something is wrong if the calm of the summer night does not sink into the heart, for it embodies the peace of God. Something is wrong in the man to whom the sunrise is not a divine glory, for therein are embodied the truth, the simplicity, and the might of the Maker. When all is true in us, we shall feel the visible presence of God's watchful eye and loving hand. For the things that he works are their signs and symbols, their clothing fact. In the gentle meeting of earth and sky, in the witnessing colors of the west, in the wind that so gently visited her cheek, in the great burst of a new morning, Mary saw the sordid affairs of Mammon, to whose worship the shop seemed to become more and more of a temple, sink to the bottom of things, as the mud, which, during the day the feet of the drinking cattle have stirred, sinks in the silent night to the bottom of the clear pool. And she saw that the sordid is all in the soul, and not in the shop. The service of Christ is help. The service of Mammon is greed.

Letty was not a good correspondent. After one letter in which she said she was perfectly happy, and another in which she said almost nothing, her communication ceased. Mrs. Wardour had been in the shop several times, but on every occasion had sought the service of another of the clerks. And once, indeed, when Mary was the only one free, she had waited until another was at liberty. Once she met Godfrey. It was in the fields. He was walking hurriedly, as usual, but with his head bent, and a gloomy gaze fixed upon nothing in particular. He started when he saw her, took his hat off, and, with his eyes seeming to look far away beyond her, passed without a word. Yet she had been to him a true pupil, and had learned more from Godfrey than Godfrey was capable of teaching. She had turned thought and feeling into life, into reality, into creation.

The so-called *creations* of the human intellect are spoken of, and of the human imagination. But there is nothing man can do that comes half so near the true "making," the true creativity of the Maker as the ordering of his own way. There is only one thing that is higher: the highest creation of which man is capable—and that is to will the will of the Father. That act indeed contains within it an element of the purely creative, and when man does will such, then is he most like God.

To do what we ought to do, as children of God, is an altogether higher, more divine, more potent, more creative thing, than to write the grandest poem, paint the most beautiful picture, carve the mightiest statue, build the most magnificent temple, dream out the most enchanting symphony.

If Godfrey could have seen the soul of the maiden into whose face his discourtesy called the hot blood, he would have beheld there simply what God made the earth for. As it was, he saw a shop girl, to whom he had once shown kindness but in whom he was now no longer interested. But the sight of his troubled face called up all the mother in her; a rush of tenderness, born of gratitude for all he had done for her, flooded her heart. He was sad, but alas! she could do nothing to comfort him!

20 / The Wedding Dress

For all her troubles, however, Mary had her pleasures, even in the shop. She had the pleasure, as real as it was simple, of pure service, reaping the fruit of the earth in the joy of the work that was given her to do. There is no true work that does not carry its reward, though there are few who do not drop it and lose it. She gathered also the pleasure of seeing and talking with people whose manners and speech were of finer grain and tone than those about her. When Hesper Mortimer entered the shop, her smile was light, and her whole presence an enchantment to Mary. The reading aloud that Wardour had led her to practice had taught her much, not only about the delicacies of speech, but in the deeper matters of motion, relation, and harmony. When Hesper entered the shop, Mary would hasten to serve her as if she had been an angel come to do a little earthly shopping. Hesper, in response all but unconscious, would be waited on by no other than Mary. And there always passed between them some sweet gentle nothings, which afforded Hesper more pleasure than she could have accounted for.

Her wedding day was now for the third time fixed. One morning she entered the shop to make some purchases. Not happy about the prospect before her, she was yet inclined to make the best of it so far as clothes were concerned, and she was now brooding over a certain idea for her wedding dress. She had altogether failed in the attempt to convey her thoughts to her London *couturiere*, and it had come into her head to see whether Mary might not grasp what she was thinking and help her to make it intelligible.

Mary listened and thought, questioned, and asked for explanations, and at length asked if she would allow her to ponder the thing a little: she did not want to venture to say anything at once. Hesper laughed, and said she was taking a small matter too seriously.

"A small matter? Your wedding dress!" exclaimed Mary.

Hesper gave a little sigh, which struck sadly on Mary's sympathetic heart. She cast a quick look in her face. Hesper caught the look, and understood it. For one passing moment she felt as if, amid all her troubles, she had found a friend. But then the next instant she saw the absurdity of imagining a friend in a mere shopgirl.

"But I must make up my mind so soon!" Hesper answered.

"I will talk to you about it as early as you wish tomorrow morning, if that will do," returned Mary.

"But I cannot have the horses tomorrow," said Hesper.

124

After a moment's silence, Mary said, "I might walk out to Durnmelling this evening after the shop is shut. By that time I shall have been able to think about it."

"Thank you!" she said sweetly. "Then I shall expect you. Ask for my maid. She will take you to my room."

As soon as she was gone, Mary set her thoughts to the dress, and even managed to cut out a sample of paper during the dinner hour. When she was free, she set out with it for Durnmelling, looking forward to seeing the old house of which she had so often heard.

The butler opened the door to her, leaving her in the entrance hall while he went to find "Miss Mortimer's maid," he said, though there was but one lady's maid in the place.

The few moments she had to wait far more than repaid Mary for the trouble she had taken: through a side door she looked into the great roofless hall, the one grand thing about the house. Its majesty laid hold upon her, and the shopkeeper's daughter felt the power of the ancient dignity far more than any of the family to which it had for centuries belonged.

She was standing lost in delight when a voice called to her from halfway up a stair: "You're to come this way, miss."

With a start, she turned and went.

It was a large room to which she was led. There was no one in it, and she walked to an open window, which had a wide outlook across the fields. A little to the right, over some trees, were the chimneys of Thornwick. It surprised her to see them—so near, and yet so far—like the memory of a sweet, sad story.

"Do you like my view?" asked the voice of Hesper behind her. "It is flat."

"I like it very much, Miss Mortimer," answered Mary, turning quickly with a bright face. "Flatness has its own beauty. I sometimes feel as if room were all I wanted, and a wide open flat space gives you all that you need. You can see over the tree tops too, and that is good—sometimes—don't you think?"

Miss Mortimer gave no other reply than a gentle stare, which expressed no curiosity, although she had a vague feeling that Mary's words meant something. Most girls of her class would hardly have got even so far as that.

The summer was backward, but the day had been fine and warm, and the evening was dewy and soft, full of evasive odor. The window Mary was peering from looked westward, and the setting sun threw long shadows toward the house. A gentle wind was moving in the tree tops and a peace filled the air. The spirit of the evening had laid hold of Mary. The day's business vanished, molten in the rest of the coming night.

"This reminds me of some beautiful verses of Henry Vaughan!" she said half dreamily.

"What do they say?" asked Hesper disinterestedly.

Mary repeated as follows:

" 'The frosts are past, the storms are gone
And backward life at last comes on.
And here in dust and dirt, O here,
The Lilies of His love appear!' "

"Whose did you say the lines were?" asked Hesper, as if in automatic response.

"Henry Vaughan's," answered Mary, with a little spiritual shiver, as of one who had dropped a pearl in the miry way.

"I never heard of him," rejoined Hesper, with complete indifference.

Ignorance is one of the many things of which a lady of position is never ashamed. And in truth, ignorance is not the thing to be ashamed of, but neglect of knowledge. Why should Hesper care anyway? What could a shopgirl know that she would have the slightest interest in.

"He lived in the time of the Charleses," Mary said, with a tremble in her voice, for she was ashamed to show her knowledge in light of the other's ignorance.

"Ah!" replied Hesper, with a vague feeling that people who kept shops read stupid old books that lay about because they could afford none better. "Are you fond of poetry?" she added, feeling as though she must say something.

"Yes," answered Mary, "when it is good."

"What do you mean by good?"

"That is a difficult question to answer," replied Mary. "I think I know good poetry by what it does to me," she added thoughtfully.

"Indeed," rejoined Hesper, not any less puzzled than before, if the word should be used where there was no effort to understand. Poetry had never done anything to her, and Mary's words conveyed no shadow of an idea.

"Sometimes," Mary went on, "it makes me feel as if my heart were too big for my body. Sometimes as if all the grand things in heaven and earth were trying to get into me at once. Sometimes as if I had discovered something nobody else knew. Sometimes as if—no, not *as if*, for then I must go and pray to God. But I am trying to tell you what I don't know how to tell. I am not talking nonsense, I hope, only I am ashamed of myself that I can't talk sense—I will show you what I have been doing about your dress.

Far more to Hesper's surprise and admiration than her attempts to make clear her thoughts, Mary took out the shape she had prepared, put it on herself, and slowly turned around before Hesper.

"How clever of you!" Hesper cried. "It is a masterpiece. Why, you are nothing less than an accomplished dressmaker!"

For the next half hour the two were busy pinning and unpinning, shifting and pinning again with a roughly cut larger shape to fit Hesper. All at once she said: "I suppose you know I am going to marry money?"

"Oh! don't say that!" cried Mary.

"You supposed I was going to marry a man like Mr. Redmain for love?" rejoined Hesper with a hard laugh.

"I cannot bear to think of it!" said Mary. "But you do not really mean it!"

"Indeed! It is very horrid, I know. But the people in our world, you know, have to do as they must. They can't pick and choose like you happy creatures. I dare say you are engaged to a young man you love with all your heart."

"Oh, dear, no!" returned Mary. "I am not engaged, nor in the least likely to be."

"And not in love either?" asked Hesper.

"No," she replied.

"No more am I," echoed Hesper. "At least that is one good thing about it all. I shall not break my heart, as some girls do."

Mary was silent. She would have been less shocked with Hesper had she known that she forced an indifference she could not feel—her last poor rampart of sand against the sea of horror rising around her. But from her heart Mary pitied her.

"Don't look at me like that," said Hesper. "Look the other way and listen. I am marrying money, I tell you—and for more. Therefore, I ought to get the good out of it. So I shall be able to do what I please. Now I have fallen in love with you, and why shouldn't I have you for my—"

She paused, hesitating. She had been going to say *maid*. But something checked her before she could utter the word. Even though Hesper Mortimer would have smiled at the very notion of a girl who served behind a counter being a lady, it was yet a vague sense of that very fact which was now embarrassing her, for she was not half lady enough to deal with it. In very truth, Mary Marston was already immeasurably more of a lady than Hesper Mortimer was ever likely to be in this world.

"—For my—my companion, or something of the sort," concluded Hesper. "And then I should be sure of always being dressed just as I liked."

"That would be nice!" responded Mary, thinking only of how kindly Hesper spoke.

"Would you really like it?" asked Hesper, in her turn pleased.

"I should like it very much," replied Mary, not imagining the proposal had in it a shadow of seriousness. "I wish it were possible."

"Why isn't it then? Why shouldn't it be possible?"

"What would they do in the shop without me?"

"They could get somebody else, couldn't they?"

"Hardly, to take my place. My father was Mr. Turnbull's partner. I am half owner of it now."

"Oh!" said Hesper. "I thought you had only to give notice and quit."

There the matter dropped, and Mary thought no more about it.

"Will you let me keep this pattern?" said Hesper.

"Of course, I made it for you," answered Mary.

Mary bade her good night. Hesper returned it kindly, but neither shook hands nor did Hesper ring the bell to have her shown out. Mary found her own way, and before long was breathing the fresh air of the twilight fields on her way home to her piano and her books.

For some time after she was gone, Hesper was entirely occupied with the dress. Yet by and by it began to melt away in her mind's eye, and was gradually replaced by the form of "that singular shopgirl." There was nothing so striking about her, yet when one had been long enough in her company to feel the charm of her individuality, the very quiet of any moment was enough to bring back the sweetness of Mary's presence.

Not only had Hesper Mortimer never had a friend worthy of the name, but no idea of pure friendship had as yet been generated in her. Sepia was the nearest to her intimacy: how far friendship could have place between two such I need not inquire. But in her fits of misery Hesper had no other to go to.

Those fits, alas! grew less and less frequent, for Hesper was on the downward incline. Yet when the next did come, she found herself haunted by a silent, invisible sense of being tended, even though it offered her no consolation. The essence of Mary's being was so purely ministration that her form could not recur to any memory without bringing with it a dreamy sense of help. More powerful than all powers is *being*. *To be* is more powerful than even *to do*. Action *may* be hypocrisy, but being is the thing itself, and is the parent of action. Had anything that Mary *said* recurred to Hesper, she would have thought of it only as the poor sentimentality of a low education. As it was, she was filled, not with words or advice or ideas that Mary had *spoken* to her, but rather with an overwhelming sense of Mary's person, her *being*, her true self.

Hesper did not think of Mary's position as low. That would have been to measure it. And it did not once suggest itself as having any relationship to any life in which she was interested. Mary was simply beyond her social horizon, and she cared not to see into the distance.

In like manner, moral differences—and that in her own class—were almost equally beyond recognition. If by neglect of its wings an eagle should sink to become a sparrow, it would then recognize only the laws of sparrow life. For the sparrows of humanity do not generally believe in a consuming fire and an outer darkness, where all that will be left is an ever-renewed *alas*! The "alas" is that they neglected their wings, neglected to try to see beyond their own horizons, neglected to do the words of Him who alone is life. It is truth and not serenity that a man's nature requires of him. It is help, not the leaving of cards at doors, that will be recognized as the test. It is love, and no amount of flattery, that will prosper. Differences wide as that between a gentleman and a cad will contract to a hair's breadth in that day. The customs of the trade and the picking of pockets will go together, with the greater excuse for the greater need and the less knowledge. Liars the most gentlemanlike and the most rowdy will go as liars. The first shall be last, and the last first.

Hesper's day drew on. She had many things to think about—things very different from any that concerned Mary Marston. She was married; found life in London somewhat absorbing; and forgot Mary.

21 / Mr. Redmain

At first Mr. Redmain accompanied his wife everywhere. No one knew better than he that not an atom of love mingled with her motives in marrying him. But for a time he seemed bent on showing her that she needed not have been so averse to him.

Whether it was his design or not, I imagine he enjoyed the admiration she roused, for she was an attractive specimen. Why should not a man take pride in the possession of a fine woman as well as in that of a fine horse? To be sure, Mrs. Redmain was not quite in the same way, nor quite so much his, as his horses were, and might one day be a good deal less his than she was now. But in the meantime she was, I fancy, a pleasant break in the gathering monotony of his existence.

As he got more accustomed to the sight of her in a crowd, however, and at the same time to her not very interesting company in private, when she took not the smallest pains to please him, he gradually lapsed into his former ways, and soon came to spend his evenings in company that made him forget his wife.

Following her cousin's advice, she had appealed to him to save her; and, when he evaded her prayer, had addressed him in certain terms too appropriate to be agreeable, and too forcible to be forgotten. Therefore, though he had loved her in a sort of way, better left undefined, he had also, almost from the first, hated her a little too. His hatred, however, if that be not too strong a name, was neither virulent nor hot, for it had no inverted love to feed and embitter it. It was more a thing of his head than his heart, revealing itself mainly in short, acrid speeches, meant to be clever and unquestionably disagreeable.

Nor did Hesper prove an unworthy antagonist in their encounters of polite abuse. The common remark, generally false, about no love being lost, was in their case true enough, for there never had been any between them to lose.

Ferdinand Goldberg Redmain—parents with low surroundings often give grand names to their children—was the son of an intellectually gifted laborer who rose rapidly. At first he was boss of a work crew who began to take portions of contracts, and through one lucky venture after another, at last reached the point where his estimate was accepted and the contract given him for a rather large affair. The result was that through his skill, his faculty for getting work out of his laborers, a toughness of heart and will that enabled him to screw wages to the lowest mark, and the judicious employment of inferior material, the contract paid him much too well for any good to come out of it. From that time, what he called his life was a continuous course of what he deemed success, and he died very rich, bequeathing great wealth to his son.

From that money, the seeds of a thousand meannesses, oppressions, and some quiet rogueries bore weeds enough in Ferdinand, but curiously, he displayed neither avarice nor—within the bounds of a modest prudence—any unwillingness to part with money. He grew, in fact, to be almost a generous fellow under the right circumstances.

It is a great thing to come of decent people, and Ferdinand Goldberg Redmain must not be judged like one who, of honorable parentage, whether noble or peasant, takes himself across to the shady side of the road. Much had been against Redmain. I do not know of what sort his mother was, but from certain embryonic virtues in him, which could hardly have been his father's, I should think she must have been better than her husband. She died, however, while he was a mere child, and the boy was sent to a certain public school that was simply a hotbed of the lowest vices and character flaws; and in poor manners and learning to please no one but himself, young Redmain was an apt pupil.

There is fresh help for the world every time a youth starts clean upon manhood's race; his very being is a hope of cleansing. This one started as foul as youth could well be, and had not yet begun to repent. His character was well known to his associates, for he was no hypocrite, and Hesper's father knew it perfectly, and was therefore worse than he. Had Redmain had a daughter, he would never have given her to a man like himself. But then, Mortimer was so poor, and Redmain was so *very* rich! Alas for the man who degrades his poverty by worshiping wealth! There is no abyss in hell too deep for him to find its bottom.

Mr. Redmain had no profession, and knew nothing of business beyond what was necessary for understanding whether his factor or steward, or whatever he called him, was doing well with his money—to that he gave heed. Wiser than many, he took some care not to spend his life at full speed. With this view he laid down and observed certain rules in the ordering of his pleasures, which enabled him to keep ahead of the vice-constable for some time longer than would otherwise have been the case. But he is one who can never be outrun, and now as Mr. Redmain was approaching the end of middle age, he heard plainly enough the approach of the wool-footed avenger behind him. Horrible was the inevitable to him; but it had not yet looked frightful enough to arrest his downward rush.

When in tolerable health, he laughed at the notion of such an out-of-the-way place as hell. Yet in his heart of hearts he was horribly afraid of it. Himself a bad man, he reasoned that God was too good to punish sin. Himself a proud man, he reasoned that God was too high to take heed of him. He forgot the best argument he could have cited——namely that the punishment he had had in this life had done him no good; from which he might have been glad to argue that none would, and therefore none would be tried.

Mr. Redmain had one intellectual passion, which—poor thing as it was, and in most of its aspects and motives totally selfish—yet did something to delay that corruption of his being which, at the same time, it powerfully aided to complete: it was a desire to understand and analyze human nature, especially insofar as it concerned evil. Quiet and observant, Redmain was always on the lookout for something, if not in himself, then in another. He would sit at his club, silent and watching, day after day, night after night, waiting to cast some light on some idea of detection, on some doubt, bewilderment, or conjecture. He would ask the farthest-off questions: who could tell what might send him into the track of discovery. He would give a conversation the strangest turns. He especially delighted in discovering the hollow full of dead man's bones under the flowery lawn of seeming goodness. All this he called the study of human nature.

Truly, next to God, the proper study of mankind is man. But to rake over the contents of an ash-pit is not to study geology. And there were motives in Redmain's own being, which he was not merely incapable of understanding, but incapable of seeing, incapable of suspecting. Therefore, for all his supposed "study" he had not an ounce the more wisdom. How shall a man who knows only the evil in himself, and does not see it as hateful, even begin to read the thousandfold more complex heart of his neighbor?

The game had for him all the pleasure of keenest speculation, for in the supposed discovery of the evil of another, he felt himself vaguely righteous.

Such was the man whom Hesper, entirely aware that none could compel her to marry against her will, had, partly from fear of her father, partly from moral laziness, partly from reverence for the Moloch of society, whose priestess was her mother, vowed to love, honor, and obey!

22 / Mrs. Redmain

In the autumn the Redmains went to Durnmelling for a visit: why they did so I should find it hard to say. If Hesper had loved either of her parents as a child, the experiences of later years had so heaped that affection with the fallen leaves of dead hopes and vanished dreams that there was now nothing in her heart recognizable to herself as love to father or mother.

She always behaved to them, of course, with perfect propriety. And in fact Lady Margaret saw great improvement in her daughter. To the maternal eye, always seeking perfection, Hesper's carriage was at length satisfactory. It was cold, and the same to her mother as everyone else, but the mother did not find it too cold. It was haughty, even repellent, but by no means in the mother's eyes repulsive. "Marriage has done everything for her," said Lady Malice to herself.

Hesper never saw herself in the wrong, and never gave herself the least trouble to be in the right. She was in good health, ate, and liked to eat; drank her glass of champagne, and would have drunk a second but for her complexion. Of her own worth she had never a doubt, and she had none yet: how was she to generate one, courted everywhere she went, both for her own beauty and her husband's wealth?

To her father she was as stiff and proud as if she had been a maiden aunt bent on destroying whatever expectations he still held for her. And who will blame her? He had done her all the ill he could, and by his own deed she was beyond his reach. Nor can I see that the debt she owed him for being her father was of the heaviest.

Her husband was not in the best of health—certain attacks to which he was subject were now coming more frequently. I do not imagine his wife offered many prayers for his restoration.

Greatly contrary to Mr. Redmain's unexpressed desire, Miss Yolland had been installed as Hesper's cousin-companion. After the marriage, Hesper ventured to unfold a little, as she had promised, but what there was yet of womanhood in her had shrunk from further acquaintance with the dimly shadowed mysteries of Sepia's story. The only life principle Sepia had, so far as I know, was to get from the moment the greatest possible enjoyment that would leave the way clear for more to follow. She had hardly been in his house a week before Mr. Redmain hated her. He was somewhat given to hating people who came near him, and Sepia came much too near. If she had not been his wife's friend, they might perhaps have gotten on pretty

133

well together. But the two were such as must either be hand in glove or hate each other.

Every time Mr. Redmain had an attack, the baldness on the top of his head widened, and the skin of his face tightened on his small, neat features. His long arms looked longer, his formerly flat back rounded yet a little, and his temper grew more spiteful. Long after he had begun to recover, he was by no means an agreeable companion.

As if at the very last, though peculiar and perhaps a bit too late, Lady Malice seemed all at once bent on teaching her daughter the duty of a married woman. Thus, from the moment Mr. Redmain arrived, taken ill on the way, she devoted herself to her son-in-law, despite the brusqueness with which he treated her, with an attention she had never shown her husband. She was the only one who showed any hint of affection for him, and the only one of the family for whom, in return, he came to show the least consideration. Every night she would visit him to see that he was left comfortable, would tuck him in as his mother might have done, and satisfy herself that the night light was shaded from his eyes. With her own hands she always arranged his breakfast on the tray. Perhaps the part in him that had never had the opportunity of behaving ill to his mother, and so had not choked up its channels with wrong, remained, in middle age and illness, capable of receiving kindness.

Hesper saw the relation between them, but without the least pleasure or the least curiosity. She seemed to care for nothing—except the keeping of her back straight. It would be difficult to know what inside that lovely form gave itself pleasure. The bear as he lies in his winter nest sucking his paw has no doubt his rudimentary theories of life, and those will coincide with a desire for its continuance. But whether what the lady of the bear counts the good of life, be really that which makes either desire its continuance, is another question. Mere life without suffering seems enough for most people, but I do not think it could go on so for ever. I cannot help fancying that, but for death, utter dreariness would at length master the healthiest in whom the true life has not begun to shine.

Partly out of respect to Mr. Redmain, the Mortimers had scarcely a visitor, for he could not endure an unknown face when he was ill. Hence the time was dull for everybody—dullest, perhaps, for Sepia, who, as well as Redmain, had a few things that required forgetting. It was no wonder then that Hesper, after two weeks of it, should think once more of the young woman in the draper's shop of Testbridge. Consequently one morning she ordered her carriage, and drove to the town.

23 / Offer and Acceptance

Things had not been going much better with Mary, though there was now more lull and less storm around her. Her position in the shop was becoming less and less endurable to her, and she had as yet no glimmer of a way out of it.

When Hesper entered, she was disappointed to see Mary so much changed. But when her pale face brightened at sight of her, and a faint, rosy flush overspread it, Mary was herself again as Hesper had known her, and the radiance cast a reflex of sunshine into the February of Hesper's heart. Hesper was human after all, though her humanity was only partially developed as yet, and it is not in the power of humanity in any stage of development to hold itself indifferent to the pleasure of being loved.

She walked up to Mary, holding out her hand.

"Oh, I am glad to see you!" exclaimed Mary.

"I am glad too," replied Hesper, genuinely though with condescension. "I hope you are well. I cannot say you look as much so as when I left you."

"I am pretty well, thank you," answered Mary. Hardly anyone expressed care about her health these days, except Beenie, who complained over her loss of plumpness, and told her if she did not eat, she would soon follow her poor father.

"Come and have a drive with me," said Hesper, moved by a sudden impulse. "It will do you good. You are indoors too much."

"It is very kind of you," replied Mary, "but—I don't think I could quite manage it today."

She looked round as she spoke. There were not many customers; but for conscience' sake she was trying hard to give as little ground for offense as possible.

"Why not? If I were to ask Mr.—"

"If you really wish it, I will venture to go for half an hour. There is no need to speak to Mr. Turnbull. Besides, it is almost dinner time."

"Do, then. I am sure you will eat a better dinner for having had a little fresh air first. It is a lovely morning. We will drive to the Roman camp on the top of Clover-down."

"I shall be ready in two minutes," said Mary, and ran from the shop.

As she passed along the outside of his counter coming back, she stopped and told Mr. Turnbull where she was going. Instead of answering her, he turned himself toward Mrs. Redmain, and went through a series of bows and smiles recognizant of favor, which she did not choose to see. She turned and walked from the shop, got into the carriage, and made room for Mary at her side.

But although the drive was a lovely one, and the view from either window delightful, Mary saw little of the sweet country because she was so much occupied with Hesper. Before they stopped again at the shop door, the two young women were nearer being friends than Hesper had ever been with anyone. The sleepy heart in her was not yet dead, but still capable of the pleasure of showing sweet condescension and gentle patronage to one who admired her, and was herself agreeable.

As they went, Mary told her something of her miserable relations with the Turnbulls. And as they returned, Hesper—this time with perfect seriousness—proposed that she should give up business, and live with her.

This suggestion was not the ridiculous thing it might at first appear. It arose from what was almost the first movement in the direction of genuine friendship Hesper had ever felt. She had been familiar with a good many, but familiarity is not friendship, and may or may not exist along with it. Hesper did not, however, recognize it as friendship—how could one in her position think of being friends with a commoner, a maid—whatever else she might choose to call her? Nevertheless, the sorely whelmed divine thing in Hesper had uttered a feeble sigh of incipient longing after the real. Mary had begun to draw out the love in her, while Hesper's conventional judgment justified the proposed extraordinary proceeding with the argument of the endless advantages that would result from having in the house, devoted to her wishes, a young woman with an absolute genius for dressmaking. Never before had she found herself the best dressed in a room: now there would be hope!

However, nothing was clear in her mind as to the position she would have Mary occupy. She had a vague feeling that one like her ought not to be expected to undertake things befitting a maid—she was after all, however common, half owner of a business, though Hesper hardly saw the value in that. But she was certainly more than a mere menial. For she could quickly see that there was no room even for comparison between Mary and her maid Folter. At the same time, she was incapable of seeing that, in the eyes of certain courtiers of a high kingdom, not much keen to the world of fashion, but not the less judges of the beautiful, there was a far greater difference between Mary and herself than between herself and her maid. For while the said beholders could hardly have been astonished at Hesper's marrying Mr. Redmain, there would, had Mary done such a thing, have been dismay and a hanging of the head before the face of her Father in heaven.

"Come and live with me, Miss Marston," said Hesper, but it was with a laugh, and that light touch of the tongue which suggests but a flying fancy spoken but for the sake of the preposterous. Mary had not forgotten that she had heard the same thing once before, and so heard it with a smile, and had no rejoinder ready. Then Hesper, who was in reality feeling her way, ventured a little more seriously.

"I would never ask you to do anything you would not like," she said.

"I don't think you could," answered Mary. "I doubt that there is anything I shouldn't like to do for you."

"My meaning was that as a regular thing I should never ask you to do anything menial," explained Hesper, venturing a little further still, and now speaking in a perfectly matter-of-fact tone.

"I don't know what you mean by *menial*," returned Mary.

Hesper did not find it so strange that Mary should not be familiar with the word, and proceeded to explain it as well as she could. That seeming ignorance may be the consequence of more knowledge, she had yet to learn.

"*Menial*, don't you know?" she said, "is what you give servants to do."

But then she remembered that Mary's help in certain things her maid was totally unsuited for was one of the main reasons for her proposal: that definition of menial would hardly do.

"I mean—I mean," she resumed, with a little embarrassment, a rare thing with her, "—things like—like—cleaning one's shoes, don't you know?—or brushing your hair."

Mary burst out laughing.

"Let me come to you tomorrow morning," she said, "and I will brush your hair so that you will want me to come again the next day. Whose hands would not be honored to handle such hair as yours?"

As she spoke, she took in her fingers a stray little drift from the masses of golden twilight that crowned one of the loveliest temples in which the Holy Ghost had not yet come to dwell.

"If cleaning your shoes be menial, brushing your hair must be royal," she added,

Hesper's heart was touched. And if at the same time her *self* was flattered, the flattery was mingled with its best antidote—love.

"Do you really mean you would not mind doing such things for me? Of course I should not be exacting."

She laughed again, afraid of showing herself too much in earnest before she was sure of Mary.

"I would no more mind cleaning your boots than my own," said Mary.

"But I should not like to clean my own boots," rejoined Hesper.

"No more should I, except it had to be done," returned Mary. "But to clean yours would be different. It is scornful to think there is anything degrading in it. I heard my father once say that to look down on those who have to do such things may be to despise them for just the one honorable thing about them, which is their servanthood. Shall I tell you what I understand by the word *menial*? You know it has come to have a disagreeable taste about it, but that is not as it should be."

"Do tell me," answered Hesper.

"I did not find it out myself," said Mary. "My father taught me. He was a wise as well as a good man, Mrs. Redmain."

"Oh!" said Hesper, with the ordinary indifference of fashionable people.

"He said," Mary went on, "that it is menial to undertake anything you think beneath you for the sake of money. And still more menial, having undertaken it, not to do it as well as possible."

"That would make out a good deal more of the menial in the world than is commonly supposed," laughed Hesper. "I wonder who would do anything for you if you didn't pay them—one way or another."

"I've taken my father's shoes out of Beenie's hands many a time," said Mary, "and finished them myself, just for the pleasure of making them shine for *him*."

"Really!" drawled Hesper, concluding that it was not such a great compliment the young woman had paid her after all in wanting to brush her hair. Evidently she had a taste for low things!—she must be naturally menial, and would do as much for her own father as for a lady like her! But the light in Mary's eyes caught her attention.

"Any service done without love, whatever it be," resumed Mary, "is slavery—neither more nor less. It cannot be anything else. So you see, most slaves are made slaves by their own attitude, not by virtue of their position. Slavery is a choice, not something imposed by others. And that is what makes me doubtful whether I ought to go on serving in the shop, for as far as the Turnbulls are concerned, I have no pleasure in it. I am only helping them to make money, not doing them any good."

"Why don't you give it up at once then?" asked Hesper.

"Because I like serving the customers. They were my father's customers, and I have learned so much from waiting on them."

"Well now," said Hesper, "if you will come to me, I will make you comfortable, and you shall do just as much or as little as you please."

"What will your maid think?" suggested Mary. "If I am doing what I please, she will soon find me trespassing on her domain."

"I never trouble myself about what my servants think," answered Hesper.

"But it might hurt her, you know—to be paid to do a thing, and then not allowed to do it."

"She may quit then. I had not thought of parting with her. But I should not be at all sorry if she went. She would be no loss to me."

"Why do you keep her then?"

"Because one is just as good—and as bad as another. She knows my ways, and I prefer not having to break in a new one. It is a bore to have to say how you like everything done."

"But you are speaking now as if you meant it," said Mary, waking up to the fact that Hesper's tone was of business, and she no longer seemed half playing with the proposal. "Do you mean you want me to come and live with you?"

"Indeed I do," answered Hesper emphatically. "You shall have a room close to my bedroom, and there you shall do as you like all day long. And when I want you, I dare say you will come."

"Fast enough," said Mary cheerily, as if all was settled. In contrast with her present surroundings, the prospect was more than attractive. "But would you let me have my piano?" she asked, with sudden apprehension.

"You shall have my grand piano whenever I am out, which will be every night in the season, I dare say. That will give you plenty of practice, and you will be able to have the best of lessons. And think of the concerts you will be able to go to."

As she spoke, the carriage drew up at the door of the shop and Mary left her. Hesper accepted her nod in the proper style of a benefactress, and returned her goodbye kindly. But not yet did she shake hands with her.

Some may wonder how Mary could for a moment dream of giving up her independence in a shop of which she was half proprietor. But everything about the shop had changed for Mary; and indeed, she hardly felt an ounce of independence while there. The very air she breathed there seemed slavish. The work had become a drudgery to her. The spirit of gain was in full blast, and whoever did not trim his sails to it was in danger of finding it rough weather. Therefore, the proposal of Mrs. Redmain looked advantageous to her in contrast to this treadmill work. In Hesper's house she could serve in love, and would have plenty of time for books and music, with a thousand means of growth unapproachable in Testbridge. But she tried hard to suppress her anxiety over the matter, for she saw that, of all poverty-stricken contradictions, a Christian with little faith is the worst.

The chief attraction to her, however, was simply Hesper herself. She had fallen in love with her—I hardly know how otherwise to describe the current that flowed between them. Few hearts are capable of loving as Mary loved. It was not merely that she saw in Hesper a grand and beautiful woman, or that she was drawn to her because of her position. Rather she saw in her one she could help, one at least who needed help, for she seemed to know nothing of what made life worth having. Without the hope of helping in the highest sense, Mary could not have taken up her abode in such a house as Mrs. Redmain's. No outward service of any kind, in and of itself, was to her service enough to *choose*. Of course, were it laid upon her, she would hasten to it; for necessity is the push, gentle or strong, as the man is more or less obedient, by which God sends him into the path he would have him take. But to help to the birth of a beautiful soul, still enveloped in all the cerecloths of its chrysalis, not yet even aware that it must get out of them, and spread great wings to the sunny wind of God. That was a thing for which the holiest of saints might well take a servant's place—the thing for which the Lord of life had done it before him. To help such a lovely sister become her real self, the self God meant her to be when he began making her, that would indeed be a thing worth having lived for.

Mary was not, by virtue of this, a particularly marvelous example of humility. She was simply a young woman who believed that the man called Jesus Christ is a real person, such as those represent him who profess to have known him. And she therefore believed the man himself—believed that, when he said a thing, he entirely meant it, knowing it to be true; believed therefore that she had no choice but to do as he told her. That man was the servant of all. Therefore, to regard any honest service as degrading would be, she saw, to deny Christ, to call the life of creation's hero a disgrace. Nor was he the first servant; he did not of himself choose his life; the Father gave it him to live—sent him to be a servant, because he, the Father, is the first and greatest servant of all. He gives it to one to serve as the rich can, to another as the poor must. The only disgrace, whether of the bank, the shop, or the family, is to think the service degrading. And if for the moment we are not yet able to serve like God from pure love, let us do it because it is his way; so shall we come to do it from pure love also.

The very next day, at four o'clock in the afternoon, Hesper again entered the shop, and to the surprise and annoyance of Mr. Turnbull, Mary led her through the counter and into the house. *What an impression,* thought the great man, *will it give for her to see Marston's shabby parlor!*

But he would have been even more astonished and more annoyed still had he been able to hear what passed between the two women. Before they came down, Mary had accepted a position in Mrs. Redmain's house, and Hesper had promised that she would mention the matter to no one. Mary judged that Mr. Turnbull would be too glad to get rid of her to mind the short notice she would give him, and she would rather not undergo the remarks that were sure to be made in contempt of her scheme. She thought it only fair, however, to let him know that she intended giving up her place behind the counter, hinting that, as she meant to leave when it suited her, it might be well for him to look out for someone to take her place.

As to her money in the business, she scarcely thought of it, believing it as safe as in the bank. It was in fact, in the power of a dishonest man who prided himself on his honesty—the worst kind of rogue of all. But she had not yet learned to think of him as a dishonest man—only as a greedy one—and the money had been there ever since she had heard of money.

Mr. Turnbull was so astonished by her communication that, not seeing at once what effect the change was likely to make upon him, he held his peace. His first feeling was of pleasure, but the man of business must take care how he shows himself pleased. On further reflection, he continued to be pleased. For as they did not seem likely to secure Mary to the family as they had wished, the next best thing would certainly be to get rid of her. But he continued careful not to show his satisfaction, for she would then go sniffing about for the cause! During the next three days, therefore, he never spoke to her. On the fourth he spoke as if nothing had ever been amiss between them, and showed some interest in her further intentions. But Mary straightforwardly told him she preferred not speaking of her plans at present. From this the cunning man concluded that she wanted a place in another shop and was looking for one.

One day she asked him whether he had yet found a person to take her place.

"Time enough for that," he answered. "You're not gone yet."

"As you please, Mr. Turnbull," said Mary. "It was merely that I would be sorry to leave you without sufficient help in the shop."

"And *I* would be sorry," rejoined Turnbull, "that Miss Marston should fancy herself indispensable to the business she turned her back upon."

From that moment, the restraint he had for the last week or two laid upon himself thus broken through, he never spoke to her except with rudeness. All the rest of the people in the place, George included, followed his example, so that when finally, in the month of November, a letter from Hesper heralded the hour of Mary's deliverance, she felt that to take any formal leave would be but to expose herself to unnecessary indignity. She therefore merely told Turnbull one evening as he left the shop that she would not be there in the morning, and she was gone from Testbridge before the doors were opened the next day.

24 / Mrs. Redmain's Drawing Room_____

Some years ago a London drawing room was seldom beautiful, and the one in the Redmain's home had had expended upon it about as much taste as on the fattening of a prize pig. The only interesting thing in it was that on all sides were doors, which must lead out of it, and might lead to a better place.

It was about eleven o'clock on a November morning—more like one in March. There might be a thick fog before the evening, but now the sun was shining like a brilliant lump of ice. Between the cold sun and the hard earth, a dust-befogged wind, plainly borrowed from March, was sweeping the street.

Mr. and Mrs. Redmain had returned to town early because their country place was in Cornwall, and there Mr. Redmain was too far from his physician. He was now considerably better, however, and had begun to go about again, for the weather did not affect him much.

Mrs. Redmain was now descending the stair, straight as a Greek goddess, and about as cold as the marble she was made of. She entered the drawing room with a slow, careless, yet stately step, which belonged to her, I cannot say by nature, for it was not natural, but by ancestry. She walked to the chimney, seated herself in a low chair by the hearth, and gazed listlessly into the fire.

There was not much to see in it, for the fire is but a reflector, and there was not much behind the eyes that looked into it for that fire to reflect. Hesper was no dreamer—the more was the pity, for dreams are often the material out of which actions are made. Had she been a truer woman, she might have been a dreamer, but where was room for dreaming in a life like hers, without heaven, therefore without horizon, with so much room for desiring, and so little room for hope? The buzz that greeted her entrance of a drawing room was the chief joy she knew; to inhabit her well-dressed body in the presence of other well-dressed bodies, her highest notion of existence. And even upon these hung ever as an abating fog the consciousness of having a husband. Education she had had but little that was worth the name, for she had never been set growing. And now, although she was well-endowed by nature, she was gradually becoming stupid.

Miss Yolland came in. No kiss, no greeting whatever passed between the ladies. Sepia began at once to rearrange a few hot-house flowers on the mantelpiece, looking herself much like some dark flower painted in an old book.

They began to talk. The conversation was about nothing and is not worth recording. The wonder is that the two managed to carry on conversation after conversation, day after day, and never say anything worth having been said.

Sepia left. The fire grew hot. Hesper thought of her complexion and pushed her chair back. Then she rose, and, having taken a hand-screen from the chimney piece, was fanning herself with it when the door opened and a servant asked if she were at home to see a Mr. Helmer. She hesitated for a moment: what an unearthly hour for a caller!

"Show him up," she answered: anything was better than her own company.

Tom Helmer entered—much the same—a little paler and thinner. He made his approach with a certain loose grace natural to him, and seated himself on the chair to which Mrs. Redmain motioned him.

Tom seldom failed to please. He was well dressed, but not too much. To the natural confidence of his shallow character had been added the assurance born of a certain small degree of success in his profession, which he took for the pledge of approaching supremacy. He carried himself better than he used to, and his legs therefore did not look so long. His hair continued to curl soft about his head. His hat was new, and he bore it in front of him like a ready apology.

It was not because of any previous acquaintance that Tom now owed his admittance. True, he had been to Durnmelling frequently, but that was in the other world of the country, and even there Hesper had taken no interest in the self-satisfied youth. It was merely that she could no longer endure a *tête-à-tête* with one she knew so little as herself, and whose acquaintance she was so little desirous of cultivating.

Tom had been to a small dinner party at the house a few evenings before, brought there by the well-known leader of a certain literary clique. In return for homage, he not seldom took younger aspirants under a wing destined never to be itself more than half-fledged. It was, notwithstanding, broad enough already so to cover Tom with its shadow, so that under it he was able to creep into several houses of a sort of distinction, and among them into the Redmain's.

Tom was anxious to make himself acceptable to ladies of social influence, and of being known to stand well with such. At the gathering already mentioned, he had chanced to hear Mrs. Redmain express pleasure with a song that was sung by a lady, not without previous maneuver on the part of Tom: he would do most anything to work his way into a position where he might be admired. The words and music to that song he had now brought her.

"I have taken the liberty," he said, "of bringing you the song I had the pleasure of hearing you admire the other evening."

"I forget."

"I would not have ventured," continued Tom, "had it not happened that both air and words were my own."

"Ah!—indeed!—I did not know you were a poet, Mr.——"

She had forgotten his name.

"Helmer."

"And a musician too?"

"At your service, Mrs. Redmain."

"I don't happen to want a poet at present—or a musician either," she said, with just enough of a smile to turn the rudeness into what Tom accepted as a flattering familiarity.

"Nor am I in want of a place," he replied with spirit.

The door opened and Mr. Redmain came in. He gave a glance at Tom and then went up to his wife where he saw the sheet in her hand.

"New music teacher, eh?" he said.

"No," answered his wife.

"Who the deuce is he?"

"I forget his name," replied Hesper. "He used to come to Durnmelling."

"That is no reason why he should not have a name."

Tom came forward, told Mr. Redmain his name, and held out his hand.

"I don't know you," said Mr. Redmain, touching his palm with two fingers that felt like small fishes.

"It is of no consequence," said his wife; "Mr. Helmer is an old acquaintance of our family."

"Only you don't quite remember his name!"

Just then Sepia again entered the room, with a dark glow that flashed into dusky radiance at the sight of Tom. She had noted him on the night of the party, and remembered having seen him at the merrymaking in the old hall of Durnmelling, but he had not been introduced to her. A minute more, while the two Redmains continued their controlled exchange of mutual indifference, they were sitting together in a bay window blazing away at each other.

25 / Mary's Reception

In the afternoon of the same day, now dreary enough, Mary arrived in the city by train, the city preferred to all cities by those who live in it, but the most uninviting, I should imagine, to a stranger, of all cities on the face of the earth. Cold seemed to have taken to itself a visible form in the thin, gray fog that filled the huge station from the platform to the glass roof. It was a mist, not a November fog, properly so called. But every breath breathed by every porter, as he ran along by the side of the slowly halting train, was adding to its mass, which seemed to Mary to grow in bulk and density as she gazed. In a short while she had her boxes on a horse-drawn cab, and was driving away.

The drive seemed interminable, and she had grown anxious and again calmed herself many times before it came to an end. The house at which the cab drew up was large, and looked as dreary as large, but scarcely drearier than any other house in London on that same night of November. The cabman rang the bell, but it was not until they had waited an altogether unreasonable time that the door at length opened and a lofty, well-built footman appeared.

Mary got out and went up the steps, saying she hoped the driver had brought her to the right house: it was Mrs. Redmain's she wanted.

"Mrs. Redmain is not at 'ome, miss," answered the man. "I didn't 'ear as 'ow she was expecting of any one," he added, with a glance at the boxes, formlessly visible on the cab, through the now thicker and gathering darkness.

"She is expecting me," returned Mary, "but of course she would not stay at home just to wait for me," she remarked with a smile.

"Oh!" returned the man in a peculiar tone, and adding, "I'll see," went away, leaving her on the top of the steps with the cabman behind her, at the bottom of them, waiting orders to get her boxes down.

"It don't appear as you was overwelcome, miss!" he remarked.

"It's all right," said Mary cheerfully.

In about a minute the footman reappeared.

"Mrs. Perkin says, miss—that's the 'ousekeeper—that, if as you're the young woman from the country—and I'm sure I beg your pardon if I make a mistake—it ain't my fault, miss—Mrs. Perkin says she did 'ear Mrs. Redmain make mention of one, but she didn't 'ave any instructions concerning 'er—But as there you are," he continued more familiarly, gathering courage from Mary's nodded assent, "you can put your boxes in the 'all, and come in and sit down, she says, till Mrs. R. com 'ome."

"Do you think she will be long?" asked Mary.

"Well, who can say, seein' it's a new play as she' gone to, an' there's no tellin' when people is likely to come 'ome."

" 'Ere, mister!" cried the cabman, who had begun getting Mary's boxes down and had found the first one too much for him, "gi' me a 'and wi' this 'ere luggage."

"Why don't you bring a man with you?" objected the footman, as he descended the steps, notwithstanding, to give the required assistance. "I ain't paid as a crane. By Jupiter! what a weight the boxes are!"

"Only that one," said Mary, apologetically. "It is full of books. The other is not half so heavy."

"Oh, it ain't the weight, miss!" returned the footman. "I believe Mr. Cabman and myself will prove equal to the occasion."

With that the book-box came down with a great bump on the pavement, and presently both were in the hall, the one on the top of the other. Mary paid the cabman, the footman closed the door, told her to take a seat, and went away full of humor to report that the young person had brought a large library with her to enliven the dullness of her new situation.

Mrs. Perkin smiled crookedly, and, in a tone of pleasant reproof, desired her laughter-compressing inferior not to forget his manners.

"Please, ma'am, am I to leave the young woman sittin' up there all by 'erself in the cold?" he asked.

"For the present," replied Mrs. Perkin.

She judged it wise to let the young woman have a lesson at once in subjection and inferiority.

Mrs. Perkin was a rather tall, rather thin, quite straight, and very dark-complexioned woman. She always threw her head back on one side and her chin out on the other when she spoke, and had about her a great deal of the authoritative, which she mingled with such consideration toward her subordinates as to secure their obedience to her, while she cultivated antagonism to her mistress. She had had a better education than most persons of her class, but was morally not an atom their superior in consequence. She had entered the service of Mrs. Redmain with such a feeling of inward superiority that she considered it her work to take care of herself against a woman whose mistress she ought to have been, had Providence but started her with her natural rights. At the same time, she would have been *almost* as much offended by a hint that she was not a Christian, as she would have been by a doubt whether she was a lady. For, indeed, she was both, if a great opinion of herself constituted the latter, and a great opinion of going to church constituted the former.

She had not been taken into Hesper's confidence with regard to Mary, had discovered that "a young person" was expected, but had learned nothing of what her position in the house was to be. Therefore, she welcomed this opportunity both of teaching Mrs. Redmain the propriety of taking counsel with her housekeeper, and of letting the young person know in time that Mrs. Perkin was in reality her mistress.

The relation of the upper servants of the house to their employers was more like that of the managers of a hotel to their guests. The butler, the lady's-maid, and Mr. Redmain's personal servant, who had been with him before his marriage, and was supposed to be deep in his master's confidence, ate with the housekeeper in her room, waited upon by the livery and maid-servants, except the second cook: the first cook only came to superintend the cooking of the dinner, and then left. To all these Mrs. Perkin was careful to be just; and, if she was precise even to severity with them, she was herself obedient to the system she had established—the main feature of which was punctuality. She not only regarded punctuality as the foremost of virtues, but, in righteous moral sequence, made it the first of her duties. The master and mistress came and went, paying no attention to each other; but their meals were ready for them to the minute, when they chose to be there to eat them. The carriage came round like one of the puppets on the Strasbourg clock. The house was quiet as a hospital. The bells were answered—all except the outside doorbell after calling hours— with swiftness. You could not dirty your fingers anywhere in the place. And the house was scarcely more of a home than one of the huge hotels characteristic of the age.

Mary sat in the hall for the space of an hour, not exactly learning the lesson Mrs. Perkin had intended to teach her, but learning more than one thing Mrs. Perkin was not yet capable of learning. I cannot say she was comfortable, for she was both cold and hungry. But she was far from miserable. She had no small gift of patience, and had taught herself to look upon the minor troubles of life as on a bad dream. There are children, though not yet many, capable, through faith in their parents, of learning not a little by their experience, and Mary was one of such. From the first she received her father's lessons like one whose business it was to learn them, and had thereby come to learn where he had himself learned. Hence she was not one to say *our Father in heaven*, and then act as if there were no such Father, or as if he cared but little for his children. She was even foolish enough to believe that that Father both knew and cared that she was hungry and cold and wearily uncomfortable. And thence she was weak enough to take the hunger and cold and discomfort as mere passing trifles, which could not last a moment longer than they ought. From her sore-tried endeavors to be patient had grown the power of active waiting—and a genuinely waiting child is one of the loveliest sights the earth has to show.

This was not the reception she had pictured to herself as the train came rushing from Testbridge to London. She had not imagined a particularly warm one, but she had not expected to be forgotten. She saw no means of reminding the household of her neglected presence, and indeed would rather have remained where she was till the morning than encounter the growing familiarity of the man who had admitted her.

She had grown very weary. There was not a sound in the house but the ticking of a clock somewhere, and she was now beginning to wonder whether everybody had gone to bed, when she heard a step approaching, and presently the footman, who was the only man at home, stood before her, and, with the ease of perfect self-satisfaction, and as if there were nothing in the neglect of her but the custom of the house to cool people well in the hall before admitting them further, said, "Step this way—miss"; the last word added after a pause of pretended hesitation, for the man had taken his cue from the housekeeper. Mary rose and followed him to the basement level, into a comfortable room, where Mrs. Perkin sat embroidering large sunflowers on a piece of coarse cloth.

"You may sit down," she said, pointing to a chair near the door.

Not a little amused in spite of her discomfort, Mary did as she was permitted, and awaited what would come next.

"What part of the country are you from?" asked Mrs. Perkin, with her usual upward toss of the chin, but without lifting her eyes from her work.

"From Testbridge," answered Mary.

"The servants in this house are in the habit of saying *ma'am* to their superiors: it is required of them," remarked Mrs. Perkin. But although the tone was one of rebuke, she said the words lightly, tossed the last of them off, indeed, almost playfully, as if the lesson were meant for one who could hardly have been expected to know better. "And what place did you apply for in the house?" she went on to ask.

"I can hardly say, ma'am," answered Mary, avoiding both inflection and emphasis, and by her compliance satisfying Mrs. Perkin as to her servant status.

"It is not usual for young persons to be engaged without knowing for what purpose."

"I suppose not, ma'am."

"What wages were you to have?" inquired Mrs. Perkin next, gradually assuming a more decidedly condescending tone as she became more assured of her position with the stranger. She would gladly get some light on the affair.

"There was nothing said about wages, ma'am," answered Mary.

"Indeed! Neither work nor wages specified? It seems rather peculiar.

We must be content to wait a little then—until we learn what Mrs. Redmain expected of you, and whether you are capable of it. We can go no further now."

"Certainly not, ma'am," assented Mary.

"Can you use your needle?"

"Yes, ma'am."

"Have you done any embroidery?"

"I understand it a little, but I am not particularly fond of it."

"You mistake; I did not ask you whether you were fond of it," said Mrs. Perkin. "I asked if you had ever done any. Here!—take off your gloves," she continued, "and let me see you do one of these loose-worked sunflowers. They are the fashion now, though, I dare say, you will not be able to see the beauty of them.

"Please, ma'am," returned Mary, "if you will excuse me, I would rather go to my room. I have had a long journey, and am very tired."

"There is no room that is yours. Nothing can be done until Mrs. Redmain comes home and she and I have had a little talk about you. But you can go to the housemaid's—the second housemaid's room, I mean—and make yourself tidy. There is a spare bed in it, I believe, which you can have for the night. Only mind you don't keep the girl awake talking to her, or she will be late in the morning, and that I never put up with."

Therewith Mrs. Perkin, believing she had laid in awe the foundation of a rightful authority over the young person, gave her a nod of dismissal, which she intended to be friendly.

"Please, ma'am," said Mary, "could I have one of my boxes taken upstairs?"

"Certainly not. I cannot have two movings of them. I must take care of my men. And your boxes, I understand, are quite heavy, absurdly so. It would look better in a young person not to have so much to carry about with her."

"I have but two boxes, ma'am," said Mary.

"Full of *books*, I am told."

"Only one of them."

"You must do your best without them tonight. When I have made up my mind what is to be done with you, I shall let you have the one with your clothes. The other shall be put away in the box room. I give my people what books I think fit for light reading. There—good night!"

Mary curtsied and left her. At the door she glanced this way and that to find some indication to guide her steps. A door was open at the end of a passage, and from the odor that met her, it seemed likely to be that of the kitchen. She approached and peeped in.

"Who is that?" cried an irate voice.

It was the voice of the second cook, who was supreme there except when the *chef* was present. Mary stepped in, and the woman advanced to meet her.

"Would you please tell me where to find the second housemaid," said Mary. "Mrs. Perkin has sent me to her room."

"Why don't Mrs. Perkin show you the way, then?" returned the woman. "There ain't nobody else in the 'ouse as knows who's fit to send to the top o' them stairs with you. A nice way Jemim' 'il be in when *she* comes 'ome, to find a stranger in 'er room!"

The same instant, however, the woman seemed to think better of the words she had spoken in haste, realizing what it might mean to her job if they were reported to Mrs. Perkin. Thereupon she assumed a more compliant tone. Casting a look at her saucepans, as if to warn them concerning their behavior in her absence, she turned again to Mary, saying: "I believe I better show you the way myself. It's easier to take you than find a girl to do it. Them hussies is never where they ought to be! *You* follow *me*."

She led the way along two passages and up a back staircase of stone— up and up, till Mary, unused to such heights, began to be aware of knees. Plainly at last in the regions of the roof, she thought her hill difficulty surmounted. But the cook turned a sharp corner, and Mary following found herself once more at the foot of a stair—very narrow and steep, leading up to one of those old-fashioned roof-turrets that had begun to appear in the new houses of that part of London.

"Are you taking me to the clouds, cook?" said Mary, willing to be cheerful, and to acknowledge her obligation for laborious guidance.

"Not yet," answered the cook. "We'll get there soon enough, anyhow."

She panted up the last few steps, and immediately at the top was the room she sought. It was a very small one, scarcely big enough for the two beds. Having lighted the gas, the cook left her, and Mary, noting that one of the beds was not made up, was glad to throw herself upon it. Covering herself with her cloak, she was soon fast asleep.

She was roused by a cry, half of terror, half of surprise. There stood the second housemaid, who, having been told nothing of her room-fellow, stared and gasped.

"I am sorry to have startled you," said Mary, who had half-risen, leaning on her elbow. "They ought to have told you there was a stranger in your room."

The girl had not been in London long, and her manners had not yet ceased to be simple. For a moment, however, she seemed capable only of panting and pressing her hand on her heart.

"I am very sorry," said Mary again, "but I won't hurt you! I don't look dangerous, do I?"

"No, miss," answered the girl, with a laugh, half hysterical. "I been to the play, and there was a fearful man in it, a thief, you know, miss!"

It was some time before Mary got her quieted, but when she did the girl was quite reasonable. She deplored that the bed was not made up, and would willingly have yielded hers. She was sorry she did not have a clean nightgown to offer her—"not that it would be fit for the likes of *you,* miss!"—and showed herself full of friendly service. From her dress, Jemima judged she must be some grand visitor's maid, vastly her superior in the social scale: if she had taken her for an inferior, she would doubtless, like most, have had some airs handy.

26 / Mary's Position

Mary seemed to have but just got to sleep again when she was startled awake by the violent ringing of a bell.

"Oh, you needn't trouble yourself for a long while, miss!" said the girl who was already dressing. "I've got ever so many fires to light before they've be a thought of you!"

Mary lay down again, and once more fell fast asleep.

At length she was awoken again by the girl telling her that breakfast was ready. She rose and made herself as tidy as she could.

"I thought," Jemima said, "as Mrs. Perkin would 'a as't you to your first meal with her, but she told me when I as't what were to be done with you, as how you must go to the room, and eat your breakfast with the rest of us."

Mary did not mind this in the least. She had before this come to understand the word of her Master, that not what enters a man defiles him, but only what comes out of him; hence, no man's dignity is affected by what another does to him, but only by what he does, or would like to do, himself.

She felt a little shy on entering the room where all the servants were already seated at breakfast. Two of the men, with a word to each other, made room for her between them, and laughed. The footman, having witnessed her reception by Mrs. Perkin, spoke boldly to Mary, expressing a hope that she was not too much fatigued by her journey. Mary thanked him in her own natural, straightforward way, and from then on he spoke to her naturally and courteously, and she received not the smallest annoyance during the rest of the meal—which did not last long: Mrs. Perkin took care of that.

For an hour or more after the rest had scattered to their respective duties, she was left alone. Then Mrs. Perkin sent for her.

When she entered her room, she found her occupied with the cook, and was allowed to stand unnoticed.

"When shall I be able to see Mrs. Redmain, ma'am?" she asked when the cook at length turned to go.

"Wait," rejoined Mrs. Perkin with a quiet dignity, "until you are spoken to, young woman!" Then first casting a glance at her, and perhaps perceiving on her face a glimmer of the amusement Mary felt, she began to gather a more correct suspicion of the sort of young woman she might possibly be, and hastily added, "Take a seat."

The idea of making a blunder was unendurable to Mrs. Perkin, and she was most unwilling to believe she had done so. But even if she had, she would never show it. That would only make it all the more difficult to recover her pride of place.

"I am sorry," she said, "I can give you no hope of an interview with Mrs. Redmain before three o'clock. She will very likely not be out of her room before one. I suppose you saw her at Durnmelling?"

"Yes, ma'am," answered Mary, "—and at Testbridge."

It kept growing on the housekeeper that she had made a mistake as to Mary's position—though to what extent she sought in vain to determine.

"Would you kindly see that Mrs. Redmain is told, as soon as she wakes, that I am here," added Mary.

"Oblige me by ringing the bell," said Mrs. Perkin.

Mary obeyed.

A rather cross-looking, red-faced, thin woman appeared, whom she requested to let her mistress know, as soon as was proper, that there was a young person in the house who said she had come from Testbridge by appointment to see her.

The woman departed and Mary followed. She spent what would have been a dreary morning to one solely dependent on her own company. It was quite three o'clock when she was at length summoned to Mrs. Redmain's room. Mrs. Folter, whom Mrs. Perkin had sent for earlier, guided Mary there, and lingered long enough in the soft closing of the door to learn that her mistress received the young person with a kiss—almost as much to Mary's surprise as Folter's annoyance. She hastened to pass on the fact to Mrs. Perkin, and succeeded thereby in occasioning no small uneasiness in the heart of the housekeeper, who was almost as much afraid of her mistress as the other servants were of her. She spent some time in expectant fear, but gradually, as nothing came of it, she concluded that her behavior to Mary must have been quite correct, seeing the girl had made no complaint.

But though Hesper received Mary with a kiss, she did not ask her a single question about her journey, or as to how she had spent the night. She was there, and looking all right, and that was enough. On the other hand, she did proceed to have her at once properly settled.

The little room given her looked out upon a small court and was dark, but otherwise very comfortable. As soon as she was left to herself, she opened her boxes, put her things away in drawers and wardrobe, arranged her books, and sat down to read a little, think, and build a few castles in the air.

About eight o'clock in the evening, Folter summoned her to go to Mrs.

Redmain. By this time she was tired. She was accustomed to tea and something to eat in the afternoon, and since her early dinner with the housekeeper she had had nothing. She found Hesper dressed for the evening. As soon as Mary entered, she dismissed Folter.

"I am going out to dinner," she said. "Are you quite comfortable?"

"I am rather cold, and should like some tea," said Mary.

"My poor girl! have you had no tea?" Hesper said with some concern and annoyance. "You are looking rather pale. When did you have anything to eat?"

"At one o'clock," replied Mary, with a rather weary smile.

"This is dreadful!" said Hesper. "What can the servants be about?"

"And please, may I have a little fire?"

"Certainly," replied Hesper. "Is it possible you have been sitting all day without one? Why did you not ring the bell?" She took one of her hands. "You are frozen!" she said.

"Oh, no!" answered Mary. "I am far from that. You see, nobody knows what to do with me—you hardly know yourself," she added with a merry look. "But if you wouldn't mind telling Mrs. Perkin where you wish me to have my meals, that would put it all right, I think."

"Very well," said Hesper, in a tone that for her was sharp. "Will you ring the bell?"

She sent for the housekeeper, who presently appeared, calm and prepared for whatever might come.

"Mrs. Perkin, I wish you to arrange with Miss Marston about her meals."

"Yes, ma'am," answered Mrs. Perkin in sedatest tone.

"Mrs. Perkin," said Mary, "I don't want to be troublesome; tell me what will suit you best."

But Mrs. Perkin did not even look at her. Standing straight as a rush, she kept her eyes on her mistress, not considering Mary worth replying to.

"Do you desire, ma'am, that Miss Marston should have her meals in the housekeeper's room?" she asked.

"Whatever Miss Marston pleases," answered Hesper. "If she prefers them in her own, you will see they are properly sent up and that she is attended to."

"Very well, ma'am!—then I will await Miss Marston's orders," said Mrs. Perkin, and turned to leave the room. But when her mistress spoke again, she turned again and stood. It was Mary, however, whom Hesper addressed.

"Mary," she said, apparently anticipating worse from the tone of the housekeeper's obedience than from the neglect she had already demonstrated, "when I am alone, you shall take your meals with me. And when

I have someone with me, Mrs. Perkin will see that they are sent to your room. That is how we will settle it."

"Thank you," said Mary.

"Very well, ma'am," said Mrs. Perkin.

"Send Miss Marston some tea immediately," said Hesper.

Scarcely was Mrs. Perkin gone when the carriage was announced. Mary returned to her room, and in a little while tea, with thin bread and butter in limited quantity, was brought to her. But it was brought by Jemima, whose face wore a cheerful smile over the tray she carried. She, at least, did not grudge Mary her superior place in the household.

"Do you think, Jemima," asked Mary, "you could manage to answer my bell when I ring?"

"I should be only too glad, miss; it would be a pleasure to me."

"If you don't answer when I ring, I shall know, as well as if you told me, that you either don't hear from being upstairs somewhere, or can't come at the moment. I sha'n't be exacting.

"Do you suppose you could bring me a loaf? I have had nothing since Mrs. Perkin's dinner, and this bread and butter is rather too delicately cut," said Mary.

"Laws, miss, you must be nigh clemmed!" said the girl, and hastened away.

She soon returned with a loaf of bread and butter and a jar of marmalade sent by the cook, who was only too glad to open a safety-valve to her pleasure at the discomfort of Mrs. Perkin.

"When would you like your breakfast, miss?" asked Jemima, as she removed the tea things.

"Any time it is convenient," replied Mary.

"You'll have it in bed, miss?"

"No, thank you. I never do."

"It makes no more trouble. And why shouldn't you have it as well as Mrs. Perkin or that ill-tempered cockatoo, Mrs. Folter?"

"You don't mean that the housekeeper and the lady's-maid have breakfast in bed?"

"Almost every blessed mornin' as I've got to take it up to 'em, miss, upon my word of honor."

"Well," said Mary, "I certainly shall not add another to the breakfasts in bed. But I hate to even ask you to bring it to me here. At least I can make my bed and tidy up the room myself."

"Oh, no indeed, miss, you mustn't do that! Think what they'd say of you downstairs!"

"I can't help it, Jemima. I'll not add to your work by my own laziness. If they were servants of the right sort, I should like to have their good opinion, and they would think all the more of me for doing my share. As it is, I should count it a disgrace to care a straw what they thought. We must do our work, and not mind what people say."

"Yes, miss, that's what my mother used to say to my father when he wouldn't be reasonable. But I must go, miss, or I shall catch it for gossiping with you—that's what *she'll* call it."

When Jemima was gone, Mary fell to thinking again. It was all very well, she said to herself, to talk about doing her work, but here she was without scarcely a shadow of an idea what her work was to entail! Had *any* work been given her to do in this house? Had it been presumptuous of her to come? Had she gotten out in front of the guidance of Providence, and was she therefore now where she had no right to be?

She could not tell. But anyhow, here she was, and no one could be anywhere without the fact involving its own duty. Even if she had put herself there, and was to blame for being there, that did not free her from the obligations of the position, and she was willing to do whatever should *now* be given her to do. God was not a hard master. If she had made a mistake, he would pardon her, and either give her work here, where she found herself, or send her elsewhere. I need not say that thinking was not all her care. For she thought in the presence of him who, because he is always setting our wrong things right, is called God our Savior.

27 / Mr. and Mrs. Helmer

Mary had heard but twice from Letty since her marriage. She had written again about a month ago, but had received no reply. Knowing the address, however, she had high hopes of being able to find her; and therefore set out the next morning to attempt a visit.

The sad fact was, that, ever since she left Testbridge, for a long time Letty had been going downhill. Her better self seemed to have remained behind with Mary. And not even if he had been as good as she thought him, could Tom himself have made up to her for the loss of such a friend.

Letty had not found marriage at all the grand thing she had expected. With the faithfulness of a woman, however, she attributed her disappointment to something inherent in marriage, nowise affecting the man whom marriage had made her husband.

In order to be near the center to which what little work he did gravitate, Tom had rented a lodging in a noisy street, as unlike all that Letty had been accustomed to as London could afford. There was no green thing to be seen in any direction. Not a sweet sound was to be heard. The sun, at this time of the year, was seldom to be seen in London anywhere, and in Lydgate Street, even when there was no fog, it was in view only for a brief portion of the day. And the noise! A ceaseless torrent of sounds—stony sounds, iron sounds, grinding sounds, clashing sounds, yells and cries.

Once a week or so, Tom would take her to see a play, and that was, indeed, a happiness—not because of the play itself mainly, though she did enjoy them, but because she had Tom all to herself, in an environment away from the discordant sounds of Lydgate Street.

Alas! Tom was not half so dependent on her as she was on him, nor did he get half so much pleasure from her company. Many evenings he spent at places where those who received him had not the faintest idea he even had a wife. And if they had, it would have made little difference: they would not have invited her. Small, silly, conceited Tom, regarding himself as a somebody, was more than content to be asked to such people's houses. He thought he went about as a lion, whereas in reality it was merely as a jackal. While Letty sat in her dreary apartment, dingily clad and lonely, Tom dressed in the height of fashion and went strolling about grand rooms, now exchanging a flying shot of recognition, now pausing to pay a compliment to this lady on her singing, to that on her verses, to a third, where he dared, on her dress. For good-natured Tom was profuse with compliments. Occasionally he would sing one of his own songs, or accompany another while she sang—for Tom could do either well enough for people without a conscience in their music. At other times he might be found in some back drawing room, talking nonsense with some lady foolish enough to be amused with his folly. Tom meant no harm and did not do much— was only a human butterfly, amusing himself with other creatures of the day, who have no notion that death cannot kill them. They think, if they think at all, that it is life, strong in them, that makes them forget death; whereas in truth, it is death, strong in them, that makes them unaware of life. Like a hummingbird, all sparkle and flash, Tom flitted through the tropical delights of such society as his good luck had gained him admission to, forming many an evanescent friendship, and taking many a graceful liberty—for Tom seemed to have been born to show what a nice sort of a person a fool, well put together, may be.

He had plenty of brains, but little wit. And to a mentality such as his, nothing could reveal to him the reason or meaning behind the fact that married life was less interesting than courtship. The reasons, of course, profound as eternity, lay in himself, and of that being, as I have said, he knew next to nothing. He had no notion that when he married all of life changed, that in a lofty and blessed sense he had forfeited his life. He did not fathom that, to save his wife's life, he must yield his own, she doing the same for him—for God himself can save no other way. But the notion of any saving, any growth, any nurturing of the one the other was far from Tom. Nor had Letty any awareness of this aspect of marriage either. Not the less did they both need saving, and the mutual growth that true marriage brings, before life could be to either of them a good thing.

Life's blossom is its salvation, its redemption, the justification of its existence—and is a thing far off with most of us. For Tom, the highest notion of life was to be recognized by the world. His goal was to die in the blessed assurance that his name would be forever on the lips and in the hearts of that idol of fools they call *posterity*—a divinity as vague as the old gray Fate, and less noble.

While Tom, therefore, was idling away time that yet could hardly be called precious, his little wife, as I have said, sat at home, inquired after by nobody, thought of by nobody, and hardly even able to keep her interest in the feeble trash she was now reading. Many a day she sat musing—if, indeed, such poor mental vagaries as hers can be called even musing!— ignorant of what was the matter with her, hardly knowing that anything was the matter, and yet pining away morally, spiritually, and intellectually. Now she would wonder when Tom would be home, then she would try to congratulate herself on his being such a favorite, and thinking what an honor it was to a poor country girl like her to be the wife of a man so much courted by society. She never doubted that the people to whose houses Tom went desired his company from admiration of his writings. She had not an idea that never a one of them or their guests cared a straw about what he wrote—except, indeed, here and there, a young lady in her first season, who thought it a grand thing to know an author, as poor Letty thought it a grand thing to be the wife of one. How blessed will be that coming time when all men will begin to see that it is far superior to *do* an inferior thing well, than to write about all the most lofty things of the universe with great insight, or to be esteemed highly by the world.

It was through some of his old college friends that Tom had thus easily stepped into the literary profession. I cannot say that they had found him remunerative employment. The best they had done for him was to bring him into such a half sort of connection with a certain weekly paper that now and then he got something printed in it, and now and then the editor would hand him what he called an honorarium, but what in reality was nothing but a five-pound note. When such an event occurred, Tom would swell with the imagined dignity of supporting a family by literary labor, and, forgetting the sparseness of his mother's doles, who delighted in making the young couple feel the bitterness of dependence, would immediately invite his friends to supper—not at the lodging where Letty sat lonely, but at some tavern frequented by people of the craft. It was at such times, and in the company of men certainly not better than himself, that Tom's hopes were brightest and his confidence greatest. Long after midnight, upon such and many other occasions, would he and his companions sit laughing and jesting and drinking their champagne, some saying witty things, and all of them foolish things and worse, inventing stories intended to reveal the foibles of friends, and relating anecdotes that grew more and more irreverent to God and women as the night advanced and the wine gained power. At last, sometime between night and morning, Tom would reel gracefully home, using all the power of his will—the best use to which it was ever put—to subdue the drunkenness of which, even in its embrace, he had the lingering honor to be ashamed, that he might face his wife with the appearance of the gentleman he was anxious she should continue to consider him.

It was an unhappy thing for Tom that his mother, having persuaded her dying husband, "for Tom's sake," to leave the money in her power, should not now have carried her tyranny further, and refused him any money altogether. He would then have been forced to work harder, and there might have been some hope for him then. As it was, his so-called profession was the mere grasping after the honor of a workman without the doing of the work. And the little he gained by it was, at the same time, more than enough to foster the self-deception that he did something in the world.

With the money he gave her, which was never more than a small part of what his mother sent him, Letty had plenty to do to make both ends meet; and while he went in debt to his tailor and bootmaker, she never had anything new to wear. She did sometimes wish he would take her out with him a little oftener. But she always reflected that he could not afford it, and it was long before she began to have any doubt or uneasiness about him. What a pity it seems that so many girls are married before they are women! The woman blossoms at length, and finds she is forestalled. But, thank God, in the faithfully accepted and encountered responsibility, the woman must at length become aware that she has under her feet an ascending stair by which to climb to the woman of the divine ideal.

There was at present, however, nothing to be called thought in the mind of Letty. She had even lost much of what faculty of thinking had been developed in her by the care of cousin Godfrey. Her whole life now was Tom. Her whole day was but the continuous and little varied hope of his presence. Most of the time she had a book in her hands, but ever and again book and hands would sink into her lap, and she would sit staring before her at nothing.

The first thing that made her aware she was not quite happy was the discovery that novels were losing their charm, that they were not sufficient to make her day pass, that they were only dessert, and she had no dinner. When it came to difficulty in going on with a new one long enough to get interested in it, she sighed heavily, and began to think that perhaps life was rather a dreary thing—at least considerably diluted with the unsatisfactory.

Tom talked of himself as on the "staff" of *The Firefly*—the name of the weekly previously mentioned, a newspaper of great pretense, which took upon itself the mystery of things, as if it were God's spy. Its writers were mostly young men, and their passion was to say clever things. Whether correct or true things hardly mattered. A scandalous rumor of any kind, especially from the region styled "High life," often false, and always incorrect, was the delight both of paper and of its readers. The interest it thus awoke, united with the fear it thus caused, was mainly what procured for such as were known to be employed upon it the *entrée* into houses and parties and social gatherings where they would never have been seen otherwise.

To do Tom justice, he wrote nothing of this sort: he was neither ill-natured nor experienced enough for that department. What he did write was clever, shallow sketches of that same society into whose charmed precincts he was lately moving closer. These sketches did more for the paper than the editor was willing to know or acknowledge.

The Firefly also produced a little art—not always very original, but at least giving the illusion of literary taste. In this branch Tom contributed regularly in the shape of verse. He had a ready faculty for it, but it was not things themselves, but the reflection of things in the art of others, that moved him to produce. He was like some young preachers who spend a part of the Saturday reading this or that author in order to get inspired enough to preach on the Sunday. He was really fond of poetry, delighted in the study of its external elements, possessed not only a good but cultivated ear for verse, had true pleasure in a fine phrase or strong word, and last of all had a special faculty for imitation. From these gifts, graces, and acquirements, it came that he could write in any style that moved him— so far, at least, as to remind one who knew it of that style, and every now and then verses of his appeared in *The Firefly*.

As often as this took place, Letty was in the third heaven of delight. For was not Tom's poetry unquestionably superior to anything else the age could produce? Was even the poetry cousin Godfrey made her read to be compared with Tom's? What a happy woman she was!

But by this time the first mist of a coming fog had begun to gather dimly in her heart. When Tom would come home happy, but talk perplexingly, when he would drop asleep in the middle of a story she could make nothing of, when he would burst out and go on laughing and refuse to explain—how was she to avoid the conclusion that he had been drinking? And when she noted that this condition was reappearing at shorter and shorter intervals, might she not well begin to be frightened and to feel that she was gradually being left alone—that Tom had struck into a diverging path, and they were slowly growing miles further apart from each other?

28 / Mary and Letty

When her landlady announced a visitor, Letty could not imagine who it could be; she had not a single friend in London. When Mary entered, she jumped to her feet and stood staring. What with being so much in the house, and seeing so few people, the poor girl, I think, had grown a little stupid. But when the fact of Mary's presence cleared itself to her, she rushed forward with a cry, fell into her arms, and burst out weeping. Mary held her tight until she had come a little to herself, then pushed her gently away to the length of her arms and looked at her.

She was not a sight to make one happy. She was no longer the plump, fresh girl that used to go singing about, nor was she merely thin and pale. Simply put, she looked sad and unhealthy. Things could not be going well with her. Her dress looked neglected, even shabby. The sadness of it all sunk to Mary's heart. Letty had apparently not found marriage a grand affair!

But Mary had not come into the world to be sad or to help another to be sad. Sorrowful we may often have to be, but to indulge in sorrow is either not to know or to deny God our Savior. True, her heart ached for Letty, and the ache immediately laid itself as close to Letty's ache as it could lie. But that was only the advance-guard of her army of salvation, the light cavalry of sympathy. The next division was help, and behind that lay patience, and strength, and hope, and faith, and joy. This joy many modern teachers fail to regard as a virtue and therefore decline to regard as a duty. But he is a poor Christian indeed in whom joy has not at least a growing share, and Mary was not a poor Christian. Her whole nature drew itself together, confronting the destroyer, whatever he might be, in possession of Letty. How to help she could not yet tell, but sympathy was already at its work.

"You are not looking your best, Letty," she said, clasping her again in her arms.

With a little choking, Letty assured her she was quite well.

"How is Mr. Helmer?" asked Mary.

"Quite well—and very busy," answered Letty—a little hurriedly, Mary thought. "—But," she added in a tone of disappointment, "You always used to call him Tom."

"Oh," answered Mary with a smile, "one must be careful how one takes liberties with married people. A certain mysterious change seems to

162

pass over some of them, and then you have to make your acquaintance with them all over again from the beginning."

"You don't have to worry about that with me, Mary. I have never ceased to love you."

"I am so glad!" answered Mary. "People don't generally take much to me—at least not to come *near* me. But you can *be* friends without *having* friends," she added.

"I don't quite understand you," said Letty sadly. "But then, I never could quite, you know. Tom finds me very stupid."

These words strengthened Mary's suspicion that all was not going well between the two, but she shrunk from any confidences with but one of the married pair, which she would have considered a breach of the unity between them. But although Mary would encourage Letty to tell nothing about her relationship with Tom, she was still anxious to discover what she could in order that, if possible, she might help. She would observe: side-lights often reveal more than direct illumination. It might be she had been sent to London for Letty, and not for Mrs. Redmain at all. He who made time in time would show.

"Are you going to be in London long, Mary?" asked Letty.

"Oh, a long time!" answered Mary, with a loving glance.

Letty's eyes fell.

"I am sorry," she said, "that I cannot ask you to stay here. We have only these two rooms, and—and—you see—Mrs. Helmer is not very generous with Tom, and—because they—don't get on very well—as I suppose everybody knows—Tom won't—he won't consent to—to—"

"You little goose!" cried Mary. "You don't think I would come here expecting you to put me up, without even letting you know!—I have got a job in London."

"A job!" echoed Letty. "What can you mean, Mary? You haven't left your own shop, and gone into somebody else's?"

"No, not exactly," replied Mary, laughing. "But I have no doubt most people would think that the more prudent thing to have done."

"Then I don't," said Letty, with a little flash of her old enthusiasm. "Whatever you do, Mary, I am sure it will always be the best."

"I am glad to have so much of your good opinion, Letty. But I am not sure I shall still have it when I tell you what I have done. Indeed, I am not quite sure myself that I have acted wisely. But if I have made a mistake, it is from listening to love more than to prudence."

"What!" cried Letty. "You're married?"

"No," replied Mary, laughing. "It is neither so bad nor so good as that. But I was not happy in the shop without my father. Then it happened that I became very attached to a lady. And as the lady took a small fancy to me at the same time, and wanted to have me about her, she offered me a situation in her house, and here I am."

"But, surely, that is hardly a job fit for one like you!" cried Letty, almost in consternation. "You are, I suppose, a kind of—of—companion to your lady friend?"

"Or a kind of lady's-maid, or a kind of dressmaker, or a kind of humble friend—something like a dog, perhaps. In truth, Letty, I do not know what I am, or what I am going to be. But I shall find out before long."

"The thing doesn't seem at all like you!—Mary Marston in a menial position! I can't get hold of it."

"You remind me," said Mary, "of what my father once said to Mr. Turnbull. You remember how my father always spoke quietly? Mr. Turnbull imagined that he did not know what he was about, for the thoughts my father was thinking could not have lived a moment in the head of one such as Mr. Turnbull. 'You see, John Turnbull,' my father said to him, 'no man can look so inconsistent as one whose principles are not understood. For hardly in anything will that man do as his friend must have thought he would.' I suppose you think, Letty," Mary went on with a merry air, "that for the sake of consistency, I should never do anything but sell behind a counter?"

"In that case," said Letty, "I ought to have married a milkman, for a dairy is the only thing I understand. I am unable to help Tom at all!"

"I suppose," said Mary, "when a man sets himself to do anything, he must have it all his own way, or he can't do it."

"I suppose that's it. I know Tom is very angry with the editor when he wants to alter anything he has written. I'm sure Tom's right. You can't think how much better Tom's way always is!—he makes that quite clear, even to poor, stupid me. But then, you know, Tom's a genius. But you haven't told me yet where you are staying."

"You remember Miss Mortimer, of Durnmelling?"

"Quite well, of course."

"She is Mrs. Redmain now, and I am with her."

"You don't mean it! Why, Tom knows her very well! He has been several times to parties at her house."

"And you too?" asked Mary.

"Oh, dear no!" answered Letty, laughing at Mary's ignorance. "It's not the fashion in London for distinguished persons like my Tom to take their wives to parties."

"Are there no ladies at those parties, then?"

"Oh, yes," replied Letty, smiling again at Mary's ignorance of the world, "the grandest of ladies—duchesses and all. You don't know what a favorite Tom is in the highest circles."

Mary could believe almost anything about Tom's being a favorite, for she herself liked him a great deal more than she approved of him. But she could see no sense of his going to parties without his wife, neither could she see that the circle in which he was a favorite made any difference. She had old-fashioned notions of a man and his wife being one, and felt a breach of the law where they were separated, whatever the custom. There could be no good reason for it. But Letty seemed much too satisfied to give her any light on the matter. The same moment, as if Letty saw inside her and understood what was passing in Mary's mind, she added, in the tone of an unanswerable argument: "Besides, Mary, how could I get a dress fit to wear at such parties? You wouldn't have me go and look like a beggar! That would disgrace Tom. Everybody in London judges everybody else by the clothes she wears. You should hear Tom's descriptions of the ladies' dresses when he comes home!"

Mary was on the verge of crying out indignantly, "Then if he can't take you, why doesn't he stay at home with you?" but she thought better of herself in time to hold her peace. She settled it with herself that Tom must have less heart, or yet more muddled brains than she had thought.

"So then," reverted Letty, as if desiring to turn definitively from the subject of Tom and the parties, "you are actually living with the beautiful Mrs. Redmain! What a lucky girl you are. You will see no end of grand people! You might even see my Tom sometimes—when I can't," she added, with a sigh that went to Mary's heart.

"Poor thing!" she said to herself. "It isn't anything so great she wants—only a little more of a foolish husband's company."

It was no wonder that Tom found Letty dull, for he had just as little of his own in him as she, and thought he had a great store—which is what sends a man most swiftly along the road to that final poverty in which even that which he has shall be taken from him.

Mary did not stay so long with Letty as both would have liked, for she did not yet know enough of Hesper's ways. When she got home, she learned that she had a headache, and had not yet made her appearance.

29 / The Evening Star

Despite her headache, Mrs. Redmain was going to a small fancy ball in the evening, meant for a sort of rehearsal to a great one when the season should arrive. The part and costume she had chosen were the suggestion of her own name: she would represent the Evening Star, clothed in the early twilight, and neither was she unfit for the part. But she had sufficient confidence neither in herself, nor her maid nor the dress she had designed not to wish for Mary's opinion. After lunch, therefore, she sent for Miss Marston to come to her bedroom.

Mary found her half dressed, Folter in attendance, and a great heap of pink lying on the bed.

"Sit down, Mary," said Hesper, pointing to a chair. "I want your advice. Where I am going I am not to be Mrs. Redmain, but Hesper. You know what Hesper means?"

Mary said she knew, and waited—a little anxious; for sideways in her eyes glowed the pink of the chosen Hesperian clouds; and, if she said she didn't like it, what could be done at that late hour.

"There is my dress," continued the Evening Star, with a glance of her eyes, for Folter was busied with her hair. "I want to know your opinion of it."

Folter gave a toss of her head that seemed to say, "Have I not already spoken?" but what it really meant, how should any mortal know, for the main obstructions to understanding are profundity and shallowness, and the latter is far the more perplexing of the two.

"I would like to see it on first," said Mary. She was in doubt whether the color would suit Hesper's complexion. She had always associated the name *Hesper* with the late solemn lovely period of twilight, having little in common with the bright pink lying on the bed.

Hesper had made the choice of the particular material with the assistance of Sepia and Folter. But although it continued delightful in the eyes of her maid, it had, upon nearer and prolonged acquaintance, become doubtful in hers. And she now waited, with no little anxiety, the judgment of Mary, who sat silently thinking.

"Have you nothing to say?" she asked impatiently at length.

"Please, ma'am," replied Mary, "I must think if I am to be of any use. I am doing my best, but you must let me be quiet."

Half annoyed, half pleased, Hesper was silent, and Mary went on thinking. All was still, except for the slight noises Folter made, as, like a machine, she went on heartlessly brushing her mistress's hair, which kept emitting little crackles of dissatisfaction with her handling. Mary would now take a good gaze at the lovely creature, and try to call up to her imagination the real Hesper, not a Hesper dressed up—a process which had in it hope for the lady, but not much for the dress upon the bed.

At last Folter had done her part.

"I suppose you *must* see it on!" said Hesper, and she rose up.

Folter jerked herself to the bed, took the dress, arranged it on her arms, got up on a chair, dropped it over her mistress's head, got down, and, having pulled it this way and that for a while, fastened it here, undid it there, and fastened it again several times, and finally exclaimed: "There, ma'am! If you don't look like the loveliest woman in the room, I shall never trust my eyes again."

Mary held her peace, for the commonplace style of the dress added all the more to her dissatisfaction with the color. It was all puffed and bubbled and blown about, here and there and everywhere, so that the form of the woman was lost in the frolic shapelessness of the cloud. The whole, if whole it could be called, was a miserable attempt at combining fancy and fashion, and resulted in an ugly nothing.

"I see you don't like it!" said Hesper, with a mingling of displeasure and dismay. "I wish you had come a few days sooner! It is much too late to do anything now. I might just as well have gone without showing it to you! Here, Folter!"

With a look almost of disgust, she began to pull off the dress, in which, a few hours later, she would yet make the attempt to enchant an assembly.

"Oh, I wish you had told me yesterday!" cried Mary. "There would have been time then—and I don't know," she added, seeing disgust change to mortification on Hesper's countenance, "but something might be done yet."

"Oh, indeed!" dropped from Folter's lips.

"What can be done?" said Hesper angrily. "There can be no time for anything."

"If only we had the material!" said Mary. "That shade doesn't suit your complexion. It ought to be much, much darker—in fact, a different color altogether."

Folter was furious, but restrained herself sufficiently to preserve some calmness of tone, although her face turned almost blue with the effort as she said: "Miss Marston is not long out of the country, ma'am, and doesn't know what's suitable to a London drawing room."

Her mistress was too dejected to pay the least attention to her impertinence. "What color were you thinking of, Miss Marston?" Hesper asked stiffly. She was annoyed with Mary from feeling certain she was right, and believing there was no remedy.

"I could not describe it," answered Mary. "And, indeed, the color I have in my mind may not be to be had at all. I have seen it somewhere, but whether in cloth or only in nature, I cannot at this moment be certain. I only know it is the color that would suit your complexion, your eyes, your hair all perfectly."

"What's the good of talking like that—excuse me, ma'am—it's more than I can bear—when the ball is in a few hours! The color to match your complexion, found out in nature—indeed!" cried Folter.

"If you would allow me," said Mary, "I should like very much to see whether I might not find something that would suit you and your idea, too. But I know nothing of the London shops."

"I should think not!" remarked Folter with emphasis.

"I would send you in my carriage, if I thought it were of any use," said Hesper. "Folter could take you to the proper places."

"Folter would be of no use to me," said Mary. "If your coachman knows the best shops, that will be enough."

"But there's no time to make up anything," objected Hesper, despondently, not the less with a glimmer of hope in her tone.

"Not like that," answered Mary. "But there is much in that dress as unnecessary as it is ugly. If Folter is good at her needle—"

"I won't take up a single stitch. It would be a mere waste of time," cried Folter.

"Then please, ma'am," said Mary, "let Folter have that dress ready, and if I don't succeed, you will have something to wear."

"I hate it. I won't go if you don't find me another."

"Some people may like it, though I don't," said Mary.

"Not a doubt of that!" said Folter.

"Ring the bell," said her mistress.

The woman obeyed. The carriage was ordered immediately, and in not more than a few minutes, Mary was standing at a counter in a large shop, looking at various samplings of material, of which the young man waiting on her soon perceived she knew the qualities and capabilities better than he.

After great pains, she left the shop well satisfied with her success. And now for the greater difficulty!

She drove straight to Letty's lodging, and, there dismissing the carriage, presented herself, with a great parcel in her arms, for the second time that day.

She knew that Letty was good with her needle, and before Mary had even finished her story, she was untying the parcel and preparing to receive her instructions. Letty had upon occasion, when her supply of novels had for a day run short, asked a dressmaker who lived above if she could help her for an hour or two. And now, before the two of them had been at work many minutes, Letty thought of calling in the woman's help. Presently there were three of them busy as bees. Mary quickly communicated her ideas to the other two, and since the design of the dress was simple, Mary got all she wanted done in shorter time than she had thought possible. The landlady sent for a cab, and Mary was in plenty of time. It was with some triumph, tempered with some trepidation, that she carried the parcel to Hesper's room.

There Folter was trying to persuade her mistress to get dressed: Miss Marston, she said, knew nothing of what she had undertaken, and even if she arrived in time, it would be with something too ridiculous for any lady to appear in. At that very moment Mary entered and was received with a cry of delight from Hesper. This pleasure increased still further as Mary began to undo the parcel and Hesper caught sight of the colors. When she lifted the dress on her arm for a first affect, she was enraptured with it— aerial in texture, of the hue of a smoky rose, deep and cloudy with overlying folds, yet diaphanous, a darkness dilute with red.

Silent and grim, Folter approached to try the filmy thing. But Mary judged her scarcely in a mood to be trusted with anything so light. It had been but held together temporarily in many places, and since she knew the weak points, she begged that she might, for that evening, be allowed the privilege of dressing Mrs. Redmain. Hesper gladly consented; Folter left the room, and Mary took her place. Presently, more to Hesper's pleasure than Mary's surprise, it was found that the dress fit quite sufficiently well. Not once, while Mary was at her work, would she allow Hesper to look, and the self-willed lady was submissive in her hands. The moment she had succeeded—for her expectations were more than realized—Mary led her to the mirror.

Hesper gazed for an instant, then, turning, threw her arms about Mary and kissed her.

"I don't believe you're a human creature at all!" she cried. "You are a fairy godmother, come to look after your poor Cinderella."

The door opened and Folter entered.

"If you please, ma'am, I wish to leave your employ this day next month," she said quietly.

"Then," answered her mistress with equal calmness, "oblige me by going at once to Mrs. Perkin and telling her that I desire her to pay you a month's wages, and let you leave the house tomorrow morning. You won't mind helping me to dress till I get another maid, will you, Mary?" she added. Folter left the room, chagrined at her inability to cause annoyance.

"I do not see why you should have another maid so long as I am with you," said Mary. "How many days' apprenticeship can it take to make one woman able to dress another?"

"Not many when she is like you, Mary," said Hesper. "I am beginning to believe that it was a special providence that sent you to me."

As they talked, Mary was giving her final touches to the arrangement. When she was done she searched Hesper's jewelry box and found a fine bracelet of the true, Oriental topaz: this she clasped upon one arm. Then she took off all the rings Hesper had just put on except a certain glorious sapphire, and then led her again to the mirror. If there, Hesper was far more pleased with herself than was reasonable or lovely, my reader need not therefore fear a sermon from the text, "Beauty is only skin-deep," for that text is out of the devil's Bible. No, the maker of all beauty is the same One who made the seven stars, and his works are past finding out. But the woman's share in her own beauty may be infinitely less than skin-deep; and there is but one greater fool than the man who worships that beauty— that is the woman who prides herself upon it, as if she were the fashioner and not the thing fashioned.

But poor Hesper had much excuse, though no justification. She had had many of the disadvantages, and hardly a single one of the benefits of poverty. She had heard constantly from childhood the most worldly and greedy talk, the commonest expression of dependence on the favors of Mammon, and thus had from the first been prepared to marry money. She had been taught no other way of doing her part to procure the things of which the Father knows we have need. She had never earned a dinner, had never done or thought of doing a day's work—of offering the world anything. She had never dreamed of being any use, even to herself. Out of it all, she had brought but the knowledge that this beauty with which she was chanced to be blessed was worth much in the world—was worth everything, in fact, the world calls fine, and the devil offers to those who, unscarred by his inherent ugliness, will fall down and worship him.

The Evening Star found herself a great success—that is, much followed by the men and much complimented by the women. Her triumph culminated with the next appearance of *The Firefly*, which contained a loose little poetic bundle of nothing, "To the Evening Star," which everybody knew to stand for Mrs. Redmain. Tom had not even been at the party, but had gathered fire enough from what he heard of Hesper's appearance there to write the verses.

In the following days, as naturally as if she had been born to that very duty, Mary slid into the office of lady's-maid to Mrs. Redmain. If Hesper was occasionally a little rude to her, Mary was not one to *accent* a rudeness—that is, to wrap it up in resentment and put it away safe in the pocket of memory. She could not help occasionally feeling things of the kind; but she made haste to send them from her, and shut the doors against them. She knew herself a far more blessed person than Hesper, and felt the obligation, from the Master himself, of keeping every channel of service open between Hesper and her. To Hesper, the change from Folter's to Mary's service was like passing from night to day. Mary was full of life and near presence, as that of dew or summer wind. To have Mary near was not only to have a ministering spirit at hand, but to have a good atmosphere all around—an air, a heaven, out of which good things must momentarily come.

There was one in the house, however, who was not pleased at the change from Folter to Mary. Because of the change, Sepia found herself less necessary to Hesper. Up till now Hesper had never been satisfied without Sepia's opinion and final approval in most things. But now she found in Mary a faculty that made appeal to Sepia unnecessary. Sepia cared for herself, not another, and thus was unable to minister to the comfort or beautification of her cousin. Her displeasure did not arise from the jealousy that is born of affection but of selfishness. Sepia did not care a straw about Hesper's true self, she only cared that the links between them remain strong for the sake of her own position. To find herself in any way less needed in Hesper's eyes would be to find herself on the inclined plane of loss, and probably ruin, particularly because she had no money of her own, and no fixed allowance from her cousin.

Hesper had always been generous enough with Sepia. There was no tightness in her, any more than in her husband. They were, of course, as became people of fashion, regular and unwearied attendants of the church of Mammon, ordering all their judgments and ways in accordance with the precepts there delivered. But they were not Mammon's money-grubbers or accumulators. They gave liberally where they gave. So Hesper behaved generously to Sepia—when she thought of it; but she did not love her enough to be love-watchful and seldom thought how her money must be going, or asked herself if she might not be in want of more. There are many who will give freely, who do not care to understand need and anticipate want. While they have a giving nature, they do not cultivate the gift of giving. Hence at times, Sepia's purse would be long empty before the giving-thought would wake in the mind of Hesper. When it woke, it was gracious and free.

Had Sepia ventured to run up bills with the tradespeople, Hesper would have taken it as a thing of course, and settled them with her own. But Sepia had a certain pride in spending only what was given her. And she saw reason to avoid any appearance of taking advantage or liberties, for with keen instinct from his first visits to Durnmelling, she had been aware that Mr. Redmain did not like her. Thus she had to run no risks that might ripen his dislike to repugnance and lead him to try to turn her out.

She was right in believing that Mr. Redmain disliked her, but she was wrong in imagining that he had therefore any objection to her being, for the present, in the house. He certainly did not relish the idea of her continuing to be his wife's inseparable companion, but there would be time enough to get rid of her after he had found her out. For she had not long been one of his *family*, before he knew, with unerring insight, that she had to be found out, and was therefore an interesting subject for the exercise of his faculty of moral analysis. He was certain her history was composed mainly of secrets. As yet, however, he had discovered nothing. He said to himself that she was a bad lot, but what sort of a bad lot was not clear; he must discover how she played her life-game. She had a history, and he must know it. But till now Sepia had shown herself nothing more than any other worldly girl who knows "on which side her bread is buttered." The moment he had found, or believed he had found, what there was to know about her, he was sure to hate her heartily.

For some time after his marriage, he appeared at his wife's parties oftener than he otherwise would have done, just for the sake of keeping an eye on Sepia. But he had seen nothing, nor the shadow of anything—until one night, by the merest chance, happening to enter his wife's drawing room, he caught a peculiar glance between Sepia and a young man—not very young—who had just entered, and whom he had not seen before.

It may seem strange that with her unquestioned powers of fascination, Sepia had not yet married. But there was something about her that both drew and repelled men. Some felt strangely uncomfortable in her presence from the very first. Though no human eye is capable of reading here and there more than a scattered hint of the twilight of history, which is the aurora of prophecy, the soul may yet shudder with an instinctive foreboding it cannot explain, and feel the presence, without recognizing the nature, of the hostile.

Sepia's eyes were her great power. Their lightest glance was not a thing to be trifled with, and their gaze a thing hardly to be withstood. They were large, but no fool would be taken with mere size. They were as dark as ever eyes of woman, but not necessarily in darkness lay their peculiar witchery. If I go on to say they were luminous, plainly there the danger begins. Sepia's eyes, I confess, were not lords of the deepest light—for she was not true. But neither was there a surface light, generated of merely physical causes. Through them, concentrating her will upon their utterance, she could establish a psychical contact with almost any man she chose. Their power was an evil, selfish shadow of original, universal love. By them she could produce at once, in the man on whom she turned their play, a sense as it were of some primordial, fatal, affinity between her and him. Into those eyes she would call up her soul, and there make it sit, flashing light, in gleams and sparkles, invading with influence as irresistible as subtle the soul of the man she chose to assail, who, from that time on, for a season, if he were such as she took him for, scarcely had choice but be her slave. She seldom exerted their full force, however, without some further motive than mere desire to captivate. There are women who fly their falcons at any game, little birds and all; but Sepia did not so waste herself: her quarry must be worth the hunt.

In more than one other country, Sepia had found the men less shy of her than here, and she had almost begun to think that her style was not generally pleasing to English eyes. Whether this had anything to do with the fact that now in London she began to amuse herself with Tom Helmer, I cannot say with certainty. But almost if not quite the first time they met, that morning, namely, when first he called and they sat in the bay-window of the drawing room in Glammis Square, she brought her eyes to play upon him. And although he addressed *The Firefly* poem to Hesper in the hope of pleasing her, it was for the sake of Sepia chiefly that he desired the door of her house to be an open one to him. Whether at that time she knew he was a married man, it is hardly necessary to inquire, seeing it would have made no difference whatever to one like her, whose design was only to amuse herself with the youth, and possibly to make of him a screen. She went so far, however, as to allow him, when there was opportunity, to draw her into quiet corners, and even to linger when the other guests were gone, and he had had his full share of champagne.

Once, indeed, they remained together so long in the little conservatory, lighted only by a pale alabaster lamp, that she had to unbolt the door to let him out. This did not take place without coming to the knowledge of both Mr. and Mrs. Redmain, but the former was only afraid there was nothing in it, and was far from any wish to control her, and Sepia herself was the informant of the latter. To her she would make game of her foolish admirer, telling how, on this and that occasion, it was all she could do to get rid of him.

31 / Honor

Having now gained a partial insight into Letty's new position, Mary thought about what she could do to make life more of life to her. Not many knew better than she that the only true way to help a human heart is to lift it up. But she also knew that if we can not do a great thing, we must be ready to do the small. If we do not help in little things, how shall we be judged fit to help in greater? We must help where we can, that we may help where we cannot. The first and the only thing she could for a time think of was to secure for Letty, if possible, a share in her husband's pleasures.

Quietly, yet swiftly, a certain peaceful familiarity had established itself between Hesper and Mary, to which the perfect balance of the latter and her sense of the only true foundation of her position contributed far more than the undefined partiality of the former.

"Do you like Mr. Helmer, ma'am?" asked Mary one morning as she was brushing her hair.

"Very well. How do you know anything of him?"

"Not many people within ten miles of Testbridge do not know Mr. Helmer," answered Mary.

"Yes, yes, I remember," said Hesper. "He used to ride about on a long-legged horse and talked to anybody that would listen to him. But there was always something pleasing about him, and he is much improved. Do you know, he is considered really very clever?"

"I am not surprised," rejoined Mary. "He used to be rather foolish, and that is a sign of cleverness—at least many clever people are foolish, I think."

"*You* can't have had much opportunity for making such an observation, Mary!"

"Clever people think as much of themselves in the country as they do in London, and that is what makes them foolish," returned Mary. "But I used to think Mr. Helmer had very good points, and was worth doing something for—if one only knew what."

"He does not seem to want anything done for him," said Hesper.

"I know one thing *you* could do for him, and it would be no trouble," said Mary.

"I will do anything for anybody that is no trouble," answered Hesper. "I should like to know something that is no trouble."

"It is only, the next time you ask him to a gathering, to ask his wife," said Mary.

"He is married, then?" returned Hesper with indifference. "Is the woman presentable? Some shopkeeper's daughter, I suppose!"

Mary laughed.

"You don't imagine the son of a lawyer would be likely to marry a shopkeeper's daughter!" she said.

"Why not?" returned Hesper, with a look of non-intelligence.

"Because a professional man is so far above a tradesman."

"Oh," said Hesper. "—But he should have told me if he wanted to bring his wife with him. I don't care who she is, so long as she dresses decently and holds her tongue. What are you laughing at, Mary?"

Hesper called it laughing, but Mary was only smiling. "I can't help being amused," answered Mary, "that you should think it such an out-of-the-way thing to be a shopkeeper's daughter, and here am I all the time, feeling quite comfortable, and proud of the shopkeeper whose daughter I am."

"Oh, I beg your pardon," exclaimed Hesper, growing embarrassed, I almost believe for the first time in her life— "How cruel of me!" she went on. "But you see, I never think of you—when I am talking to you—as one of that class."

Mary laughed outright this time: she was amused, and thought it better to show it, for that would also show that she was not hurt.

"Surely, dear Mrs. Redmain," said Mary, "you cannot think the class to which I belong in itself so objectionable that it is rude to refer to it in my hearing."

"I am very sorry," repeated Hesper, but in a tone of some offense: it was one thing to confess a fault; another to be regarded as actually guilty of the fault. "Nothing was further from my intention than to offend you. I have no doubt that shopkeepers are a most respectable class in their way—"

"Excuse me, Mrs. Redmain," said Mary again, "but you quite mistake me. I am not in the least offended. I don't care what you think of the class. There are a great many shopkeepers who are anything but respectable—as bad, indeed, as any of the nobility."

"I was not thinking of morals," answered Hesper. "In that, I dare say, all classes are pretty much alike. But, of course, there are differences."

"Perhaps one of them is that in our class we make respectability more a question of the individual than you do in yours."

"That may be very true," returned Hesper. "So long as a man behaves himself, we ask no questions."

"Will you let me tell you how the thing looks to me?" said Mary.

"Certainly. You do not suppose I care for the opinions of the people about me. I too have my own way of looking at things."

So said Hesper. Yet it was just the opinions of the people about her that ruled all those of her actions that could be said to be ruled at all. No one boasts of freedom except the willing slave—the man so utterly a slave that he feels nothing irksome in his chains. Yet, perhaps, but for the opinions of those about her, Hesper would have been worse than she was.

"Am I right then in thinking," began Mary, "that people of your class care only that a man should wear the look of a gentleman, and carry himself like one?—that, whether his appearance be a reality or a mask, you do not care, so long as no mask is removed in your company?—that he may be the lowest of men, but, so long as other people receive him, you will, too, counting him good enough?"

Hesper held her peace. She had by this time learned some facts concerning the man she had married which, besides Mary's question, were embarrassing.

"It is interesting," she said at length, "to know how the different classes in a country regard each other." But she spoke wearily: it was interesting in the abstract, not interesting to her.

"The way to try a man," said Mary, "would be to turn him the other way, as I saw the gentleman who is taking your portrait do yesterday trying a frame—completely change his position and then see how much he continued to look a true man. He would show something of his real self then, I think. Make a nobleman a shopkeeper, for instance, and see what kind of a shopkeeper he made. If he showed himself just as honorable when a shopkeeper as he had seemed when a nobleman, there would be good reason for counting him an honorable man."

"What odd fancies you have, Mary!" said Hesper, yawning.

"I know my father would have been as honorable as a nobleman as he was when a shopkeeper," persisted Mary.

"That I can well believe—he was your father," said Hesper, kindly, meaning what she said so far as her poor understanding of the honorable reached.

"Would you mind telling me," asked Mary, "how you would define the difference between a nobleman and a shopkeeper?"

Hesper thought a little. The question to her was a stupid one. She had never had interest enough in humanity to care a straw what any shopkeeper ever thought or felt. Such people inhabited a region so far below her as to be practically out of her sight. They were not of her kind. It had never occurred to her that life must look to them much as it looked to her, that they too had feelings and would bleed if cut with a knife. But, although she was not interested, she peered about sleepily for an answer. Her thoughts, in a lazy fashion, tumbled in her, like waves without wind—which, indeed, was all the sort of thinking she knew. At last, with the decision of conscious superiority, and the judicial air afforded by the precision of utterance belonging to her class—a precision so strangely conjoined with the lack of truth and logic both—she said, in a tone that gave to the most insignificant childish issue the consequence of a judgment between contending sages: "The difference is that the nobleman is born to ease and dignity and affluence, and the shopkeeper to buy and sell for his living."

"Many a nobleman," suggested Mary, "buys and sells without the necessity of making a living."

"That is the difference," said Hesper.

"Then the nobleman buys and sells to make money, and the shopkeeper to make a living?"

"Yes," granted Hesper lazily.

"Which is the nobler end—to live, or to make money?"

But this question was too far beyond Hesper. She did not even choose to hear it.

"*And*," she said, resuming her definition instead, "the nobleman deals with great things, the shopkeeper with small."

"When things are finally settled," said Mary—

"Gracious, Mary!" cried Hesper, "what do you mean? I am afraid I have been harboring an awful radical!—a—what do they call it?—a communist!"

She would have ended the whole thing right there, for she was tired of it.

"Things will hardly remain forever just as they are at this moment," said Mary. "How could they, when from the very making of the world, they have been going on changing and changing, hardly ever even seeming to stand still?"

"You frighten me, Mary! You will do something terrible in my house, and I shall be blamed for it!" said Hesper, forcing a laugh.

She did in truth feel a little uncomfortable. The shadow of dismay, a formless apprehension overclouded her.

"When I tell you what I was really thinking of, you will not be alarmed at my opinions," said Mary, not laughing now, but smiling a deep, sweet smile. "I do not believe there ever will be any settlement of things but one. They cannot and must not stop changing, until the kingdom of heaven is come. Into that they must change, and rest."

"You are leaving politics for religion now, Mary. That is the one fault I have to find with you—you won't keep things in their own places! You are always mixing them up—like that Mrs.—what's her name?—who is determined to mix religion and love in her novels, though everybody tells her they have nothing to do with each other. It is so irreverent!"

"Is it irreverent to believe that God rules the world he made, and that he is bringing things to his own mind in it?"

"You can't persuade me religion means turning things upside down."

"It means a good deal more than people think. Did not our Lord say that many that are first shall be last, and the last first?"

"What has that to do with this nineteenth century?"

"Perhaps that the honorable shopkeeper and the mean nobleman will one day change places."

Oh, thought Hesper, *that is why the lower classes take so to religion!* But what she *said* was: "Oh, yes, I dare say! But everything will be so different that it won't mean anything. When we are all angels, nobody will care who is first and who is last. I'm sure, for one, it won't be anything to me."

Hesper was a tolerable attendant at church—I will not say whether high or low church, because that would make it seem that I care. When she went, she went to the Church of England, and that is all.

"In the kingdom of heaven," answered Mary, "things will always look to be exactly what they are. My father used to say people will grow their own dresses there, as surely as a leopard grows his spots. He had to do with dresses, you know, as a livelihood. There, not only will an honorable man look honorable, but a mean or less than honorable man must look just what he is, no matter what he may have been while he was here, no matter what sort of social clothes he wore to cover up the dishonorableness inside him. All our social clothes here will fall away there, and we will be left clothed only in our true selves, that which we really *are*."

"But how can you talk about the dishonorable people who will be there? Surely there will be no mean persons in heaven!"

"Then a good many won't be there who are called honorable here."

"Oh, I have no doubt there will be a good deal of allowance made for such people," said Hesper. "Society makes such demands!"

32 / The Party

When Letty received Mrs. Redmain's card inviting her with her husband to an evening party, it raised in her a bewildered flutter—of pleasure, of fear, of pride, of shyness, of dismay. How would she dare show her face in such a grand assembly? She would not know a bit how to behave herself. And it was impossible, for she had no dress fit to go anywhere! What would Tom say if she looked dowdy? He would be ashamed of her, and she dared not think what might come of it!

Not long after the postman came Mary, and a long talk followed. Letty was full of trembling delight, but Mary was a little anxious inside about how Tom would take it.

The first matter, however, was Letty's dress. She had no money, and seemed afraid to ask for any.

Their council of ways and means lasted a good while, including many digressions. At last, though somewhat unwillingly, Letty accepted Mary's proposal that a certain dress—indeed, Mary's best, but she did not say so—which she had hardly worn and was not likely to miss, should be made to fit Letty. It was a lovely black silk, the best her father had been able to choose for her the last time he was in London. A little pang did shoot through her heart at the thought of parting with it, but she had too much of that father in her not to know that the greatest honor that can be shown any *thing* is to use it to serve a *person*, that the dearest gift of love, withheld from human necessity, is handed over to the moth and the rust. But little idea had Letty, much as she appreciated her kindness, what a sacrifice Mary was making for her that she might look her own sweet self, and worthy of her renowned Tom!

When Tom came home that night, however, the look of the world and all that is in it changed quickly for Letty. He arrived in great good humor, for somebody had been praising his verses, and the joy of the praise overflowed on his wife. But when, pleased as any little girl with the prospect of a party and a new dress, she told him, with gleeful gratitude, of the invitation and the heavenly kindness that had made it possible for her to accept it, the countenance of the great man changed.

He immediately rejected the idea of her going with him to any gathering of his grand friends—objected most of all to her going to Mrs. Redmain's. Alas! he had begun to allow to himself that he had married in too great haste—and beneath him. Wherever he went, his wife could be no credit to

180

him, and her presence would take from him all sense of liberty! Not choosing, however, to acknowledge either of these objections, and not willing to appear selfish in the eyes of the woman who had given herself to him, he put everything on another ground of impossibility. Controlling his irritation for the moment, he set forth with lordly kindness that it was absolutely out of the question for him to accept such an offer as Mary's. Could she for a moment imagine, he said, that he would degrade himself by taking his wife out in a dress that was not her own?

Here Letty interrupted him.

"Mary has given me the dress," she sobbed, "—for my very own."

"A secondhand dress! A dress that has been worn!" cried Tom. "How could you dream of insulting me so? The thing is absolutely impossible. Why, Letty, just think!—there should I be, going about as if the house were my own, and there would my wife be in the next room, or perhaps at my elbow, dressed in a cast-off from the lady's-maid of the house! It won't bear thinking of!"

"It's not a cast-off," sobbed Letty, laying hold of the one fact within her reach; "it's a beautiful black silk!"

"It matters not a straw what it is," persisted Tom, adding humbug to cruelty. "You would be nothing but a sham!—a live dishonesty! A jackdaw in peacock's feathers!—I am sorry, Letty, that your own sense of truth and uprightness should not prevent even the passing desire to act out such a lie. I have been taking too much for granted with you. I must bring you no more novels. A volume or two of Carlyle is what *you* need."

This was too much. To lose her novels and her new dress together, and be threatened with nasty moral medicine besides in the form of Carlyle's stern books, was bad enough; but to be so reproved by her husband was more than she could bear. If she was a silly and ignorant creature, she had the heart of a woman-child; and that precious thing in the sight of God, wounded and bruised by the husband in whom lay all her pride, went on beating laboriously for him only. She did not blame him. Anything was better than that.

She wept and wailed like a sick child, until at length the hard heart of selfish Tom was touched, and he sought, after the fashion of a foolish mother, to read the inconsolable a lesson of wisdom. But the truer a heart, the harder it is to console with the false. By and by, however, sleep, the truest of things, did for her what even the blandishments of her husband could not.

When she woke in the morning, he was gone. He had thought of an emendation in a poem that had been type-set the day before, and made haste to the office, lest it should be printed without the precious betterment.

Mary came before noon, and found sadness where she had left joy.

When she had heard as much as Letty thought proper to tell her, she was filled with indignation, and her first thought was to arrange for the tyrant's own exclusion from the paradise whose gates he closed against his wife. But second thoughts are sometimes best, and the next moment she saw not only that punishment did not belong to her, but that the weight of it would fall on Letty. The only thing she could think of to comfort her was to ask her to spend the same evening with her in her room. The proposal brightened Letty up at once. Some time or other in the course of the evening she would, she imagined, see, or at least catch a glimpse of Tom in his glory!

The evening came, and with beating heart Letty went up the back stairs to Mary's room. She was dressing her mistress, but did not keep her waiting long. She had provided tea beforehand, and when Mrs. Redmain had gone down, the two friends had a pleasant time together. Mary took Letty to show her many splendors, which moved no envy in her simple heart, yet made her sad thinking of Tom. As she passed to the drawing room, Sepia looked in and saw them together.

But as the company kept arriving, Letty grew very restless. She could not talk of anything for two minutes without getting up and creeping out of the room and halfway down the stair to look over the banister-rail for a bird's eye peep at a portion of the great landing, where indeed she caught many a glimpse of beauty and state, but never a glimpse of her Tom. What she saw made her feel as if her idol were miles away, and she could never be near him again.

Worn out at last, and thoroughly disappointed, she wanted to go home. It was by then past midnight. Mary went with her, and saw her safely into bed before she left her.

On her return, as she went up to her own room, she saw, through the door by which the gardener entered the conservatory, Sepia standing there, and Tom, with flushed face, talking to her eagerly.

Letty cried herself to sleep, and dreamed that Tom had disowned her before a great company of grand ladies, who mocked her from their sight.

Tom came home while she slept, and in the morning was cross and miserable—in part because he had been so abominably selfish to her. But the moment that, half-frightened, half-hopeful, she told him where she was the night before, he broke into the worst anger he had ever yet shown her. His shameful pride could not imagine the idea that, where he was a guest, his wife was being entertained by one of the domestics!

"How dare you be guilty of such a disgraceful thing!" he cried.

"Oh, don't, Tom—dear Tom!" pleaded Letty in terror. "It was you I wanted to see—not the great people, Tom! I don't care if I never see one of them again."

"Why should you ever see one of them again. I should like to know!

What are they to you, or you to them?"

"But you know I was asked to go, Tom."

"That's quite another thing! A man has to cultivate connections his wife need not know anything about. It is one of the necessities of my position."

Letty supposed it all truer than it was either intelligible or pleasant, and said no more. She merely let poor, self-abused, fine-fellow Tom scold and argue and reason away till he was tired. She was not sullen, but bewildered and worn out. He got up and left her without a word.

Even at the risk of hurt to his dignity, of which there was no danger from the presence of his sweet, modest little wife in the best of company, it would have been well for Tom to have allowed Letty the pleasure within her reach. It might have protected him from worse than he imagined himself susceptible to. For that night Sepia's artillery played on him ruthlessly. It may have been merely for her amusement—time, you see, moves so slowly with such as have no necessities they must themselves supply, and recognize no duties they must perform. Without these two main pillars of life, necessity and duty, how shall the temple stand, when the huge, weary Samson comes tugging at it? The wonder is that there is not a great deal more wickedness in the world. For listlessness and boredom and nothing-to-doness are the best of soils for the breeding of the worms that never stop gnawing; and parents especially, who would keep their children from becoming the future Toms and Sepias of the world, would do well to provide them with plenty of material to make the pillars of their temples strong, in the form of necessities and duties.

Anyhow, Sepia had flashed on Tom. The tinder of Tom's heart had responded, and any day when Sepia chose, she might blow up a wicked as well as a foolish flame. And if it should suit her purpose, Sepia was not one to hesitate in the use of the fire-fan. All the way home her eyes haunted him, and it is a more dreadful thing than most are aware of to be haunted by anything, good or bad, except the being who is out of life. And those eyes, though not good, were beautiful. Evil, it is true, has neither part nor lot in beauty; it is absolutely hostile to it, and will at last destroy it utterly. But the process is a long one, so long that many imagine badness and beauty vitally associable. Tom yielded to the haunting, and it was in part the fault of those eyes that he used such hard words on his wife in the morning. Wives often suffer sorely for discomforts and wrongs in their husbands of which they know nothing. But the thing will be set right one day, and in a better fashion than if all the women's-rights committees in the world had their will of the matter.

About this time in *The Firefly* it appeared that Twilight had given place to Night. The first of many verses began to show themselves in which

Twilight, or Hesper, or Vesper, or the Evening Star, was no more mentioned, but only and always Nox, or Hecate, or the dark Diana. *Tenebrious* was a great word with Tom about this time. He was also very fond of the word *interlunar*. I will not trouble my reader with any specimen of the outcome of Tom's new inspiration, partly for this reason, that the verses not infrequently came so near being good, nay, sometimes were really so good that I do not choose to set them down here where I could hardly keep from treating them with a mockery they do not in themselves deserve. He did not direct his wife's attention to them, nor did he compose them at home or at the office.

Of all that read them, and here was a Nemesis awful in its poetic justice, there was not one *less* moved by them than she who had inspired them. It is true, she saw in them a reflex of her own power—and that pleased her. But it did not move her. She took the devotion and pocketed it, as a greedy boy might an orange or a prized marble. The verses in which Tom delighted were but the merest noise in the ears of the lady to whom of all he would have had them acceptable. One momentary revelation as to how she regarded them would have been enough to release him from his foolish enthrallment. Indignation, chagrin, and mortification would have soon been the death of such poor love as Tom's selfish infatuation.

Mary and Sepia were on terms of politeness—of readiness to help on the one side, and condescension upon the other. Sepia would have condescended to the Mother Mary. The pure human was an idea beyond her, as beyond most people. They have not enough religion toward God to know there is such a thing as religion toward their neighbor.

But Sepia never made an enemy if she could help it. She could not afford the luxury of hating—openly, at least. But I imagine she would have hated Mary heartily could she have seen the way she regarded her—the look of pitiful love, of compassionate and waiting helpfulness which her soul would now and then cast upon her. Of all things she would have resented pity; but she took Mary's readiness to help for servility—and naturally, seeing in herself that willingness came from nothing else, though she called it prudence and necessity, she thus saw no shame because of it. Her children justify the heavenly wisdom, but the worldly wisdom justifies her children. Mary could not but feel how Sepia regarded her service. But service, to be true, must be divine, that is, to the just and the unjust together, like the sun and the rain.

Between Sepia and Mr. Redmain continued a distance too great for either difference or misunderstanding. They met with a cold good morning, and parted without any good night. Their few words were polite, and their demeanor was civil. At the breakfast table, Sepia would silently pass things to Mr. Redmain. He would thank her, but never trouble himself to do much

for her. His attentions, indeed, were seldom wasted at home. But he was
not often rude to anybody except his wife and his servant, other than when
he was ill.

It was a long time before Mr. Redmain began to feel any interest in
Mary. He knew nothing of her except that she was a nice-looking maid his
wife had gotten—rather a prim-looking face, he would have said, had he
had occasion to describe her. What Mary knew of him was merely the
reflection of him in the mind of his wife. But the first time she saw him,
she felt she would rather not have to speak to him.

33 / A New Life

Mary went to see Letty as often as she could. But she had scarcely a chance of seeing Tom; either he was not up, or had gone—to the office, Letty supposed. She had no more idea of where the office was, or of the other places haunted by Tom, than he himself had of what spirit he was of.

One day, when Mary could not help remarking upon her pale, weary looks, Letty burst into tears, and confided to her a secret of which she was not the less proud that it caused her anxiety and fear. As soon as she began to talk about it, the joy of its hope began to gain the upper hand, and before Mary left her she was filled with great happiness at the prospects. But to any thoughtful heart it must be sad to think what a little time the joy of so many mothers lasts—not because their babies die, but because they live. Mary's mournfulness was caused by the fear that the splendid dawn of mother-hope would soon be swallowed in dismal clouds of father-fault. For mothers and wives there is no redemption, no unchaining of love, except by the coming of the kingdom—*in themselves*. Oh, why do not mothers, sore-hearted mothers at least, if none else on the face of the earth, rush to the feet of the Son of Mary!

Yet every birth is but another link in the golden chain by which the world shall be lifted to the feet of God. It is only by the birth of new children, ever fresh material for the creative Spirit of the Son of Man to work upon, that the world can finally be redeemed.

Letty had no *ideas* about children, only the usual instincts of appropriation and indulgence. Mary had a few, for she recalled with delight some of her father's ways with herself. Him she knew as, next to God, the source of her life, so well had he fulfilled that first duty of all parents—the transmission of life. About such things she tried to talk to Letty, but soon perceived that not a particle of her thought found its way into Letty's mind. She cared nothing for any duty concerned—only for the joy of being a mother.

She grew paler yet and thinner. Dark hollows came about her eyes; she was parting with her life to give it to her child. She lost the girlish gaiety Tom used to admire, and the something more lovely that was taking its place, he was not capable of seeing. He gave her less and less of his company. His countenance did not shine upon her. In her heart she grew aware that she feared him, and ever as she shrunk, he withdrew. Had it not now been for Mary, she would likely have died. She did all for her that friend could. As often as she seemed able, she would take her for a drive, or on the river, that the wind, like a sensible presence of God, might blow upon her, and give her fresh life to take home with her. So little progress did she make with Hesper, that she could not help thinking it must have been for Letty's sake she was allowed to go to London.

Mr. and Mrs. Redmain went to Durnmelling for a time, but Mary begged Hesper to leave her behind. She told her the reason, without mentioning the name of the friend she desired to tend. Hesper shrugged her shoulders, as much as to say she wondered about her taste in companions. Inside, Hesper did not believe such to really be the cause of Mary's wish. She concluded that she did not want to show herself in Testbridge in her new position as a maid. But as she was afraid of losing her if she opposed her, she let her have her way. Nor, indeed, was she so necessary at Durnmelling where there were few visitors and comparatively little social activity. Jemima was enough; she had now and then been called by Mary to her aid, had proved herself handy and capable, and had learned a great deal.

So all through the hottest of the late summer and autumn weather, Mary remained in London, where every street seemed like the floor of a baker's oven, and, for all the life with which the city swarmed, the little winds that wandered through it seemed to have lost their vitality. How she longed for the fields and the woods, where the very essence of life seemed to dwell in the atmosphere even when stillest, and the joy that came pouring from the throats of the birds seemed to flow first from her own soul into them. The very streets and lanes of Testbridge looked like paradise to Mary in London. But she never wished herself in the shop again, although almost every night she dreamed of the glad old time when her father was in it with her, and when, although they might not speak from morning to night, their souls kept talking across crowd and counters, and each was always aware of the other's supporting presence.

Longing, however, is not necessarily pain—it may, indeed, be intense bliss. And if Mary longed for the freedom of the country, it was not to be miserable that she could not have it. Her mere thought of it was to her a greater delight than the presence of all its joys is to many who desire them the most. That such things, and the possibility of such sensations from them, should be in the world, was enough to make Mary jubilant. But then, she was at peace with her conscience, and had her heart full of loving duty. Besides, an active patience is a heavenly power. Mary could not only walk along a pavement dry and lifeless as the Sahara, enjoying the summer that brooded all about and beyond the city, but she bore the refreshment of blowing winds and running waters into Letty's hot room, with the clanging street in front and the little yard behind, where, from a cord stretched across between the walls, hung a few pieces of poorly-washed linen, motionless in the glare, with two plump sparrows picking up crumbs in their shadow. Into this live death Mary would carry a tone of breeze, and sailing cloud, and swaying tree-top. In her the life was so concentrated and active that she was capable of communicating life—the highest of human endowments.

One evening, as Letty was telling her how the dressmaker upstairs had been ill for some time, and Mary was feeling reproachful that she had not told her before that she might have seen what could be done for her, they became aware, it seemed gradually, of the softest, sweetest, faintest tone of music coming from somewhere. Mary went to the window: there was nothing capable of music within sight. It came again; and intermittingly came and went several times. For a while they would hear nothing at all, and then again the most delicate of tones would creep into their ears, bringing with it more, it seemed to Mary in the surprise of its sweetness, than she could have believed a single tone capable of carrying. Once or twice a few consecutive sounds made a division strangely sweet, and then again, for a time, nothing would reach them but a note here and a note there of what she tried to imagine a wonderful melody. The visitation lasted for about an hour, then ceased. Letty went to bed, and all night long dreamed she heard the angels calling her. She woke weeping that her time was come so early, while as yet she had tasted so little of the pleasure of life. But the truth was, she had as yet, poor child, got so little of the good of life, that it was not at all time for her to go.

When her time drew near, Tom condescended—unwillingly, I am sorry to say, for he did not take the trouble to understand her feelings—to leave word where he might be found if he should be wanted. Even this assuagement of her fears Letty had to plead for. Mary's being so much with her was to him reason, and he made it an excuse, for his absence; he had begun to dread Mary. And when at length he was sent for, he showed no great haste to come, and all was well over when he arrived. But he was a little touched when, drawing his face down to Letty's, she feebly whispered, "He's as like to you, Tom, as ever small thing was to great!" She saw the slight emotion, and fell asleep comforted.

It was night when she awoke. Mary was sitting by her.

"Oh, Mary!" she cried, "the angels have been calling me again. Did you hear them?"

"No," answered Mary. "Why do you think the angels should call you? Do you suppose them desirous of your company?"

"They do call people," returned Letty, "and I don't know why they might not call me. I'm not such a very wicked person."

Mary's heart smote her; she was refusing Letty the time God was giving her.

She could not wake her up, and, while God was waking her, she was impatient.

"I heard the call too, Letty," she said. "But it was not the angels. It was the same instrument we heard the other night. Who can there be in the house to play like that? It was clearer this time. I thought I could listen to it a whole year."

"Why didn't you wake me?" said Letty.

"Because the more sleep you get the better. And the doctor says I mustn't let you talk. I will get you something, and then you must go to sleep again."

Tom did not appear any more that night. And if they had wanted him now, they would not have known where to find him. He was about nothing very bad—only drinking with some friends—such friends as he did not even care to tell that he had a son.

He was ashamed of being in London at this time of the year when no social events were going on, and, but that he had not money enough to go anywhere except to his mother's, he would have gone and left Letty to shift for herself.

He was pleased with his child, and would occasionally take him for a few moments. But when he cried, he was cross with him, and showed himself the unreasonable baby of the two.

The angels did not want Letty just yet, and she slowly recovered.

For Mary it was a peaceful time. She was able to read a good deal, and, although there were no books in Mr. Redmain's house, she generally succeeded in getting such as she wanted. She was also able to practice as much as she pleased, for now the grand piano was entirely at her service, and she took the opportunity of having a lesson every day.

34 / The Musician

One evening, soon after the baby's arrival, as Mary sat with him in her lap, the sweet tones they had heard twice before came creeping into her ears so gently that she seemed to be aware of their presence only after they had been for some time coming and going. She laid the baby down, stole from the room, and listened on the landing. Certainly the sounds were born in the house, but whether they came from below or above she could not tell. She went first down the stair, and then up, and soon satisfied herself that they came from above, and therefore ventured a little farther up the stair.

She had already been to see the dressmaker, whom she had come to know through Letty, had found her far from well, and had done what she could for her. But she was in no financial need, and of more than ordinary independence—a Yorkshire woman, about forty years of age, delicate, but of great patience and courage. She was a plain, fair, freckled woman, with a belief in religion rather in God. Very strict, therefore, in her observances, she thought a good deal more of the Sabbath than of man, a great deal more of the Bible than of the truth, and ten times more of her creed than of the will of God. Of course, if she had heard anyone utter such words as I have just written, she would have said he was an atheist.

She was a worthy creature, notwithstanding. As has already been shown with respect to her friendship with Letty, she was only too willing to lend a helping hand when it lay within her power. Only she was very unpleasant if one happened to step on the toes of a pet ignorance. Mary soon discovered that there was no profit in talking with her on the subjects she loved the most, especially any matter of doctrine. Plainly she knew little about them, except secondhand—that is, through the forms of other minds than her own. Such people seem intended for the special furtherance of the saints in patience; being utterly unassailable by reason, they are especially trying to those who desire to stand on brotherly terms with all men, and so are the more sensitive to the rudeness that always goes with moral stupidity; intellectual stupidity may coexist with the loveliness of an angel.

As Mary climbed the stairs the music ceased. Hoping Miss Byrom would be able to enlighten her concerning its source, she continued on, and knocked at her door. A voice invited her to enter.

Ann sat near the window, for, although it was quite dusk, a little use might yet be made of the lingering ghost of the daylight. About all Mary

190

could see of her was the reflection from the round eyes of a pair of horn spectacles.

"How do you do, Miss Byrom?" she said.

"Not at all well," answered Ann.

"Is there anything I can do for you?" asked Mary.

"We are to owe no man anything but love, the apostle tells us."

Before Mary could answer she was startled by a sound. She turned quickly, but before she could see anything through the darkness, the softest of violin tones came again through the air close beside her, and then she saw, seated on the corner of Ann's bed, the figure of a man—young or old, she could not tell. His bow was wandering slowly about over the strings of his violin. "I came," said Mary, turning again to Ann, "hoping you might be able to tell me where the sweet sounds came from which we have heard now two or three times. But I had no idea there was anyone in the room besides yourself. They come at intervals a great deal too long," she added, turning toward the figure in the darkness.

"I am afraid my ear is out sometimes," said the man, mistaking her remark. "I suppose it comes of the anvil."

The voice was manly, though gentle, and gave an impression of utter directness and simplicity. It was Mary's turn, however, not to understand, and she made no answer.

"I am very sorry," the musician went on, "if I annoyed you, miss."

Mary began to assure him that the fact was quite the other way around, when Ann prevented her.

"I told you so!" she said. "You make an idol of your foolish playing, but other people take it only for the nuisance it is."

"Indeed, you were never more mistaken," said Mary. "Both Mrs. Helmer and myself are charmed with the little that reaches us."

"Now don't go flattering his folly, miss," cried Ann, "or before long not a word I say will be of the smallest use."

"If your words are not wise," said Mary, "the less he heeds them the better."

"It's hardly wise, to my judgment, miss, to make a man think himself something when he is nothing. It's quite enough a man should deceive his own self, without another come to help him."

"To speak the truth is not to deceive," replied Mary. "I have some knowledge of music, and I say only what is true."

"What good can it be spending his time scraping horse-hair against cat-gut?"

"They must think some good in it up in heaven," said Mary, "or they wouldn't have so much of it there."

"There's no fiddles in heaven," said Ann with indignation. "They've nothing there but harps and trumpets."

Mary turned to the man who had not said another word.

"Would you mind coming downstairs with me," she said, "and playing a little, very softly, to my friend? She has a little baby, and is not strong. It would do her good."

"She'd do better to read her Bible," said Ann, who was lighting a candle in the dark.

"She does read her Bible," returned Mary, "and a little music would perhaps help her to get more out of it."

"There, Ann!" cried the player.

The woman replied with a scornful grunt.

"Two fools don't make a wise man, however much they may agree," she said.

But Mary had once more turned toward the musician, and in the light of the candle was met by a pair of black eyes, keen yet soft, looking out from under an overhanging ridge of forehead. The rest of the face was in shadow, but she could see by the whiteness, through a beard that clouded all the lower part of it, that he was smiling to himself. Mary had said what pleased him, and his eyes sought her face, and seemed to rest on it with a kind of trust, and a look as if he was ready to do whatever she might ask of him.

"You will come?" said Mary.

"Yes, miss, certainly," he replied, and flashed a full smile that rested upon Ann, and seemed to say he knew her not so hard as she looked.

He rose, tucked his violin under his arm, and showed himself ready to follow.

"Good night, Miss Byrom," said Mary.

"Good night, miss," returned Ann grimly. "I'm sorry for you both, miss, but until the spirit is poured out from on high, it's nothing but a stumbling in the dark."

Her last utterance was a reflection rather than a remark.

Mary made no reply. She did not care about having the last word. She ran down the stair, and at the bottom stood waiting for her new acquaintance, who descended more slowly, careful to make no noise.

By the gaslight that burned on the landing, Mary could see a little more of what the man was like. He was powerfully built, rather over middle height, and about the age of thirty. His complexion was dark, and the hand that held the bow was dirty. He bore himself well, but a little stiffly, with a care over his violin like that of a man carrying a baby. He was decidedly handsome, in a rugged way—mouth and chin but hinted at through a thick beard of darkest brown.

"Come this way," said Mary, leading him into Letty's parlor. "I will tell my friend you have come. Her room opens off this and she will hear you delightfully. Please, take a seat."

"Thank you, miss," said the man, but remained standing.

"I have caught the bird, Letty," said Mary, loud enough for him to hear, "and he has come to sing a little to you—if you feel strong enough for it."

"It will do me good," said Letty. "How kind of him!"

The man was already tuning his violin when Mary came back out from the bedroom, and sat down on the sofa. The instant he had gotten it to his mind, he turned, and, going to the farthest corner of the room, closed his eyes tight and began to play.

How shall I describe what followed? If you could imagine some music-loving sylph attempting to guide the wind among the strings of an Aeolian harp, every now and then succeeding, and then again for a while the wind having its own way, you will gain, I think, something like a dream-notion of the man's playing. Mary tried hard to get hold of some clue to the combinations and sequences, but the motive of them she could not find. Whatever their source, there was, either in the composition itself or in his mode of playing, not a little of the lawless. Yet every now and then would come a passage of exquisite melody. But ever as she sought to get some insight into the movement of the man's mind, still would she be swept away on the storm of some change, seeming of mood incongruous.

At length came a little pause. He wiped his forehead with a blue cotton handkerchief, and seemed ready to begin again. But Mary interrupted him: "Will you please tell me whose music you have been playing?"

He opened his eyes, which had remained closed, and, with a smile that seemed especially sweet because of the rugged face out of which it came, answered: "It's nobody's, miss."

"Do you mean you have been making all this up as you go?"

"Yes, miss."

"You have no notes, you learned it from nowhere?"

"I couldn't read them if I had notes put in front of me," he answered.

"Do you ever play the same melody twice?"

"Oh yes, miss."

"Then what an ear and what a memory you must have!"

"Not being able to read, and seldom hearing any music I care for, I'm forced to be content with what runs out at my fingers when I shut my eyes. It all comes of shutting my eyes. I couldn't play a thing but for that. It's wonderful what comes of shutting your eyes. Did you ever try it, miss?"

Mary was so astonished both by what he said and the simplicity with which he said it, that she was silent, and the man, after a moment's returning, began to play again. Then Mary gathered all her powers, and braced her attention to the tightest—but at first with no better success.

And indeed, that was not the way to understand. It seems to me, at least in my great ignorance, that one cannot understand music unless he is humble toward it, and consents, if need be, not to understand. When one is quiet, submissive, and opens the ears of the mind and demands nothing more than the hearing—when the rising waters of question retire to their bed and individuality is still, then the dews and rains of music, finding the way clear for them, soak and sink through the sands of the mind, down, far down, below the thinking-place, down to the region of music, which is the hidden workshop of the soul, the place where lies ready the divine material for man to become the creative reflection of his Maker.

Weary at last with vain effort, Mary stopped trying to understand the structure of the music, and in a little while was herself being molded by it. It awoke pictures in her mind, not thoughts.

First there was a crowd in slow, then rapid movement. Cries and entreaties arose. Hurried motions came, disruption, and running feet. A pause followed. Then woke a lively melody, changing to the prayer of some soul too grateful to find words. Next came a bar or two of what seemed calm, lovely speech, then a few slowly delivered chords, and all was still.

She came to herself, and then first knew that, like sleep, the music had seized her unawares, and she had been understanding, or at least enjoying without knowing it. The man was approaching her from his dark corner. His face was shining, but plainly he did not intend more music, for his violin was already under his arm. He made her a little awkward bow—not much more than a nod, and still Mary was unable to speak. For Letty, she was fast asleep.

From the top of the stair came the voice of Ann, grating against the peaceful memory of the music: "Here's your hat, Joe. I knew you'd be going when you played that last one. I knew you'd forget your hat."

Mary heard the hat come tumbling down the stair.

"Thank you, Ann," returned Joe. "Yes, I'm going. The ladies don't care much for my music. Nobody does but myself. But then, it's good enough for me."

The last two sentences were spoken to himself, and quietly. But Mary heard them, for he stood with the handle of the door in his hand. He closed it, picked up his hat, and went softly down the stair.

The spell was broken, and Mary darted to the door. But, just as she opened it, the outer door closed behind the strange musician, and she had not even learned his name.

35 / A Change

As soon as Letty had strength enough to attend to her baby without help, to the surprise of her mistress and the destruction of her theory concerning her stay in London, Mary presented herself at Durnmelling, found that she was more welcome than looked for, and that very day resumed her duties about Hesper.

It was with curiously mingled feelings that she gazed from her window out onto the chimneys of Thornwick. How much had changed in her life since, in the summer-seat at the end of the hedge of yew trees, Mr. Wardour first opened to her the door of literature! It was now autumn and the woods, to get young again, were dying their yearly death. For the moment she felt as if she too had begun to grow old. Ministration had tired her a little— but, oh! how different its weariness from that which came from other forms of labor. She regretted nothing that had come, nothing that had gone. She believed more and more that not anything worth having is ever lost; that even the most evanescent shades of feeling are safe for those who grow after their true nature, toward that for which they were made—in other and higher words, after the will of God.

It was with some sadness that, one day, on the footpath to Testbridge, she met Mr. Wardour, and, looking at her, and plainly recognizing her, he passed without a greeting. Like a sudden wave the blood rose to her face, and then sank to the depths of her heart; and from somewhere came the conviction that one day the destiny of Godfrey Wardour would be in her hands. He had done a great deal for her intellectually, and when that day was come, he should not find her fail him.

She was then on her way to the shop. She did not at all relish entering it, but, as she had a large money-interest in the business, she said to herself that she ought at least to pay the place a visit. When she entered, Turnbull did not at first recognize her, and, taking her for a customer, blossomed into repulsive suavity. The change that came over his countenance when he gradually began to recognize her was a shadow of such mingled and conflicting shades that she felt there was something peculiar in it which she must attempt to analyze. It remained hardly a moment to encounter question, but was almost immediately replaced with a politeness evidently false. Then, for the first time, she began to be aware of distrusting the man.

Asking a few questions about the business, to which he gave satisfactory answers, she kept looking about the shop, unable to account for the impression the look of it made upon her. Either her eyes had formed for themselves another scale and could no more rightly judge between past or present, or the look of the place was actually different. Was there less in it? she asked herself—or was it only not so well kept as when she left it? She could not tell. Neither could she understand the profound but distant consideration with which Mr. Turnbull endeavored to behave to her, treating her like a stranger to whom he must, against his inclination, show all possible respect. She bought a pair of gloves of the young woman who seemed to have taken her place, paid for them, and left the shop without speaking to anyone else. All the time, George was standing behind the opposite counter staring at her, but to her relief showed no other sign of recognition.

Beenie was still in Testbridge, in a cottage of her own. But Mary felt she must think her observations over before visiting her. Therefore, she left the town and walked homeward.

What did it all mean? She knew very well that they must look down on her ten times more than ever, because of the menial position in which she had placed herself. But if that were so, why did the man behave so seemingly respectfully? That did not use to be Mr. Turnbull's way with someone he looked down upon. And then, what did the shadow that passed over his face prior to this behavior mean? She had never seen that look upon him!

Then there was the impression the shop made on her. Somehow it seemed to have acquired a shabby look. Could it be possible anything was going wrong with the business? Her father had always spoken with great respect of Mr. Turnbull's business faculties, but she knew he had never troubled himself to look into the books or know how they stood with the bank. She also knew that Mr. Turnbull was greedy after money, and that his wife was ambitious and hated the business.

Halfway back, she turned and walked back to the town, and went for a visit with Beenie.

The old woman was naturally a gossip. Thus Mary was hardly seated before she began to pour out the talk of the town, in which presently came certain rumors concerning Mr. Turnbull—mainly hints at speculation and loss.

The result was that Mary went from Beenie to the lawyer in whose care her father had left his affairs. He was an old man, and had been ill; had no suspicion of anything being wrong, but would look into the matter at once. She went home, and tried to think about it no more.

She had been at Durnmelling but a few days when Mr. Redmain, wishing to see how things were on his estate in Cornwall and making up his mind to run down, carelessly asked his wife if she would accompany him. It would be only for a few days, he said, and a breeze or two from the

Atlantic would improve her complexion. He was always more polite in the company of Lady Margaret, who continued to show him the kindness no one else dared or was inclined to do.

Mary was delighted with the proposal, and delighted to be able to see more of her country. She had traveled very little, but was capable of gathering ten times more from a journey to Cornwall than most travelers from one through Switzerland itself. The place to which they went was lonely and lovely, and Mary enjoyed it unspeakably for the first few days.

But then suddenly Mr. Redmain was taken ill. For some reason or other, he had sent his man to London, and the only other they had with them besides the coachman was useless in such a need, while the housekeeper who lived at the place was nearly decrepit. Thus, of the entire household Mary alone was capable of fit attendance in the sickroom. Hesper shrunk almost with horror, certainly with disgust, from the idea of having anything to do with her husband as an invalid. When she had the choice of her company, she said, she would not choose his. Mr. Redmain's man Mewks was sent for at once, but did not arrive before the patient had had some experience of Mary's tendance. The attack was a long and severe one, delaying for many weeks their return to London, where Mr. Redmain declared he positively had to be, no matter what the risk, before the end of November.

36 / Lydgate Street

Letty's whole life was now gathered about her baby boy, and she thought comparatively little about Tom. And Tom thought so little about her that he did not perceive the difference.

When he came home he was always in a hurry to be gone again. He always had something important to do, but it never showed itself to Letty in the shape of money. He gave her a little now and then, of course, and she made it go incredibly far, but it was ever with more of a grudge that he gave it.

Sepia's influence over him was scarcely less now that she was gone north with Mary and Hesper. But if she cared for him at all, it was mainly that, being now a little stale-hearted, his devotion reminded her pleasurably of a time when other passions than those of self-preservation were strongest in her. On Tom's part, he had begun by now to consider life a rather poor affair. Across the cloud of this death gleamed the flashing of Sepia's eyes, or the softly infolding dawn of her smile, but only the next hour, nay, the next moment, to leave all darker than before. But Sepia was prudent for herself, and knew, none better, what she was about, so far as the near future was concerned. Therefore, she held him at arm's length, where Tom basked in a light that was of hell—for what is a hell, or a woman like Sepia, but an inverted creation?

His nature, in consequence, was in all directions dissolving. He drank more and more strong drink, fitting fuel to such his passion, and Sepia liked to see him approach with his eyes blazing. There are not many women like her; she is a rare type—but not, therefore, to be passed over in silence. It is little consolation that the man-eating tiger is a rare animal, if one of them be actually on the path. And to the philosopher a possibility is a fact. But the true value of the study of abnormal development is that it is in and through studying such persons as Sepia that we get glimpses, down the gulf of the moral volcano, to the infernal possibilities of the human—the lawless rot of that which, in its *attainable* idea, is nothing less than divine, imagined, foreseen, cherished, and labored for by the Father of the human. Such inverted possibility, the infernal possibility, I mean, lies latent in every one of us, and, except we stir ourselves up to the right, will gradually, from a possibility, become an energy. The wise man dares not yield to a temptation, were it only for the terror that, if he does, he will yield the more readily again. The commonplace critic, who recognizes life solely upon

198

his own conscious level, mocks equally at the ideal and its opposite, incapable of recognizing the art of Shakespeare himself as true to the human nature that will not be human.

I have said that Letty did her best with what money Tom gave her. But when she came to find that he had not paid the lodging's rent for two months, that the payment of various things he had told her to order and he would see to had been neglected, and that the tradespeople were getting persistent in their applications; that when she mentioned to him anything of the sort, he treated it as a matter of no consequence that he would quickly set right, and then another time ranted on about the unreasonableness of the impertinent creditor whom he would punish by making him wait his time—then finally her heart began to sink within her. As sparing as she had been from the first, she was more sparing than ever now. She even upon occasion went without proper food, grew very thin, and, indeed, if she had not been of the healthiest, could not have stood her own treatment many weeks.

Her baby soon began to show signs of suffering, but this did not make her alter her methods of conservation, or drive her to appeal to Tom. She was ignorant of the simplest things a mother needs to know, and never imagined her abstinence could hurt her baby. So long as she went on nursing him, it was all the same, she thought. He cried so much that Tom made it a reason with himself, and indeed gave it as one to Letty, for not coming home at night. The child would not let him sleep; and how was he to do his work if he didn't have his night's rest? It hardly mattered with semi-mechanical professions like medicine or the law, but how was a man to write articles such as he wrote, not to mention poetry, unless he had the repose necessary to reinvigorate his exhausted brain?

But the baby went on crying, and the mother's heart was torn. The woman of the house said he must already be cutting his teeth and recommended some devilish syrup. Letty bought a bottle with the next money she got, and thought it did him some good—because, lessening his appetite, it lessened his crying, and also made him sleep more than he should.

At last one night Tom came home very much the worse for drink, and in drunken affection insisted on taking the baby from its cradle. The baby shrieked. Tom was angry with the weakling, yelled at him for ingratitude to "the author of his being," and shook him roughly to teach him the good manners of the world he had come to.

Up sprang the mother in Letty, erect and fierce. She ran toward Tom, snatched the child from his arms, and turned to carry him into the bedroom. But as the mother rose in Letty, the devil rose in Tom. If what followed was not the doing of the real Tom, it was the doing of the devil to whom the real Tom had opened the door. With one stride he overtook his wife, and suddenly mother and child lay together on the floor. I must say for him that, even in his drunkenness, he did not strike his wife as he would have struck a man. It was an openhanded blow he gave her, what, in familiar language, is called a box on the ear; but for days she carried the record of it on her cheek in five red fingermarks.

When he saw her on the floor, Tom's bedazed mind came to itself; he knew what he had done, and was sobered. But even then he thought more of the wrong he had done to himself as a gentleman than of the grievous wound he had given his wife's heart. He took the baby, who had stopped crying as soon as he was in his mother's arms, and laid him on the rug, and then lifted the bitterly weeping Letty, placed her on the sofa, and knelt beside her—not humbly to beg her pardon, but, as was his habit, to justify himself by proving that all the blame was hers, and that she had wronged him greatly in driving him to do such a thing. Never having had from him a fuller acknowledgment of wrong, this poor Letty was willing to accept as an apology. She turned on the sofa, threw her arms about his neck, kissed him, and clung to him with an utter forgiveness. But all it did for Tom was to restore him his good opinion of himself, and enable him to go on feeling as much of a gentleman as before.

Reconciled, they turned to the baby. He was pale, his eyes were closed, and they could not tell whether he was breathing. In a horrible fright, Tom ran for the doctor. Before he returned with him, the child had come to, and the doctor could discover no injury from the fall they told him he had had. At the same time, he said he was not properly nourished, and must have better food.

This presented a new difficulty to Letty, for it meant more money. And now their landlady, who had throughout been very kind, was in trouble about her own rent, and began to press for part at least of theirs. Letty's heart seemed to labor under a stone. She forgot that there was a thing called joy. She looked so sad that the good woman, full of pity, assured her that, come what might, she should not be turned out, but at the worse would only have to go a story higher, to smaller rooms. The rent could wait, she said, until better days. But this kindness relieved Letty only a little, for the rent past and the rent to come hung upon her like a cloak of lead.

And this was not even the worst debt that now oppressed her. For, possibly from the fall, but more from the prolonged want of suitable nourishment and wise treatment after that terrible night, the baby grew worse. Many were the tears the sleepless mother shed over the sallow face and wasted limbs of her slumbering treasure—her one antidote to countless sorrows; and many were the foolish means she tried to restore his sinking vitality.

Mary had written to her, and she had written to Mary. But she had said nothing of the straits to which she was reduced; that would be to bring blame upon Tom. But with her fine human instinct, Mary felt that things must be going worse with her than before, and when she found that her return to the city was indefinitely postponed by Mr. Redmain's illness, she decided at last to attempt a daring measure. She was not overly hopeful about the results it might bring, yet she did not know what else she could possibly do. Therefore, she wrote to Mr. Wardour, telling him she had reason to fear things were not going well with Letty Helmer, and suggesting, in the gentlest way, whether it might not now be time to let bygones be bygones, and make some inquiry concerning her.

Godfrey returned no answer to this letter. For all her denial, he had never stopped believing that Mary had been Letty's accomplice throughout that miserable affair. And now the very name—the Letty and the Helmer— stung him to the quick. He took it as a piece of utter presumption in Mary to write to him about Letty, and that in the tone, as he interpreted it, of one reading him a lesson of duty. But while he was thus indignant with Mary, he was also angry with Letty for not writing him herself, forgetting that he had never hinted at any door of communication open between him and her. His heart quivered at the thought that she might be in distress; he had known for certain, he said, that the fool would bring her misery.

For himself, the thought of Letty was an ever-open wound—with an ever-present pain, now dull and aching, now keen and stinging. The agony of desertion, he said, would never cease gnawing at his heart until it was laid in the grave. Like most heathen Christians, he thought of death as the end of all the joys, sorrows, and interests generally of this life.

But while he thus brooded, a fierce and evil joy awoke in him at the thought that now at last the expected hour had come when he would heap coals of fire on her head. He was still fool enough to think of her as having forsaken him, although he had never given her ground for believing, and she had never had conceit enough to imagine, that he cared the least for her person. If he could but let her have a glimmer of what she had lost in losing him! She knew by this time what she had gained in Tom Helmer.

He spent a troubled night, dreamed painfully, and started awake to renewed pain. Before morning he had made up his mind to take the first train to London. But he thought far more of being her deliverer than of bringing her deliverance.

37 / Godfrey and Letty

It was a sad, gloomy, kindless November night when Godfrey arrived in London. The wind was cold, the pavements were cold, the houses seemed to be not only cold but feeling it. The very dust that blew in his face was cold.

Now cold is a powerful ally of the commonplace, and imagination therefore was not very busy in the heart of Godfrey Wardour as he went to find Letty Helmer, which was just as well, in the circumstances. He was cold to his very bones when he walked up to the door indicated by Mary, and rung the bell. Mrs. Helmer was at home: would he walk up the stairs?

It was not a house of ceremonies. He was shown up and up and into the room where she sat, without a word carried before to prepare her for his visit. It was so dark that he could see nothing but the figure of one at work by a table, on which stood a single candle. There was but a spark of fire in the dreary grate, and Letty was colder than anyone could know.

She looked up. She had thought it was the landlady and had waited for her to speak. She gazed for a moment in bewilderment, saw who it was, and jumped up half frightened, half ready to go wild with joy. All the memories of Godfrey rushed in a confused heap upon her, and overwhelmed her. She ran to him, and the same-moment was in his arms, with her head on his shoulder, weeping tears of such gladness as she had not known since the first week of her marriage.

Neither spoke for some time; Letty could not because she was crying, and Godfrey would not because he did not want to cry. Those few moments were pure, simple happiness to both of them; to Letty because she had loved him from childhood, and hoped that all was to be as of old between them; to Godfrey because, for the moment, he had forgotten himself, and had neither thought of injury nor hope of love, remembering only the old days and the Letty that used to be. It may seem strange that, having never once embraced her all the time they lived together, he should do so now. But Letty's love would any time have responded to the least show of affection, and when, at the sight of his face, into which memory had called up all his tenderness, she rushed into his arms, how could he help kissing her?

But the embrace was not a long one. Godfrey was the first to relax its strain, and Letty responded with an instant collapse. Instantly she feared she had done it all and disgusted Godfrey. But he led her gently to the sofa, and sat down beside her on the hard old slippery horsehair. Then first he perceived what a change had passed on her. She was pale and thin, and sad, with such big eyes, and the bone tightening the skin upon her forehead! He felt as if she were a specter—Letty, not the same Letty he had loved. Glancing up, she caught his troubled gaze.

"I am not ill, cousin Godfrey," she said. "Do not look at me so or I shall cry again. You know you never liked to see me cry."

"My poor girl!" said Godfrey, in a voice which, if he had not kept it lower than natural, would have broken. "You are suffering."

"Oh no," replied Letty, with a pitiful effort at the cheerful. "I'm only glad to see you again."

She sat on the edge of the sofa, and had put her open hands, palm to palm, between her knees in a childish way. For a moment Godfrey sat gazing at her, with troubled heart and troubled looks, then between his teeth muttered, "Damn the rascal!"

Letty sat straight up and turned upon him eyes of appeal, scared, yet ready to defend. Her hands were now clinched, one on each side of her.

"Cousin Godfrey!" she cried, "if you mean Tom, you must not, you must not. I will go away if you speak a word against him. I will—I *must*, you know."

Godfrey made no reply—neither apologized nor sought to cover his words.

"Why, child!" he said at last. "You are half-starved!"

The pity and tenderness of both word and tone were too much for her. She had not been at all pitying herself, but such an utterance from the man she loved like an elder brother so worked upon her weakened condition that she broke into a cry. She struggled to suppress her emotion. In her agony she would have rushed from the room, had not Godfrey caught her, drawn her down beside him, and kept her there.

"You shall not leave me," he said, in that voice Letty had always been used to obeying. "Who has a right to know how things go with you, if I have not? Come, you must tell me all about it."

"I have nothing to tell, cousin Godfrey," she replied with some calmness, for Godfrey's decision had enabled her to conquer herself, "except that the baby is sick, and looks as if he will never get better, and it is likely to break my heart. Oh, he is such a darling, cousin Godfrey!"

"Let me see him," said Godfrey, in his heart detesting the child—the visible sign that another was nearer to Letty than he.

She jumped up, almost ran into the next room, and, coming back with the little one, laid him in Godfrey's arms. The moment he felt the weight of the little, sad-looking, sleeping thing, he grew human toward him, and saw in him Letty and not Tom.

"Good God! the child is starving too!" he exclaimed.

"Oh no, cousin Godfrey!" cried Letty. "He is not starving. He had a fresh egg for breakfast this morning, and some arrowroot for dinner, and some bread and milk for tea—"

"London milk!" said Godfrey.

"Well, it is not like the milk at the dairy in Thornwick," admitted Letty. "If he had milk like that, he would soon be well!"

But Godfrey dared not say, "Bring him to Thornwick." He knew his mother too well for that!

"When were you anywhere in the country?" he asked.

"Not since we were married," she answered sadly. "You see, poor Tom can't afford it."

Now Godfrey happened to have heard, "from the best authority," that Tom's mother was far from ungenerous to him.

"Mrs. Helmer allows him so much a year—does she not?" he said.

"I know he gets money from her, but it can't be much," she answered.

Godfrey's suspicions against Tom increased every moment. He must learn the truth. He *would* have it, if even by a cruel experiment! He sat a moment in silence—then said, with assumed cheerfulness: "Well, Letty, I suppose, for the sake of old times, you will give me some dinner?"

Then indeed, her courage gave way. She turned from him, laid her head on the end of the sofa, and sobbed so that the room seemed to shake with the convulsions of her grief.

"Letty," said Godfrey, laying his hand on her head, "it is no use trying to hide the truth from me anymore. I don't want any dinner. I ate long ago. But you would not be open with me, and I was forced to find out for myself. You do not have enough to eat, and you know it. I will not say a word about who is to blame—for anything I know, it may be no one—I am sure it is not you. But this must not go on! I have brought you a little purse. I will call again tomorrow, and you will tell me then what more you need."

He laid the purse on the table. There was ten times as much in it as Letty had ever had at once. But she never knew what was in it. She rose with instant resolve. All the woman in her woke at once. She felt that a moment had come when she must be resolute, or lose hold on life.

"Cousin Godfrey," she said, in a tone he scarcely recognized as hers, "if you do not take that purse away, I will throw it in the fire without opening it. If my husband cannot give me enough to eat, I can starve as well as another. If you loved Tom, it would be different, but you hate him, and I will have nothing from you. Please, take it away."

Mortified, hurt, and miserable, Godfrey took the money, and, without another word, walked from the room. Somewhere down in his secret heart was dawning an idea of Letty beyond anything he used to think of her. But in the meantime he was only blindly aware that his heart had been shot through and through. Nor was this the time for him to reflect that, under his training, Letty, even if he had married her, would never have grown to such dignity.

It was, indeed, only in that moment that she had become capable of the action. She had been growing as no one, not even Mary, still less herself, knew under the heavy snows of affliction, and this was her first blossom. Some of my readers will no doubt mistake me. Had it been in Letty pride that refused help from such an old friend, that pride I should never consider a blossom of her strengthening character. But the dignity of her refusal was in this—that she would accept nothing in which her husband had and could have no share. She had married him because she loved him, and she would hold by him wherever that might lead her. Not wittingly would she allow the finest edge, even of ancient kindness, to come between Tom and herself. To accept from her cousin Godfrey the help her husband ought to provide her, would be to let him, however innocently, step into his place!

There was no reasoning in her resolve. As the presence of death will sometimes change even an ordinary man to a prophet, in times of sore need the childlike nature may well receive a vision sufficing to direct the doubtful step. Letty felt that the taking of that money would be the opening of a gulf to divide her and Tom forever.

The moment Godfrey was out of the room, she threw herself on the floor and sobbed as if her heart would break. But her sobs were tearless. And agony of agonies! unsought came the conviction, and she could not send it away—to this had finally sunk her lofty idea of Tom!—that he would have had her take the money!

The baby began to cry. She rose and took him from the sofa where Godfrey had laid him when he was getting out the purse, and held him tightly to her bosom, as if by laying their two aching lives together they might both be healed, and rocking him to and fro, said to herself, for the first time, that her trouble was greater than she could bear. "O baby! baby! baby!" she cried, and her tears streamed on the little pale face. But as she sat with him in her arms, the blessed sleep came, and the storm sank to a calm.

It was utterly dark when she awoke.

For a minute she could not remember where she was. The candle had burned out: it must be late. The baby was still on her lap—still, very still. One faint gleam of satisfaction crossed her mind at the thought that he slept so peacefully, hidden from the gloom which, somehow, appeared to be all the same gloom outside and inside of her. In that gloom she sat alone.

Suddenly a prayer was in her heart. It was moving there as of itself. It had come there by no calling of it on her part, by no conscious will of hers. "O God," she cried, "I am desolate! Is there no help for me?" And in that moment she knew that she had prayed, and knew that never in her life had she so prayed before.

She jumped to her feet: a horrible fear had taken possession of her. With one arm she held the child fast to her bosom, with the other she searched in vain to find a match. And still, as she searched, the baby seemed to grow heavier upon her arm, and the fear sickened more and more at her heart.

At last she had light! and the face of the child came out of the darkness. But the child himself had gone away into it. The unspeakable had come while she slept—had come and gone, and taken her child with him. What was left of him was more good to kiss than the last doll of her childhood!

When Tom came home, there was his wife on the floor as if dead, and a little way from her the child, dead indeed, and cold with death. He lifted Letty and carried her to the bed, amazed to find how light she was. It was long since he had had her thus in his arms. Then he laid her dead baby by her side, and ran to rouse the doctor. He came and pronounced the child quite dead—from lack of nutrition, he said. To see Tom, no one could have helped contrasting his dress and appearance with the look and surroundings of his wife. But few would have been ready to lay blame on him. And as for himself, he was not in the least awake to the fact of his guilt.

The doctor gave the landlady, who had responded at once to Tom's call, full directions for the care of the bereaved mother. Tom handed her the little money he had in his pocket, and she promised to do her best. And she did it, for she was one of those, not a few, who, knowing nothing of religion toward God, are yet full of religion toward their fellows, and with the Son of Man that goes a long way. As soon as it was light, Tom went to see about the burying of his baby.

He went first to the editor of *The Firefly*. He told him his baby was dead, and he needed money. It was forthcoming at once, for literary men, like all other artists, are in general as ready to help one another as the very poor themselves. There is less generosity, I think, among businessmen than in any other class. The more honor to the exceptions!

"But," said the editor, who had noted the dry, burning palm, and saw the glazed fire in Tom's eyes, "my dear fellow, you ought to be in bed yourself. It's no use talking on about the poor little baby: *you* couldn't help what happened. Go home to your wife and tell her she's got to nurse you. And if she's in any fix about money, tell her to come to me."

Tom went home, but did not give his wife the message. She lay all but insensible, never asked for anything, or refused anything that was offered her. She never said a word about her baby, or about Tom, or seemed to be more than when she lay in her mother's lap. Her baby was buried, and she knew nothing of it. Not until nine days were over did she begin to revive.

For the first few days Tom moved with undefined remorse, trying to take a hand in nursing her. She took things from him, as she did from the landlady, without heed or recognition. Just once, opening her eyes suddenly wide upon him, she uttered a feeble wail of *"Baby,"* then turned her head and did not look at him again. Then for the first time, Tom's conscience gave him a sharp sting.

He was himself far from well. The careless and in many respects dissolute life he had been leading had more than begun to tell on a constitution by no means strong. But he had never become aware of his weakness, nor had he ever felt really ill until now. But that sting, although the first sharp one, was not his first warning of a waking conscience. Ever since he took his place at his wife's bedside, he had been fighting off the conviction that he was a brute. He would not, he could not believe it. How could he, Tom Helmer, the fine fellow he had always known himself to be, cower before his own conscience as an unworthy man, greatly to be despised!

With that pitiful cry of his wife after her lost child, disbelief in himself got within the lines of his defense. He could do no more, and began to loathe that conscious self that had hitherto been his pride.

Whatever the effect of illness may be upon the temper of some, it is most certainly an ally of the conscience. All pains, and all sorrows, all demons, and even all sins themselves under the suffering care of the highest minister are but the ministers of truth and righteousness.

But conscience reacts on the body—for sickness until it is obeyed, for health thereafter. The moment conscience spoke thus plainly to Tom, the little that was left of his physical endurance gave way. His illness got the upper hand, and he took to his bed—all he could have for a bed, that is—namely, the sofa in the sitting room, widened out with chairs, and a mattress over the whole. There he lay, and their landlady had enough to do. Not that either of her patients were exacting; they were both too ill and miserable for that. It is the self-pitiful, self-coddling invalid that is exacting. Such, I suspect, require something sharper still.

Tom groaned and tossed and cursed himself and soon passed into delirium. His visions, animate with shame and confusion of soul, were more distressing than even his tongue could have told. Dead babies and ghastly women pursued him everywhere. His fever increased. The cries of terror and dismay that he uttered reached the ears of his wife, and were the first thing that roused her from her lethargy. She rose from her bed, and, just able to crawl, began to do what she could for him. If she could but get near enough to him, the husband would yet be dearer than any child. She had him carried to the bed, and thereafter took on the sofa what rest there was for her. To and fro between bed and sofa she crept—let the landlady say what she might—gave him all the food he could be coaxed to take, cooled his burning hands and head, and cried over him because she could not take him on her lap like the baby that was gone. Once or twice, in a quieter interval, he looked at her and seemed about to speak. But the fever carried away the word of love for which she listened so eagerly. The doctor came daily, but Tom grew worse, and Letty could not get well.

39 / Words of Righteousness

When the Redmains went to Cornwall, Sepia was left at Durnmelling, expecting to join them in London within two weeks at the latest. The illness of Mr. Redmain, however, caused her stay to be prolonged, and she was worn out with boredom.

The self she was so careful over was not by any means good company. Not seldom during her life had she found herself capable of almost anything to get rid of it, short of suicide or repentance. This autumn at Durnmelling, she would even occasionally, when the weather was nice, go for a solitary walk—a thing, I need hardly say, she hated in itself, though now it was her forlorn hope to possibly fall in with some distraction. But the hope was not altogether a vague one. For was there not a man somewhere underneath those chimneys she saw over the roof of the laundry? She had never spoken to him, but Hesper and she had often talked about him, and often watched him ride—never man more to her mind. In her wanderings she had come upon the breach in the wall, and, clambering up, found herself on the forbidden ground of a neighbor whom the family did not visit. To no such folly would Sepia be a victim.

In one of her rambles on his ground she had her desire, and met Godfrey Wardour. He lifted his hat, and she stopped and addressed him by way of apology.

"I am afraid you will think me very rude, Mr. Wardour," she said. "I know I am trespassing, but this field of yours is higher than the ground about Durnmelling, and seems to take pounds off the weight of the atmosphere."

For all he had gone through, Godfrey was not yet less than courteous to ladies. He assured Miss Yolland that Thornwick was as much at her service as if it were a part of Durnmelling. "Though, indeed," he added with a smile, "it would be more correct to say, 'as Durnmelling were a part of Thornwick'—for that was the real state of the case once upon a time."

The statement interested, or seemed to interest Miss Yolland, giving rise to many questions, and a long conversation followed. Suddenly she woke, or seemed to wake to the consciousness that she had forgotten herself and the proprieties together. Hastily, and to all appearance with some confusion, she wished him a good morning; but she was not too much confused to thank him again for the permission he had given her to walk on his ground.

It was not by any intention on the part of Godfrey that they met several times after this, but they always had a little conversation before they parted. And Sepia did not find it at all difficult to get him sufficiently within range to make him feel the power of her eyes. She was too prudent, however, to bring to bear upon any man all at once the full play of her mesmeric battery. Things had gotten no further when she went to London—a week or two before the return of the Redmains, ostensibly to get things in some special readiness for Hesper. That this may have been a pretense appears possible from the fact that Mary came from Cornwall on the same mission a few days later.

There was an acquaintance of Sepia's, mentioned in passing earlier as having attracted the notice and roused the peculiar interest of Mr. Redmain, because of a look he saw pass between them. This man spoke both English and French with a foreign accent, and passed himself off as a Georgian— Count Galofta, he called himself: I believe he was a prince in Paris. At this time he was in London, and during the ten days that Sepia was alone came to see her several times—called early in the morning, first, the next day in the evening, when they went together to the opera, and once came and stayed late. Whether from her dark complexion making her look older than she was, or from the subduing air which her experience had given her, or merely from the fact that she belonged to nobody much, Miss Yolland seemed to have *carte blanche* to do as she pleased, and come and go when and where she liked, as one knowing well enough how to take care of herself.

Arriving unexpectedly at the house in Glammis Square, Mary met him in the hall as she entered. He had just taken leave of Sepia, who was going up the stair at that moment. Mary had never seen him before, but something about him caused her to look at him again as he passed.

Somehow Tom also had discovered Sepia's return, and had gone to see her more than once.

When Mr. and Mrs. Redmain arrived, there was so much to be done for Hesper's wardrobe, that for some days Mary found it impossible to go and see Letty. Her mistress seemed harder to please than usual, and more doubtful of humor than ever before. This may have arisen—but I doubt it—from the fact that the Sunday before they had heard a different sort of sermon from any she had heard in her life before.

The morning after her arrival, Hesper found herself in want of Mary's help. Instead of calling her as she generally did, she opened the door that connected their rooms and saw Mary on her knees by her bedside. Now Hesper had heard of saying prayers—night and morning both—and when she was a child she had been expected to say her own. But to be found on one's knees in the middle of the day looked to her a thing exceedingly odd.

Actually Mary was not in the habit of kneeling at such a time: she had to pray much too often to kneel always, and God was too near her, wherever she happened to be, for the fancy that she must seek him in any particular place. But so it happened now. She rose, a little startled, and followed her mistress into her room.

"I am sorry to have disturbed you, Mary," said Hesper, herself a little annoyed, it is not quite easy to say why; "but people do not generally say their prayers in the middle of the day."

"I say mine when I need to say them," answered Mary.

"For my part, I don't see any good in being righteous overmuch," said Hesper.

"I don't know what that means," returned Mary. "I believe it is somewhere in the Bible, but I am sure Jesus never said it, for he tells us to be righteous as our Father in heaven is righteous."

"But the thing is impossible," said Hesper. "How is one, with such claims on her as I have, to attend to these things? Society has claims, you cannot deny that."

"And God has none?" asked Mary.

"Many people now think there is no God at all," returned Hesper.

"If there is no God, that settles the question," answered Mary. "But if there is one, what then?"

"Then I am sure he would never be hard on one like me. I do just like other people. One must do as people do. If there is one thing that must be avoided more than another, it is peculiarity. How ridiculous it would be of anyone to set herself against society."

"Then you think the Judge will be satisfied if you say, 'Lord, I had so many names in my visiting book, and so many invitations I could not refuse, that it was impossible for me to attend to those religious kinds of things'?"

"I don't see that I'm at all worse than other people," persisted Hesper. "I can't go and pretend to be sorry for sins I should commit again the next time there was a necessity. I don't see what I've got to repent of."

Nothing had been said about repentance: here, I imagine, the sermon may have come in.

"Then, of course, you can't repent," said Mary.

Hesper recovered herself a little.

"I am glad you see the thing as I do," she said.

"I don't see it at all as you do," answered Mary gently.

"Why!" exclaimed Hesper, taken by surprise. "What have I got to repent of?"

"Do you really want me to say what I think?" asked Mary.

"Of course I do," returned Hesper, getting angry, and at the same time uneasy. She knew Mary's freedom of speech upon occasion, but felt that to draw back would be to yield to some unspoken sin. "What have I done to be ashamed of, pray tell me!"

Some ladies are ready to plume themselves upon not having been guilty of certain great crimes. Some thieves, I dare say, console themselves that they have never committed murder.

"If I had married a man I did not love," answered Mary, "I would be more ashamed of myself than I can tell you."

"That is the way of looking at such things in the class you belong to, I dare say," rejoined Hesper. "But with us it is quite different. There is no necessity laid upon *you*. *Our* position obliges us."

"But what if God should not see it as you do?"

"If that is all you have got to bring against me!—" said Hesper with a forced laugh.

"But that is not all," replied Mary. "When you married, you promised many things, not one of which you have ever done."

"Really, Mary, this is intolerable!" cried Hesper.

"I am only doing what you asked me," said Mary. "And I have said nothing that every one associated with Mr. Redmain does not know as well as I do."

Hesper now wished heartily that she had never challenged Mary's judgment.

"But," she resumed more quietly, "how could you, or anyone—how could God himself ask me to act the part of a loving wife to a man like Mr. Redmain?"

"But you promised," persisted Mary. "It belongs to the very idea of marriage."

"There are a thousand promises made every day which nobody is expected to keep. It is the custom, the way of the world. How many of the clergy believe the things they say?"

"They must answer for themselves. We are not clergymen, but women, who ought never to say a thing except we mean it, and when we have said it, to stick to it."

"But just look around you and see how many there are in precisely the same position as me. Will you dare to say they are all going to be lost because they do not behave like angels to their brutes of husbands?"

"I say they have got to repent of behaving to their husbands as their husbands behave to them. What someone else does has nothing to do with it. The responsibility of a Christian is clear no matter that everyone else goes their own selfish way."

"And what if they don't repent?"

Mary paused a little.

"Do you expect to go to heaven, ma'am?" she asked.

"I hope so."

"Do you think you will like it?"

"I must say, I think it will be rather dull."

"Then, to use your own word, you must be very like lost anyway. There does not seem to be a right place for you anywhere, and that is very like being lost—is it not?"

Hesper laughed.

"I am pretty comfortable where I am," she said.

Husband and all! thought Mary, but she did not say that. What she said was: "But you know you can't stay here. God is not going to keep up this way of things for you. And how can you expect it when you don't care a straw what he wants of you? I have sometimes thought—What if hell were just a place where God gives everybody everything they want, and lets everybody do whatever they like, without once coming to interfere! What a hell that would be! For God's presence in the very being, and nothing else, is bliss. That, then, would be the very opposite of heaven, and very much the opposite of this world. Such a hell would go on, I suppose, till every one had learned to hate everyone else in the world."

This was beyond Hesper, and she paid no attention to it.

"You can never, in your sober senses, Mary," she said, "mean that God requires of me to do things for Mr. Redmain that the servants can do a great deal better. That would be ridiculous—not to mention that I oughtn't and couldn't and wouldn't do them for any man!"

"Many a woman," said Mary, "has done many more trying things for persons of whom she knew nothing."

"I dare say! But such women go in for being saints, and that is not my line. I was not made for that."

"You were made for that, and far more," said Mary.

"There are such women, I know," persisted Hesper, "but I do not know how they find it possible."

"I can tell you how they find it possible. They love every human being just because he is human. Your husband might well be a demon from the way you behave to him."

"I suppose *you* find it agreeable to wait upon him. He is civil to you, I dare say."

"Not very," replied Mary with a smile. "But the person who can not bear with a sick man or a baby is not fit to be a woman."

"You may go to your own room," said Hesper.

For the first time, a feeling of dislike toward Mary awoke in the heart of her mistress—very naturally I am sure my readers will allow. The next few days she scarcely spoke to her, sending directions for her work through Sepia, who discharged the office with dignity.

At length one morning, when she believed Mrs. Redmain would not be up before noon, Mary felt she must go and see Letty. She did not find her in the quarters where she had left her, but a story higher, in a shabby room, sitting with her hands in her lap. She did not lift her eyes when Mary entered: where hope is dead, curiosity dies. Not until she had come quite near did she raise her head, and then she seemed to know nothing of her. When she did recognize her, she held out her hand in a mechanical way, as if they were two specters met in a miserable dream, in which they were nothing to each other, and neither could do, or cared to do, anything for the other.

"My poor Letty!" cried Mary, greatly shocked, "what has come to you? Are you not glad to see me? Has anything happened to Tom?"

She broke into a low, childish wail, and for a time that was all Mary heard. Presently, however, she became aware of a feeble moaning in the adjoining room, the sound of a human sea in trouble—mixed with a wandering babble, which to Letty was but as the voice of her own despair, and to Mary was a cry for help.

She abandoned the attempt to draw anything from Letty and went to the next room, the door of which stood wide open. There lay Tom, but so changed that it took Mary a moment to be certain it was he. She went softly to him and laid her hand on his head. It was burning. He opened his eyes, but she saw their sense was gone. She went back to Letty, and, sitting down beside her, put her arm about her, and said: "Why didn't you send for me, Letty? I would have come to you at once. I will come now, tonight, and help you take care of him. Where is the baby?"

Letty gave a shriek and jumped from her chair. She began walking wildly about the room, wringing her hands. Mary went after her, and taking her in her arms, said: "Letty, dear, has God taken your baby?"

Letty gave her a lackluster look.

"Then," said Mary, "he is not far away, for we are all in God's arms."

But what is the use of the most powerful of medicines while they stand on the sick man's table? What is the mightiest of truths so long as it is not believed? The spiritually sick still mocks at the medicine offered; he will not know its cure. Mary saw that, for any comfort to Letty, God was nowhere. It went to her very heart. Death and desolation and the enemy were in possession.

She turned to go, that she might return able to begin her contest with ruin. Letty saw that she was going, and imagined her offended and abandoning her to her misery. She ran to her, stretched out her arms like a child, but was so feeble that she tripped and fell. Mary lifted her, and laid her wailing on the couch.

"Letty," said Mary, "you didn't think I was going to leave you! But I must go for an hour, perhaps two, to make arrangements for staying with you till Tom is over the worst."

Then Letty clasped her hands in her old beseeching way, and looked up with a faint show of comfort.

"Be courageous, Letty," said Mary. "I shall be back as soon as I can. God has sent me to you."

She went straight home, and heard that Mrs. Redmain was annoyed that she had gone out.

"I offered to help dress her," said Jemima, "and she knows I can quite well. But she would not get up till you came, and made me fetch her a book. So there she is, waiting for you."

"I am sorry," said Mary, "but I had to go, and she was fast asleep."

When she entered her room, Hesper gave her a cold glance over the top of her novel, and went on with her reading. Mary proceeded to get her things ready for dressing. But by this time she had gotten interested in the story.

"Then please, ma'am," replied Mary, "would you mind letting Jemima dress you? I want to go out again, and should be glad if you could do without me for some days. My friend's baby is dead, and both she and her husband are very ill."

Hesper threw down her book and her eyes flashed.

"What do you mean by using me so, Miss Marston?" she said.

"I am very sorry to put you to any inconvenience," answered Mary, "but the husband seems to be dying, and the wife is scarcely able to crawl."

"I have nothing to do with it," interrupted Hesper. "When you made it necessary for me to part with my maid, you undertook to perform her duties. I did not engage you as a sicknurse for other people."

"No, ma'am," replied Mary, "but this is an extreme case, and I cannot believe you would object to my going."

"I do object. Pray tell me, how is the world to go on, if this kind of thing is permitted! I may be going out to dinner, or the opera, tonight, for anything you know, and who is there to help dress me? No, on principle, and for the sake of example, I will not let you go!"

"I thought," said Mary, greatly disappointed in Hesper, "that I did not stand to you quite in the relation of an ordinary servant."

"Certainly you do not. I look for a little more devotion from you than from a common, ungrateful creature who thinks only of herself. But you are all alike.''

More and more distressed to find one she had loved so long herself so selfish, Mary's indignation had by now almost gotten the best of her. But a little heightening of her color was all the show it made.

"Indeed, it is quite necessary, ma'am," she persisted, "that I should go."

"The law has fortunately made provision against such behavior," said Hesper. "You cannot leave without giving me a month's notice."

"The understanding on which I came to you was very different," said Mary sadly.

"It was. But since then you consented to become my maid."

"It is ungenerous to take advantage of that," returned Mary, growing angry again.

"I have to protect myself and the world in general from the consequences that must follow were such lawless behavior allowed to pass."

Hesper spoke with calm severity, and Mary, making up her mind, answered now with almost equal calmness.

"The law was made for both sides, and as you bring the law to me, I will take refuge in the law. It is, I believe, a month's warning or a month's wages; and, as I have never had any wages, I imagine I am at liberty to go. Goodbye, ma'am. I am sorry it must be this way, for I have been privileged to serve you. But I have higher duties that even my love for you cannot touch."

Hesper made her no answer, and Mary left the room. She went to her own, stuffed her immediate necessities into a bag, let herself out of the house, called a cab, and, with a great lump in her throat, drove to the help of Letty.

First, she had a talk with the landlady and learned all she could tell. Then she went up and began to make things as comfortable as she could. All was in sad disorder and neglect.

With the mere inauguration of cleanliness, and the first dawn of coming order, the courage of Letty began to revive a little. The impossibility of doing all that ought to be done, had, in her miserable weakness, so depressed her that she had not done even as much as she could—except where Tom was immediately concerned.

Mary next went to the doctor to get instructions, and then to buy what things were most wanted. And now she almost wished Mrs. Redmain had paid her for her services, for she must write to Mr. Turnbull for money, and that she disliked having to do. But by the very next post she received, enclosed in a business envelope in George's writing, the check for fifty pounds she had requested.

She did not dare write to Tom's mother, because she was certain, were she to come, her presence would only add to his misery and take away half the possibility of his recovery, and Letty's too. In the case of both, nourishment was the main thing, and to provide and administer it, she turned all her energy.

For a day or two she felt at times as if she could hardly get through what she had undertaken. But she soon learned to drop asleep at any moment, and wake immediately when she was wanted. And thereafter she was able to remain more rested in the midst of the unending work.

Under her skillful nursing—skillful, not from experience, but simply from her faith, whence came both conscience of and capacity for doing what the doctor told her—things went well. It is from their want of this faith and their consequent arrogance and conceit that the ladies who aspire to help in hospitals give the doctors so much trouble. They have not yet learned *obedience*, the only path to any good, the one essential to the saving of the world. One who cannot obey is the merest slave—essentially and in himself a slave.

The crisis of Tom's fever was at length passed, but the result remained doubtful. By late hours and strong drink, he had done not a little to weaken his constitution, in itself, far from strong. While the unrest of what is commonly and foolishly called a bad conscience stirred, with the misery over the death of his child and the conduct that had disgraced him in his own eyes and ruined his wife's happiness, all this combined to retard his recovery.

While he was still delirious, and grief and shame and consternation operated at will on his poetic nature, the things he kept saying over and over were very pitiful. But they would have sounded more miserable yet in the ears of one who did not look so far ahead as Mary. She had been trained to regard all things in their true meaning and importance, and was therefore rejoiced to find him loathing his former self, and beyond the present suffering saw the gladness at hand for the sorrowful man, the repenting sinner. Had she been mother or sister to him, she could hardly have waited on him with more devotion or tenderness.

One day, as his wife was doing some little thing for him, he took her hand in his feeble grasp, and pressing it to his face, wet with the tears of reviving manhood, said: "We might have been happy together, Letty, if I had but known how much you were worth, and how little I was worth myself!"

He burst into a wail that tortured Letty with its likeness to the crying of her baby.

"Tom! my darling Tom!" she cried, "when you speak as if I belonged to you, it makes me happy as a queen. When you are better, you will be happy too. Mary says you will."

"But, Letty!" he sobbed—"the baby!"

"The baby's all right, Mary says. And some day, she says, he will run into your arms, and know you for his father."

"And I shall be so ashamed to look at him!" said Tom.

An hour or so after this, he woke from a short sleep, and his eyes searched about for Letty's watching face.

"I have seen the baby," he said, "and he has forgiven me. I dare say it was only a dream," he added, "but somehow it makes me happier. At least I know how the thing might be."

"It was true, whether it was a dream, or something more," said Mary, who happened to be near by.

"Thank you, Mary," he returned. "You and Letty have saved me from what I dare not think of. I could die happy now—if it weren't for one thing."

"What is that?" asked Mary.

"I am ashamed to say it," he replied. "But I ought to, for the man who does shamefully ought to be ashamed. It is that, when I am in my grave, it is horrid to think that people up here will still have a hold on me because of debts I shall never be able to pay them."

"Don't be too sure of that, Tom," said Mary cheerfully. "I think you will pay them yet. But I have heard it said," she went on, "that a man in debt never tells the truth about his debts—as if he had only the face to make them, not talk about them. Can you make a clean breast of it, Tom?"

"I don't exactly know what they are; but I always did mean to pay them, and I have some idea about them. I don't think they would all come to more than a hundred pounds."

"Your mother would not hesitate to pay that for you," said Mary.

"I know she wouldn't, but then, I'm thinking of Letty."

He paused, and Mary waited.

"You know, when I am gone," he resumed, "there will be nothing for her but to go to my mother. And it breaks my heart to think of it. Every sin of mine she will lay upon her."

"Then I will pay your debts, Tom, and gladly," said Mary, "if they don't come to much more than you say—than you *think*, I mean."

"But don't you see, Mary? That would only be a shifting of my debt from them to you. Except for Letty, it would not make the thing any better."

"What?" said Mary. "Surely you don't mean to say there is no difference between owing a thing to one who loves you and one who does not? To one who would always be wishing you had paid him and one who is glad to have even the poor bond of a debt between you and her? All of us who are sorry for our sins are brothers and sisters."

"Oh, Mary!" said Tom.

"But I will tell you what will be better: let your mother pay your debts, and I will look after Letty. I will care for her like my own sister, Tom."

"Then I shall die happy," said Tom. From that day on he began to recover.

Many who would pay money to keep a man alive or to deliver him from pain would pay nothing to take a killing load off the shoulders of his mind. Hunger they can pity—not mental misery.

Tom would not hear of his mother being written to.

"I have done Letty wrong enough already," he said, "without subjecting her to the cruel tongue of my mother. I have conscience enough left not to have anybody else abuse her."

"But, Tom," argued Mary, "if you want to be good, one of your first duties is to be reconciled to your mother."

"I am very sorry things are all wrong between us, Mary," said Tom. "But if you want her to come here, you don't know what you are talking about. She must have everything her own way, or else she storms from morning to night. I would gladly make it up with her, but live with her, or die with her, I could not. To make either possible, you must convert her too. When you have done that, I will invite her at once."

"Never mind me, Tom," said Letty. "So long as you love me, I don't care even what your mother thinks of me. I will do everything I can to make her comfortable and satisfied with me."

"Wait till I am better, Letty, for I won't have a chance if my mother comes. I will tell you what, Mary: if I get better I promise you I will do what is possible to be a son to my mother, and for the present I will dictate a letter, if you will write it, bidding her good-bye, and asking her forgiveness for everything I have done wrong by her, which you will please send if I should die. I cannot and I will not promise more."

After this he was exhausted, and Mary dared not say another word. And for the moment she did not see what more there was to be said. Where all relation has been perverted, things cannot be set right by force. Perhaps all we can do sometimes is to be willing and wait.

The letter was written—a lovely one, Mary thought: it made her weep as she wrote it. Tom signed it. Mary folded, sealed, and addressed it, and laid it away in her desk.

The same evening Tom said to Letty, putting his thin long hand in hers—"Mary thinks we shall know each other there, Letty."

"Tom!" interrupted Letty, "don't talk like you are going to die. I can't bear it!"

"All I wanted to say," persisted Tom, "was that I should sit all day looking out for you, Letty."

41 / The Music Again

The faint, sweet, luminous sound of bow and string, as between them they tore the silky air into a dying sound, came hovering—neither could have said whether it was in the soul only, or there and in the outer world too.

"What is that?" asked Tom.

"Mary!" Letty called into the other room. "There is our friend with the violin again. Don't you think Tom would like to hear him?"

"Yes I do," answered Mary, rising at once. She went up the one flight of stairs—all that now divided them, and found the musician with his sister—his half-sister she was.

"I thought we should have you in upon us!" said Ann. "Joe thinks he can play so as nobody can hear him; and I was fool enough to let him try. I am sorry."

"I am glad," rejoined Mary, "and I have come to ask him downstairs, for Mrs. Helmer and I think it will do her husband good to hear him. He is very fond of music."

"Much help music will be to him, poor young man!" said Ann.

"Wouldn't you give a sick man a flower, even if it only made him a little happier for a moment with its scent and its loveliness?" asked Mary.

"No, I wouldn't. It would only be to help the deceitful heart to be more desperately wicked."

I will not continue the conversation. Ann's father had been a preacher among the followers of Whitefield, and Ann was a follower of her father. She laid hold upon the garment of a hard master, a tyrannical God. Happy he who has learned the gospel according to Jesus, as reported by John— that God is light and in him is no darkness at all! Happy is he who finds God his refuge from all the lies that are told for him and in his name! But it is love that saves, and not opinion that damns, and let the Master himself deal with the weeds in his garden as with the tares in his field.

"I read my Bible a good deal," said Mary at last, "but I never found one of those things you say in it."

"That's because you were never taught to look for them," said Ann.

"Very likely," returned Mary. "In the meantime I prefer the violin— that is, with one like your brother to play it."

She turned to the door, and Joseph Jasper, who had not spoken a word, rose and followed her. As soon as they were outside, Mary turned to him and asked if he would play the same piece with which he had ended the last time.

"I thought you did not care for it. I am so glad," he said.

"I liked it very much," replied Mary, "and have often thought of it since. But you left so hurriedly, before I could find words to thank you."

"You mean the ten lepers, don't you?" he said. "But of course you do. I always end my playing with them."

"Is that what you call it?" returned Mary. "Then you have given me the key to it, and I shall understand it much better this time, I hope."

"That is what I call it," said Joseph, "—to myself, I mean, not to Ann. She would consider it blasphemy. God has made so many things that she thinks must not be mentioned in his hearing."

When they entered the room, Joseph cast a quick look round it, and made at once for the darkest corner. Three quick strides took him there, and without more introduction than if he had come upon a public platform to play, he closed his eyes and began.

And now at last Mary began to understand at least this specimen of his strange music, and was able to fill up the blanks in the impression it had made upon her earlier. Alas that my helpless ignorance should continue to make it impossible for me to describe it.

A movement even and rather slow, full of unexpected chords, wonderful to Mary, who did not know that such things could be made on the violin, brought before her mind's eye the man who knew all about everything, and loved a child more than a sage, walking in the hot day upon the border between Galilee and Samaria. Sounds arose which she interpreted as the stir of village life, the crying and calling of domestic animals, and of busy housewives at their duties, carried on half out of doors, in the homeliness of country custom. Presently the instrument began to tell the gathering of a crowd, with bee-like hum, and the crossing of voice with voice—but, at a distance, the sounds confused and obscure. Swiftly then they seemed to rush together to blend and lose themselves in the unity of an imploring melody, in which she heard the words, uttered afar, with uplifted hands and voices, drawing nearer and nearer as often repeated, "Jesus, Master, have mercy upon us." Then came a brief pause, and then what, to her now fully aroused imagination, seemed the voice of the Master saying, "Go show yourselves unto the priests." Then followed the slow, half-unwilling, not hopeful march of timeless feet. Then a clang as of something broken, then a silence as of sunrise, then air and liberty—long-drawn notes divided with quick, hurried ones; then the trampling of many feet, going farther and farther—merrily, with dance and song. Once more a sudden pause— and a melody in which she read the awe-struck joyous return of one. Steadily yet eagerly the feet drew nigh, the melody growing at once in awe and jubilation, as the man came nearer and nearer to him whose word had made him clean, until at last she saw him fall on his face before him, and heard his soul rushing forth in a strain of adoring thanks, which seemed to end only because it was choked in tears.

The violin ceased, but, as if its soul had passed from the instrument into his, the musician himself took up the strain, and in a mellow tenor voice, with a mingling of air and recitative, and an expression which to Mary was entrancing, sang the words, "and he was a Samaritan."

At the sound of his own voice, he seemed to wake up, hung his head for a moment, as if ashamed of having shown his emotion, tucked his instrument under his arm, and walked from the room, without a word spoken on either side. All the time he played, Mary had not once seen the face of the man; her soul sat only in the porch of her ears, and not once looked from the window of her eyes.

42 / Mary and Mr. Redmain_____

A few rudiments of righteousness lurked, in their original undevelopment, but still in a measure active, in the being of Mr. Redmain. There had been in the soul of his mother, I suspect, a strain of generosity, and she had left a mark of it upon him, and it was the best thing about him. But in action these rudiments took an evil shape.

Preferring inferior company, and full of that suspicion which puts the last edge upon what the world calls knowledge of human nature, he thought no man his equal in penetrating the arena of motive, and reading actions in the light of motive. With this candle, not that of the Lord, he searched the dark places of the soul. But where the soul was light, his candle could show him nothing. In fact, it served only to blind him yet further, if possible, to what was there present. And because he did not seek the good, never yet in all his life had he come near enough to a righteous man to recognize that in something or other that man was different from himself.

As for women—there was his wife—of whom he was willing to think as well as she would let him. And he firmly believed she was an angel beside Sepia. He believed he knew Sepia's self, although he did not yet know her history, and ever since his marriage had been scheming how to get rid of her—only, however, through finding her out. There would be no satisfaction otherwise! He had, therefore, almost all the time more or less been on the watch to uncover the wickedness he felt sure lay at no great depth beneath her surface. And in the meantime, for the sake of this end, he lived on terms of decent domiciliation with her. She had no suspicion how thin was the crust between her and the lava.

In Cornwall, he began at length to puzzle himself about Mary. Of course she was just like the rest! but he did not at once succeed in fitting what he saw to what he believed of all people—namely, that they were out for their own good and no one else's. That someone could actually live for the sake of others was an idea foreign to him, because it had no part in his own nature. Thus Mary remained to him, like Sepia, a riddle to be solved. He was not so ignorant as his wife concerning the relations of the different classes, and he felt certain there must be some reason, of course a discreditable one, for Mary's having left her former position, to step down into her present one. The attack he had in Cornwall afforded him the unexpected opportunity of finding her out, as he called it.

It was here too that Mary first ventured to speak to her mistress on the neglect of her husband.

"Brought up as you have been," Hesper replied, "you cannot possibly know how it feels to one in my position, to whom the very tone of coarse language is odious. It makes me sick. I cannot endure it—no lady can. I beg you will not mention Mr. Redmain to me again."

"Dear Mrs. Redmain," said Mary, "as ugly as such language is, there are many things worse. It seems to me worse that a wife should not go near her husband when he is suffering than that he should in his pain speak out bad words."

She had been on the point of saying that a thin skin was not purity, but she thought better of it in time.

"You are scarcely in a position to lay down the law for me, Mary," said Hesper. "We will, if you please, drop the subject."

Mary's words were overheard, as was a good deal more in the house than was thought, and reached Mr. Redmain, whom they perplexed: what could the young woman hope from taking his part?

One morning after the arrival of his man Mewks, Mary heard Mr. Redmain calling him in a tone which betrayed that he had been calling for some time. The house was an old one and the bells were neither in good trim, nor was his in a convenient position. At first she thought of going to try to locate Mewks, but then she decided to go to Mr. Redmain's door herself. She ran there; it stood half open.

"Can I not do something for you, sir?" she said.

"Yes you can. Go and tell that lumbering idiot to come to me instantly. No! here, you!—that's a good girl!—Oh, damn!—Just give me your hand and help me to turn an inch or two."

The change of posture relieved him a little.

"Thank you," he said. "That is better. Wait a few moments, will you— till the rascal comes?"

Mary stood back, a little behind him, thinking not to annoy him with the sight of her.

"What are you doing there?" he cried. "I like to see what people are about in my room. Come in front here, and let me look at you."

Mary obeyed, and with a smile took the position he pointed out to her. Immediately followed another agony of pain, in which he looked beset with demons, whom he not feared but hated. Mary hurried to him, and in the compassion which she inherited long back of Eve, took his hand, the fingers of which were twisting themselves into shapes like tree roots. With a hoarse roar, he dashed hers from him, as if he had been a serpent. She returned to her place and stood.

"What did you mean by that?" he said, when he came to himself. "Do you want to make a fool of me?"

Mary did not understand him, and made no reply. Another fit came. This time she kept her distance.

"Come here," he howled, reaching out his hand to her.

She obeyed.

"Damned nice hands you've got!" he gasped; "much nicer than my wife's, by Jove!"

Mary took no notice. Gently she withdrew her hands, for the fit was over.

"I see! that's the way of you!" he said, as she stepped back. "But come now, tell me how it is that a nice, well-behaved, handsome girl like you should leave a position where, they tell me, you were your own mistress, and take a cursed place as a lady's-maid to my wife."

"It was because I liked Mrs. Redmain so much," answered Mary. "And I was very uncomfortable where I was."

"What the devil did you see to like in her? I never saw anything!"

"She is so beautiful!" said Mary.

"Is she! ho! ho!" he laughed. "What is that to another woman! You are new to the trade, my girl, if you think that will go down! One woman taking to another because she is beautiful! Ha! ha! ha!"

His laugh carried an insulting tone, but it trailed off in a cry of suffering.

"Hypocrisy mustn't be too barefaced," he resumed, when again his torture abated. "Come, tell me honestly what is the real reason you are waiting on my wife?"

"She was kind to me," said Mary. "That may be a better reason, but not necessarily truer."

"It's more than she ever was to me! What wages does she give you?"

"I have not spoken about that yet, sir."

"You haven't had any?"

"I haven't wanted any yet."

"Then what the deuce ever made you come to this house?"

"I hoped to be of some service to Mrs. Redmain," said Mary, growing troubled.

"And you aren't of any? Is that why you don't want wages?"

"No, sir. That is not the reason."

"Then what *is* the reason? Come! Trust me. I will be much better to you than your mistress. Out with it! I knew there was something!"

"I would rather not talk about it," said Mary.

"You needn't mind telling *me*! I know all about such things. Look here! Give me that pocketbook on the table."

Mary brought him the pocketbook. He opened it, and, taking from it some bank notes, held them out to her.

"If your mistress won't pay you your wages, I will. There! take that. What does it matter who pays you?"

"I don't know yet," answered Mary, "whether I shall accept wages from Mrs. Redmain. Something might happen to make it impossible. Or, if I had taken money, to make me regret it."

"I like that! There you keep a hold on her!" said Mr. Redmain in a confidential tone, while in his heart he was more puzzled than ever. "Deuced clever of you! But there's no occasion for it with me," he went on. "You might as well have your money when you can have it and she be nothing the wiser. There—take it. I will swear you any oath you like not to tell my stingy wife."

"She is not stingy," said Mary, "and if I don't take wages from her, I certainly shall not from anyone else. Besides," she added, "it would be dishonest."

"Oh! that's the dodge!" said Mr. Redmain to himself. But aloud he said, "Where would be the dishonesty, when the money is mine to do with as I please?"

"To take wages from you and pretend to Mrs. Redmain I was going without."

"Ha! ha! The first time, no doubt, you ever pretended anything of such nature?"

"It would be," said Mary, "so far as I can remember at the moment."

"Get out of here," cried Mr. Redmain, losing, or pretending to lose, his patience with her. "You are too unscrupulous a liar for me to deal with."

Mary turned and left the room. As she went, his keen glance caught the expression of her face, and noted the indignant red that flushed her cheeks, and the lighting of wronged innocence in her eyes.

"I ought not to have said it," he remarked to himself.

He did not for a moment fancy that she had spoken the truth; but the look of her went to a deeper place in him than he knew even the existence of.

"Hey! stop!" he cried as she was disappearing. "Come back, will you?"

"I will find Mr. Mewks," she answered, and went.

After this, Mary naturally dreaded seeing Mr. Redmain, especially alone. And he, thinking she must have time to get over the offense he had given her, made for the present no fresh attempt to get a bird's eye view of her character and scheme of life.

His curiosity, however, being in no degree satisfied concerning the odd human animal whose spoor he had for the moment failed to track, meditated on how best to renew the attempt when they returned to London. Not small was his annoyance, therefore, when he found, a few days after his arrival, that she was no longer in the house. He questioned his wife as to the cause of her absence, and told her she was utterly heartless in refusing her leave to go and nurse her friend. From this, neither from a desire to do right nor from any regard to her husband's opinion, Hesper resolved to write to Mary—as if taking it for granted she had meant to return as soon as she was able. Hesper was concerned to have her back—once her irritation for being refused was past—chiefly because she now saw that, because Mary did not now dress her, she no longer caused the same sensation upon entering a room. But as will be seen from the letter she wrote, she pricked the sides of her intent with another spur designed to insure her against any further willfulness on the part of Mary.

Dear Mary, can you tell me what has become of my large sapphire ring? I have never seen it since you brought my case with you from Cornwall. I have been looking for it all morning, but in vain. You must have it. I shall be lost without it, for you know it has not an equal for color and brilliance. I do not believe you intended for a moment to keep it, but only to punish me for thinking I could do without you. If so, you have your revenge, for I find I cannot do without either of you—you or my ring—so you will carry the joke further than I can bear. If you cannot come at once, write and tell me it is safe, and I shall love you more than ever. I am dying to see you again. Yours faithfully, H.R.

By this time Letty was much better and Tom no longer required such continuous attention. Therefore, Mary went at once to Mr. Redmain's. Hesper was out shopping, and Mary went to her own room to wait for her, where she was glad for the opportunity of getting at some of the things she had left behind her.

While she was looking for what she wanted, Sepia entered, and was, or pretended to be, astonished to see her. In a strange, sarcastic tone: "Ah, you are here!" she said. "I hope you will find it."

"If you mean the ring, that is not likely, Miss Yolland," Mary answered.

Sepia was silent a moment or two, then said: "How is your cousin?"

"I have no cousin," replied Mary.

"I mean the person you have been staying with."

"Better, thank you."

"Almost a pity, is it not—if there should come trouble about this ring."

"I do not understand you. The ring will of course be found," returned Mary.

"In any case the blame will come on you: it was in your charge."

"The ring was in the case when I left Cornwall."

"You will have to prove that."

"I remember quite well."

"No one will question that."

Beginning at last to understand her insinuations, Mary became angry.

"But that will hardly go far to clear you." Sepia went on. "Don't imagine I mean you have taken it. I am only warning you how the matter will look, so that you may be prepared. Mr. Redmain is one to believe the worst things of the best people."

"I am obliged to you," said Mary, "but I am not worried."

"It is necessary you should know also," continued Sepia, "that there is some suspicion attached to a female friend of yours as well, a young woman who used to visit you—the wife of the other, it is supposed. She was here, I remember, one night when there was a party. I saw you together in my cousin's bedroom. She had just dressed and gone downstairs."

"I remember," said Mary. "It was Mrs. Helmer."

"It is very unfortunate, certainly, but the truth must be told. A few days before you left, one of the servants, hearing someone in the house in the middle of the night, got up and went down, but only in time to hear the front door open and shut. In the morning a hat was found in the drawing room, with the name *Thomas Helmer* in it: that is the name of your friend's husband, I believe?"

"I am aware Mr. Helmer was a frequent visitor," said Mary, trying to keep cool for what was to come.

This that Sepia told her was true enough, though she was not accurate as to the time of its occurrence. I will relate briefly how it came about.

43 / The Hat and the Ring _____

On a certain evening a few days before Mary's return from Cornwall, Tom would have gone to see Miss Yolland had he not known that she meant to go to the play with a Mr. Emmet, a cousin of the Redmains. Before the hour arrived, however, Count Galofta called, and Sepia went out with him, telling the man who opened the door to ask Mr. Emmet to wait. The man was rather deaf, and did not catch with certainty the name she gave. Mr. Emmet did not appear, and it was late before Sepia returned.

Tom, jealous even to hatred, spent the greater part of his evening in a tavern on the borders of the city—in gloomy solitude, drinking brandy and water, and building castles of the most foolish type—for castles are as different as the men that build them. Through all the rooms of them glided the form of Sepia, his evil genius. He grew more and more excited as he built, and as he drank. At last he rose, paid his bill, and, a little suspicious of his equilibrium, stalked out into the street. There, almost unconsciously, he turned and walked westward. It was getting late. Before long the theaters would be emptying. He might have a look at Sepia as she came out!—but what would be the good of it when that fellow was with her! *But*, thought Tom, growing more and more daring as in an adventurous dream, *why should I not go to the house, and see her after he has left her at the door?*

He went to the house and rang the bell. The man came, and said immediately that Miss Yolland was out, but had desired him to ask Mr. Helmer to wait. Tom immediately walked in and up the stair to the drawing room, and from there into a second and third drawing room, and from the last into the conservatory. The man went down and finished his second pint of ale.

From the conservatory, Tom, finding himself in danger of havoc among the flower pots, turned back into the third room, threw himself on a couch, and fell fast asleep.

He woke in the middle of the night in pitch darkness. It was some time before he could remember where he was. When he did, he recognized that he was in an awkward predicament. But he knew the house well, and would make the attempt to get out undiscovered. It was foolish, but then Tom was foolish.

Feeling his way, he knocked down a small table with a great crash of china, and, losing his equanimity, rushed for the stair. Happily the hall lamp was still lit, and he found no trouble with bolts or lock, for the door was not any way secured.

The first breath of the cold night air brought with it such a gush of joy as he had rarely experienced. He walked the silent streets with something of the pleasure of an escaped criminal, until, alas! the wind, at the first turning to face it, let him know that he had left his hat behind him! He felt as if he had committed a murder, and left his calling card with the body!

A vague terror grew upon him as he hurried along. Justice seemed following on his track. He had found the door on the latch: if anything was missing, how would he explain the presence of his hat without himself to go with it? The devil of the brandy he had drunk was gone out of him, and only the gray ashes of its evil fire were left in his sick brain. But it had helped first to kindle another fire, which was now beginning to glow unsuspected in the depths of his brain—that of a fever whose fuel had been slowly gathering for some time.

He opened the door with his pass-key and hurried up the stair, his long legs taking three steps at a time. Never before had he felt as if he were fleeing to a refuge when going home to his wife.

He opened the door of the sitting room—and there on the floor lay Letty and little Tom, as I have already told.

"Why have I heard nothing of this before?" said Mary when Sepia had told her about the finding of Tom's hat.

"I am not aware of any right you have to know what happens in this house."

"Not from you, of course, Miss Yolland—perhaps not from Mrs. Redmain. But the servants talk of most things, and I have not heard a word—"

"How could you," interrupted Sepia, "when you were not in the house?—And so long as nothing was missed, the thing was of no consequence," she added. "Now it is different."

Mary found herself a little confused. She stopped to think a moment. One thing was clear—that, if the ring was not lost until after she left the house—and of this much she was sure—it could not be Tom who had taken it, for he was then ill in bed. The night of his escapade in the house, she had still not arrived back in Glammis Square from Cornwall, with the ring supposedly in Mrs. Redmain's case. Something to this effect she managed to say.

"I told you already," returned Sepia, "that I had no suspicion of him—at least I desire to have none, but you may be required to prove all you say. And it was well to let you understand—though there is no reason why I should take the trouble—that your going to those very people at the time, and their proving to be friends of yours, adds to the difficulty."

"How?" asked Mary.

"I am not on the jury," replied Sepia with indifference.

The scope of her remarks seemed to Mary intended to show that any suspicion of her would only be natural. For the moment, the idea amused her. But Sepia's way of talking about Tom, whatever she meant by it, was disgraceful!

"I don't see how you can be so indifferent," Mary said, "if the character of a gentleman whom you know is as seriously threatened as you would imply. I know he has been to see you more than once while Mr. and Mrs. Redmain had still not returned."

Sepia's countenance changed. An evil fire glowed in her eyes, and she looked at Mary as if she would search her to the bone.

"How do you *know* that?" she asked with cold hatred in her voice.

"The servants will talk," replied Mary, "as I mentioned."

"The foolish fellow," Sepia returned with a smile of contempt; "falling in love with me! A married man, too!"

"If you understood that, how did he come to be here so often?" asked Mary, looking her in the face.

But Sepia knew better than to declare war, a moment before it was unavoidable.

"Have I not told you," she said in a haughty tone, "that the man was in love with me?"

"And have you not just told me he was a married man? Could he have come to the house so often without at least your permission?"

Mary was actually taking the upper hand with her! Sepia felt it with scarcely repressible rage. "He deserved the punishment," she replied with calmness.

"You do not seem to have thought of his wife."

"Certainly not. She never gave me offense."

"Is offense the only ground for regarding a fellow human being?"

"Why should I think of her?"

"Because she was your neighbor, and you were doing her a wrong."

"Once and for all, Miss Marston," cried Sepia, overcome at last, "this kind of thing will not do with me. I may not be a saint, but I have honesty enough to know the genuine thing from humbug. You have thrown dust in a good many eyes in this house, but none in mine! I know you for what you are!"

By this time Mary had got her temper quite back in hand, taking a lesson from the serpent, who will often keep his when the dove loses hers. She hardly knew what fear was, for she had in her something a little stronger than what generally goes by the name of faith. She was therefore able to see that she ought, if possible, to learn Sepia's object in talking thus to her.

"Why are you telling me all this?" she asked quietly. "I will not flatter myself that it is from friendship."

"Certainly not. But the motive may be worthy, for all that. You are not the only one involved. People who would pass for better than their neighbors will never believe any good purpose in one who does not choose to talk their slang."

Sepia had repressed her rage, and through it looked aggrieved. "She confesses for some purpose," said Mary to herself, and waited.

"They are not all villains who are not saints," Sepia went on. "This man's wife is your friend?"

"She is."

"Well, the man himself is my friend—in a sort of sense."

A strange shiver went through Mary, and seemed to make her angry. Sepia went on.

"I confess, I did allow the poor boy—he is little more—to talk foolishly to me. I was amused at first, but perhaps I have not quite escaped unhurt. And as a woman, you must understand that, when a woman has once felt in that way, if but for a moment, she would at least be—sorry—" Here her voice faltered, and she did not finish the sentence, but began afresh: "What I want of you is, through his wife, or any way you think best, to let the poor fellow know he had better slip away—to France, say—and stay there till the thing has blown over."

"But why should you imagine he has anything to do with the matter? The ring will be found, and then the hat will mean nothing."

"Well," replied Sepia, putting on an air of openness, and for that sake an air of familiarity, "I see I must tell you the whole truth. I never did for a moment believe Mr. Helmer had anything to do with the business, though when you made me angry I pretended to believe it, and that you were in it as well: that was merely from my irritation. But there is sure to be trouble, for my cousin is miserable about her sapphire, which she values more than anything she has. And if it is not found, the affair will be put into the hands of the police, and then what will become of poor Mr. Helmer, be he as innocent as you and I believe him! Even if the judge should declare that he leaves the court without a blot on his character, Newgate mud is sure to stick, and he will be *half* looked upon as a thief for the rest of his days. The world is so unjust! And that is not all, for they will put you in the witness box and make you confess the man an old friend of yours from the same part of the country, whereupon the counsel for the prosecution will not fail to hint that you ought to be standing beside the accused. Believe me, Mary, that, if Mr. Helmer is taken up on charges for this, you will not come out of it clean."

"Still, you explain nothing," said Mary. "You would not have me believe it is for my sake you are giving yourself all this trouble?"

"No. But I thought you would see where I was leading you. For—and now for the *whole* truth—although nothing can touch the character of one in my position, it would be worse than awkward for me to be spoken of in connection with the poor fellow's visits to the house. *My* honesty would not be called into question as yours would, but what is dear to me as my honesty—nay, it certainly would. My reputation, you know, might not hold up so well were it known I had had anything to do with such a fellow. You see now why I came to you!—You must go to his wife, or, better still, to Mr. Helmer himself, and tell him what I have been saying to you. He will at once see the necessity of disappearing for a while."

Mary had listened attentively, and she could not help fearing that something worse than unpleasant might be at hand. But she did not trust Sepia, and in no case could she consent that Tom should compromise himself. Danger of this kind must be met, not avoided. Still, whatever could be done ought to be done to protect him, especially in his present critical state. A breath of such a suspicion as this reaching him might be the death of him, and of Letty too.

"I will think over what you have said," she answered. "But I cannot give him the advice you wish me to. What I shall do I cannot say—the thing has come upon me with such suddenness."

"You have no choice that I can see," said Sepia. "He either disappears or is ruined. I give you fair warning that I will stop at nothing where my own reputation is concerned. You and yours shall be trod in the dirt before I allow a spot on my character!"

To Mary's relief they were here interrupted by the hurried entrance of Mrs. Redmain. She almost ran up to her, and took her by both hands.

"You dear creature! You have brought me my ring!"

Mary shook her head with a little sigh.

"But you have come to tell me where it is?"

"Alas! no, dear Mrs. Redmain. I am sorry!" said Mary.

"Then you must find it," she said, and turned away with an ominous-looking frown.

"I will do all I can to help you find it."

"Oh, you *must* find it! My jewel case was in your charge."

"But there has been time to lose everything in it, the one after the other, since I gave it up. The sapphire ring was there, I know, when I left the house."

"That cannot be. You gave me the box, and I put it away myself, and the next time I looked in it, it was not there."

"I wish I had asked you to open it when I gave it to you," said Mary.

"I wish you had," said Hesper. "But the ring must be found, or I shall send for the police."

"I will not make matters worse, Mrs. Redmain," said Mary, with as much calmness as she could assume, and much was needed, "by pointing out what your words imply. If you really mean what you say, it is I who must insist on the police being sent for."

"I am sure, Mary," said Sepia, speaking for the first time since Hesper's entrance, "that your mistress had no intention of accusing you."

"Of course not," said Hesper. "Only what am I to do? I must have my ring. Why did you come, if you had nothing to tell me about it?"

"How could I stay away when you were in trouble? Have you searched everywhere?"

"Everywhere I can think of."

"Would you like me to help you look? I feel certain it will be found."

"No, thank you. I am sick of looking."

"Shall I go then?—What would you like me to do?"

"Go to your room, and wait till I send for you."

"I must not be away from my invalids long," said Mary, as cheerfully as she could.

"Oh, indeed! I thought you had come back to your work!"

"I did not understand from your letter that you wished that, ma'am. Though indeed, I could not have come just yet in any case."

"Then you mean to go and leave things just as they are?"

"I am afraid there is no help for it. If I could do anything—but I will call again tomorrow, and every day till the ring is found, if you like."

"Thank you," said Hesper dryly. "I don't think that would be of much use."

"I will call anyhow," returned Mary, "and inquire whether you would like to see me. I will go to my room now, and while I wait will get some things I want."

"As you please," said Hesper.

Scarcely was Mary in her room, however, when she heard the door, which had the trick of falling shut of itself, closed and locked, and she knew that she was a prisoner. For one moment a frenzy of anger overcame her; the next, she remembered where her life was hid, knew that nothing could touch her, and was calm. While she took from her drawers the things she wanted, and put them in her handbag, she heard the door unlocked, but, as no one entered, she sat down to wait what would come next.

As soon as she was aware of her loss, Mrs. Redmain had gone in distress to tell her husband, who had given her the ring as a gift in the first place. Unlike his usual self, he had showed interest in the affair. She attributed this to the value of the jewel, and the fact that he himself had chosen it. He thought himself very knowing in stones, and he was somewhat, and the sapphire was in truth a most rare one. But it was for quite other reasons that Mr. Redmain cared about its loss: it would, he hoped, like the famous carbuncle, cast a light all round it into the persons involved.

He was as yet by no means well, and had not been out of the house since his return.

The moment Mary was out of the room, Hesper rose.

"I should be a fool to let her leave the house," she said.

"Hesper, you will do nothing but mischief," cried Sepia.

Hesper paid no attention, but locked the door of Mary's room, and then ran to her husband's and told him she had made her a prisoner.

No sooner was she in her husband's room than Sepia hastened to unlock Mary's door. But just as she did so, she heard someone on the stair above, and retreated without going in. She would then have turned the key again, but now she heard steps on the stair below, and once more withdrew.

Mary heard a knock at her door. Mewks entered. He brought a request from his master that she would go to his room.

She rose and went, taking her bag with her.

"You may go now, Mrs. Redmain," said her husband when Mary entered. "Get out, Mewks," he added, and both lady and valet disappeared.

"So!" he said with a grin of pleasure. "Here's a pretty business! You may sit down, though. You haven't got the ring in that bag there?"

"Nor anywhere else, sir," answered Mary. "Shall I shake it all out on the floor?"

"Nonsense! You don't imagine me such a fool as to suppose, if you had it, you would carry it about in your bag!"

"You don't really believe I have it, sir—do you?" she returned.

"How am I to know what to believe? There is something dubious about you—you have yourself all but admitted that: how am I to know that robbery might not be your little dodge? All that rubbish you talked at Lychford about honesty, and taking no wages, and loving your mistress, and all that rot, looks devilish like something off the square! That ring now, the stone of it alone is worth seven hundred pounds: one might let pretty good wages go for a chance like that!"

Mary looked him in the face, and made him no answer. He spied a danger: if he irritated her, he would get nothing out of her.

"My girl!" he said, changing his tone, "I believe you know nothing about the ring; I was only teasing you."

Mary could not help a sigh of relief, and her eyes fell, for she felt them beginning to fill. She could not have believed that the judgment of such a man would ever mean so much to her. But the unity of the race is a thing that cannot be broken.

Now although Mr. Redmain was by no means so sure of her innocence as he had pretended, he did at least wish and hope to find her innocent— from no regard for her, but because there was another he would be more glad to find concerned in the ugly affair.

"Mrs. Redmain," he went on, "would have me hand you over to the police. But I won't. You may go home when you please, and you need fear nothing."

He had the house where the Helmers lodged already being watched, and knew this much, that someone was ill there, and that the doctor came almost every day.

"I certainly shall fear nothing," said Mary, not quite trusting him. "My fate is in God's hands."

"We know all about that," said Mr. Redmain. "I'm up to most dodges. But look here, my girl; it wouldn't be prudent in me, lest there should be such a personage as you have just mentioned, to be hard upon any of my fellow creatures. I am pretty sure one day to be in misfortune myself. You might not think it of me, but I am not quite a heathen, and do reflect a little at times. You may be as wicked as I am myself, or as good as Joseph for anything I know or care, for, as I say, it isn't my business to judge you. Tell me now what you are up to, and I will make it the better for you."

Mary had been trying hard to get at what he was "up to," but found herself quite bewildered.

"I am sorry, sir," she faltered, "but I haven't the slightest idea what you mean."

"Then you go home," he said. "I will send for you when I want you."

The moment she was out of the room, he rang his bell violently. Mewks appeared.

"Go after that young woman—do you hear? You know her—Miss—damn, what's her name?—Harland or Cranston, or—oh, hang it! you know well enough, you rascal!"

"Do you mean Miss Marston, sir?"

"Of course I do! Why didn't you say so before? Go after her. I tell you, and be quick about it. If she goes straight home—you know where—come back as soon as she's inside the door."

"Yes, sir."

"Go, confound you, or you'll lose sight of her!"

"I'm listening for the street-door, sir. There it is now!"

And with the word he left the room.

Mary was too much absorbed in her own thoughts to notice that she was followed by a man with the collar of his overcoat up to his eyes, and a woolen comforter round his face. She walked on steadily for home, scarcely seeing the people that passed her. It was clear to Mewks that she had not a suspicion of being kept in sight. He saw her in at the door, and went back to his master.

There was one other fact that Mewks carried to his master—namely, that as Mary came near the door of the house, she was met by "a rough looking man" who came walking slowly along, as if he had been going up and down the sidewalk waiting for her. He made her an awkward bow as she drew near, and she stopped and had a long conversation with him— such it seemed to Mewks, at least, annoyed that he could hear nothing of it, and afraid of attracting their attention. After this the man went away, and Mary went into the house. This report made his master grim, for, through the description Mewks gave, he suspected a thief disguised as a workman. But his hopes were against the supposition, and he dwelt not long on it.

The man who stopped Mary, and whom indeed she would have stopped, was Joseph Jasper, the violin-playing blacksmith. That he was rough in appearance no one would deny, but one less likely thief would have been hard to find. His hands were very rough and ingrained with black. His fingers were long, but square at the points, and had no resemblance to the long, tapering fingers of an artist or pickpocket. His clothes were of corduroy, not especially grimy because of the huge apron of thick leather he wore at his work. But they looked none the better that he had topped them off with his tall Sunday hat.

His complexion was a mixture of brown and browner. His black eyebrows hung far over the blackest of eyes, the brightest flashing of which was never seen because all the time he played he kept them closed tightly. His face wore its natural clothing—a mustache thick and well-shaped, and a beard not too large, of a color that looked like black burned brown. His hair was black and curled all over his head. His whole appearance was that of a workman; a quick glance could never have suspected him a poet-musician. But as little could even such a glance have failed to see in him an honest man. He was powerfully built, over the middle height, but not tall. He spoke very fair, old-fashioned English, with the Yorkshire tone and accent. His walk was rather plodding, and his movements slow and stiff; but in communion with his violin they were free enough, and the more delicate for the strength that was in them; at the anvil they were as supple as powerful. On his face dwelt an expression that was not to be read by the indifferent—a waiting in the midst of work, as of a man to whom the sense of the temporary was always present, but present with the constant reminder that, just therefore, work must be as good as work can be that things may last their due time.

The following was the conversation Mewks was unable to hear.

Mary held out her hand to Jasper, and it disappeared in his. He held it for a moment with a great but gentle grasp, and, as he let it go, said: "I took the liberty of watching for you, miss. I wanted to ask a favor of you. It seemed to me you would take no offense."

"You might be sure of that," Mary answered. "You have a right to anything I can do for you."

He fixed his gaze on her for a moment, as if he did not understand her.

"I've done nothing for you," he finally said. "It's all very well to go on playing, but that's not doing anything. And if *he* had done nothing, there would have been no fiddling at all. I know you understand me, miss: work comes before music, and makes the soul of it; it's not the music that makes the doing. I'm a poor hand at saying without my fiddle, miss. You'll excuse me."

Mary's heart was throbbing. She had not heard a word like this—not since her father went to what people call "the other side." She felt as if the spirit of her father had descended on the strange workman, and had sent him to her. She looked at him with shining eyes, and did not speak. He resumed, as fearing he had not conveyed his thought.

"What I mean is, miss, that the poor gentleman in there must need all the help you can give him, and more. There must surely be left something for a man to do. He must need lifting done at times, and that's not fit for either of you ladies."

"Thank you," said Mary heartily. "I will mention it to Mrs. Helmer, and I am sure she will be very glad for your help sometimes."

"Couldn't you ask her now, miss? I should like to know when I should call. But perhaps the best way would be to walk about here in the evening, after my day's work is over, and then one of you could run down any time if you needed me."

To Tom and Letty it seemed quite peculiar that such a stranger would be ready to walk about the street in order to be at hand to help them. But Mary was only delighted, not surprised, for what the man had said to her was both intelligible and absolutely reasonable. One who is the servant of the Lord will often be found doing things the world cannot understand.

Joseph did not, however, have to wander the street. The arrangement was made that as soon as his work was over, he should come and see whether there was anything he could do for them. And he never came but there was something, and if nothing else was wanted of him, he was always ready to discourse on his violin. When Tom was not in the mood for music, sometimes Mary would read to him.

Joseph was a man of very little education, but showed signs of being what men call a genius. His father, who was a blacksmith before him, and a local preacher, had married a second time, and Joseph was the only child of the second marriage. His father had brought him up to his own trade, and, after his death, Joseph came to work in London, mainly because his sister had preceded him. He was now thirty, and had from the first been saving what he could of his wages in the hope of one day having a smithy of his own, and his time more at his own ordering than someone else's.

Mary saw that in his violin he possessed a grand fundamental undeveloped education. He was like a man going about the world with a ten-thousand-pound note in his pocket, but not enough sixpences to pay for his daily needs. But there was another education working in him far deeper, and already more developed, than that which divine music even was giving him. This Mary recognized also—this was what chiefly attracted her to him, and was simply this: the man was one of those childlike natures that may indeed lack formal education or training, but which take everything to themselves, and the moment they do become aware of a thing, strive immediately to put it into practical reality in their life.

Mary had taken for herself the rooms below, formerly occupied by the Helmers, with the hope of seeing them reinstated in them before long. There she had a piano, the best she could afford to rent, and she found herself wishing that Joseph might be given some training in the mechanics of violin playing so that they might one day play together. Thus she hoped to do what she could toward the breaking of the invisible bonds that tied the wings of Jasper's genius.

Mary was too wise to hurry anything, but gradually, when he came, sat down at her piano and asked him to join her, if he was not immediately needed upstairs.

"How nice it would be," she said one evening, "if we could play together sometimes."

"Oh, that could hardly be, miss," he replied. "I know nothing but my own songs, and they're not written down. I've heard tell of the notes and all that, but I don't know how to work or read them."

"You have heard the choir in the church—all keeping with the organ," said Mary.

"Scarcely since I was a child. My mother took me sometimes then. But I was always wanting to get out again, and paid no attention."

"Do you never go to church now?"

"No, miss—not for years. Time's too precious to waste."

"How do you spend it then?"

"As soon as I've had my breakfast—that's on a Sunday, I mean—I get up and lock my door and set myself to have a day of it. Then I read the next thing in my Bible where I stopped last—whether it be a chapter or a verse—till I get the sense of it—if I can't get that, it's no use to me. I don't read so well, but well enough to get under the words a bit if I stick to it long enough. Then I take my fiddle and bow, and go stirring and stirring about at the story, and the music keeps coming and coming. And when it stops, which it does sometimes all at once, then I go back to the book."

"But you don't go on like that all day, do you?" said Mary.

"I generally go on till I'm hungry. Then I stop for something to eat, and come back and begin again."

"Will you let me teach you to read music?" said Mary, more and more delighted with him, and desirous of contributing to his growth—the one great service of the universe.

"If you would, miss, perhaps I might be able to learn. You see, I never was like other people. Mother was the only one that didn't take me for backward—you know, slow. She gave me her large Testament when she was dying. But Ann tells me I'm a heathen and worship my fiddle because I don't go to church with her, but it does seem such a waste of good time. I'd go to church, though, if I knew it to be the right thing to do, only it's hard to work all the week and have to be wearied out on Sunday too. I would be longing for my fiddle the whole time. You don't think that a great person like God cares whether we pray to him in a room or a church, do you, miss?"

"No, I don't," answered Mary. "For my own part, I find I can pray best at home."

"So can I," said Joseph. "Though sometimes I can't pray at all till I get my fiddle under my chin, and then it says all the prayers for me till I grow able to pray myself. And sometimes, when I seem to have gotten to the outside of prayer, and my soul is hungrier than ever, only I can't tell what I want, all at once I'm at my fiddle again, and it's praying for me."

Mary thought of all the "groanings that cannot be uttered." Perhaps that is just what music is meant for—to say the things that have no shape, therefore have no words, yet are intensely alive—the unembodied children of thought, the eternal child. Certainly the musician can groan the better with the aid of his violin. Surely this man's instrument was the gift of God to him. All God's gifts are a giving of himself. The Spirit can better dwell in a violin than in an ark or in the mightiest of temples.

"But you know, Mr. Jasper," said Mary, "when many violins play together, each taking a part in relation to all the rest, a much grander music is the result than any single instrument could produce."

"I've heard about such things, but I've never heard them."

He had never been to a concert, an oratorio, or a play.

"Then you shall," said Mary, her heart filling with delight at the thought. "—But what if in the same way the prayers of all souls may blend like many violins? We are all brothers and sisters, you know—and what if the gathering together in church be one way of making up a concert of souls?—imagine one mighty prayer, breaking like a huge wave against the foot of his throne!"

"There would be some force in a wave like that!" said Joseph. "But it seems to me that churches can't be the places to tune the fiddles for that kind of consort. The kind of prayer wave you're talking about must involve people praying in a bigger way than any of the single church-houses recognize. You see, miss, I'm sure there are praying folk all throughout the world like me, who aren't in churches. And then there are churches here and churches there that almost seem set up like enemies of one another, judging from the way they argue about all the little things God doesn't himself seem to care much about. And that's one of the reasons why I don't care to go into them. I never heard a sermon that didn't seem to make of Christ nothing like a live man at all. It always seemed to me more like a fellow they had dressed up and called by his name than the man I read about in my mother's Bible."

"How my father would have delighted in this man!" said Mary to herself.

"You see, miss," Jasper resumed. "I was brought up in a church, my father being a local preacher, and a very good man. Perhaps, if I had been as clever as sister Ann, I might be thinking now just as she does. But it seems to me a man that is born stupid has much to be thankful for. He can't take in things before his heart's ready for believing them, and so they don't get spoiled, like a child's book before he is able to read it. All that I heard when I went with my father to his preaching was to me no more than one of the chapters full of names in the Book of Chronicles. I wasn't even frightened at the awful things my father said about hell and the certainty of our going there if we didn't lay hold upon the Savior. For all the time he showed but such a ghost of a man that he called the Savior as it wasn't possible to lay hold upon. Not that I reasoned about it that way then; I only felt no interest in it all."

"So what happened to change that?" asked Mary.

"After my father and mother were gone, and I was at work and away from the church—well, I needn't trouble you with what set me thinking— only it was a great disappointment, such as I suppose most young fellows have to go through. What came of it, however, was that I began to read my mother's big Testament in earnest, and then my conscience began to speak. Here was a man who said he was God's Son, and sent by him to look after us, and we must do what he told us or we should never be able to see our Father in heaven. That's what I made out of it, at least. And my conscience said to me that I must do as he said, seeing he had taken all that trouble, and come down to look after us. If he spoke the truth, and nobody could listen to him without being sure of that, there was nothing left but just to do the thing he said. So I set about getting a hold of anything he did say, and trying to do it. And then it was that I first began to be able to play on the fiddle, though I had been muddling away at it for a long time before. I knew I could play then, because I understood what it said to me, and got help out of it. I don't really mean that, you know, miss, for I know well enough that the fiddle in itself is nothing, and nothing is anything but the way God takes to teach us. And that's how I came to know you, miss."

"How do you mean that?" asked Mary.

"I used to be frightened of Sister Ann. After I came to London, at first I wouldn't go near her. But I thought Jesus Christ would have me go, and if I hadn't gone to see her, I should never have seen you. When I went to see her, I took my fiddle with me, and when she would start going on at me for not going to church, I would just give my fiddle a squeeze under my arm, and that gave me patience."

"But we heard you playing to her."

"That was because I always forgot myself while she was talking. The first time, I remember, it was from her making God out not fit for any honest man to believe in. I was so miserable listening to her that I began to play without knowing it, and it couldn't have been very loud, for she went on about the devil picking up the good seed sown in the heart. Off I went into that, and there I saw no end of birds with long necks and short legs gobbling up the grain. But a little way off there was the long beautiful stalks growing strong and high, waving in God's wind, and the birds did not go near them."

Mary drew a long breath, and thought to herself: *The man is a poet!*—"You're not afraid of your sister now?" she said to him.

"Not a bit," he answered. "Since I knew you, I feel as if we had in a sort of a way changed places, and she was a little girl that must be humored, and made the best of. When she scolds, I laugh, and try to make a bit of fun with her. But she's always so sure she's right that you wonder how the world got made before she was up."

They parted with the understanding that when he came next she should give him his first lesson in reading music.

Within a short time he was able to learn the notes, and then grew so delighted with some of the music Mary got for him, entering into every nicety of severest law, that for a while he ceased to play anything of his own.

"How can I go on playing such loose, skinning things," he would say, "when here are such perfect shapes all ready for my hand!"

But Mary said to herself that, if these were shapes, his were odors.

45 / The Sapphire

One morning as Mary sat at her piano, Mewks was shown into the room. He brought the request from his master that she would go see him. She did not much like it, but did not hesitate.

She was shown into the room Mr. Redmain called his study, which was connected by a dressing room with his bedroom. He was seated, evidently waiting for her.

"Ah, Miss Marston!" he said. "I have a piece of good news for you— so good that I thought I should like to give it you myself."

"You are very kind, sir," Mary answered.

"There!" he went on, holding out what she saw at once was the lost ring.

"I am so glad," she said, and took it in her hand. "Where was it found?"

"There's the point!" he returned. "That is just why I sent for you. Can you suggest any explanation of the fact that it was found, after all, in a corner of my wife's jewel box? Who searched the box last?"

"I do not know, sir."

"Did you search it?"

"No, sir. I offered to help Mrs. Redmain look for the ring, but she said it was of no use. Who found it, sir?"

"I will tell you who found it, if you will tell me who put it there."

"I don't know what you mean. It must have been there all the time."

"That's the point again! Mrs. Redmain swears it was not, and could not have been there when she looked for it. It is not like a small thing, you see. There is something mysterious about it."

He looked hard at Mary.

Mary had often admired the ring, as anyone who had an eye for stones would have. And now as they were talking she kept gazing at it. When Mr. Redmain ended, she stood silent. In her silence, her attention concentrated itself upon the sapphire. She stood long, looking closely at it, moving it about a little, and changing the direction of the light. And while her gaze was on the ring, Mr. Redmain's gaze was on her, watching her with equal attention. At last, with a sigh, as, if waking from a reverie, she laid the ring on the table. But Mr. Redmain still stared in her face.

"Now what is it you've got in your head?" he said at last. "I've been watching you. Come, out with it!"

"I was only plaguing myself between my recollection of the stone and the actual look of it," answered Mary. "It is so annoying to find what seemed to be a clear recollection proves a deceitful one. It may appear a presumptuous thing to say, but my recollection seems of a finer color."

While she spoke, she had again taken the ring, and was looking at it. Mr. Redmain snatched it from her hand.

"The devil!" he cried. "You haven't the face to hint that the stone has been changed?"

Mary laughed.

"Such a thing never came into my head. But now that you have put it there, I could almost believe it."

"Get out with you!" he cried, casting at her a strange look, which she could not understand, and the same moment he pulled the bell-rope hard.

That done, he began to examine the ring intently, as Mary had been doing, and did not speak a word. Mewks came.

"Show Miss Marston out," said his master, "and tell my coachman to bring the hansom around immediately."

"For Miss Marston?" inquired Mewks, who had learned not a little cunning in the service.

"No!" roared Mr. Redmain, and Mewks darted from the room, followed more leisurely by Mary.

"I don't know what to come of him!" ventured Mewks, as he led the way down the stair.

But Mary took no notice and left the house.

For about a week she heard nothing.

In the meantime, Mr. Redmain had been prosecuting certain inquiries he had some time ago begun, and another quite new one besides. He was acquainted with many people of many different sorts, and had been to jewelers and pawnbrokers, gamblers and lodging-house keepers, and had learned some things to his purpose.

Once more Mary received from him a summons, and once more, against her liking, obeyed. She was less disinclined to go this time, however, for she felt a growing curiosity about the ring.

"I want you to come back to the house," he said abruptly the moment she entered his room.

Mary was hardly prepared for such a request. Ever since the ring was found, so long a time had passed that she never expected to hear from the house again. But Tom was now so much better, and Letty so much like her former self, that, if Mrs. Redmain had asked her, she might perhaps have consented.

"Mr. Redmain," she answered, "you must see that I cannot do so only at your desire."

"Oh rubbish!—humbug!" he returned with annoyance. "Don't fancy I am asking you to go fiddle-faddling about my wife again. I don't see how you *can* do that, after the way she has used you! But I have reasons for wanting to have you within call. Go to Mrs. Perkin. I won't take a refusal."

"I cannot do it, Mr. Redmain," said Mary; "the thing is impossible." She turned to leave the room.

"Stop!" cried Mr. Redmain, jumping from his chair.

He would not have succeeded in preventing her had not Mewks met her full face in the doorway. She had to draw back, and the man, perceiving at once how things were, closed the door the moment he entered, and stood with his back against it.

"He's in the drawing room, sir," said Mewks.

A scarcely perceptible sign of question was made by the master, and answered in kind by the man.

"Show him here directly," said Mr. Redmain. Then turning to Mary, "Go out that way, Miss Marston, if you will go," he said, and pointed to the dressing room.

Without a suspicion, Mary obeyed. But just as she discovered that the door into the bedroom beyond was locked, she heard the door behind her locked also. She turned and knocked.

"Stay where you are," said Mr. Redmain, in a low but imperative voice. "I cannot let you out until this gentleman is gone. You must hear what is said: I want you for a witness."

Bewildered and annoyed, Mary stood motionless in the middle of the small room, and presently heard a man, whose voice seemed not quite strange to her, greet Mr. Redmain like an old friend. The latter made a slight apology for having sent for him to his study—claiming the privilege, he said, of an invalid, who could not for a time have the pleasure of meeting him either at the club or his wife's parties. The visitor answered agreeably, with a touch of merriment that seemed to indicate a soul at ease with itself and with the world.

Suddenly Mary came to herself, and was aware that she was in quite a false position. She withdrew to the farthest corner, sat down, closed her ears with the palms of her hands, and waited.

She had sat thus for a long time, not weary, but occupied with such thoughts as could hardly for a century or two cross the horizon line of such a soul as Mr. Redmain's, even if he were at once to repent, when she heard a loud voice calling her name from a distance. She raised her head, and saw the white, skin-drawn face of Mr. Redmain grinning at her from the open door. When he spoke again, his words sounded like thunder, for she had removed her hands from her ears.

"I fancy you've had a dose of it!" he said.

As he spoke, she rose to her feet, her countenance illumined both with righteous anger and the tender shine of prayer. Her look went to what he had of a heart, and the slightest possible color rose to his face.

"Gone a step too far, curse it all!" he murmured to himself. "There's no knowing one woman by another."

"I see!" he said. "It's been a trifle too much for you, and I don't wonder! You needn't believe a word I said about myself. It was all humbug to make the villain show his game."

"I did not hear a word, Mr. Redmain," she said.

"Oh, you needn't trouble yourself!" he returned. "I meant you to hear it all. What did I put you there for, but to get your oath to what I drew out of the fellow? A fine thing if your pretended squeamishness should ruin my plot! What do you think of yourself, hey?—but I don't believe it."

He looked at her keenly, expecting a response, but Mary made him none. For some moments he regarded her curiously, then turned away into the study, saying: "Come along. By Jove! I'm ashamed to say it, but I half begin to believe you. I did think I was past being taken in, but it seems possible once again. Of course, you will return to Mrs. Redmain now that all is cleared up."

"It is impossible," Mary answered. "I cannot live in a house where the lady mistrusts and the gentleman insults me."

She left the room and Mr. Redmain did not try to prevent her. As she left the house she burst into tears; and this fact Mewks carried to his master.

The man was all the more careful to report everything about Mary. But there was one in the house of whom he never reported anything, but to whom, on the contrary, he told everything he thought she would care to know. Till Sepia came, he had been conventionally faithful—faithful with the faith of a lackey, that is—but she had found no difficulty in making of him a spy upon his master.

While Mary sat deaf in the corner of the dressing room, what passed was the following:

Mr. Redmain asked his visitor what he would have. He made choice of brandy and soda-water, and the bell was rung. A good deal of conversation followed about a disputed point in a recent game of cards at one of the clubs.

The talk then veered in another direction—that of personal adventure, so guided by Mr. Redmain. He told extravagant stories about himself and his doings, in particular various ruses by which he had contrived to lay his hands on money. And whatever he told, his guest capped, narrating trick upon trick to which on different occasions he had had recourse. At all of them Mr. Redmain laughed heartily, and applauded their cleverness extravagantly, though some of them were downright swindling.

At last Mr. Redmain told how he had once gotten money out of a lady. I do not believe there was a word of truth in it. But it was capped by the other with a narrative that seemed especially pleasing to the listener. In the midst of a burst of laughter, he rose and rang the bell. Count Galofta thought it was to order something more in the way of "refreshment," and was surprised when he heard his host ask the man to request the favor of Miss Yolland's presence. But the Count had not studied non-expression in vain, and had brought it to a degree of perfection not easily disturbed. Casting a glance at him as he gave the message, Mr. Redmain could read nothing. But this was in itself suspicious to him—and justly, for the man ought to have been surprised at such a close to the conversation they had been having.

Sepia had been told that Galofta was in the study, and therefore received the summons—a thing that had never happened before—with the greater alarm. She tried to make what preparation she could against showing her surprise. Thoroughly capable of managing her features, her anxiety was still sufficient to deprive her of power over her complexion, and thus, she entered the room with her face revealing her emotion. Having greeted the Count with the greatest composure, she turned to Mr. Redmain with question in her eyes.

"Count Galofta," said Mr. Redmain in reply, "has just been telling me a curious story of how a certain rascal got possession of a valuable jewel from a lady with whom he pretended to be in love, and I thought the opportunity a good one for showing you a strange discovery I have made with regard to the sapphire Mrs. Redmain missed for so long. Very odd tricks are played with gems—such gems, that is as are of enough value to make it worth a rogue's while."

So saying, he took the ring from one drawer, and from another a bottle, from which he poured something into a crystal cup. Then he took a file, and, looking at Galofta, in whose well-drilled features he believed he read something that was more than mere curiosity, said, "I am going to show you something very curious," and began to file away that part of the setting which immediately clasped the sapphire.

"What are you doing?" cried Sepia. "You are destroying the ring! What will cousin Hesper say?"

Mr. Redmain paid no attention, but filed away, then with the help of a pair of pincers, freed the stone and held it up in his hand.

"You see this?" he said.

"A splendid sapphire!" answered Count Galofta, taking it in his fingers, but, as Mr. Redmain saw, not looking at it closely.

"I have always heard it called a splendid stone," said Sepia, whose complexion, though not her features, passed through several changes while all this was going on: she was obviously nervous.

Her inquisitor did not fail to surprise the uneasy glances she threw, furtively though involuntarily, toward the face of the Count—who never once looked in hers: tolerably sure of himself, he was not sure of her.

"That ring, when I bought it—the stone of it," said Mr. Redmain, "was a star sapphire, and worth seven hundred pounds. Now, the whole thing is worth about ten."

As he spoke, he threw the stone into the cup, let it lie a few moments, and took it out again. Then, almost with a touch, he divided it in two, the one a mere scale.

"There!" he said, holding out the thin part on the tip of a finger, "that is a slice of genuine sapphire. And there!" holding out the rest of the seeming stone to which the gem had been glued, "that is glass."

"What a shame!" cried Sepia.

"Of course," said the Count, "you will prosecute the jeweler."

"I will not prosecute the jeweler," answered Mr. Redmain. "But I have taken some trouble to find out who changed the stones."

With that he threw both the bits of blue into a drawer, and the contents of the cup into the fire. A great flame flew up the chimney, and, as if struck at the sight of it, he stood gazing for a moment after it had vanished.

When he turned, the Count was gone, as he had expected, and Sepia stood with eyes full of anger and fear. Her face was set and colorless, and strange to look upon.

"Very odd—isn't it?" said Mr. Redmain, and, opening the door of his dressing room, called out: "Miss Marston!"

When he turned, Sepia too was gone.

I would not have my reader take Sepia for an accomplice in the robbery. Even Mr. Redmain did not believe that: she was much too prudent! His idea was that she had been wearing the ring and that, with or without her knowledge, the fellow had gotten hold of it and carried it away, then brought it back, treating the thing as a joke, when she was only too glad to restore it to the jewel-case, hoping the loss of it would then pass for an oversight on the part of Hesper. If he was right in this theory of the affair, then the Count had certainly a hold upon her, and she dared not or would not expose him.

He had before discovered that about this time the Count had had losses, and was said to be unable to meet them, when all of a sudden had showed himself "flush" again, and from that time on had had an extraordinary run of luck.

When he went out of the door of Mr. Redmain's study, he vanished from the house and almost as quickly from London altogether. Turning the first corner he came to, and the next and the next, he slipped into a mews, the court of which seemed empty, and slipped behind the gate. He wore a new hat and was clean shaven except for his upper lip. Presently a man came out of the mews in a Scotch cap and full beard.

What became of him Mr. Redmain did not care. He had no desire to punish him. It was enough that he had found him out, proved his suspicion correct, and obtained evidence against Sepia. He did not at once make up his mind how he would act; he had a certain pleasure in watching his victim. But he did not like the notion of Hesper—free, rich, and beautiful, and far from wise—with Sepia for a counselor.

For the present, the thing seemed to blow over. Mr. Redmain, who took pleasure in behaving generously so far as money was concerned, bought his wife the best sapphire he could find, and, for once, really pleased her.

But Sepia now knew that Mr. Redmain had to himself justified his dislike of her, and, as he said nothing, she was all the more certain he meant something. Therefore, she lived in constant dread of his sudden vengeance. But she could take no precaution against it, for she had not so much as a conjecture as to what form it might assume. From that time on, she was never at peace in his presence.

Nor was it a small addition to her misery that she imagined Mary fully aware of Mr. Redmain's opinion and intention with regard to her. For, whatever had passed first between the Count and Mr. Redmain, she did not doubt that Mary had heard, and was prepared to bring charges against her when the determined moment should arrive. How much the Count might or might not have said, she could not tell. But seeing their common enemy had permitted him to escape, she more than dreaded he had sold her secret for his own freedom, and had laid upon her a burden of lies as well.

46 / More Changes

With all Mr. Redmain's faults, there was a certain love of justice in the man. It was, however, as is the case with most of us, ten times the more in reference to the action of other people than to his own. He was much more indignant at any shortcoming of another's that crossed any desire or purpose of his own than he was anxious in his own person to fulfill justice when that fulfillment in its turn would cross any wish he cherished.

Badly as he had behaved to Mary, he was now furious with his wife for having treated her so heartlessly that she could not return to her service; for he began to think she might be one to depend upon, and to desire her alliance in the matter of ousting Sepia from the confidence of his wife.

Therefore, the moment Mary was out of the study, he walked into his wife's room and shut the door behind him. His presence there was enough to make her angry, but he took no notice of it.

"I want you to get that girl of yours back, and in double-quick time," he said.

"How dare you walk in here and proceed to order me about!" she retorted. "I no longer have the least use for the likes of her."

"If you do not do as I say, I shall know how to make you."

"If such a thing as this occurs again, Mr. Redmain," she said haughtily, "I shall go to Durnmelling."

She spoke with a vague idea that he stood in some awe of the father and mother whose dread, however well she hid it, she would never, while she lived, succeed in shaking off. But to the husband it was a rare delight to gain the upper hand over his wife in such a skirmish of words. He burst into a loud and almost merry laugh.

"Why you goose! If I send a telegram before you, they won't so much as open the door to you! They know better which side their bread is buttered on."

Hesper jumped up in a rage. This was too much—and the more too much that she believed it would be as he said.

"Mr. Redmain, if you do not leave the room, I will."

"Oh, don't!" he cried, in a tone of pretended alarm. His pleasure was great, for he had succeeded in stinging the impenetrable. But just as quickly his voice went cold. "I swear to you, madam, if you don't fetch that girl home within the week, I will discharge your coachman, sell your carriage, and leave you penniless. Good morning!"

She had no doubt he would do as he said. He would probably enjoy selling her horses! But she could not give in at once. I say "could not" because hers was the weak will that can hardly bring itself to do what it knows it must, and is continually mistaken for the strong will that defies and endures. She had a week to think about it, and she took all seven days, knowing all the time that she would capitulate in the end.

At length a letter of forced apology—and request to return—was written to Mary, then dispatched, received, and answered. Mary would not return. She had lost all hope of being of any true service to Mrs. Redmain, and she knew that, with Tom and Letty, she was really of use for the present.

After her reply, Mary lay awake one night and thought of many things she might have said and done better when she was with Hesper, and would gladly have given herself another chance. She could no longer flatter herself that she would ever be of any real good to her. She believed, in fact, that there was more hope even for Mr. Redmain. For had she not once, for one brief moment, seen him look a trifle ashamed of himself, while Hesper was and remained, so far as she could tell, altogether satisfied with herself? Equal to her own demands upon herself, there was nothing in her to begin with—no soil to work upon.

Meanwhile, for some time Tom made progress toward health, and was able to read a good part of the day. Most evenings he asked Joseph to play for him a while. When Joseph was through, Mary was always ready to give him a lesson; and, even had he been less gifted than he was, he could not have failed to make progress with such a teacher. And it was not long before he began to write out some of the things that came into his mind. To the first such that he brought to Mary, she managed to put a simple little accompaniment, and his delight over their first attempt to play it together was touching, and not a little amusing. Never was a pupil more humble or more obedient. Thinking nothing of himself or of anything he had done or could do, his path was open to the swiftest and highest growth. It matters little where a man may be at this moment; the point is whether he is growing. The next point will be whether he is growing at the ratio given him. The key to the whole thing is *obedience*, and nothing else.

The gift of such an instructor was to Joseph nothing less than a gift from on high. He was like a man seated on the grass outside the heavenly gate, from which every evening as the sun went down an angel would come to teach and teach, until he too should be fit to enter in. An hour would arrive when she would no longer have to come out to him where he sat. Under such an influence all that was gentlest and sweetest in his nature might well develop with rapidity, and every accidental roughness—and in him there was no other—by swift degrees vanish from both speech and manners. The angels do not need tailors to make their clothes: their habits come out of themselves.

As to falling in love with a lady like Mary, such a thing was as far from Jasper's consciousness as if she had been a queen. She belonged to another world from his, a world at which his world gazed from afar. Her absence might for him darken the universe as if the sun had withdrawn his brightness. But who thinks of falling in love with the sun, or dreams of climbing nearer to his radiance?

The day will come—or what of the long-promised kingdom of heaven?—when a woman, instead of spending anxious thought on the adornment of her own outward person, will seek with might the adornment of the inward soul of another, and will make that her crown of rejoicing. Nay, are there none such even now? The day will come when a man, rather than build a great house for the overflow of a mighty hospitality, will give himself, in the personal labor of outgoing love, to build spiritual houses like St. Paul—a higher art than any of man's invention. Oh, my brother and sister, what is there higher than to have a hand in making thy brother beautiful in God's sight!

Those who believe in such a calling believe that such growth, such creation, is all God cares about. They have become so blind with this fixed idea that they cannot see how God could care for anything else. They actually believe that the very Son of the life-making God lived and died for that and for nothing else. That such men and women are fools has been widely believed. But the end will alone reveal the beginning.

There soon came a change, however, and the lessons ceased altogether.

Tom had come down to his old quarters, and, in the arrogance of convalescence, had presumed on his imagined strength, had begun to get up and go about, and so caught cold. An alarming relapse was the result. The cold settled into his lungs, and the patient sank rapidly.

Joseph, whose violin was useless now, was not the less in attendance. Every evening when his work was over, he came knocking gently at the door of the parlor, and never left until Tom was settled for the night. They took turns watching Tom through the night, and when it was his turn, he never closed an eye, but at daybreak would rouse Mary, and go straight to his work, without so much as tasting food until the hour arrived for his mid-day meal.

Tom soon became aware that his days were numbered—what a phrase of unbelief that is, for are they not numbered from the beginning? Are our hairs numbered, and our days forgotten—till death gives a hint to the doctor? He was sorry for his past life, and thoroughly ashamed of much of it. For my part, I think he was taken away to have a little more of that care and nursing which neither his mother nor his wife had been woman enough to give the great baby.

Is it strange that one so used to bad company and bad ways should so alter in such a short time, and without any great struggle? The assurance of death at the door, and a wholesome shame of things that are past, may, I think, lead up to such a swift change, even in a much worse man than Tom. For there is the Life itself, all-surrounding, and ever-pressing in upon the human soul, wherever that soul will afford a chink of entrance; and Tom had not yet sealed up all his doors.

When he lay there dead, Letty had him already enshrined in her heart as the best of husbands—as her own Tom who had never said a hard word to her—as the cleverest as well as kindest of men, who had written poetry that would never die while the English language was spoken. Nor did *The Firefly* spare its dole of homage to the memory of one of its greatest writers. Indeed, all about its office had loved him, each in his own way. The print of him was deep in the heart of Letty, and not shallow in the affection of Mary; and such as these were not insignificant records for any man to leave behind him, as records go. Happy was he to have left behind him any love, especially such a love as Letty bore him. For what is the loudest praise of posterity to the quietest love of one's own generation?

For his mother, her memory was mostly in her temper. She had never understood her wayward child, just because she had given him her waywardness, and not parted with it herself, so that between the two of them they made havoc of love. She who gives her child all he desires, in the hope of thus binding his love to herself, no less than she who thwarts him in everything, may rest assured of the neglect she has richly earned. When she heard of his death, she howled and cursed her fate, and the woman, meaning poor Letty, who had parted her and her Tom, swearing she would never set eyes upon her, and never let her touch a farthing of Tom's money. She would not hear of paying Tom's debts, until Mary told her she then would, whereupon the fear of public disapprobation wrought for right if not righteousness.

But what was Mary now to do with Letty? She was little more than a baby herself. Children must learn to walk, but not by being turned out alone on the street.

Some perplexity was relieved for the present by the arrival of a letter from Mrs. Wardour to Letty, written in a tone of stiffly condescendent compassion—not so unpleasant to Letty as to Mary. But on the whole the letter was kind—perhaps a little repentant. It is hard to say, for ten persons will repent of a sin for every one who will confess it—I do not mean to the priest, that may be an easy matter, but to the only one who has a claim to the confession, namely, the person wronged. Yet such confession is in truth far more needful to the wronger than to the wronged; it is a small thing to be wronged, but a horrible thing to wrong.

The letter contained a poverty-stricken expression of sympathy, and an invitation to spend the summer months with them at her old home. It might, the letter said, prove but a dull place to her after the gaiety of London to which she had of late been accustomed, but it might still suit her present sad situation, and possibly uncertain prospects.

Letty's heart felt one little throb of gladness at the thought of being again at Thornwick, and in peace. With all the probable unpleasant side effects of the visit, she still thought there to be nowhere else that she could feel the same sense of shelter as where her childhood had passed.

Mary also was pleased. For although Letty might not be altogether comfortable, the visit would end, and by that time, she might know what could be devised best for her comfort and well-being.

47 / Turnbull and Marston

It was now Mary's turn to feel that she was, for the first time in her life, about to be cut adrift—adrift, that is, as a world is adrift on the surest of paths, though without eyes to see. For ten days or so, she could form no idea of what she should do next. But when we are in such perplexity, the fact seems plain that decision is not required of us—perhaps just because our way is at the moment being made straight for us.

Joseph called once or twice, but for Letty's sake they had no music.

One day Mary received an unexpected visit from Mr. Brett, her lawyer. He had been searching into the affairs of the shop and had discovered enough to make him uneasy, and indeed fill him with reproach at himself for not looking into things more thoroughly immediately after her father's death. He had come to tell her all he knew, and talk matters over with her that they might agree as to what proceedings should be taken.

I will not weary myself or my readers with business detail, for which I have no great aptitude and a good deal of ignorance. But in brief, Mr. Brett found that Turnbull had been speculating in several companies, trying to become rich in haste, and had instead lost what he had saved of the profits of the business, and all of Mary's as well. He had even borrowed against the original capital of the firm, allowed the stock to run down and deteriorate, so that the monthly business had fallen off as well. But what displeased Mary more than anything was that he had used money of her father's to speculate with in more than one bar and public-house. And she knew that, if such had been done in her father's lifetime, it would have been enough to make him insist on dissolving the partnership the moment the thing came to his knowledge, even had the investment been highly successful.

Therefore, it was impossible to allow her money to remain any longer in the power of such a man, and she gave authority to Mr. Brett to make the necessary arrangements for putting an end to the partnership between them.

It was a somewhat complicated and tedious business, and things looked worse the more they were searched into. Unable to varnish over the facts any longer, Mr. Turnbull wrote Mary a letter almost cringing in its tone, begging her to remember the years her father and he had been as brothers, how she had grown up in the shop, and had been to him, until misunderstandings arose, almost as a daughter, and insisting that her withdrawal from the shop had had no small share in the ruin of the business. He entreated her to leave things as they were, to trust him to see after the interests of the daughter of his old friend, and not insist upon measures which must end in a forced sale, in the shutting up of the shop of Turnbull and Marston, and the disgracing of her father's name along with his.

Mary replied that she was acting on the advice of her father's lawyer, and with the regard she owed her father's memory, in severing all connection with a man in whom she no longer had confidence, and insisted that the business be completed and put an end to as soon as possible.

She told Mr. Brett that, if it could be managed, she would prefer getting the shop, even at considerable loss, into her own hands, with what stock might be in it. Then she would attempt to conduct the business on principles her father would have approved of. She did not doubt she would soon be able to restore it to good repute. It would be necessary, however, to keep her desire a secret, otherwise Mr. Turnbull would be certain to frustrate it somehow.

Mr. Brett approved of her plan, for he knew she was widely respected and had many friends. Mr. Turnbull would be glad, he said, to give up the whole thing to escape prosecution—that at least was how Mary interpreted his somewhat technical statement of affairs between them.

The swindler wrote again, begging for a personal interview, which she declined, except in the presence of her lawyer.

Mary made up her mind that she would not go near Testbridge till everything was settled. A few days before Letty was to leave for Thornwick, Jasper called and heard about their plans. When Mary said to him she would miss her pupil, he smiled in a sort of abstracted way, as if not quite apprehending what she said.

So Mary was left alone—more alone than she had ever been in her life. But she did not feel lonely, for the best of reasons—that she never fancied herself alone, but knew that she was not. Joseph Jasper never came near her. She could not imagine why, and was disappointed and puzzled.

She went up to see Ann Byrom now and then. But how very different she seemed from the time when they first worked together over Hesper's twilight dress! Ever since Mary had made the acquaintance of her brother, she seemed to have changed toward her. Perhaps she was jealous; perhaps she believed Mary was confirming him in his bad ways.

It was the middle of the summer before the affairs of the firm were wound up, and the shop in the hands of the London man whom Mr. Brett had employed in the purchase.

Lawyer as he was, however, Mr. Brett had not been sharp enough for Turnbull.

The very next day, a shop in the same street that had been for rent for some time displayed above its now open door the sign, *John Turnbull, late*—then a very small *of—Turnbull and Marston*. Mr. Brett immediately saw the oversight of which he had been guilty. There was nothing in the shop when it was opened, but even that Turnbull utilized for advertising by making a to-do over it. He had so arranged that within an hour the goods began to arrive, and kept arriving, by every train, for days and days after, while all the time he made a great public show of himself, fussing about, the most triumphant man in the town. It made people talk, and if not always as he would have liked, yet it was talk, and in the matter of advertisement, that is the main thing.

When he told the news to Mary, it gave her not the smallest uneasiness. She only saw what had several times seemed on the point of happening in her father's lifetime. She would not have moved a finger to prevent it. Let the two principles meet, let business be conducted in two different ways according to two different sets of priorities, with what result God pleased!

Whether he had suspected Mary's design and had determined to challenge her before the public, I cannot tell. His wife continued to hate the business, but things appeared to go on with them just as before. They still inhabited the villa, the wife scornful of her surroundings, and the husband driving a good horse to his shop every morning. How he managed it all, nobody knew but himself, and whether he succeeded or not was a matter of small interest to any except his own family and his creditors. He was a man nowise beloved, although there was something about him that carried simple people with him—for his ends, not theirs. To those who alluded to the change, he represented it as entirely of his own doing, to be rid of the interference of Miss Marston in matters of which she knew nothing. He knew well that a confident lie has all the look of truth, and, while fact and falsehood were disputing together in men's mouths, he would be busy selling his drapery. The country people were flattered by the confidence he seemed to put in them by giving them this explanation, and those who liked him before sought the new shop as they had frequented the old one.

Unlike most men, not to mention lawyers, Mr. Brett fully admitted to Mary his oversight and took full responsibility upon himself for it. He was greatly relieved when she said she would not have had the thing any other way: she would gladly meet Mr. Turnbull in a fair field. Not that she would in the least think of him as a rival; she would simply carry out her own ideas of right, without regard to him or any measures he might take: the result should be as God willed. Mr. Brett shook his head. He knew her father, and saw the daughter prepared to go even further. Theirs were principles that did not come within the range of his practice! He said to himself and his wife that the world could not go on for twelve months if such ways were to become universal: whether by the world he meant his own profession, I will not inquire. Certainly he did not make the reflection that the new ways are intended to throw out the old ways, and the worst argument against any way is that the world cannot go on so; for that is just what is needed—that the world should not go on so.

Mr. Brett nevertheless admired not only Mary's pluck, but the business sense that she manifested. There is a holy way of doing business, and, little as business men may think it, that is the standard by which they must be tried. For their judge in business affairs is not their own trade or profession, but the man who came to convince the world concerning right and wrong and the choice between them; or, in the older speech—to reprove the world of sin, and of righteousness, and of judgment.

48 / Thornwick

It was almost with bewilderment that Letty Helmer revisited Thornwick.

The near past seemed to have vanished like a dream that leaves a sorrow behind it, and the far past to take its place. She had never been accustomed to reflect on her own feelings; things came, were welcome or unwelcome, proved better or worse than she had anticipated, passed away, and were mostly forgotten. With plenty of intelligence, Letty had not yet emerged from the cocoon condition. She lived much as one in a dream, with whose dream mingle sounds and glimmers from the waking world. Very few of us are awake, very few even alive in the true, availing sense. "Pooh! what nonsense!" says the sleeper, and will say it still until the true waking begins to come.

On the threshold of her old home, then, Letty found her old self awaiting her. She crossed it, and was once more just Letty, a Letty wrapped in the garments of sorrow, and with a heaviness at the heart, but far from such a miserable Letty as during the last of her former life there. Little joy had been hers since the terrible night when she fled from its closed doors, and now that she returned, she could take up everything where she had left it, except the gladness. But peace is better than gladness, and she was on the way to find that.

Mrs. Wardour, who, for all her severity, was not without a good-sized heart, and whose conscience had spoken to her about Letty, was touched with compassion at sight of her worn and sad look. She granted to herself that the poor thing had been punished enough, even for her lack of respect to the house of Thornwick, broke down a little, and took her to her bosom. Letty, loving and forgiving as always, nestled in it a moment, and after she went to her own room, wept quietly for a long time.

By degrees, rapid yet easy, she slid into all her old ways, took charge again of the dairy as if she had never left it, attended to the washing of the linen, darned the socks, and in everything but her pale, thin face and heavy heart was the young Letty again. She even went to the harness-room to look after cousin Godfrey's stirrups and bits.

Mrs. Wardour continued to be kind to her, but every now and then would allow a tone as of remembered naughtiness to be sub-audible in speech or request. Letty never resented it. She had been so used to it in the old days that it seemed only natural. And to balance it, her aunt considered her health in the kindest way. Now that Letty had known some of the troubles of marriage, she felt more sympathy with her, did not look down upon her from quite such a height, and to Letty this was strangely delightful.

When Godfrey saw her moving about the house as in former days, but changed, like one of the ghosts of his saddest dreams, a new love began to rise out of the buried seed of the old. In vain he reasoned with himself against it. The image of Letty, with her trusting eyes and her watching looks full of ministration, haunted him, and was too much for him. She was never the sort of woman he could have fancied himself falling in love with, for she was not even a *lady*, and not at all his ideal. A woman like Hesper, uplifted and strong, broad-fronted and fearless, large-limbed, and full of latent life was more of the ideal he could have written poetry about. But we are deeper than we know. Who is capable of knowing his own ideal? The ideal of a man's self is hid in the bosom of God, and may lie ages away from his knowledge; and his ideal of woman is the ideal belonging to this unknown self: the ideal only can bring forth an ideal. Gladly would Godfrey now have taken Letty to his arms. But he forced restraint upon himself, remembering the fact of his and her position, as well as the jealousy of his mother. Therefore, he kept out of her way as much as he could, went more about the farm, and took long rides.

Nothing could have been further from Letty's mind than any hint of what Godfrey felt toward her. Her poet was gone from her. To her, Tom was the greatest, the one poet of the age. He had been hers—was hers still, for did he not die telling her that he would go on watching till she came to him? He had loved her, she knew; he had learned to love her better before he died. She must be patient; the day would come when, as he had told her, she would soar aloft in search of her mate. The sense of wifehood had grown one with her consciousness. If she did not read poetry, she read her New Testament, and if she understood it only in a childish fashion, she obeyed it in a childlike one, whence the way of all wisdom lay open before her. It is not where one is, but in what direction he is going. Before her too was her little boy—borne in his father's arms, she pictured him, and hearing from him of the mother who was coming to them by and by, when God had made her good enough to rejoin them!

But while she continued thus simple, Godfrey could not fail to see how much more of a woman she had become. But he was not yet capable of seeing that she could never have gotten so far with him, even if he had married her.

Love and marriage are of the Father's most powerful means for the making of his foolish ones into sons and daughters. But so unlike in many cases are the immediate consequences to those desired and expected, that it is hard for many to believe that he is anywhere looking after their fate.

And the doubt would be a reasonable one, if the end of things was marriage. But the end is life—that we can become the children of God; after which all things can and will go their grand, natural course. The heart of the Father will be content for his children, and the hearts of the children will be content in their Father.

The Redmains were again at Durnmelling, and had been for some weeks. Sepia had taken care that she and Godfrey should meet—on the footpath to Testbridge, in the field accessible by the breach in the dike— here and there anywhere suitable for a little detention and talk that should seem accidental, and be out of sight. Nor was Godfrey the man to be insensible to the influence of such a woman, brought to bear at close quarters. A man less vulnerable—I hate the word, but it is the right one with Sepia concerned, for she was in truth, an enemy—might perhaps have yielded to the suspicion that these meetings were not so accidental as they appeared. But no glimmer of such a thought passed through the mind of Godfrey. Had it not been for the return of Letty, Sepia would by this time have had him her slave. But although he was always glad to meet her, and his heart had begun to beat a little faster at the sight of her approach, the glamor of her presence was nearly destroyed by the arrival of Letty. Sepia was more than sharp enough to perceive a difference in the expression of his eyes the next time she met him. At the very first glance she suspected some hostile influence at work! And as the two worst enemies she could have were the truth and a woman, she was alternately jealous and terrified. The truth and a woman together she had not yet begun to fear; that would, indeed, bring ruin upon her!

She soon found there was a young woman at Thornwick, who had but just arrived, and before long learned who she was—one, indeed, who had already a shadowy existence in her life. She had heard of Tom's death through *The Firefly*, but she had not once thought of his widow.

For some time now, as I have already more than hinted, Sepia had been fashioning a man to do her bidding—Mewks, namely, the body-servant of Mr. Redmain. It was a very gradual process she had adopted, and it had been very successful. It had gotten so far with him that whatever Sepia showed the least wish to understand, Mewks would take endless trouble to learn for her. The rest of the servants, both at Durnmelling and in London, were none of them very friendly with her—least of all Jemima, who was now with her mistress as lady's-maid.

The more she thought about it, the more Sepia began to conclude that the only way out of her present position—with which she was growing increasingly bored and anxious, seeing as how Mr. Redmain could well turn her out of the house at any moment, without so much as a penny— was marriage. If she could secure for a husband this gentleman-yeoman, she thought, she might hold her head up with the best.

From all she could learn, there was nothing that amounted even to ordinary friendship between Mr. Wardour and the young widow. She was in the family but as a distant poor relation—*Much as I am myself!* thought Sepia, with a bitter laugh that even in her own eyes she should be comparable to a poor creature like Letty. The fact remained, however, that Godfrey was a little altered toward her: she must have been telling him something against her—something she had heard from that detestable little hypocrite who was turned away on suspicion of theft!

One morning Letty found she had an hour's leisure, and wandered out to the oak on the edge of the bank, so memorable with the shadowy presence of her Tom. She had not been seated under it many minutes before Godfrey caught sight of her from his horse's back. Knowing his mother was gone to Testbridge, he yielded to the longing, took his horse to the stable, and crossed the grass to where she sat.

Letty was thinking of Tom. All the enchantment of the first days of her love had come back upon the young widow, and all the ill that had crept in between had drifted out of her memory, as the false notes in music melt in the air that carries the true ones across ravine and river, meadow and grove, to the listening ear. For indeed, Letty lived in a dream of her husband—one, perhaps, not factually altogether accurate, but not without many elements of the true nevertheless.

She was sitting with her back toward the tree and her face to Thornwick, and did not see Godfrey till he was within a few yards of her. She smiled, expecting his kind greeting, but was startled to hear from behind her instead the voice of a lady greeting him. She turned her head involuntarily. There was the head of Sepia rising above the breach in the stone wall, and Godfrey had turned aside to give her his hand.

Now Letty knew Sepia by sight, from the evening she had spent at the old hall. But she knew nothing more of her; Mary had told her nothing concerning Sepia and Tom. Therefore, Letty had no feeling toward her but one of admiration for her grace and beauty, which she could appreciate the more that they were so different from her own.

"Thank you," said Sepia, holding tightly to Godfrey's hand, and climbing over with a little pant. "What a lovely day it is for your haymaking. How can you afford the time to play knight-errant to a distressed damsel?"

"The hay is nearly independent of my presence," replied Godfrey. "Sun and wind have done their parts too well for my being of much use."

"Take me with you to see how they are getting on."

"I will, with pleasure," said Godfrey, perhaps a little consoled in the midst of his disappointment, and they walked away, neither taking notice of Letty.

What passed between them is scarcely worthy of record. It is enough to say that Sepia found her companion distracted, and he felt her a little evasive. In a short while they came back together, and Sepia saw Letty under the great bough of the Durnmelling oak. Godfrey handed her across the dike, careful not to invade Durnmelling with so much as a single plant of his foot. She ran home, and up to a certain window with her opera-glass. But the branches and foliage of the huge oak would have concealed many couples.

Godfrey turned toward Letty. She had not moved.

"What a beautiful lady Miss Yolland is," she said, looking up with a smile of welcome, and a calmness that prevented the slightest suspicion of a flattering jealousy.

"I was coming to see *you*," returned Godfrey. "I didn't see her till her head came up over the dike.—Yes, she is beautiful—at least she has good eyes."

"They are splendid! What a wife she would make for you, cousin Godfrey."

Letty's words drove a stake to Godfrey's heart. He turned pale. But not a word would he have spoken had not Letty, in her innocence, gone on to torture him. She jumped up from the ground.

"Are you ill, cousin Godfrey?" she asked in alarm, and with that sweet tremor of the voice that shows the heart is near. "You are very pale!—Oh dear! I've said something I oughtn't to have said! Do forgive me, cousin Godfrey."

In her childlike anxiety she would have thrown her arms round his neck. He drew back. Quickly he mastered himself, but then, alarmed in his turn at the idea of having possibly hurt her, caught her hands in his. As they stood regarding each other with troubled eyes, the embankment of his prudence gave way, and the stored passion broke out.

"You don't mean you would like to see me married, Letty?" he groaned.

"Yes, indeed I do, cousin Godfrey! You would make such a lovely husband."

"I never knew you cared for me, Letty."

He dropped her hands and turned half aside.

"I care for you more than anybody in the world—except perhaps Mary," said Letty. Truthfulness was part of her now.

"And I care for you more than all the world! Oh, Letty, your eyes haunt me day and night! I love you with my whole being!"

"How kind of you, cousin Godfrey!" faltered Letty, trembling, and not knowing what she said. She was very frightened, but hardly knew why, for the idea of Godfrey in love with her was all but inconceivable. Nevertheless, its approach was terrible. Like a fascinated and terrified bird she could not take her eyes off his face. Her knees began to fail her. But Godfrey was full of himself and had not the most shadowy suspicion of how she felt. He took her emotion for a favorable sign, and stupidly went on.

"Letty, I can't help it! I know I shouldn't speak to you like this—but I can't keep quiet any longer. I love you more than the universe. A thousand times rather would I cease to live than live without you to love me. I have loved you for years. I was loving you with heart and soul when you went away and left me."

"Cousin Godfrey!" shrieked Letty, "don't you know I belong to Tom?" She dropped like one lifeless on the grass.

Godfrey felt as if suddenly condemned for eternity; and his hell was death. He stood gazing on the white face. The world, heaven, God, and nature were dead, and that was the soul of it all, dead before him! But such death is never born of love. This agony was but the fog of disappointed self-love, and out of it suddenly rose what seemed a new power to live, but from a lower world: it was all a wretched dream.

Mechanically he stooped and lifted the death-defying lover in his arms and carried her to the house. He felt no thrill as he held the treasure to his heart. It was the merest material contact. He took her to the room where his mother sat, laid her on the sofa, and said he had found her under the oak tree. Then he went to his study. On a chair in the middle of the floor he sat like a man bereft of all. Nothing came between him and suicide but an infinite scorn. A slow rage devoured his heart. From this moment forward he would live above what God or woman could do to him! He rose and went out to the hayfield, from which he did not return till after midnight.

He did not sleep, but he came to a resolution. In the morning he told his mother that he wanted a change. Now that the hay was safely in, he would go—possibly to the Continent. She must not be uneasy if she did not hear from him for a week or two. Perhaps he would have a look at the pyramids.

The old lady was filled with dismay. But scarcely had she begun to expostulate when she saw in his eyes that something was seriously amiss, and held her peace—she had had to learn that with both father and son.

Godfrey went, and courted distraction. Ten years before he would have brooded, but that he would not do now: the thing was not worth it. His pride was strong as ever, and both helped him to get over his suffering, and prevented him from gaining the good of it. He entrenched himself in his pride. No one should say he had not had his will! He was a strong man, and was going to prove it!

Thus thought Godfrey. But in reality it is a weak man who must have recourse in pride to carry him through. Only, if a man does not have love enough to make a hero of him, what is he to do?

He was away a month, and came back in seeming health and good spirits. But he was greatly relieved to find on his arrival that Letty was no longer at Thornwick.

She had gone through a sore time. To have made Godfrey unhappy made her miserable. But how was she to help it? She belonged to Tom. Not once had she ever entertained the thought of ceasing to be Tom's. But what was she to do? She could not remain where she was. And she could not tell his mother why she must go away.

She wrote to Mary and told her she could not stay longer. They were very kind, she said, but she must be gone before Godfrey came back.

Mary suspected the truth. The fact that Letty did not give her any reason was almost enough. The supposition also shed much light on the strange mixture of misery and hardness in Godfrey's behavior at the time of Letty's old mishap. She answered, begging her to keep her mind easy about the future and to keep her informed.

This much from Mary was enough to set Letty at comparative ease. She began to recover strength and was able to write a letter to Godfrey, to leave where he would find it in his study.

It was a lovely letter—the utterance of a simple, childlike spirit. She poured out on Godfrey the affection of a woman-child. She told him what a reverence and love he had been to her, but told him too that it would change her love into fear, if he tried to make her forget Tom. She told him he was much too grand for her to dare love him in that way, but she could look up to him like an angel—only he must not come between her and Tom. Nothing could be plainer, simpler, more honest, or stronger than the way the little woman wrote her mind to the great man. Had he been worthy of her, he might even yet, with her help, have gotten above his pride and passion, and been a great man indeed. But as so many do, he only sat upon himself, kept himself down, and sank below his passion.

When he went to his study the day after his return, he saw the letter. His heart leaped like a wild thing in a trap at sight of the poorly shaped, childish writing. When he read it, however, it was with a curling lip of scorn at the childishness of the creature to whom he had offered the heart of Godfrey Wardour. Instead of admiring the lovely devotion of the girl-widow to her boy-husband, he scorned himself for having dreamed of a creature who could love a fool like Tom Helmer, and go on loving him after he was dead.

The worst devil a man can be possessed with is himself; the presiding, indwelling, inspiring spirit of him is himself, and that is the hardest of all to cast out. Godfrey rose from the reading of that letter *cured* once and for all, as he called it. But it was a cure that left the wound open as a door to the entrance of evil things. He tore the letter into a thousand pieces, and threw them into the empty grate—not even showing it the respect of burning it with fire.

Mary had gotten her affairs settled, and was once again in the old place, the hallowed temple of so many holy memories. At once she wrote to Letty, saying the room that had been hers for so long was at her service as soon as she would like to occupy it. She would take her father's.

Letty breathed a deep breath of redemption, and made haste to accept the offer. But to let Mrs. Wardour know her resolve was a severe strain on her courage.

I will not give the conversation that followed her announcement that she was going to visit Mary Marston. Her aunt met it with scorn and indignation. Ingratitude, laziness, love of low company, all the old words of offense she threw afresh in her face. But Letty could not help being pleased to find that her aunt's storm no longer swamped her boat. When she began, however, to abuse Mary, calling her a low creature, who actually gave up an independent position to put herself at the beck and call of a lady, Letty grew angry.

"I will not sit and hear you call Mary names, Aunt," she said. "When you cast me out, she stood by me. You do not understand her. She is the only friend I ever had—except Tom."

"You thankless hussy, do you dare to say such a thing in the house where you've been clothed and fed and sheltered for so many years! You're the child of your father with a vengeance! Get out of my sight!"

"Aunt—" said Letty, rising.

"No aunt of yours!" interrupted the wrathful woman.

"Mrs. Wardour," said Letty with dignity, "you have been my benefactor, but hardly my friend. Mary has taught me the difference. I owe you more than you will ever give me the chance of repaying you. But what friendship could have stood for an hour the hard words you have been in the way of giving me, as far back as I can remember. Hard words take all the sweetness from shelter. Mary is the only true Christian I have ever known."

"So we are all pagans, except your low-lived lady's-maid, is that it?"

"She makes me feel, many times," said Letty, her eyes filling with tears, "as if I were with Jesus himself—as if he must be in the room somewhere."

So saying, she left her, and went to pack up her things. Mrs. Wardour locked the door of the room where she sat, and refused to speak to her again. Letty left the house with her bag and walked to Testbridge.

"Godfrey will do something to make her understand," she said to herself, weeping as she walked.

Whether Godfrey ever did, I cannot tell.

49 / William and Mary Marston _____

The same day on which Turnbull opened his new shop, a man was seen on a ladder painting out the sign above the old one. But the paint took time to dry.

The same day Mary returned to Testbridge, entered in by the kitchen door to the back of the shop, and went up to her father's room, to which she had kept the keys the entire time—to Turnbull's great indignation. But for all his bluster, he was afraid of Mary, and did not dare touch anything she had left.

That night she spent alone in the house. But she could not sleep. She got up and went down to the shop. It was a bright, moonlit night, and all the house, even where the moon could not enter, was full of glimmer and gleam, except the shop. There she lit a candle, sat down on a pile of goods, and let the memories of the past sweep over her. Back and back went her thoughts as far as she could send them. God was everywhere in all the story, and the clearer she saw him there the surer she was that she would find him as she went on. She was neither sad nor fearful.

Wherever she turned, her father seemed near all the time. Wherever she looked she saw the signs of him, and she pleased herself to think that perhaps he was there to welcome her. She knew that, in spite of time and space, she was and must be near him so long as she loved and did the truth. She knew there is no bond so strong, none so close, none so lasting as the truth. In God alone, who is the truth, can creatures truly meet.

The place was left in sad confusion and dirty, but she began that night to restore order in what little ways she could. At length she was tired, and went to her room.

On the first landing there was a window to the street. She stopped and looked out, candle in hand, but drew back with a start. On the opposite side stood a man, looking up at the house, or so she thought. She hastened to her room, and to bed. If God was not watching, no staying awake was of use. And if God was watching, she might sleep in peace. She did sleep, and woke refreshed.

Her first care in the morning was to write to Letty—with the result as I have given it. The next thing she did was to go and ask Beenie to come back to the house. The old woman was delighted to see her, and ready to lock her door at once and go back to her old quarters. They returned together, while Testbridge was yet but half awake.

267

Many things had to be done before the shop could be opened. Beenie went after some cleaning women, and soon a great bustle of scouring and sweeping arose. But the door and front windows were kept shut.

In the afternoon Letty came fresh from misery into more than counter-balancing joy. She took but time to take off her bonnet and coat, and was presently at work helping Mary, cheerful as hope and a good conscience could make her.

Mary was in no hurry to open the shop. There was inventory to be taken, many things had to be rearranged, and not a few things added before she could begin with comfort. And she must see to it all herself, for she was determined to hire no assistant until she could give her orders without hesitation.

She was soon satisfied that she could not do better than make a proposal to Letty that she had for some time contemplated—namely, that she should take up her permanent residence with her, and help her in the shop. Letty was charmed, and never even thought of the annoyance it would be to her aunt. A new spring of life seemed to bubble up in Letty the moment Mary mentioned the matter, and in serving she soon proved herself one after Mary's own heart. Many customers were even more pleased with her than with Mary. Before long, besides her salary Mary gave her a small share in the business.

Mrs. Wardour carried her business to the Turnbulls.

When the paint was dry which obliterated the old sign, people saw the new one begin with an *M*, and the sign-writer went on until there stood in full, *Mary Marston*. Mr. Brett hinted he would rather have seen it without her first name, but Mary insisted she would do and be nothing she would not hold her "Christian" name to, and on the sign her own name, neither more nor less, should stand. She would have liked it better to make it *William and Mary Marston*, for the business was to go on exactly as her father had taught her; the spirit of her father should never be out of the place. But people were too dull to understand such a thing, and she therefore set the sign so in her heart only.

Her old friends soon began to come about her again, and it was not many weeks before she saw fit to go to London to add to her stock.

The evening of her return, as she and Letty sat over a late tea, a silence fell.

"I wonder how cousin Godfrey is getting on?" she said at length, smiling sadly.

"How do you mean *getting on*?" asked Mary.

"I was wondering whether Miss Yolland and he—"

"Letty!" exclaimed Mary in a voice of utter dismay, "you don't mean that woman is—is making friends with *him*?"

"I saw them together more than once, and they seemed—well, on very good terms."

"Then it is all over with him!" said Mary in despair. "Oh, Letty! what *is* to be done? He'll be madly in love with her by this time!"

"But what's the harm, Mary? She's a very handsome lady, and of a good family."

"We're all of good enough family," said Mary. "But that Miss Yolland, Letty, is a bad woman."

"I never heard you say such a hard word about anybody before, Mary! It frightens me to hear you."

"It is true of her, Letty."

"How can you be so sure?"

"I cannot tell you, Letty," Mary answered. "You know the two bonds of friendship are the right of silence and the duty of speech. I dare say you have some things which, truly as I know you love me, you neither wish nor feel at liberty to tell me."

Letty thought of what had so recently passed between her and her cousin Godfrey. She never thought of one of the many things Tom had done or said that had cut her to the heart; those no longer had any existence. They were swallowed in the gulf of forgetful love—dismissed even as God casts the sins of his children behind his back: behind God's back is nowhere. She did not answer, and again there was silence for a time, during which Mary kept walking about with great anxiety on her face.

"Oh, Letty! what *am* I to do?" she said at last.

"Mary dear, *you* can't be to blame. One would think you fancied yourself accountable for cousin Godfrey!"

"I *am* accountable for him. He has done a great deal for me, and for you too. And I know things about her that he does not know, and the ignorance of them could well be his ruin. I must do something!"

It was so unlike her to be so discomposed that Letty began almost to be frightened. She sat silent and looked at her. Then spoke the spirit of truth in the scholar, for the teacher was too troubled to hear. She rose, and went up to Mary from behind, put her arm round her, and said: "Mary, why don't you ask Jesus?"

Mary stopped short, and looked at Letty. But she was not thinking about Letty at all. With the very words she was questioning within herself. Something must be wrong with her: why *had* she not done as Letty said? Why had she not thought of her first duty in all matters above anything? She threw herself on the couch. Letty watched her in silence, and not without fear that she had been wrong to say what she did.

In a few minutes Mary rose. Her face was wet with tears, but the perplexity had vanished from it, and resolution had taken its place. She threw her arms round Letty and kissed her.

"Thank you, Letty, dear," she said. "You are a true sister."

"What have you found out, Mary?"

"I have found out why I did not go at once to ask him what I ought to do. It was because I was afraid of what he would tell me to do."

"Then you know now what to do?" asked Letty.

"Yes," answered Mary, and sat down, the tears beginning to run down her cheeks again.

50 / A Hard Task

The next morning Mary left the shop to Letty and set out for Thornwick immediately after breakfast.

The duty she had to perform there was so distasteful that she felt her very limbs trying to refuse the office required of them. All the way, as she went, she was hoping she might be spared an encounter with Mrs. Wardour. But the old lady saw her coming, imagined that she wanted to bring Letty back to her in some new trouble, and hastened to prevent her from entering the house by meeting her on the porch.

"Good morning, Mrs. Wardour," said Mary, trying to speak without betraying emotion.

"Good morning, Miss Marston," returned Mrs. Wardour grimly.

"Is Mr. Wardour at home?"

"What is your business with him?" rejoined the mother.

"Yes, it is with him," returned Mary, as if she had mistaken her question.

"About that hussy?"

"I do not know whom you mean," replied Mary.

"You know well enough whom I mean. Who should it be but Letty Lovel?"

"My business has nothing to do with her," answered Mary.

"Whom does it have to do with then?"

"With Mr. Wardour."

"What is it?"

"Only Mr. Wardour himself must hear it. It is his business, not mine."

"I will have nothing to do with it."

"I have no desire to give you the least trouble about it," rejoined Mary.

"You can't see Mr. Wardour. He's not one to be at the beck and call of every silly woman that wants him."

"Then I will write and tell him I called, but you would not allow me to see him."

"I will give him a message if you like."

"Then tell him what I have just said. I am going home to write. Good morning."

She was half way down the drive again, when Mrs. Wardour, reflecting that it must be something of consequence to have brought her there so early, spoke out again to her back.

271

"I will tell him you are here. But you must not blame me if he does not choose to see you. We don't feel you have behaved well about that girl."

"Letty is my friend," said Mary, turning back toward the house. "I have behaved to her as if she were my sister."

"You had no business to behave to her as if she were your sister. You had no right to tempt her down to your level. You had nothing to do with her."

"Excuse me, ma'am, but I have some right in Letty. I am sorry to have to say it, but she would have been dead long ago if I had behaved to her as you would have me."

"That was her own fault."

"I will not talk with you about it: you know nothing about the circumstances I am referring to. I request to see Mr. Wardour. I have no time to waste in useless argument."

Mary was angry, and it did her good; it made her fitter to face the harder task before her.

That moment the sound of Godfrey's step approaching through a long passage in the rear could be heard. His mother went into the parlor, leaving the door, to which Mary had returned, opened. Godfrey, reaching the hall, saw Mary, and came up to her with a formal bow, and a face flushed with displeasure.

"May I speak to you alone, Mr. Wardour?" said Mary.

"Can you not say what you have to say here?"

"It is impossible."

"Then I am curious to know—"

"Let your curiosity plead for me then."

With a sigh of impatience he yielded, and led the way to the drawing room, which was at the other end of the hall. Mary turned and shut the door he left open.

"Why all this mystery, Miss Marston?" he said. "I am not aware of anything between you and me that can require secrecy."

He spoke with unconcealed scorn.

"When I have made my communication, you will at least allow secrecy to have been necessary."

"No doubt it will seem so to the likes of you!" said Wardour in a tone of insult.

"Mr. Wardour," returned Mary, "I am here for your sake, not my own. Please do not make a painful duty all the more difficult."

"May I beg, then, that you will be as brief as possible? I am more than doubtful whether what you have to say will seem to me of so much importance as you suppose."

"I shall be very glad to find it so."

"I will give you ten minutes, no more."

Mary looked at her watch.

"You have recently become acquainted with Miss Yolland, I am told," she began.

"Whew!" whistled Godfrey, yet hardly as if he were surprised.

"I have been compelled to know a good deal of that lady."

"As a lady's-maid in her family, I believe."

"Yes," said Mary—then changing her tone after a slight pause, went on: "Mr. Wardour, I owe you more than I can ever thank you for. You opened much in the world of literature to me. I strongly desire to fulfill the obligation, and for the sake of it—for your sake, I am risking much—namely, your opinion of me."

He made a gesture of impatience.

"I *know* Miss Yolland to be a woman without principle. I have seen it with my own eyes, and from her own confession. She is capable of playing a cold-hearted game for her own ends. Be persuaded to consult Mr. Redmain before you commit yourself to anything with regard to her. Ask him if Miss Yolland is fit to be the wife of an honest man."

There was nothing in Godfrey's countenance but growing rage. Turning to the door, Mary would have gone without another word.

"Stay!" cried Godfrey, in a voice of suppressed fury. "Don't you dare go until I have told you that you are a vile slanderer. If anything more than the character of your statement was necessary to satisfy me of the falsehood of every word of it, you have given it me in your reference to Mr. Redmain—a man whose very life has made him unfit for the acquaintance, not to say the confidence of any decent woman. This is no doubt a plot—for what final object God knows! Leave the house!"

"I am sorry you find it so hard to distinguish between truth and falsehood," said Mary as she went to the door.

She walked out, and back to town, went into the shop, and served the rest of the morning. But in the afternoon she had to lie down, and she did not appear again for three days.

The reception she had met with did not much surprise her: plainly Sepia had been before her. She had pretended to make Godfrey her confidant, had invented, dressed, and poured out injuries to him, and so blocked up the way to all testimony unfavorable to her.

It added to Godfrey's rage that he had not a doubt Mary knew what had passed between Letty and him. That, he reasoned, was at the root of it all: she must be trying to bring them together, in order to make her bosom friend mistress of Thornwick and thus get her own clutches somehow upon it! He should never even have been civil to her! What a fool he was to ever have cared a straw for such a low-minded creature as that Letty!

And now what more could Mary do? Just one thing was left: Mr. Redmain could satisfy Mr. Wardour of the fact he would not hear from her!—so, at least, thought Mary yet. If Mr. Redmain would take the trouble to speak to him, Mr. Wardour would surely be convinced, however true might be what Mr. Wardour said about Mr. Redmain.

She sat down and wrote the following letter:

> Sir: I hardly know how to address you without seeming to take a liberty. At the same time I cannot help hoping you will trust me enough to believe that I would not venture such a request without good reason. Should you kindly think me not too presumptuous, and should you be well enough in health, would you mind coming to see me here in my shop? I think you must know it—it used to be Turnbull and Marston—the Marston was my father. You will see my name over the door. Any hour will do for me, only please let it be as soon as you can make it convenient.
>
> I am, sir,
> Your humble and grateful servant,
> MARY MARSTON

"What the deuce is she grateful to me for?" grumbled Mr. Redmain when he read it. "I never did anything for her! By Jove, the gypsy wouldn't let me! I vow she's got more brains of her own than any half-dozen women I ever had to do with before!"

The least thing bearing the look of plot or intrigue, or secret to be discovered or heard was enough for Mr. Redmain. What he had of pride was not of the same sort as Wardour's: it made no pretense to dignity, and was less antagonistic, so long at least as there was no talk of good motive or righteous purpose. Far from being offended with Mary's request, he got up at once, though indeed he was rather unwell and dreading an attack, ordered his carriage, and drove to Testbridge. There, careful of secrecy, he went to several shops, and bought something at each, but pretended not to find the thing he wanted.

He then said he would lunch at the inn, told his coachman to put up, and, while his meal was getting ready, went to Mary's shop, which was but a few doors away. There he asked for a certain outlandish stuff and insisted on looking over a bale not yet unpacked. Mary understood him, and whispered to Letty to take him to the parlor. She followed herself a minute later.

As soon as she entered—

"Come now, what's it all about?" he said.

Mary began at once to tell him, as directly as she could, that she was under obligation to Mr. Wardour of Thornwick, and that she had reason to fear Miss Yolland was trying to get a hold of him—"And you know what that would be for any man!" she said.

"No, by Jove! I don't," he answered. "What would it be?"

"Utter ruin," replied Mary.

"Then go and tell him so, if you want to save him."

"I have told him. But he does not like me, and won't believe me."

"Then let him take his own course and be ruined."

"But I have just told you, sir, I owe him a great deal."

"Oh! I see! You want him yourself!—well, as you wish it. I would rather you should have him than that she-devil."

"I do not want him," she answered with a smile.

"Well, now, that's a pity. I might have done a good deal for you—I don't know why, for you're a little humbug if ever there was one! But I can't help liking you anyway. But if you don't care about the fellow, I don't see why I should take the trouble. Confess now—you're just a little bit in love with him—aren't you now? Confess to that and I will do what I can."

"I can't confess to something that's not true. I owe him a debt of gratitude—that is all—but it is no light thing, you will allow."

"I don't know; I never tried its weight. Anyhow, I should make haste to be rid of it."

"I have tried to talk to him, but he thinks me only a spreader of lies. Miss Yolland has been to him before me."

"Then, by Jove! I don't see but that you're quits with him. You've done what you can. I don't see why you should trouble your head about him further. Let him take his way, and to—to Sepia and the devil together."

"But, what a dreadful thing."

"I don't see it. I've no doubt he's just as bad as she is. We all are. We're all the same. And if not, it's all the better a joke on him!"

"But he's of good family," said Mary, foolishly thinking that would weigh with him.

"Good old fiddlestick! Nothing but a worn-out broom-end! *She's* of a good old family—quite good enough for his, you may take your oath! Why, my girl, the thing's not worth burning your fingers with. You've brought me here on a goose-errand."

He rose to go.

"I'm sorry to have vexed you, sir," said Mary, greatly disappointed. "I suppose I'll have to try something else."

"I wouldn't advise you. The man's only the surer to hate you and stick to her. Let him alone. There's one good thing in it, my wife'll be rid of her. But I don't know! They'll be next door when Durnmelling is mine! But I can sell it."

"If he *should* come to you, will you tell him the truth?"

"I don't know that. It might spoil my own little game."

"Will you let him think me a liar and slanderer?"

"No, by Jove! I won't do that. I don't promise to tell him all the truth, or even that what I do tell him shall be exactly true. But I won't let him think ill of my little puritan; that would spoil *your* game."

He went out, with his curious grin, amused, and enjoying the idea of a proud fellow like that being taken in with Sepia.

"I hope he'll marry her!" he said to himself as he went to his lunch. "Then I shall hold a rod over them both, and perhaps buy that miserable little Thornwick. Mortimer would give the skin off his back for it."

Mary had done the thing that ought to have been done: was there nothing left for her to do further?

51 / A Summons

One hot Saturday afternoon, in the sleepiest time of the day, when nothing was doing, and nobody in the shop, except a poor boy who had come asking for some string to fly his kite, though for the last month wind had been more scarce than string, Jemima came in from Durnmelling. She greeted Mary with the warmth of the friendship that had always been true between them, and gave her a letter.

"Who is it from?" asked Mary.

"Mr. Mewks gave it to me," said Jemima. "He said nothing about it."

Mary opened it, though not without an instinctive distrust of everything that passed through Mewks's hands, and feared that, much as his master trusted him, he was not true to him. She found the following note from Mr. Redmain:

> DEAR MISS MARSTON: Come and see me as soon as you can; I have something to talk to you about. Send word by the bearer when I may look for you. I am not well.
>
> Yours truly,
> F.G. REDMAIN

Mary went to her desk and wrote a reply, saying she would be with him the next morning about eleven o'clock. She would have gone that same night, she said, but as it was Saturday she had to remain open long enough for her country customers.

"Give it to Mr. Redmain himself, if you can, Jemima," she said.

"I will try, but I doubt if I can, miss," answered the girl.

"Between ourselves, Jemima," said Mary, "I do not trust that man Mewks."

"Nobody does, miss, except the master and Miss Yolland."

"The thing may be worse than I thought," said Mary to herself.

"I'll do what I can, miss," Jemima went on. "But he's so sharp!—Mr. Mewks, I mean."

After she was gone, Mary wished she had given her a verbal message, that she might have insisted on delivering it in person.

With circumspection, Jemima managed to reach Mr. Redmain's room unencountered. But just as she knocked at the door, Mewks came behind her from somewhere and snatched the letter away, for she was carrying it in her hand ready to justify her entrance to the first glance of her irritable master. He then pushed her rudely away, and immediately went in. But as he did so he put the letter in his pocket.

"Who took the note?" asked his master.

"The girl that waits on the mistress, sir."

"Has she not come back yet?"

"No, sir, not yet. She'll be in a minute, though. I saw her coming up the avenue."

"Go and bring her here."

"Yes, sir."

Mewks went, and in two minutes returned with the letter, and the message that Miss Marston hadn't time to address it.

"You rascal! I told you to bring the messenger here."

"She ran the whole way, sir, and not being very strong, was so tired that the moment she got in the poor thing dropped in a dead faint."

His master gave him one look straight in the eyes, then opened the letter and read it.

"Miss Marston will call here tomorrow morning," he said. "See that she is shown up at once—here, to my sitting room. I hope that is clear enough."

When the man was gone, Mr. Redmain nodded his head three times, and grinned, the skin tight as a drum-head over his cheek-bones. "There isn't a bloody one of them to be trusted!" he said to himself, and sat silent and thoughtful.

What he was thinking would be hard to say. Times of reflection arrive to most men, and a threatened attack of the illness he believed must one day take his life might well have disposed him to think a bit more than usual.

In the evening he was worse.

By midnight he was in agony, and Lady Margaret was up all night with him. In the morning came a lull, and Lady Margaret went to bed. His wife had not come near him. But Sepia might have been seen, more than once or twice, hovering about his door.

Both she and Mewks thought, after such a night, he must have forgotten his appointment with Mary.

When he had had some chocolate, he fell into a doze. But his sleep was far from profound. Often he woke and again dozed off.

The clock in the dressing room struck eleven.

"Show Miss Marston up the moment she arrives," he said. His voice was almost like that of a man in good health.

"Yes, sir," replied the startled Mewks, and felt he must obey.

Mary was at once shown to the chamber of the sick man.

To her surprise, for Mewks had given her no warning about his condition, he was in bed, and looking as ill as she had ever seen him. His small head was like a skull covered with parchment. He made the slightest of signs to her to come nearer—and again. She went close to the bed. Mewks sat down at the foot of it, out of sight. It was a great four-post bed, with curtains.

"I'm glad you've come," he said with a feeble grin, all he had for a smile. "I want to have a little talk with you. But I can't while that brute is sitting there. I have been suffering horribly. Look at me, and tell me if you think I am going to die—not that I take your opinion as worth anything. That's not what I wanted you for though. I wasn't so ill then. But I want you the more to talk to now. You have a bit of a heart, even for people that don't deserve it—at least I'm going to believe you have. And if I am wrong, I almost think I would rather not know it till I'm dead and gone!—Good God! Where shall I be then?"

I have already said that whenever his sufferings reached a certain point, Mr. Redmain was subject to fits of terror at the thought of hell. He laughed at the notion when he was well, and shook when he was suffering. In vain he accused himself of cowardice—the thing was there—in him—and nothing could drive it out. And verily, even a madman may be wiser than the prudent of this world; and the courage of not a few would forsake them if they dared but look the danger in the face. Wait till the thing stares you in the eyes, and then, whether you be brave man or coward, you will at all events care little about courage or cowardice. The nearer a man is to being a true man, the sooner will conscience of wrong make a coward of him; and herein Redmain had a far-off kindred with the just. After the night he had just passed, he was now in one of his terror-fits. And this much may be said for his good sense—that if there was anywhere a hell for the use of anybody, he was justified in anticipating a free entrance.

"Mewks!" he called suddenly, and his tone was loud and angry.

Mewks was by his bedside instantly.

"Get out with you. If I find you in this room again without having been called, I will kill you! I am strong enough for that, even without this pain! They won't hang a dying man, and where I am going they will rather like it."

Mewks vanished.

"You need not mind, my girl," he went on to Mary. "Everyone knows I am very ill. Sit down there, on the foot of the bed, only take care you don't shake it. I want to talk to you. People nowadays, you know, say there isn't any hell—or perhaps none to speak of?"

"I should think the former more likely than the latter," said Mary.

"You don't believe there is a hell then? I am glad of that! for you are a good girl and ought to know."

"You mistake me, sir. How can I imagine there is no hell when he said there was?"

"Who's *he?*"

"The man who knows all about it, and means to keep you out of it."

"Oh yes, I see!—But I don't for the life of me see what a fellow is to make of all that—don't you know? Those parsons! They all insist there's no way but theirs, and I never could see a handle anywhere to that door!"

"I don't see what the parsons have got to do with it, or what you have got to do with the parsons. If the thing is true, you have as much to do with it as any parson in England. If it is not true, neither you nor they have anything to do with it."

"But I tell you, if it be all true that—that we are all sinners, I don't know what to do."

"It seems to me a very simple thing. *He* as much as said he knew all about it, and came to find men that were lost, and take them home."

"He can't well find one more lost than I am! But how am I to believe it? How *can* it be true? It's ages since he was here, if he ever was at all, and there hasn't been a sign of him ever since the whole time!"

"There you may be quite wrong. I think I could find you some who believe him just as near them now as he was to his own brothers and disciples—who believe that he hears them when they speak to him, and heeds what they say."

"That's bosh! You would have me believe contrary to what my good senses tell me!"

"You must have strange senses, Mr. Redmain, that give you evidence where they can't possibly know anything. If that man spoke the truth when he was in the world, he *is* near us now. And if he is not near us and did not speak the truth, that is the end of it all."

"The nearer he is, the worse for me!" sighed Mr. Redmain.

"The nearer he is, the better for the worst man that ever breathed."

"That's an odd doctrine! It seems a cowardly thing to go asking him to save you, after you've all your life been doing what ought to damn you— if there be a hell, mind you, that is."

"But think," said Mary, "if that should be your only chance of being able to make up for the mischief you have done? No punishment you can have will do anything for that. No suffering of yours will do anything for those you have made suffer. But it is so much harder to leave the old way than to go on and let things take their chance."

"There may be something in what you say. But still I can't see it any better than sneaking—to do a world of mischief, and then slink away into heaven, leaving all the poor wretches to look after themselves."

"I don't think Jesus Christ is worse pleased with you for feeling like that," said Mary.

"What? What's that you say?—Jesus Christ worse pleased with me?

That's a good one! As if he ever thought about a fellow like me!"

"If he did not think about you, you would not be thinking about him just this minute, I suspect. He said himself he didn't come to call the righteous, but sinners to repentance."

"I wish I could repent."

"You can, if you will."

"I can't make myself sorry for what's gone and done with."

"No, you need him to do that. But you can turn from your old ways and ask him to have you for a pupil. Aren't you willing to learn, if he is willing to teach you?"

"I don't know. It's all so dull! I never could bear going to church."

"I said nothing about church. It's not one bit like that! It's like going to your mother and saying you're going to try to be a good boy, and not disobey her any more."

"Well, I've had as much of it as I can stand for now. You see, I'm not used to such things. You go away and send Mewks. Don't be far off though, and mind you don't go home without letting me know. There! Go along."

She had just reached the door when he called her again.

"I say, mind whom you trust in this house. There's no harm in Mrs. Redmain, only she seems to grow stupider. But that Yolland—that woman's the devil! I know more about her than you or anyone else. I can't bear her to be about Hesper. But if I told her the half I know, she would not believe the half of that. I shall find a way, though. But I am forgetting, you know her as well as I do—that is, you would, if you were wicked enough to understand. But don't say a word. Go along, and send Mewks."

With all his suspicions, Mr. Redmain did not suspect just how false Mewks was. He did not know that Sepia had bewitched him for the sake of having an ally in the enemy's camp. All he could hear—and the dressing-room door was handy—the fellow reported to her.

Mary went and sat on the lowest step of the stair just outside the room.

"What are you doing there?" said Lady Margaret, coming from the corridor.

"Mr. Redmain will not have me go yet, my lady," answered Mary, rising. "He asked me to wait till he sends for me."

Lady Margaret swept past her murmuring, "Most peculiar!" Mary sat down again.

In about an hour Mewks came and said his master wanted her.

He was very ill and could hardly talk, but he would not let her go. He made her sit where he could see her, and now and then stretched out his hand to her.

Even in his pain he showed a quieter spirit. *Something may be working—who can tell!* thought Mary.

It was late in the afternoon when at length he sought further conversation.

"I have been thinking, Mary," he said, "that if I do wake up in hell when I die, no matter how much I deserve it, nobody will be the better for it, and I shall be all the worse."

He spoke with coolness, but it was by a powerful effort for he had waked from a frightful dream, drenched from head to foot. Coward? No. He had good reason to fear.

"Whereas," rejoined Mary, taking up where he left off, "everybody will be the better if you keep out of it—everybody," she repeated, "God, and Jesus Christ, and all their people."

"How do you make that out?" he asked. "God has more to do than look after such as me."

"You think he has so many worlds to look to. But why does he care about his worlds? Is it not because they are the schools of his souls? And why should he care for the souls? Is it not because he is making them children—his own children to understand him, and be happy with his happiness."

"I can't say I care for his happiness. I want my own. And yet I don't know anything that's worth the worry of it. No, I would rather be put out like a candle."

"That's because you have been a disobedient child, insisting on your own way, and turning God's good things to evil. You don't know what a splendid thing life is. You actually and truly don't know, never experienced in your being the very thing you were made for."

"My father had no business to leave me so much money."

"You had no business to misuse it."

"I didn't know what I was doing."

"You do now."

Then came a pause.

"You think God hears prayers—do you?"

"I do."

"Then I wish you would ask him to let me off—I mean, to let me die right out when I do die. What's the good of making a body miserable?"

"I am sure it would be of no use to pray that. He certainly will not throw away a thing he has made because that thing may be foolish enough to prefer the dust-hole to a cabinet."

"Wouldn't you do it now, if I asked you?"

"What—let you off, let you die and that be the end?"

"Yes, surely *you* would not torture me."

"I would do nothing but what God will do, which is always the best. I would leave you in God's hands rather than inside the gate of heaven."

"I don't understand you. You wouldn't say such a thing if you cared for me! Only, why should you care for me?"

"I would give my life for you."

"Come, now! Bosh! I don't believe that!"

"Why, I wouldn't be a Christian if I wouldn't."

"You are being downright absurd!" he cried. But the look on his face did not seem exactly as if he thought it.

"Absurd!" repeated Mary. "Isn't that what makes him our Savior? How could I be his disciple if I wouldn't do as he did?"

"You are saying a good deal."

"But to follow Jesus, I have no choice."

"I wouldn't do that for anybody under the sun."

"You are not his disciple. You have not been going about life with him."

"And you have?"

"Yes—for many years. Besides, I cannot help thinking there is one for whom you would do it."

"If you mean my wife, you were never more mistaken. I would do nothing of the sort."

"I did not mean your wife. I mean Jesus Christ."

"Oh, I dare say! Well, perhaps, if I knew him as you do, and if I were quite sure he wanted it done for him."

"He does want it done for him—always and every day—not for his own sake, though it does make him very glad. To give up your way for his is to die for him. And when any one will do that, then he is able to do everything for him. For then, and not until then, he gets such a hold of him that he can lift him up, and set him down beside himself. That's how my father used to teach me, and now I see it for myself to be true."

"It's all very grand, no doubt. But it's nowhere, you know. It's all in your own head, and nowhere else. You don't, you can't possibly believe all that moonshine!"

"I believe it so thoroughly that I live in the strength and hope it gives me, and order my ways according to it every day in everything I do. At least I try to do so."

"Why didn't you teach my wife so?"

"I tried, but she didn't care to think. I could not get any further with her. She has had no trouble yet to make her listen."

"By Jove! I should have thought marrying a wretch like me might have been trouble enough to make a saint of her."

It was impossible to fix him to any line of thought, and Mary did not attempt it. To move the child in him was more than all argument.

A pause followed.

"I don't love God," he said.

"I dare say not," replied Mary. "How should you, when you don't know him?"

"Then what's to be done? I can't very well show myself where I hate the master of the house!"

"If you knew him, you would love him."

"You are judging me by yourself. But there is as much difference between you and me as between light and darkness."

"Not quite that much," replied Mary with a smile. "If you knew Jesus Christ, you could not help loving him, and to love him is to love God."

"*Know Jesus Christ*! How am I to go back two thousand years?"

"What he was then he is now," answered Mary. "And you may even know him better than they did at the time. For it was not until they understood him better, by his being taken from them, that they wrote down his life."

"I suppose you mean I must read the New Testament?" said Mr. Redmain.

"Of course!" answered Mary, a little surprised. She was unaware of how few people have a notion what the New Testament is, or is meant for.

"Then why didn't you say so at first? There I have you! That's just where I learn that I must be damned forever!"

"I don't mean the Epistles. Those you can't understand—yet."

"I'm glad you don't mean *them*. I hate them."

"I don't wonder. You have never seen a single shine of what they are. And what most people think about them is hardly the least like them. What I would have you do is read the life and death of the Son of Man, the master of men."

"I can't read. I should only make myself twice as ill."

"I will read it to you, if you will let me."

"How did you come to be such a theologian?"

"I am no theologian. This is one of those cases where those who call themselves his followers do not always believe the very thing the Master said. He said God hid these things from the wise and prudent and revealed them to babes. I had a father who was child enough to know them, and I was child enough to believe him, and so grew able to understand them for myself. The whole secret is to do the thing the Master tells you: then you will understand what he tells you. The opinion of the wisest man, if he does not do the things he reads, is not worth a straw. He may be partly right, but you have no reason to trust him."

"Well, you shall be my chaplain. Tomorrow, if I'm able to listen, you shall see what you can make of the old sinner."

"*I* shall be able to make nothing of you. It is *He* who does all the making."

"Ah, yes! Tut, tut! Of course! You know what I mean in any case."

Mary did not waste words. What would have been the use of correcting the poor spiritual dullard with every lumbering step, at any word inconsistent with the holy manners of the high countries? Once get him to court, and the power of the presence would subdue him, and make him over again from the beginning, without which absolute renewal the best observance of religious etiquette is worse than worthless. Many good people are such sticklers for the proprieties! For myself, I take joyous refuge with the grand, simple, everyday humanity of the man I find in the story—the man with the heart like that of my father and my mother and my brothers and sisters. If I may but see and help to show him a little as he lived to show himself, and not as church talk and church ways and church ceremonies and church theories and church plans of salvation and church worldliness generally have obscured him for hundreds of years, and will yet obscure him for hundreds more, until he comes himself to remove the scales from the eyes of his own church-bound sons and daughters!

Toward evening, when she had just given him one of the many attentions he required, and which there was no one that day but herself to give him, for he would scarcely allow Mewks to enter the room, he said to her: "Thank you. You are very good to me. I shall remember you. Not that I am going to die just yet. I've often been as bad as this, and got quite well again. Besides, I want to show that I have turned over a new leaf. Don't you think God will give me one more chance, now that I really mean it? I never did before."

"God can tell whether you mean it without that," she answered, not daring to encourage him where she knew nothing. "But you said you would remember me, Mr. Redmain. I hope you didn't mean in your will."

"I did mean in my will," he answered, but in a tone of displeasure. "I must say, however, I should have preferred you had not shown quite such an anxiety about it. I shall not be in my coffin tomorrow, and I'm not in the habit of forgetting things."

"I beg you," returned Mary, flushing, "to do nothing of the sort. I have plenty of money, and don't care about more. I would rather not have any from you."

"But think how much good you might do with it!" said Mr. Redmain. "It was come by honestly—so far as I know."

"Money can't do half the good people think. It is stubborn stuff to turn to any good. And in this case it would be directly against good."

"Nobody has a right to refuse what comes honestly in his way. There's no end to the good that may be done with money—to judge, at least, by the harm I've done with mine," said Mr. Redmain, this time with seriousness.

"Good is not in money," persisted Mary. "If it had been, our Lord would have used it, and he never did."

"Oh, but he was an exception!"

"On the contrary, he is the only man who is no exception. We are the exceptions. Everyone but him is more or less out of straight. Don't you see?—He is the very one we must all come to be like, or perish! No, Mr. Redmain! don't leave me any money, or I shall be altogether bewildered what to do with it. Mrs. Redmain would not take it from me. Miss Yolland might, but I would not dare give it to her. And for societies, I have small faith in them."

"Well, well! I'll think about it," said Mr. Redmain, who by now was quite capable of believing that when Mary said a thing she meant it, though he was utterly incapable of understanding the true relations of money. Few indeed are the Christians capable of that! Most of them are just where Peter was, when, the moment after the Lord had honored him as the first to recognize him as the Messiah, he took it upon himself to object to his Master's way of working salvation in the earth. The Roman emperors took up Peter's plan, and the devil has been in the church ever since—Peter's Satan, whom the Master told to get behind him. They are poor prophets, and no martyrs, who honor money as an element of any importance in the salvation of the world. Those preachers and evangelists and missionaries who turn their focus toward the accumulation of money in order to "further the gospel," as they say, demonstrate a profound lack of understanding of the Father's work in the life of his Son, namely, that he knows our need even before we ask. For did the Son not teach us to pray, "Give us this day our daily bread"? Hunger itself does incomparably more to make Christ's kingdom come than ever money did, or ever will do while time lasts. Of course, money has its part, for everything has. And whoever has money is bound to use it as best he knows. But his best is generally an attempt to do saint-work by devil-proxy. And simple obedience—treating everyone you encounter as Christ would treat him, in the next five minutes, all your life long—will do more to further the coming of God's true kingdom, than all you could do with a million pounds, were it handed you to spend "in his work" the moment you finish this sentence.

"I can't imagine where on earth you got such a sackful of extravagant notions!" said Mr. Redmain.

"I told you before, I had a father who set me thinking," answered Mary.

"I wish I had had a father like yours," he rejoined.

"There are not many such to be had."

"I fear mine wasn't just what he ought to be, though he can't have been such a rascal as his son. He hadn't time; he had his money to make."

"He had the temptation to make it, and you have the temptation to spend it: which is the more dangerous, I don't know. Each has led to many crimes."

"Oh, as to crimes—I don't know about that! It depends on what you call crimes."

"It doesn't matter whether men call a deed a crime or a fault. The thing is how God regards it, for that is the only truth about it. What the world thinks goes for nothing, because it is never right. It would be worse in me to do some thing the world considers perfectly honorable, than it would be for some other man to commit a burglary, or still another a murder. I mean my guilt might be greater in committing a respectable sin, than theirs in committing a disreputable one. God judges every man, and every woman on the basis of the decisions they make according to their own conscience, and the level of obedience he is at that moment requiring of them."

Had Mary known anything of science, she might have said that, in morals as well as in chemistry, the qualitative analysis is easy, but the quantitative another affair.

Sepia, who was listening, heard the latter part of this conversation, and misunderstood utterly.

All the rest of the day Mary was with Mr. Redmain, mostly by his bedside, sitting in silent watchfulness when he was unable to talk with her. Nobody entered the room except Mewks, who, when he did, seemed to watch everything, and try to hear everything. Once Lady Margaret came in. When she saw Mary seated by the bed, though she must have known well enough she was there, she drew herself up with grand English repellence, and looked scandalized. Mary rose, and was about to leave the room, but Mr. Redmain motioned her to sit still.

"This is my spiritual advisor, Lady Margaret," he said.

His ladyship cast a second look on Mary, such as few but her could cast, and left the room.

On into the gloom of the evening Mary sat. No one brought her anything to eat or drink, and Mr. Redmain was too much taken up with himself, soul and body, to think of her. She was now past hunger. Late in the night, through the settled darkness, the words came to her from the bed: "I should like to have you near me when I am dying, Mary."

The voice was softer than she had yet heard from Mr. Redmain, and its tone went to her heart.

"I will certainly be with you, if God please," she answered.

"There is no fear of God," returned Mr. Redmain. "It's the devil who will try to keep you away. But never you heed what anyone may do or say

to prevent you. Do your very best to be with me. By that time I may not
be having my own way any more. Be sure, the first moment they can get
the better of me, they will. And you mustn't place confidence in a single
soul in this house. I don't say my wife would play me false so long as I
was able to swear at her, but I wouldn't trust her one moment longer. You
come and be with me in spite of the whole batch of them.''

"I will try, Mr. Redmain,'' she answered softly. "But indeed, you must
let me go now, otherwise I may be unable to come tomorrow.''

"What's the matter?'' he asked hurriedly, half lifting his head with a
look of alarm. "There's no knowing,'' he went on, muttering to himself,
"what may happen in this cursed house.''

"Nothing,'' replied Mary, "but I have not had anything to eat since I
left home. I feel rather faint.''

"They've given you nothing to eat!'' cried Mr. Redmain. "Ring the
bell!''

"Indeed, I would rather not have anything now till I get home,'' said
Mary. "I don't feel inclined to eat where I am not welcome.''

"Right! Right!'' said Mr. Redmain. "Stick to that. Never eat where
you are not welcome. Go home directly. Only say when you will come
tomorrow.''

"I can't very well during the day,'' answered Mary. "There is so much
to be done, and I have so little help. But if you should want me, I would
rather shut up the shop than not come.''

"There is no need for that. Indeed, I would much rather have you in
the evening. The first look of the night is worst of all. It's then the devils
are out—look here,'' he added, after a short pause, during which Mary
hesitated to leave him, "—being in business, you've got a lawyer, I suppose?''

"Yes,'' she answered.

"Then you go to him tonight and tell him to come to me tomorrow,
about noon. Tell him I am ill and in bed, and particularly want to see him.
And he mustn't let anything they say keep him from me, not even if they
tell him I am dead.''

"I will,'' said Mary, and, stroking the thin hand that lay outside the
blanket, turned and left him.

"Don't tell anyone you are gone,'' he called after her, with a voice far
from feeble. "I don't want any of their cursed company.''

Mary left the house and saw no one on her way out.

The night was very dark. There was no moon, and the stars were hidden by thick clouds. She would have to walk all the way to Testbridge. She felt weak, but the fresh air revived her some.

She had not gone far when the moon rose, and from behind the clouds diminished the darkness a little. The first part of her journey lay along a narrow lane, with a small ditch, a rising bank, and a hedge on each side. About halfway to town there was a farmyard, and a little way farther a cottage. Soon after passing the gate of the farmyard, she thought she heard steps behind her, seemingly soft and swift. She naturally felt a little apprehension, so she quickened her pace. As she drew near the common, she heard the steps more plainly, still soft and swift, and almost wished she had sought refuge in the cottage she had just passed. When she reached the spot where the paths united, she stopped to listen.

Behind her were the footsteps plain enough!

The same moment the clouds thinned about the moon, and a pale light came filtering through upon the open pastureland in front of her. She cast one look over her shoulder, saw something turn a corner in a lane, and sped on again. She would have run, but there was no place of refuge now nearer than the corner of the turnpike road, and she knew her breath would fail her long before that. How lonely the common looked! The soft steps came nearer and nearer.

Was that music she heard?

She dared not stop to listen. But immediately again came to her ears on the dim air such a stream of faint pearly sounds as if all the necklaces of some heavenly choir or woman-angels were broken, and the beads came pelting down in a cataract of hurtless hail. From no other source could they come except the violin and bow of Joseph Jasper! Where could he be? She was so happy to know that he must be somewhere near that she nearly stopped. But then she remembered her fear, and ran on again.

She was now near the ruined hut in the middle of the common. The moon had gradually been growing out of the clouds, clearer and clearer. The hut came in sight, but the look of it was somehow altered—with an undefinable change, such as might appear on a familiar object in a dream. Leaning against the side of the door stood a figure she could not mistake. Absorbed in his music, he did not see her.

"Joseph! Joseph!" she called out. He started, threw his bow down, tucked his violin under his arm, and bounded to meet her. She tried to stop, but the same moment glanced back to look behind her. She tripped and fell—but the same moment was in the smith's arms.

That instant a man appeared running. He half stopped, then turned off the path, and took off across the flat moor.

Joseph handed his violin to Mary, and darted after him. The chase did not last a minute. The man was already spent and could keep it up no longer. Joseph seized him by the wrist, saw something glitter in his other hand, suddenly felt a slash of sharp pain, and turned sick. The fellow had stabbed him.

With indignation, as if it were a snake that had bit him, the blacksmith flung from him the hand he held, twisting the arm as he did. The man gave a cry, staggered backward, recovered himself, and ran.

Joseph would have followed again, but fell, and for a minute or two lost consciousness. When he came to himself, Mary was binding up his arm.

"What a fool I am!" he said, trying to get up, but yielding at once to Mary's hands which, gently but firmly, kept him down. "It's ridiculous that a man of my size, and ready to work a sledge with any man in Yorkshire, should get sick from a little bit of a job with a knife. But my father was just the same, and he was a stronger man than I'm likely to be."

"It is no wonder," said Mary. "The cut is deep, and you have lost a good deal of blood."

Her voice faltered. It was not easy to get the edges of the wound properly together.

"You've stopped it—haven't you, miss?"

"I think so."

"Then I'll be after the fellow."

"No, no! You mustn't. You must lie still a while. But I don't understand at all! That cottage used to be a mere hovel, without door or window. It can't be you who lives in it."

"Ay, that I do! and it's not a bad place either," answered Joseph. "That's what I went to Yorkshire to get my money for. It's mine—bought and paid for."

"But what made you think of coming here?"

"Let's go into the smithy," said Joseph, "—I won't presume to call it a house, though it has a lean-to for the smith. I'll tell you everything about it. But really, miss, you oughtn't be out like this after dark. There's too many vagabonds about."

With a little help from Mary, Joseph got up and led her into what was now a respectable little smithy, with forge and bellows and anvil and bucket.

Opening a door where there had been none before, he brought a chair, made her sit down, began to blow the covered fire on the hearth, and before long had boiled his kettle for tea. Then he closed the door, lit a candle, and, looking around, Mary could scarcely believe the change that had come upon the miserable little place. Joseph sat down on his anvil, asked to know where she had been, and how far she had run from the rascal. When he learned something of the peculiar relations in which Mary stood to the family at Durnmelling, he began to think there might have been something more in the pursuit than a chance assault by a ruffian, and greater were his regrets that he had not secured the man.

When Mary had told him what she had been about and the necessity of her going again—how many times more God only knew—to Durnmelling, he said, "Anyhow, miss, you'll never come from there alone in the dark again!"

"But I cannot take you from your work, Joseph."

"Work's not everything," he answered. "And it's seldom pressing—except I be shoeing a horse. I can leave it when I choose. Any time you want to go anywhere, just you send for me. You won't have to wait long till I come."

Part of this conversation, and a good deal more, passed on their way to Testbridge. Mary had insisted on setting back out as soon as she knew Joseph was all right, and he had been equally insistent to accompany her safe to her own door.

In her turn she questioned him, and learned that, as soon as he knew she was going to settle at Testbridge, he started off to find a place in the neighborhood, if possible, humble enough for him to afford, and yet near enough for the hope of seeing her sometimes, and having what help with his music she might please to give him. The explanation afforded Mary more pleasure than she cared to show. She had a true friend near her—one ready to help her on her own ground—one who understood her because he understood the things she loved! He told her that he already had enough work to keep him going, that the horses he once shod were always brought to him again, that he had not nearly the expenses he had in town, and that he had plenty of time both for his violin and his books.

When they came to the outskirts of Testbridge, she sent him home, and went straight to Mr. Brett with Mr. Redmain's message. Happily, it was not so late that the good lawyer had already retired. He undertook to be at Durnmelling at the time appointed, and to let nothing prevent him from seeing his new client.

53 / The Next Night_____

Mr. Brett found no difficulty in obtaining his interview, for Mr. Redmain had given Mewks instructions he dared not disobey. His master had often been sick before and recovered again, and he must not venture too far. As soon as he had shown the visitor into the room, he was dismissed, but not before he had satisfied himself that the man was a lawyer.

He carried the news at once to Sepia, and it brought about no little anxiety in the house. There was a will already in existence, and no reason for thinking a change in it meant anything good. Mr. Redmain never shared his thoughts or anxieties or hopes with any of his people. The ladies, however, met in deep consultation, although of course there was nothing to be done. The only operative result was that it let Sepia know that, though for different reasons, her anxieties were shared by the others. Unlike theirs, her sole desire was *not* to be mentioned in the will; that could only be for the sake of leaving her a curse! Mr. Redmain's utter silence after having gathered denouncing facts to her discredit had long convinced her he was but biding his time. She was certain he would not depart this world without leaving his opinion of her and the proofs of its justice behind him. She also knew Hesper well enough to be certain that, however she might delight in opposition to the desire of her husband, she would never carry that opposition to a point where it became injurious to her own interests. Sepia's one thought, therefore, was to somehow prevent the making of another will, or the leaving of any new document behind. She could not help what he might already have done, but what he might yet do, it would be well to prevent. Thus she impressed upon Mewks the absolute necessity of learning as much as possible of what might pass between his master and the lawyer.

Mewks was driven to the end of his wits, and they were not a few, to find excuses for going into the room, and for delaying his departures, while he listened with all his ears. But both client and lawyer were almost too careful for him, and he had learned positively nothing when the latter rose to depart. He instantly left the room, with the door a trifle ajar, and listening intently heard his master say that Mr. Brett must come again the next morning; that he felt better, and would think over the suggestions he had made; and that he must leave the memoranda within his reach, on the table by his bedside. Before the lawyer exited, Mewks was on his way with all this to his tempter.

Sepia concluded there had been some difference of opinion between

Mr. Redmain and his advisor, and hoped nothing had been finally settled. Was there any way to prevent the lawyer from seeing him again? Could she possibly steal a peak at the memoranda mentioned? She dared not suggest the thing to Hesper or Lady Malice, and she dared not show herself in Mr. Redmain's room. Was Mewks to be trusted to the point of such danger as grew in her thought?

The day wore on, and toward evening he had a dreadful attack. Another man would have sent before now for what medical assistance the town could afford him, but Mr. Redmain hated having a stranger about him, and, as he knew how to treat himself, it was only when extremely ill that he would send for his own doctor to the country. But now Lady Margaret took upon herself to send a telegram.

An hour before her usual time for closing the shop, Mary set out for Durnmelling, and at the appointed spot on the way found her squire of low degree waiting. At first sight, however, she did not quite recognize him. I would not have my reader imagine Joseph one of those fools who delight in appearing something other than they are. But while every workman ought to look a workman, it ought not to be by looking less of a man, or of a *gentleman* in the true sense. And Joseph, out of respect to her who would honor him with her company, dressed himself in a new suit of unpretending gray, with a nice hat; and at first sight looked more like a country gentleman having a stroll over his farm than a man whose hands were hard with the labors of the forge. He took off his hat as she approached—if not with ease, yet with the clumsy grace peculiar to him. For unlike many whose manners are unobjectionable, he had in him something that might be called his own. But the best of it was that he knew nothing about his manners, beyond the desire to give honor where honor was due.

He walked with her to the door of the house, for they had agreed that, from whatever quarter had come the pursuit, and whatever might have been its object, it would be well to show that she was attended. They had also arranged at what hour, and what spot close at hand, he was to be waiting to accompany her home. But though he said nothing about it, Joseph was determined not to leave the place until she rejoined him.

It was nearly dark when he left her, and when he had wandered up and down the avenue a while, it seemed dark enough to return to the house and see what he might see.

He had already made the acquaintance of the farmer who occupied a portion of the great square, behind the part where the family lived. He had had several of his horses to shoe, and had not only given satisfaction by the way he had shod them, but had interested their owner with descriptions of more than one rare method of shoeing. Therefore he was less nervous of being discovered about the place.

From the back he found the way into the large roofless hall, and there paced quietly up and down, measuring the floor, and guessing at the thickness of the walls and the sort of roof they had once had. He noted that the walls of the house rose higher than those of the ruin with which it was in contact, and that there was a window in it just over one of those walls. As he was thinking whether it had been there when the roof was on, he saw through it the flickering of a fire, and wondered whether it could be the window of Mr. Redmain's room.

Mary had given no notice of her arrival, and had entered the hall door quietly and walked straight to Mr. Redmain's bedroom. When she opened the door of it, Mewks came hurriedly to meet her, as if he would have made her go out again, but she scarcely looked at him, and advanced to the bed. Mr. Redmain was just waking from the sleep into which he had fallen after a severe paroxysm.

"Ah! there you are!" he said, smiling her a feeble welcome. "I am very glad you have come. I have been looking for you. I am very ill. If it comes again tonight, I think it will be the end of me."

She sat down by the bedside. He lay quite still for some time, breathing like one very weary after a prolonged exertion. Then he seemed to grow easier, and said with much gentleness: "Can't you talk to me?"

"Would you like me to read to you?" she asked.

"No," he answered. "I can't bear the light. It makes my head throb."

"Shall I talk to you about my father?" she asked.

"I don't believe in fathers," he replied. "They're always after some notion of their own. It's not their children they care about."

"That may be true of some fathers," answered Mary. "But it is not the least true of mine."

"Where is he? Why don't you bring him to see me if he is such a good man? He might be able to do something for me."

"There is none but your own father who can do anything for you," said Mary. "My father is gone home to him, but if he were here, he would only tell you about *him*."

There was a moment's silence.

"Why don't you talk?" said Mr. Redmain crossly. "What's the good of sitting there saying nothing! How am I to forget that the pain will be here again if you don't say a word to help me?"

Mary lifted up her heart and prayed for something to say to the sad human soul that had never known the Father. But she could think of nothing to talk about except the death of William Marston. So she began with the dropping of her watch, and told him whatever seemed at the moment fit to tell, ending with the dream she had the night of his funeral. By that time the hidden fountain was flowing in her soul, and she was able to speak straight out of it.

"I cannot tell you," she said, closing the story of her dream, "what a feeling it was! The joy of it was beyond all expression."

"You're surely not going to offer me a dream in proof of anything!" muttered the sick man.

"Yes," answered Mary, "—in proof of what it can prove. The joy of a child over a new toy or piece of candy shows of what bliss the human soul is made capable."

"Oh, capable, I dare say!"

"And more than that," Mary went on, adding instead of replying, "no one ever felt such gladness without believing in it. There must be somewhere the justification of such gladness. There must be the father of it somewhere."

"Well! I don't like to say, after your kindness in coming here to take care of me, that you talk the worst rubbish I ever heard. But just tell me of what use it all is to me, in the state I am in! What I want to be is free of pain, and have some pleasure in life—not to be told about a father."

"But what if the father you don't want is determined that you shall not have what you do want? What if your desire is not worth keeping you alive for? And what if he is ready to help your smallest effort to be the thing he wants you to be—and in the end to give you your heart's desire?"

"It sounds very fine, but it's all so thin, so up in the clouds! It doesn't have a leg of provable fact to stand on. Why, if it were true, everybody would be good. There would be nothing but saints in the world! What's in it, I'm sure I don't know."

"It will take ages to know what is in it. But if you should die now, you will be glad to find, on the other side, that you have made a beginning. For my part, if I had everything my soul could desire, except God with me, I could but pray that he would come to me, or not let me live a moment longer. For it would be but the life of a devil. There is no true life without him."

"What do you mean by a devil?"

"A power that lives against its life," said Mary.

Mr. Redmain answered nothing. He did not perceive a speck of meaning in the words. They gave him not a glimmer. Neither will they to many of my readers; while not a few will think they see all that is in them, and see nothing.

He was silent for a long time—whether he was awake or asleep, she could not tell.

The annoyance was great in the home conclave when Mewks brought the next piece of news—namely, that there was that designing Marston in the master's room again, and however she got into the house he was sure *he* didn't know.

"All the same thing over again, miss!—hard at tryin' to convert 'im!—And what's the use, you know, miss? If a man like the master's to be converted and get off, I don't for my part see where's the good o' keepin' up a devil."

"I am quite of your opinion, Mewks," said Sepia.

But in her heart she was ill at ease.

All day long she had been haunted with an ever-recurring temptation, which, instead of dismissing it, she kept like a dog on a string. Different kinds of evil affect people differently. Ten thousand will do a dishonest thing, who would indignantly reject the dishonest thing favored by another ten thousand. They are not sufficiently used to its ugly face not to dislike it, though it may not be quite so ugly as their *protege*. A man will feel grandly honest against the dishonesties of another trade than his, and be eager to justify those of his own. Here was Sepia, who did not care the dust on a butterfly's wing for causing any amount of family misery, who would without a pang have sacrificed the genuine reputation of an innocent man to save her own false one—shuddering at a vague idea in her brain—an idea which, however, she did not dismiss, and so grew able to endure.

Sepia was unnatural—as every one is unnatural who does not set his face in the direction of the true Nature; but she had gone further in the opposite direction than many people have yet reached. Everyone is always progressing in the one direction or the other. Every tiniest choice we make propels us along the eternal road, a step at a time, either toward the likeness of our true Nature—that is, our Father—or the likeness of the great destroyer of truth. And whoever has not faced about in the direction our elder Brother has trod before us is on the way to a capacity for worse things than even our enemies would believe of us.

Her very existence seemed at stake to her now. If by his dying act Mr. Redmain should drive her from under Hesper's roof, what was to become of her! All hope of marrying Godfrey Wardour would be gone the moment the truth about her past was known. He would never speak to her again if he learned but the half of what Mr. Redmain was certain to record against her!

Since the beginning of this last attack, Sepia had scarcely slept. For some time she had been awake half the night generally, and all the last night she had been wandering here and there about the house, not infrequently positioned where she could hear every motion in Mr. Redmain's room. She was the slave of tomorrow, the undefined, ever about to bring forth no one knows what.

She had become very thin during these trying days. Her great eyes were larger yet, and filled with a troubled anxiety. Not paleness, for that her complexion was incapable of, but a dull pallor possessed her cheek. If one had met her as she roamed the house that night, he might well have taken her for some naughty ancestor, whose troubled conscience, not yet able to shake off the madness of some evil deed, made her wander still about the place where she had committed it.

She believed in no supreme power who cares that right should be done in his worlds. Of those who do not believe, some have never had a noble picture of God presented to them. But whether their phantasm is of a mean God because they refuse him, or they refuse him because their false image of him is mean, who can tell? Anyhow, mean notions must come of meanness within those who imagine them, and, uncharitable as it may appear, I cannot but think there is a moral root to all chosen unbelief. But let God himself judge his own.

Sepia had in her time heard a good deal about *euthanasia*. Being one who did not believe in God, to believe in this spoke no more against her than for advocating cremation, which she also did. But the notion of *euthanasia* might well work for evil in a mind that had not a thought for the ease of the irremediable ills of the human race any more than for the betterment of humanity. Opinions, like drugs, work differently on different constitutions. Hence the man is foolish who goes scattering vague notions regardless of the soil on which they fall.

She was used to asking the question, What's the good? but always in respect of something she wanted out of her way.

"What's the good of an hour or two more if you're not enjoying it?" she said to herself again and again that Monday. "What's the good of living when life is pain—or fear of death, from which no fear can save you?" But the question had no reference to her own life: she was judging for another—and not for that other's sake, or from his point of view, but from her own sake, and from where she stood.

All day long she wandered about the house, such thoughts as these in her heart, and in her pocket a bottle of that concentrate that Mr. Redmain was taking much diluted for medicine. But she hoped *not to have to use it*, she said to herself. If only Mr. Redmain would yield the conflict, and depart without another interview with the lawyer!

She had not learned to fear temptation. She feared poverty, dependence, humiliation, labor, boredom, and misery. The thought of the life that would surely follow in the case of the dreaded disclosure was unendurable. The thought of what she might have to do to frustrate that disclosure was not *so* absolutely unendurable. That was something she *could* bear, if need be. And as she thought about the deed itself, it was one moment with resistance and fear, and yet the next with a cold, scornful smile of triumphant success.

Was she so exceptionally bad? You who think ill of your brother and sister—do you not feel wicked for the thought? Have you forgotten the words of him who said that with the thought comes the deed?

All the afternoon Sepia hovered about Mr. Redmain's door, down upon Mewks every moment he appeared. Her head ached and she was tired, but rest she could not. Once when Mewks told her his master was asleep, she crept in, softly approached the head of the bed, looked at him from behind, and then stole out again.

"He seems dying, Mewks," she said.

"Oh no, miss! I've often seen him as bad. He's better."

"Who's that whispering?" murmured the patient angrily, though half asleep.

Mewks went in and answered: "Only me and Jemima, sir."

"Where's Miss Marston?"

"She's not yet come, sir."

"I want to go to sleep again. You must wake me the moment she comes."

"Yes, sir."

Mewks went back to Sepia.

"His voice is much changed," she said.

"He most always speaks like that now, miss, when he wakes—very different from I used to know him! He'd always swear bad when he woke, but Miss Marston does seem to have got a good deal of that out of him. Anyhow, this last two days he's scarce swore enough to make it feel home-like."

"It's death that has gotten it out of him," said Sepia. "I don't think he can last through the night. Fetch me at once if—and don't let that Marston into the room again, whatever you do."

She spoke with the utmost emphasis, plainly clinching instructions previously given, then went slowly up the stair to her own room. Surely he would die tonight, and she would not be led into temptation! She would then but have to get hold of the paper! It was absurd to talk of a Providence! She must be her own providence!

She stole down the stairs again. Her cousin was safe with a novel, and there was Mewks fast asleep in an easy-chair in the study, with the doors of the dressing-room and chamber ajar!

She crept into the sick room. There was the tumbler with the medicine! Her fingers were on the vial in her pocket. The dying man slept soundly.

She drew near the table by the bed. He stirred as if about to awake. Her limbs, her brain seemed to rebel against her will. But what folly it was! The man was not for this world a day longer anyway— what could it matter whether he left it a few hours earlier or later? The drops on his forehead revealed his agony. Every breath was torture to him. It would be merciful to help him across the verge—if to more life, he would owe her thanks, if to endless rest, he would never accuse her.

She took the vial from her pocket. She heard a hand on the lock of the door! She turned and fled quickly through the dressing-room and study, waking Mewks as she passed. He jumped up, hurried into the chamber, and saw Mary already entered.

When Sepia learned who it was that had scared her, she felt she could kill her with less compunction than she could Mr. Redmain. She hated her far worse.

"You *must* get the viper out of the house, Mewks," she said. "It's your fault she got into the room."

"I'm sure I'm willing enough to keep her out," he answered. "But what am I to do? She's that brazen, you wouldn't believe, miss! And he insists on having her about."

"No doubt, no doubt," responded Sepia. "But surely," she went on, "the next time he has an attack, and he's certain to have one soon, you will be able to get her hustled out."

"No, miss—least of all then. She'll make a pretense for not moving a yard from the bed—as if me who's been about him so many years didn't know what ought to be done with him in his seizures of pain better than the likes of her! The only way is to be quiet, and seem to trust her, and watch for the chance of her going out—then shut her out, and keep her out."

"I believe you are right," returned Sepia.

Hence in part it came that Mary met with little interruption to her watching and ministering. Mewks kept coming and going—watching her, and waiting for his opportunity. Mr. Redmain scarcely heeded him, only once and again saying in sudden anger, "What can the idiot be about? He might know by this time I'm not likely to want *him* so long as *you* are in the house!"

Mary said to herself, "Who knows what good the mere presence of one who trusts may be to him, even if he shouldn't seem to take much of what she says! Perhaps he may think of some of it after he is dead—who knows?"

Patiently she sat and waited, full of help that would have flowed in a torrent, but which she felt only trickling from her heart like a stream that is lost on the face of the rock down which it flows.

All at once she looked at her watch and realized Joseph had been waiting for her more than an hour and would not, she knew, go away without her even if it meant his waiting all night. Mr. Redmain was lying very still. She would slip out and send Joseph away, and get quickly back before the patient or any one else should miss her!

She went softly from the room and glided down the stairs and out of the house, seeing no one—but not unseen. Hardly was she out of the room when the door was closed and locked behind her, and hardly from the house when the house-door was also closed and locked behind her. But she heard nothing, and without the least foreboding ran to the corner where Joseph was to meet her.

There he was, waiting as patiently as if the hour had not yet come.

"I can't leave him, Joseph. My heart won't let me," she said. "I cannot go back before morning. I will look in on you as I pass."

So saying, and without giving him time to answer, she bade him good night and ran back to the house. But to her dismay she found the door locked, concluding that the hour must have arrived when the house was shut up for the night. She rang the bell, but there was no answer—for there was Mewks himself standing close on the other side of it, grinning like his master an evil grin. As she knocked and rang in vain, the thought finally flashed on her that she had been intentionally shut out. She turned away in despair. There stood Joseph! She ran back to him and told him she had been locked out.

"Why do you think they have done it?" he asked.

"I don't know," answered Mary. "None of them like me but Jemima— not even Mrs. Redmain now, I'm afraid. I can't stand the thought of him needing me and me nowhere to be found—as they're sure to tell him. There's no telling what lies they may tell about me. Everything I've been telling him will seem like idle tales if he thinks I have deserted him!"

"This is a serious affair," said Joseph. "To have a dying man believe you false to him would be dreadful! We must find some way in. Let us go to the kitchen door."

"If Jemima happened to be near, then perhaps," rejoined Mary. "But if they want to keep me out, you may be sure Mewks has taken care of one door as well as another. He knows I'm not so easy to keep out."

"If you did get in," said Joseph, speaking in a whisper as they went, "would you feel quite safe after this?"

"I'm not afraid. I dare say they would lock me up somewhere if they could, before I got to Mr. Redmain's room. Once in, however, they would not dare touch me."

"I will not go out of hearing so long as you are in that house," said Joseph with decision. "Not until I have you out again do I leave the premises. If anything makes you uncomfortable, you cry out, and I'll make such a noise at the door that everybody at Thornwick over there shall hear me."

"It is a large house, Joseph. One might call in many a part of it and never be heard outside. I don't think you could hear me from Mr. Redmain's room," said Mary, with a little laugh, for she was amused as well as pleased at the protection Joseph would give her. "It is up two flights, and he chose it for himself for the sake of being quiet when he was ill."

As she spoke they reached the door they sought—the most likely of all to still be open: it was locked tight and dark as if it had not been unbolted for years. One or two more entrances they tried, but with no better success.

"Come this way," whispered Joseph. "I know a place where we shall at least be out of their sight, and where we can plan what to do at our leisure."

He led her to the back entrance to the old hall. Alas! even that was closed.

"This is disappointing," he said; "for, if we were only in there, I think something might be done."

"I believe I know a way," said Mary, and led him to a place nearby, used for a woodshed.

At the top of a great heap of sticks and kindling was an opening in the wall that had once been a window, or perhaps a door.

"I know that to be the wall of the tower," she said, "and there can be no difficulty of getting through there. Once in, it will be easy to reach the hall—that is, if the door of the tower is not locked."

In an instant Joseph was at the top of the heap, and through the opening, hanging on and feeling with his feet. He found footing, and presently Mary was beside him. They descended softly, and found the door into the hall wide open.

"Can you tell me what that window is," whispered Joseph, "just above the top of the wall?"

"I can't," answered Mary. "I never could go about the house as I did at Mr. Redmain's in London. Lady Margaret always looked so fierce if she saw me trying to understand the place. But why do you ask?"

"You see the flickering of a fire? Could it be Mr. Redmain's room?"

"I can't tell. I don't think so. That has no window in this direction, as far as I know. But I could not be certain."

"Think how the stairs turn as you go up, and how the passages go into the room. Think in what direction you look at every corner you turn."

Mary was silent and thought a while. In her mind she followed every turn she had to take from the moment she entered the house till she got to the door of Mr. Redmain's room, and then thought how the windows lay when she entered it. Her conclusion was that one side of the room must be against the hall, but she could remember no window in it.

"But," she added, "I never was in that room when I was here before, and the twice I have been in it now, I was too much occupied to take much notice of things around me. I know two windows look into a quiet little corner of the courtyard, where there is an old pump covered with ivy. I remember no other."

"Is there any way of getting to the top of that wall from this tower?" asked Joseph.

"Certainly. People often walk round the top of those walls. They are more than thick enough for that."

"Are you able to do it?"

"Yes, quite. I have been round them more than once. But I don't like the idea of looking in at a window."

"Neither do I. But you must remember, if it is his room, it will only be your eyes going where the whole of you has a right to be. And if it should not be that room, they have driven you to it: such a necessity will justify it."

"You must be right," answered Mary, then turned and led the way up the stair of the tower and through a gap in the wall out upon the top of the great walls.

It was a sultry night. A storm was brooding between heaven and earth. The moon was not yet up, and it was so dark that they had to feel their way along the wall, glad of the protection of a fence of thick ivy on the outer side. Looking down into the court on the one hand, and across the hall to the lawn on the other, they saw no living thing in the light from various windows, and there was little danger of being discovered. In the gable there was only the one window, for which they were heading. Mary went first, as knowing the path better, also as having the better right to look in. Through the window, as she went, she could see the flicker, but not the fire. All at once came a great blaze. It lasted but a moment—long enough, however, to let them see plainly into a small closet, the door of which was partly open.

"That is the room, I do believe," whispered Mary. "There is a closet, but I never was in it."

"If only the window is unbolted," returned Joseph.

The same instant Mary heard the voice of Mr. Redmain call in a tone of annoyance—"Mary! Mary Marston! I want you. Who is in the room?— Damn you! who are you?"

"Let me pass you," said Joseph, and making her hold to the ivy edged past her and to the window. The blaze was gone and the fire was back to its old flicker. He lifted the sash. A moment more and he was in. The next, Mary was beside him.

Something, known only to her as an impulse, induced Mary to go softly to the door of the closet and look into the next room. She saw Hesper, as she thought, standing—sideways to the closet—by a chest of drawers invisible from the bed. A candle stood on the farther side of her. In one hand she held the tumbler from which, repeatedly that evening, Mary had given the patient his medicine. Into this she was pouring something from a small dark bottle.

With a sudden suspicion of foul play, Mary glided swiftly into the room and to where she stood. It was Sepia!

She started with a smothered shriek, turned white, and almost dropped the bottle. Then seeing who it was, she recovered herself, casting upon Mary a look of hate out of her great black eyes. Mary thought for a moment she might attack her, but then she turned away and walked swiftly to the door. But from behind Mary, Joseph too had caught sight of the bottle and tumbler, also of Sepia's face. Seeing her now leaving with the bottle in her hand, he sprang after her, and, thanks to the fact that she had locked the door, was in time to snatch it from her. She turned like a wild beast, and a terrible oath came hissing as from a feline throat. However, when she saw the unknown figure of a powerful man rather than Mary, she turned again to the door and fled. Joseph shut and locked it, and went back to the closet. Mary drew near the bed.

"What have you been about all this time?" asked the patient, "and who was that who went out of the room just now? What's all the hurry about?"

Anxious that he should be neither frightened nor annoyed, Mary replied to the first part of his question only.

"I had to go tell a friend, who was waiting for me, that I shouldn't be home tonight. But I am here now, and I will not leave you again."

"How did the door come to be locked? And who was that who went out of the room?"

While he was thus questioning, Joseph crept softly out of the window, and all the rest of the night he lay on the top of the wall under it.

"It was Miss Yolland," answered Mary.

"What business did she have in my room?"

"She shall not enter it again while I am here."

"Don't let Mewks in either," he rejoined. "I heard the door unlock and lock again. What did it mean?"

"Wait till tomorrow. Perhaps we shall find out then."

He was silent a little.

"I must get out of this house, Mary," he sighed at length.

"When the doctor comes, we shall see," said Mary.

"What! Is the doctor coming? I am glad of that. Who sent for him?"

"I don't know. I only heard he was coming."

"But your lawyer, Mary—what's his name?—will be here first. We'll talk the thing over with him, and take his advice. I feel better, and shall go to sleep again."

All night long Mary sat by him and watched. Not a step, so far as she knew, came near the door. Certainly not a hand was laid upon the lock. Mr. Redmain slept soundly, and in the morning was beyond a doubt better.

But Mary could not think of leaving him until Mr. Brett came. At Mr. Redmain's request she rang the bell. Mewks made his appearance, with the face of a ghost. His master told him to bring his breakfast.

"And see, Mewks," he added in a tone of gentleness that terrified the man, so unaccustomed was he to such from the mouth of his master—"see that there is enough for Miss Marston as well. She has had nothing all night. Don't let my lady have anything to do with it—"stop!" he cried as Mewks was going, "I won't have you touch it either. I am fastidious this morning. Tell the young woman they call Jemima to come here to Miss Marston."

Mewks slunk away. Jemima came, and Mr. Redmain ordered her to get breakfast for himself and Mary. It was done speedily, and Mary remained in the sick-chamber until the lawyer arrived.

54 / Breakings Up

"I am afraid I must ask you to leave us now, Miss Marston," said Mr. Brett, seated with pen, ink, and paper, to receive his new client's instructions.

"No," said Mr. Redmain. "She must stay where she is. I fancy something happened last night that she has got to tell us about."

"Ah, what was that?" asked Mr. Brett, facing round on her.

Mary began her story with the incident of her having been pursued by someone, and rescued by the blacksmith, whom she told her listeners, she had known in London. Then she narrated all that had happened the night before, from first to last, not forgetting the flame that lighted the closet as they approached the window.

"Just let me see those memoranda," said Mr. Brett to Mr. Redmain, rising, and looking for the paper where he had left it the day before.

"I was thinking of that paper this very moment," answered Mr. Redmain.

"It is not here!" said Mr. Brett.

"I thought as much! The fool! There was a thousand pounds there for her! I didn't want to drive her despairing to suicide: a dying man must mind what he is about. Ring the bell and see what Mewks has to say about it."

Mewks came, in evident anxiety.

I will not record his examination. Mr. Brett took it for granted he had deliberately and intentionally shut Mary out, and Mewks did not attempt to deny it. When examined as to the missing paper, he swore by all that was holy he knew nothing about it.

Mr. Brett next requested the presence of Miss Yolland. She was nowhere to be found. The place was searched throughout, but there was no trace of her.

When the doctor arrived, the bottle Joseph had taken from her was examined, and its lethal contents discovered.

Lady Malice was grievously hurt at the examination she found had been going on.

"Have I not cared for you like my own brother, Mr. Redmain?" she said.

"You may be glad you have escaped a coroner's inquest in your house, Lady Margaret!" said Mr. Brett.

"For me," said Mr. Redmain, "I have not many days left me, but

305

somehow a fellow wants to have his days be his own, and not taken from him!''

Hesper sought Mary and greeted her with some appearance of gratitude. She saw what a horrible suspicion, perhaps even accusation, she had saved her from. The behavior and disappearance of Sepia seemed to give her little trouble.

Mr. Brett got enough out of Mewks to show the necessity of his dismissal, and the doctor sent from London a man fit to take his place.

Almost every evening, until he left Durnmelling, Mary went to see Mr. Redmain. She read to him, and tried to teach him, as one might an unchildlike child. And something did seem to be getting into, or waking up in him. The man had never before submitted in the least. But now it looked as if the watching spirit of life were feeling through the dust-heap of his low thoughts, bad life, and wrong judgments to find the thing that spirit had made. When the two met and joined, then would the man be saved— God and he would be together.

Sometimes he would utter the strangest things—such as if all the old evil ways of thinking and feeling were in full operation again. And sometimes for days Mary would not have an idea what was going on in him. When he was suffering, he would occasionally break into fierce and evil language, then be suddenly silent. God and Satan were striving for the man, and the victory would be with him with whom the man would side.

For some time it remained doubtful whether this attack was not going to be, as he kept saying, the last. The doctor was doubtful, and, having no reason to think his death would be a great grief in the house, did not hesitate to express his doubt about the gravity of Mr. Redmain's condition. And indeed, it caused no gloom. For there was little love in the attentions the Mortimers paid him, and in what other hope could Hesper have married than that one day she would be free, with a freedom complete with the power of money! But to the mother's suggestions as to possible changes in the future, the daughter never responded: she had no thought of plans in common with her. Strange rumors circulated abroad. Godfrey Wardour heard something of them and laughed them to scorn. There was a conspiracy in that house to ruin the character of the loveliest woman in creation. But when week after week passed, and he heard nothing of or from her, he became anxious, and at last lowered his pride so far as to call on Mary, under the pretense of buying something in her shop.

His troubled look filled her with sympathy, but she could not help being glad that he had escaped the snares laid for him. He looked at her with searching expression, and at last murmured a request that she would allow him to have a little conversation with her.

She led the way to her parlor, closed the door, and asked him to take a seat. But Godfrey was too proud, or perhaps agitated to sit.

"You will be surprised to see me on such an errand, Miss Marston," he said.

"I do not yet know your errand," replied Mary, "but I may not be as surprised as you think."

"Do not imagine," continued Godfrey stiffly, "that I believe a word of the reports in circulation. I have come only to ask you to tell me the real nature of the accusations brought against Miss Yolland: your name is, of course, coupled with them."

"Mr. Wardour," said Mary, "if I thought you would believe what I told you, I would willingly do as you ask me. As it is, allow me to refer you to Mr. Brett, the lawyer, whom I dare say you know."

Happily the character of Mr. Brett was well known in Testbridge, and all the country round, and from him Godfrey learned what sent him traveling on the Continent again—not in the hope of finding Sepia, but rather trying to forget, again; this time trying to forget what a fool he had been to be thus duped by such a woman. What became of her, none of the family ever learned.

Sometime after, it came out that the same night on which the presence of Joseph rescued Mary from her pursuer, a man speaking with a foreign accent went to one of the doctors in Testbridge to have his shoulder set, which he said had been dislocated by a fall. When Joseph heard it, he smiled, and thought he knew what it meant.

Hesper was no sooner in London than she wrote to Mary, inviting her to come visit her. But Mary answered that she could no more leave home, and must content herself with the hope of seeing Mrs. Redmain when she came to Durnmelling.

So long as her husband lived, the time for such a visit did not again arrive. But when Mary went to London, she always called on her, and generally saw Mr. Redmain. They had not had anymore talk about the things Mary loved most. But he always received her kindly, and she hoped he was continuing to think about those things. He also seemed to wear a gentler manner. Whether the change was caused by something better than physical decay, who knows except he who can use even decay for redemption? He lived another two years, and then died rather suddenly. After his death, and that of her father, which soon followed, Hesper went again to Durnmelling, and behaved better to her mother than before. Mary sometimes saw her, and a flicker of genuine friendship began to appear on Hesper's part.

Mr. Turnbull was soon doing what he called a roaring trade. He bought and sold a great deal more than Mary, but she had business sufficient to keep her days busy, and leave her nights free, and bring her and Letty enough to live on as comfortably as they desired—with a little left over to use, when needed, for others, and something to lay aside for the time of lengthening shadows.

Turnbull seemed to have taken a lesson from his late narrow escape, for he gave up the worst of his speculations, and confined himself to "genuine business principles"—the more contentedly that, all Marston folly swept from his path, he was free to his own interpretation of the phrase. He grew to be a rich man and died happy—so his friends said, and said as they saw. Mrs. Turnbull left Testbridge and went to live in a small country town where she was unknown. There she was regarded as the widow of an officer in her Majesty's service, and, as there was no one within a couple hundred miles to support an assertion to the contrary, she did not think it worth her while to make one. Was not the supposed label a truer index to her own estimation of herself than the actual ticket ill luck had attached to her—widow of a linen draper?

George carried on the business. When he and Mary happened to pass in the street, they nodded to each other.

Letty was diligent in business, but it never got into her heart. She continued to be much liked, and in the shop was delightful. If she ever had another offer of marriage, the fact remained unknown. She lived to be a sweet, gracious little old lady—and often forgot that she was a widow, but never that she was a wife. All the days of her appointed time she waited till her change should come, and she should find her Tom on the other side, looking out for her, as he had said he would. Her mother-in-law could not help dying, but she never forgave her—for what, nobody knew.

After a year or so, Mrs. Wardour began to take a little notice of her again, but she never asked her to Thornwick until she found herself dying. Perhaps she then remembered a certain petition in the Lord's prayer. But will it not be rather a dreadful thing for some people if they are forgiven as they forgive?

Old Mr. Duppa died, and a young man came to minister to his congregation who thought the baptism of the spirit of more importance than the most correct opinions concerning even the baptizing spirit. From him Mary found she could learn, and would be much to blame if she did not learn. From him Letty also heard what increased her desire to be worth something before she went to rejoin Tom.

Joseph Jasper once more became Mary's pupil. She was now no more content with her little cottage piano, but had an instrument of quite another capacity on which to accompany the violin of the blacksmith.

To him trade came in steadily, and before long he had to build a larger shoeing shed. From a wide neighborhood horses were brought to him to be shod, cartwheels to be tired, axles to be mended, plowshares to be sharpened, and all sorts of odd jobs to be done. He soon found it necessary to make arrangement with a carpenter and wheelwright to work on his place. Before two years were over, he was what people call a flourishing man, and laying by a little money.

"But," he said to Mary, "I can't go on like this, you know. I don't want money. It must be meant to do something with, and I must find out what that something is."

55 / The Song of Love

One winter evening, as soon as his work was over for the day, Joseph locked the door of his smithy, washed himself well, put on clean clothes, took his violin, and set out for Testbridge: Mary was expecting him to tea. It was the afternoon of a holiday, and she had closed early.

Was there ever a happier man than Joseph that night as he strode along the footpath? A day of invigorating and manly toil behind him, folded up in the sense of work accomplished; a clear sky overhead, beginning to breed stars; the pale amber hope of tomorrow's sunrise low down in the west; a frosty air around him, challenging to the surface the glow of the forge which his day's labor had stored in his body; his heart and brain at rest with his Father in heaven; his precious violin under his arm; before him the welcoming parlor, where two sweet women awaited his coming, one of them the brightest angel in or out of heaven; and the prospect of an evening of music between them—who, I repeat, could have been more blessed, heart, soul, and body, than Joseph Jasper? God only knows how blessed he could make us if we would but let him! He pressed his violin case to his heart, as if it were a living thing that could know that he loved it.

Before he reached the town the stars were out, and the last of the sunset had faded away. Earth was gone and heaven only was left. "There lie the fields of my future," he said to himself, "when this chain of gravity is unbound from my feet! Blessed am I here now, my God, and blessed shall I be there then."

When he reached the suburbs of the town, the light of homes was shining through curtains of all colors. When he reached the streets, all the shops he passed were closed, except the beer-shops and the druggists.

He reached Mary's shop, turned into the court to the kitchen door, and was in a mood for music. One might imagine the violin under his arm was possessed by an angel, and, ignoring his ears, was playing straight into his heart!

Beenie let him in, and took him up to the parlor. Mary came halfway toward him to greet him. He laid down his violin, and seated himself where Mary told him, in her father's armchair by the fire. Gentle nothings with a down of rainbows were talked until tea was over, and then without a word they set to their music—Mary and Joseph, with their own hearts, and Letty for their audience.

They had not gone far on the way to fairyland, however, when Beenie called Letty from the room, to speak to a friend and customer, who had come from the country on a sudden necessity for something from the shop. Letty found herself unable to find quite the right thing, and came in her turn to call Mary. She rose and went as quietly as if she were leaving a tiresome visitor. The music was broken, and Joseph left alone with the silent instruments.

But in his hands, solitude and a violin were sure to marry in music. He began to play, forgot himself utterly, and, when the customer had gone away satisfied, and the ladies returned to the parlor, there he stood with his eyes closed, playing on, not even suspecting they were in the room again. They sat down and listened in silence.

Mary had not listened long before she found herself strangely moved. Her heart seemed to swell up into her throat, and it was all she could do to keep from weeping. A little longer and she was compelled to yield, and the silent tears flowed freely. Letty, too, was overcome—more than she had ever been by music. She was not so open to its influences as Mary, but her eyes were full, and she sat thinking of her Tom, far in the regions that are none the less true that we cannot see them.

A mood had taken shape in the mind of the blacksmith, and wandered from its home, seeking another country. Thus, in a garment of mood whose color and texture was music, did the soul of Joseph Jasper that evening, like a homeless ghost, come knocking at the door of Mary Marston. It was the very being of the man praying for admittance. Now he was telling no story of old with his strange melodies, but rather telling a story that was coming from deep within him. And as Mary watched, Joseph stood and played, thinking himself alone with his violin. The violin was his mediator with her, and it was pleading and pleading for the admittance of its master. It prayed, it wept, it implored. It cried aloud that eternity was very long to spend alone, like a great palace without a quiet room. "Oh, rather a thousand-fold let me love thee," it sang, "than be content with all else the world gives, free of this pang that tells me of a bliss yet more complete, fulfilling the gladness of heaven!"

All the time Joseph knew nothing of where his soul was. He thought Mary was still in the shop and beyond the hearing of his pleader. And this was, indeed, not even the shape the thing took to the consciousness of the musician. He seemed to himself to be standing alone in a starry and moonlit night, among roses, and sweet peas, and apple blossoms—for the soul cares little for the seasons, and will make its own month out of many. On the bough of an apple tree, in the fair moonlight, sat a nightingale, swaying to and fro like one mad with the wine of his own music, singing as if he wanted to break his heart and be done with it, for the delight was too much for the mortal creature to endure. And the song of the bird grew to be the prayer of the man in the brain and heart of the musician, and thence burst, through the open fountain of the violin, and worked what it could work. "I love you! I love you! I love you!" cried the violin, and the worship was entreaty that knew not itself. On and on it went, ever beginning before it ended, as if it could never come to a close. And the two sat listening as if they cared for nothing but to hear, and would listen forever—listening as if, when the sound ceased, all would be at an end.

Ah, do not blame me too quickly, you who love God but fear to love the human too much. You have yet to learn that the love of the human *is* love, is divine, is but a lower form of a part of the love of God. When you love man, or woman, or child, yea, or even dog aright, then will you no longer need that I tell you how God and his Christ would not be content with each other alone in the glories even of the eternal original love, because they could create more love. For that more love, together they suffered and patiently waited. He that loves not his brother whom he has seen how shall he love God whom he has not seen?

A sob, like a bird new-born, burst from Mary's heart.

It broke the enchantment in which Joseph was bound. That enchantment had possessed him so completely that he started at the sound. For a moment his arms and legs were hardly his own. His violin fell to his side, and he stumbled and all but fell.

Mary darted to him, threw her arms round him, laid her head on his great chest, and burst into tears. Tenderly he laid his violin on the piano, and, like one receiving a gift straight from the hand of God, folded his arms around the woman. Music had spoken enough that night; now two hearts were silently shouting their joy to each other. Joseph's violin was still, but his being was made whole!

56 / The End of the Beginning_____

Joseph Jasper and Mary Marston were married the next summer.

Mary did not leave her shop, nor did Joseph leave his forge. Mary was proud of her husband, not merely because he was a musician, but because he was a blacksmith. With the true taste of a right woman, she honored the manhood that could do hard work. The day will come when the youth of our country will recognize that it is a more manly thing to follow a good craft, if it makes the hands black as coal, than to spend the day in keeping books, and making accounts, and investing money, and making fortunes at the expense of other people. Of course from a higher point of view still, all work set by God and divinely done is of equal honor. But where there is a choice, I would gladly see a son of mine choose rather to be a blacksmith, a watchmaker, a bookbinder, a cobbler, a woodworker, than a banker or broker. Making things is higher in the scale of reality than any mere transmission, than buying and selling, to whatever godly end that may be done as well. Besides, it is easier to do honest work than to buy and sell honestly. The more honor, of course, to those who are honest under the greater difficulty! But the man who knows how important is the prayer, "Lead us not into temptation," knows that he must not be tempted into temptation even by the glory of duty under difficulty. In humility we must choose the easiest, as we must hold our faces unflinchingly to the hardest, even to the seeming impossible, when it is given us to do.

I must show the blacksmith and shopkeeper once more—two years after marriage—long enough to have made common people as common to each other as the weed by the roadside. But these are not common to each other yet, and never will be.

They will never complain of being disillusioned, for they have never been illuded. They look up each to the other still, because they were right in looking up each to the other from the first. Each was, and therefore is and will be, real.

It was a lovely morning in summer. The sun was but a little way above the horizon, and the dew-drops seemed to have come scattering from him as he shook his locks when he rose. The foolish larks were up, of course, for they fancied, come what might of winter and rough weather, the universe was founded in eternal joy, and themselves were endowed with the best of all rights to be glad, for there was the gladness inside, and struggling to get outside of them. And out it was coming in a divine profusion!

How many baskets would not have been needed to gather up the lordly waste of those scattered songs! In all the trees, in all the flowers, in every grassblade, and every weed, the sun was warming and coaxing and soothing life into higher life. And in those two on the path through the fields outside Testbridge, the same sun, light from the Father of lights, was nourishing highest life of all, that for the sake of which the Lord came, that he might set it growing in hearts of whose existence it was the very root.

Joseph and Mary were taking their walk together before the day's work should begin. Those who have a good conscience and are not at odds with their work can take their pleasure any time—as well before their work as after it. But the joy of the sunrise would linger about Mary all the day long in the gloomy shop; and for Joseph, he had but to lift his head to see the sun hastening on to the softer and yet more hopeful splendors of the evening. The wife, who did not have to begin work so early, was walking with her husband, as was her custom even when the weather was not of the best, to see him well started on his day's work. It was with something very much like pride, yet surely nothing evil, that she would watch the quick blows of his brawny arm, as he beat the cold iron on the hard anvil till it was all aglow like the sun that lighted the world—then stuck it into the middle of his coals, and blew softly with his bellows till the flame on the altar of his work-offering was awake and keen. The sun might shine or not, the wind might blow or be still, the path might be crisp with frost or soft with mud, but the lighting of her husband's forge-fire, Mary never omitted to turn by her presence into a holy ceremony. It was to her the "Come let us worship and bow down," of the daily service of God-given labor.

That done, she would kiss him, and leave him: she had her own work to do. Filled with prayer she would walk steadily back the well-known way to the shop, where, all day long, ministering with gracious service to the wants of her people, she would know the evening and its service drawing nearer and nearer, when Joseph would come, and the delights of heaven would begin afresh at home, in music, in books, in trustful talk. Every day was a life, and every evening a blessed death—type of that larger evening rounding our day with larger hope. But many Christians are such pagans that they will hardly believe it possible such a loving pair should think of that evening of earthly life except with misery at the thought of growing old.

That morning, as they went, they talked something like this:

"Listen to the larks, Mary," said Joseph. "They are all saying that I would have been nothing without you."

"You would have been a true man, Joseph, whatever the larks may say."

"A solitary melody at best, with no harmony to go with it."

A pause followed.

"I shall be rather shy to meet your father," said Joseph. "What if he isn't content with me?"

"Even if you weren't what you are, my father would love you because I love you. But I know my father as well as I know you. And I know you are just the man it must make him happy, even in heaven, to think of his Mary marrying."

"That was a curious statement of Letty's yesterday. You heard her say, didn't you, that if everybody was so good in heaven, she was afraid it would be rather dull?"

"We mustn't make too much of what Letty says, either when she's merry or when she's miserable. She speaks both times only out of halfway down."

"Yes. I wasn't meaning to find fault with her. I only wanted to know what you would say."

"Well, perhaps it is because we know so little about good that it seems to us not enough sometimes. For my part, I don't feel that strife of any sort is necessary to make me enjoy life; of all things, strife leads to misery. Certainly effort and struggle add immeasurably to the enjoyment of life, but those I look upon as labor, not strife. There may be whole worlds for us to help bring into order and obedience. And I suspect there must be no end of work in which there is yet much strife. There must be millions of spirits in prison that need preaching to. Anyhow there will be plenty to do, and that's the main thing. Seeing we are made in the image of God, and he is always working, we could not be happy without work. It will, in any case, hardly be dull."

"But you don't want to die, do you, Mary?" said Joseph.

"No, I want to live. And I've got such a blessed plenty of life while waiting for more that I am quite content to wait. But I do wonder that some people I know should cling to what they call life as they do. They profess to believe in the gospel, but they are constantly complaining about their sufferings, are not in the least submitted to the will of God from how hard they imagine themselves dealt with, and speak of death as the one paramount evil. In the utmost weariness, they seem incapable of understanding the apostle's desire to depart and be with Christ, or of imagining that to be with him can be at all so good as remaining where they are."

"Don't you think, though," said Joseph, "that some people put their clothes on wrong side out, and so appear more heartless than they actually are? My sister Ann used to go on scolding people for not believing, all the time saying they could not believe till God made them, and then talking about God so that I don't see how, even if they could, anyone would have believed in such a monster as she made of him. And then if you objected to belief in such a God, she would tell you it was all from the depravity of your own heart. And yet this sister of mine, I know, once went for months without enough to eat in order to feed the children of a neighbor, of whom she knew next to nothing, when their father lay ill of a fever. And she looked for no thanks, except it was from that same God she would have to be a tyrant from the beginning—one who would calmly stand by and watch the unspeakable misery of creatures whom he had compelled to exist, whom he would not permit to cease, and for whom he would do a great deal, but not all that he could. Such people, like Ann, are indeed a paradox to the faith."

"You're right, Joseph. There are many whose beliefs are as false to God as they can be, yet who are a little faithful to him through their actions."

"Just as truly as the opposite is the case!"

"Yes, those whose beliefs may be true but whose lives are false. But for those such as poor Ann, if we don't take their testimony against God, neither must we take it against themselves. Only why is it they are always so certain they are in the right?"

"For the perfecting of the saints," suggested Joseph, with a curious smile.

"Perhaps," answered Mary. "Anyhow, we may get that good out of them, whether they be here for the purpose or not. I remember Mr. Turnbull once accused my father of irreverence, because he spoke about God in the shop. My father said to him, 'Our Lord called the old temple his father's house and a den of thieves in the same breath.' Mr. Turnbull saw nothing but nonsense in the answer. Then my father said, 'You will admit that God is everywhere?' 'Of course,' replied Mr. Turnbull. 'Except in this shop, I suppose you mean?' said my father. 'No, I don't. That's just why I wouldn't have you speak as you do.' 'Then you wouldn't have me think about him either?' 'Well, there's a time for everything!' Then my father said, very solemnly, 'I came from God, and I'm going back to God, and I won't have any gaps of death in the middle of my life.' And that was nothing to Mr. Turnbull either."

To one in ten of my readers it may be something.

Just before they came in sight of the smithy, they saw a lady and a gentleman on horseback flying across the common.

"There go Mrs. Redmain and Mr. Wardour!" said Joseph. "They're to be married next month, they say. Has Hesper been to see you in the shop?"

"No, but the customers are talking about it. It must be true."

"Well, it's a handsome couple they'll make. And the two properties together will make a fine estate."

"I hope she'll learn to like the books he does," said Mary. "Her tastes used to be quite different. I never could get her to listen to anything for three minutes."

"I suppose they deserve each other," mused Joseph.

Mary was silent. She knew far too much about either of them to dispute her husband's remark. Sadly, she thought, never was a truer word spoken. She only hoped the day would come when they would each get past their selves enough to do the other some good.

Though Joseph generally stopped work long before Mary closed the shop, she not infrequently managed to meet him on his way home. Joseph always kept looking out for her as he walked.

That very evening they were gradually nearing each other—the one from the smithy, the other from the shop—with another pair between them on its way to Testbridge—Godfrey Wardour and Hesper Redmain.

"How strange," said Hesper, "that after all its changes and breakings, old Thornwick would be joined up again at last."

Partly by a death in the family, partly through the securities her husband had taken on the property, partly by the will of her father, the whole of Durnmelling now belonged to Hesper.

"It is strange," answered Godfrey with an involuntary sigh. He was thinking of all he had been through in recent years, loving then losing, then loving and losing again. Now he found himself almost doubting that Hesper would really be his. Was he in reality but walking in his sleep? Would he be able to fully love—either a woman or the property—again?

They had talked of Mary more than once. Now that she was to marry Godfrey, much of what Mary used to say about loving her husband gradually had come back to the mind of Hesper; she now found herself occasionally repenting of having so scorned her words. And in part through what Hesper had told him of her, Godfrey had come to see that he had been unjust to her. I do not mean he had come to know the depth and extent of his injustice—that would imply a full understanding of Mary herself, which was yet far beyond him. A thousand things had to grow, a thousand things to shift and shake themselves together in Godfrey's mind before he could begin to understand one who cared only for the highest.

Godfrey and Hesper made a glorious pair to look at—but would their's be a happy union? Happy, I dare say—but not too happy. There were fine elements in both, and, if indeed they could learn to love outside of themselves, then by degrees—by slow degrees most likely—all could begin to come right with them. Whether this would happen depended upon their own choices, and nothing else.

If they had both been born again before they began, so to start fresh, then like two children hand in hand they might have run in through the gates into the city. But what is love, what is loss, what are pains and hopes and disappointments, what is sorrow and death and all the ills of the flesh, but means to this very end, to this waking of the soul to seek the home of our being—the life eternal? Verily we must be born from above, and be good children, or become, even to our self-loving selves, a scorn and endless reproach.

If they had only had Mary to talk to them! If they had only listened—or would only now listen—to her when she had talked to them in the past. But they did not want her. To them she was a good sort of creature, who, with all her disagreeableness, meant them well, and whom they had misjudged a little and made cry. But they had no suspicion that she was one of the lights of the world—one of the wells of truth, whose springs are fed by the rains on the eternal hills.

Turning past a clump of bushes on the common, they met Mary. She stepped off the path. Mr. Wardour took off his hat to her. They stopped.

"Well, Mary," said Hesper, holding out her hand, and speaking in a tone reminiscent of the friendly relations in which they had once stood with each other, "where are you going?"

"To meet my husband," answered Mary. "I see him coming."

With a deep, loving look at Hesper, and a bow and a smile to Godfrey, she left them, and hastened to meet her workingman.

Behind Godfrey Wardour and Hesper Redmain walked Joseph Jasper and Mary Marston toward Testbridge, half of them at least forming a procession of love toward a far-off, eternal goal. But which of them was to be first in the kingdom of heaven, Mary or Joseph or Hesper or Godfrey, is not to be told. They had yet a long way to walk, and there are first that shall be last, and last that shall be first.